SURFACE RESCUE

"I'm really stuck here," Molina called, a hint of desperation in his voice. "I need you to help me. What are you doing up there?"

Alexios heard himself say, "I'm coming down. It'll take a few minutes. Hang in there."

"Well for Christ's sake don't dawdle! I'm sloshing in my own sweat inside this frigging suit."

Alexios smiled again. You're not helping yourself, Victor. You're not making it easier for me to come to your aid.

But he pushed the door of the tractor's cab open and jumped to the ground, almost hoping that he'd snap an ankle or twist a knee and be unable to save Victor's self-centered butt. Angry with himself, furious with Victor and the other two, irritated at the world in general, Alexios marched to the winch and wrapped the cable around both his gloved hands.

Slowly he began lowering himself down the steep side of the gully.

"What are you doing?" Molina demanded. "Are you coming?"

"I'll be there in a few minutes," Alexios said between gritted teeth.

I'll save your ass, Victor, he thought. I'll save your body. I won't let you die. I'll bring you back and let you destroy yourself. That's just as good as killing you. Better, even. Destroy yourself, Victor. With my help.

TOR BOOKS BY BEN BOVA

MERCURY

BEN BOVA

TOR®

A TOM DOHERTY ASSOCIATES BOOK
NEW YORK

This is a work of fiction. All the characters and events portrayed in this book are either products of the author's imagination or are used fictitiously.

MERCURY

Copyright © 2005 by Ben Bova

Edited by Patrick Nielsen Hayden

A Tor Book
Published by Tom Doherty Associates, LLC
175 Fifth Avenue
New York, NY 10010

www.tor-forge.com

Tor® is a registered trademark of Tom Doherty Associates, LLC.

ISBN 978-0-7653-4314-7

First Edition: May 2005
First Mass Market Edition: March 2006

Printed in the United States of America

0 9 8 7 6 5 4 3

To the memory of my friend and colleague,
the star-seeker Robert Forward;
and to A.D., of course;
but most of all to the beauteous Barbara.

History will remember the inhabitants of [the twentieth] century as the people who went from Kitty Hawk to the moon in sixty-six years, only to languish for the next thirty in low-Earth orbit. At the core of the risk-free society is a self-indulgent failure of nerve.

—Buzz Aldrin,
Apollo 11 astronaut

A species with all its eggs in one planetary basket risks becoming an omelet.

—Stephen Webb
Where Is Everybody (Copernicus Books, 2002)

MERCURY

PROLOGUE:
THE LONG SEARCH

When, in disgrace with Fortune and men's eyes,
I all alone beweep my outcast state . . .

As he had every night for more than twelve years, Saito Yamagata wearily climbed the winding dark stone stairway to the top of Chota Lamasery's highest tower. He could feel the cold winter wind whipping down from the low entrance to the platform at the top. It was going to be a long, bitterly cold night. No matter. Yamagata was seeking atonement, not comfort. Atonement— and something more.

Once he had been a giant of global industry. Yamagata Corporation had even reached beyond the Earth to build the first solar-power satellites. Men trembled at his slightest frown; fortunes were made when he smiled. Then he had been struck down by an inoperable brain cancer and died.

That had been Yamagata's first life. Yamagata's only legitimate son, Nobuhiko, had personally administered the lethal injection that allowed the doctors to pronounce him clinically dead. More carefully than an ancient Pharaoh, Yamagata was preserved in a stainless steel sarcophagus filled with liquid nitrogen to await the day when his tumor could be safely removed and he might be brought back to life.

By the time he was cured and revived, Nobu was physically the same age as his father. Yamagata burst into laughter when he first saw his son: it was like looking into the mirror when he shaved. With great wisdom, he thought, Yamagata declined to resume his position at the head of the corporation. Nobu had done well, and to demote him now would shame his son intolerably. So the elder Yamagata retired to this lamasery carved into the distant Himalayas to contemplate his first life.

However, he did not live as the lamas did; he had comfortable furniture and decorations carried laboriously up the mountains to his bare stone cell. He maintained contact with the outside world through the latest electronic communications systems, including a satellite relay lofted especially for him alone. To the despair of the grand lama, who earnestly wanted to teach Yamagata the way to enlightenment, he brought in his own cook and even managed to gain weight. And he began to write his memoirs.

Perhaps because he dwelt on his former life, Yamagata found it impossible to stay entirely away from the corporation he had founded. He spoke to his son often over the videophone system in his quarters. He began to offer advice to Nobu. He envisioned a grand plan for Yamagata Corporation, a plan that extended far beyond the Earth. He led the corporation into the Asteroid Wars.

It took the slaughter of the *Chrysalis* habitat to shock Yamagata into realizing what he had done. More than a thousand helpless men, women, and children were massacred senselessly, needlessly.

I did not order the attack, he told himself. Yet he found that he could not sleep. Even his cook's most tempting preparations became tasteless, unappetizing to him. In his mind's eye he kept seeing those terrified, innocent people screaming in helpless horror as their space habitat was torn apart.

It took Yamagata many weeks to realize that he felt more than guilt. For the first time in his lives he felt shame. He was ashamed of what he had set in motion. I did not order the attack, he repeated to himself. Still, it was the inevitable consequence of the war that I willingly started.

Unsure of himself for the first time in his life, racked by a sense of shame he had never felt before, Yamagata begged for a private audience with the grand lama, hoping the old man could soothe his inner turmoil.

"There has been a tragedy," he began, hesitantly.

The grand lama waited for him to continue, sitting in silent patience on the low couch of his chamber, his head shaved bald, his ascetic face bony, hollow-cheeked, his dark mahogany eyes squarely on Yamagata.

"There is a war going on in space," Yamagata continued. "Far from here. In the Asteroid Belt."

"Even here, such rumors have been whispered," said the grand lama, his voice little more than a soft murmur.

"A few days ago more than a thousand people were killed," Yamagata stumbled on. "Slaughtered. In a space habitat."

The lama's lean face went gray.

His heart pounding, Yamagata finally blurted, "It may have been my fault! I may have caused their deaths!"

The grand lama clutched at his saffron robe with both hands. Yamagata thought the old man was having a heart attack. He stood before the lama, stiff with shame and guilt, silent because he had no words to express what he felt.

When at last the grand lama recovered his self-control he looked into Yamagata's eyes with a stare that pierced to his very soul.

"Do you accept responsibility for these murders?" he asked, his voice now hard as iron.

It was not easy for a man of Yamagata's pride and power to stand there humbly asking forgiveness from this aged, robed lama. He feared that the old man would expel him from the lamasery, shame him, accuse him of polluting the very air they were breathing.

"I do," he whispered.

The grand lama said, "For more than four years you have lived among us, but not as one of us. You have used our sanctuary and our way of life for your personal convenience."

Yamagata said nothing. It was true.

Slowly, in words as hard and unyielding as the stones of the mountain aerie itself, the grand lama told Yamagata that he must seek true atonement or suffer the deadly weight of guilt forever.

"How do I do that?" Yamagata asked.

The lama was silent for many moments. Then, "Become one of us, not merely among us. Accept our way. Seek your path to atonement. Seek enlightenment."

Yamagata bowed his acceptance.

Heavy with remorse, Yamagata started out on the path to atonement. He sent his cook back to Japan, got rid of his comfortable furniture and electronic equipment, moved into a bare cell, and tried to live as the lamas did. He fasted with them, prayed with them, slept on a hard wooden pallet. And every night, winter or summer, he climbed the high tower to spend hours alone in contemplation, trying to meditate, trying to find true atonement in his soul.

The grand lama died, since the sect did not believe in rejuvenation treatments, and was replaced by a younger man. Still every night Yamagata climbed his weary way and sat cross-legged on the cold stone floor of the tower's platform, waiting for—what? Forgiveness? Understanding?

No. Yamagata realized over the slow passage of the years that what he truly sought was enlightenment, a satori, a revelation of the path he must follow.

Nothing. Night after night, year after year, not a glimmer of a hint. Yamagata prayed to the deaf heavens and received nothing in return. He wondered if the fault was in him, if he was not worthy of a sign from the vast universe. Deep in his soul, though, he thought that perhaps all this meditation and mortification was nothing more than cleverly packaged nonsense. And this troubled him, because he realized that as long as he harbored such thoughts, he would never find the path he so desperately sought.

So he hunkered down against the stone rail as the cold night wind gusted by, his teeth chattering despite the padded coat he had wrapped around himself, his fur hat pulled down over his ears, his chin sunk on his chest, his inner voice telling him that he was a fool for going through all this pain and humiliation. But doggedly he remained there, waiting, hoping, praying for a revelation.

It was a bitterly cold night. The moaning wind was like daggers of ice that cut through him mercilessly. Yamagata sat alone and miserable, trying to ignore the freezing wind, trying to find the path to atonement. Nothing. Only darkness and the glittering points of thousands of stars staring down at him from the black bowl of night.

He stared back at the stars. He could make out the Big Dipper, of course, and followed its Pointers to the North Star. Polaris was a thousand light years distant, he remembered from an astronomy lecture many years ago.

The nearest star was Alpha Centauri, but it was too far south to be seen from these frigid mountains.

Suddenly Yamagata threw his head back and laughed, a hearty, full-throated roar of delight that he hurled back into the teeth of the keening night wind. Of course! he said to himself. The answer has been all around me for all these years and I was too blind to see it. The stars! My path must lead to the stars.

BOOK I
THE REALM OF FIRE

No, Time, thou shalt not boast that I do change:
Thy pyramids built up with newer might
To me are nothing novel, nothing strange;
They are but dressings of a former sight.

ARRIVAL

Saito Yamagata had to squint against the Sun's overwhelming glare, even through the heavily tinted visor of his helmet.

"This is truly the realm of fire," he whispered to himself. "Small wonder our ancestors worshiped you, Daystar."

Despite his instinctive unease, Yamagata felt physically comfortable enough inside his thickly insulated spacesuit; its cooling system and the radiators that projected from its back like a pair of dark oblong wings seemed to be working adequately. Still, the nearness, the overpowering brightness, the sheer *size* of that seething, churning ball of roiling gases made his nerves flutter. It seemed to fill the sky. Yamagata could see streamers arching up from the Sun's curved limb into the blackness of space, huge bridges of million-degree plasma expanding and then pouring back down onto the blazing, searing surface of the photosphere.

He shuddered inside the cramped confines of his suit. Enough sight-seeing, he told himself. You have proven your courage and audacity for all the crew and your guests to see and remember. Get back inside the ship. Get to work. It is time to begin your third life.

Yamagata had come to Mercury to seek salvation. A strange route to blessedness, he thought. I must first pass through this fiery inferno, like a Catholic serving time in purgatory before attaining heaven. He tried to shrug philosophically, found that it was impossible in the suit, so instead he lifted his left arm with the help of the suit's miniaturized servomotors and studied the keyboard wrapped around his wrist until he felt certain that he knew which keys he must touch to activate and control his suit's propulsion unit. He could call for assistance, he knew, but the loss of face was too much to risk. Despite the lamas' earnest attempts to teach him humility, Yamagata still held to his pride. If I go sailing out into infinity, he told himself, then I can call for help. And blame a suit malfunction, he added, with a sly grin.

He was pleased, then, when he was able to turn himself to face *Himawari*, the big, slowly rotating fusion torch ship that had brought him and his two guests to Mercury, and actually began jetting toward it at a sedate pace. With something of a shock Yamagata realized this was the first time he had ever been in space. All those years of his first life, building the power satellites and getting rich, he had remained firmly on Earth. Then he had died of cancer, been frozen, and reborn. Most of his second life he had spent in the lamasery in the Himalayas. He had never gone into space. Not until now.

Time to begin my third life, he said to himself as he neared *Himawari*. Time to atone for the first two.

Time for the stars.

LANDFALL

E ven with three subordinates assisting him, it took Yamagata nearly an hour to disencumber himself of the bulky, heavily insulated spacesuit. He was dripping wet with perspiration and must have smelled ripe, but none of his aides dared say a word or show the slightest expression of distaste. When they had helped him into the suit Yamagata had thought of a Spanish toreador being assisted in donning his "suit of lights" for the bullring. Now he felt like a medieval knight taking off his battered armor after a bruising tournament.

Going outside the ship in the spacesuit had been little more than a whim, Yamagata knew, but a man of his wealth and power could be indulged his whims. Besides, he wanted to impress his subordinates and guests. Even though his son Nobu actually ran Yamagata Corporation and had for decades, the elder Yamagata was treated deferentially wherever he went. Despite the years of patient instruction that the lamas had spent on him, Yamagata still relished being fawned upon.

Money brings power; he understood that. But he wanted more than that. What he wanted now was respect, prestige. He wanted to be remembered not merely as a wealthy or powerful man; he wanted to go down in history for his vision, his munificence, his drive. He wanted to be the man who gave the stars to the human race.

Yamagata Corporation's solar power satellites were bringing desperately needed electrical power to an Earth devastated by greenhouse flooding and abrupt climate shifts. Under Nobuhiko's direction, the corporation was helping to move Japan and the other nations crippled by the global warming back onto the road toward prosperity.

And freedom. The two went hand in hand, Yamagata knew. When the greenhouse cliff struck so abruptly, flooding coastal cities, collapsing the international electrical power grid, wrecking the global economy, Earth's governments became repressive, authoritarian. People who are hungry, homeless, and without hope will always trade their individual liberties for order, for safety, for food. Ultraconservative religious groups came to power in Asia, the Middle East, even Europe and America; they ruled with an absolute faith in their own convictions and zero tolerance for anyone else's.

Now, with the climate stabilizing and some prosperity returning, many of the world's peoples were once again struggling for their individual rights, resuming the age-old battle that their forebears had fought against kings and tyrants in earlier centuries.

All to the good, Yamagata told himself. But it is not enough. The human race must expand its frontier, enlarge its horizons. Sooner or later, humankind must reach out to the stars. That will be my gift to humanity.

Can I do it? he asked himself. Do I have the strength and the will to succeed? He had been tough enough in his earlier lives, a ruthless industrial giant before the cancer had struck him down. But that had been for myself, he realized, for my corporation and my son's legacy. Now I am striving to accomplish greatness for humanity, not merely for my own selfish ends. Again he smiled bitterly. Foolish man, he warned himself. What you do now you do for your own purposes. Don't try to delude yourself. Don't try to conceal your own ambitions with a cloak of nobility.

Yet the question remained: Do I have the determination, the strength, the single-minded drive to make this mad scheme a success?

Finally freed of the suit with all its paraphernalia and boots and undergarments, Yamagata stood in his sweat-soaked sky-blue coveralls, which bore on its breast the white flying crane symbol of his family and his corporation. He dismissed his subordinates with a curt word of thanks. They bowed and hissed respectfully as Yamagata turned and started up the corridor that led to his private compartment and a hot shower.

Yamagata was a sturdily built man, slightly over 175 centimeters tall, who appeared to be no more than fifty-some years old, thanks to rejuvenation therapies. In his youth he had been as slim as a samurai's blade, but the years of good living in his first life had softened him, rounded his body and his face. The cancer ate away much of that, and his years in the lamasery had kept him gaunt, but once he left the Himalayas to begin his third life he soon reverted to his tastes in food and drink. Now he was slightly paunchy, his sodden, stained coveralls already beginning to strain at the middle. His face was round, also, but creased with laugh lines. In his first life Yamagata had laughed a lot, although during those years of remorse and penance he had spent with the lamas in their stone fortress high in the Himalayas there was precious little laughter.

Freshly showered and dressed in a crisply clean open-necked shirt and fashionable dark trousers, Yamagata made his way to the ship's bridge. He thought about dropping in on his two guests, but he would see them later at dinner, he knew. As soon as he stepped through the open hatch into the bridge the Japanese crew, including the captain, snapped to respectful attention.

Waving a hand to show they should return to their duties, Yamagata asked the captain, "Are we ready to send the landing craft to the planet?"

The captain tried to keep his face expressionless, but it was clear to Yamagata that he did not like the idea.

"It is not necessary for you to go down to the surface, sir," he said, almost in a whisper. "We have all the necessary facilities here on the ship—"

"I understand that," said Yamagata, smiling to show that he was not offended by the captain's reluctance. "Still, I wish to see the surface installation for myself. It's near the north pole, I understand."

"Yes, sir. Borealis Planitia."

"Near the crater Goethe," said Yamagata.

The captain dipped his chin to acknowledge Yamagata's understanding of the geography. But he murmured, "It is very rugged down there, sir."

"So I have been told. But personal comfort is not everything, you know. My son, Nobuhiko, enjoys skiing. I cannot for the life of me understand why he would risk his life and limbs for the joy of sliding down a snowy mountain in all that cold and wet, but still he loves it."

The captain bowed his head. But then he added one final warning: "Er . . . They call it 'Dante's Inferno' down there. Sir."

DATA BANK

The closest planet to the Sun, Mercury is a small, rocky, barren, dense, airless, heat-scorched world.

For centuries astronomers believed that Mercury's rotation was "locked," so that one side of the planet always faced the Sun while the other side always looked away. They reasoned that the sunward side of Mercury must be the hottest planetary surface in the solar system, while the side facing away from the Sun must be frozen down almost to absolute zero.

But this is not so. Mercury turns slowly on its axis, taking 58.6 Earth days to make one revolution. Its year—the time it takes to complete one orbit around the Sun—is 87.97 Earth days.

This leads to a strange situation. Mercury's rotation rate of nearly fifty-nine Earth days is precisely two-thirds of the planet's year. A person standing on the surface of the planet would see the huge Sun move from east to west across the dark airless sky, but it would slow down noticeably, then reverse its course and head back east for a while before resuming its westerly motion. At some locations on Mercury, the Sun rises briefly, then dips down below the horizon before finally rising again for the rest of the Mercurian day. After sunset the Sun peeks back up above the horizon before setting for the length of the night.

Counting the Mercurian day from the time the Sun appears directly overhead (local noon) to the next time it reaches that point, it measures one hundred seventy-six Earth days. From the standpoint of noon-to-noon, then, the Mercurian day is twice as long as its year!

The Sun looms large in Mercury's sky. It appears twice as big as we see it from Earth when Mercury is at the farthest point from the Sun in its lopsided orbit and three times larger at the closest point.

And it is *hot*. Daytime temperatures soar to more than 400° Celsius, four times higher than the boiling point of water, hot enough to melt zinc. At night the temperature drops to -135°C because there is no atmosphere to retain the day's heat; it radiates away into space.

With a diameter of only 4,879 kilometers, Mercury is the smallest planet in the solar system except for distant-most Pluto. Jupiter and Saturn have moons that are larger than Mercury. The planet is slightly more than one-third larger than Earth's own Moon.

Yet Mercury is a dense planet, with a large iron core and a relatively thin overlay of silicon-based rock. This may be because the planet formed so close to the Sun that most of the silicate material in the region was too hot to condense and solidify; it remained gaseous and was blown away on the solar wind, leaving little material for the planet to build on except iron and other metals.

Another possibility, though, is that most of Mercury's rocky crust was blasted away into space by the impact of a mammoth asteroid early in the solar system's history. Mercury's battered, airless surface looks much like the Moon's, testimony to the pitiless barrage of asteroids and larger planetesimals that hurtled through the solar system more than three billion years ago. Caloris Basin is a huge bull's-eye of circular mountain ridges some 1,300 kilometers in diameter. This gigantic impact crater is the center of fault lines that run for hundreds of kilometers across the planet's rocky surface.

An asteroid roughly one hundred kilometers wide smashed into Mercury nearly four billion years ago, gouging out Caloris Basin and perhaps blasting away most of the planet's rocky crust.

Despite the blazing heat from the nearby Sun, water ice exists at Mercury's polar regions. Ice from comets that crashed into the planet has been cached in deep craters near the poles, where sunlight never reaches. Just as on the Moon, ice is an invaluable resource for humans and their machines.

DANTE'S INFERNO

Yamagata rode the small shuttle down to the planet's airless surface in his shirtsleeves, strapped into an ergonomically cushioned chair directly behind the pilot and copilot. Both the humans were redundancies: the shuttle could have flown perfectly well on its internal computer guidance, but *Himawari*'s captain had insisted that not merely one but two humans should accompany their illustrious employer.

The shuttle itself was little more than an eggshell of ceramic-coated metal with a propulsion rocket and steering jets attached, together with three spindly landing legs. Yamagata hardly felt any acceleration forces at all. Separation from *Himawari* was gentle, and landing in Mercury's light gravity was easy.

As soon as the landing struts touched down and the propulsion system automatically cut off, the pilot turned in his chair and said to Yamagata, "Gravity here is only one-third of Earth's, sir."

The copilot, a handsome European woman with pouty lips, added, "About the same as Mars."

The Japanese pilot glared at her.

Yamagata smiled good-naturedly at them both. "I have never been to Mars. My son once thought of moving me to the Moon, but I was dead then."

Both pilots gaped at him as he unstrapped his safety harness and stood up, his head a bare centimeter from the cabin's metal overhead. Their warning about the Mercurian gravity was strictly pro forma, of course. Yamagata had instructed *Himawari*'s captain to spin the fusion torch vessel at one-third normal gravity once it reached Mercury after its four-day flight from Earth. He felt quite comfortable at one-third g.

Leaning between the two pilots' chairs, Yamagata peered out the cockpit window. Even through the window's tinting, it looked glaring and hot out there. Pitiless. Sun-baked. The stony surface of Mercury was bleak, barren, pockmarked with craters and cracked with meandering gullies. He saw the long shadow of their shuttle craft stretched out across the bare, rocky ground before them like an elongated oval.

"The Sun is behind us, then," Yamagata muttered.

"Yes, sir," said the pilot. "It will set in four hours."

The copilot, who still had not learned that she was supposed to be subordinate to the pilot, added, "Then it will rise again for seventy-three minutes before setting for the night."

Yamagata saw the clear displeasure on the pilot's face. The man said nothing to his copilot, though. Instead, he pointed toward a rounded hillock of stony rubble.

"There's the base," he informed Yamagata. "Dante's Inferno."

Yamagata said, "They are sending out the access tube."

A jointed tube was inching toward them across the uneven ground on metal wheels, reminding Yamagata of a caterpillar groping its way along the stalk of a plant on its many feet. He felt the shuttle rock slightly as the face of the tube thumped against the craft's airlock.

The pilot watched the display on his panel, lights flicking on and off, a string of alphanumerics scrolling across the screen. He touched a corner of the screen with one finger and a visual image came up, with more numbers and a trio of green blinking lights.

"Access tube mated with airlock," he announced, reverting to the clipped jargon of his profession. To the copilot he commanded, "Check it and confirm integrity."

She got up from her chair wordlessly and brushed past Yamagata to head back to the airlock. He appreciated the brief touch of her soft body, the hint of flowery perfume. What would she do if I asked her to remain here at the base with me? Yamagata wondered. A European. And very independent in her manner. But I have a dinner appointment with my two guests, he reminded himself. Still, the thought lingered.

After a few silent moments, the pilot rose from his chair and walked a courteous three steps behind Yamagata to the airlock's inner hatch. The copilot stepped through from the opposite direction, a slight smile curving her generous lips.

"Integrity confirmed," she said, almost carelessly. "The tube is airtight and the cooling system is operational."

Yamagata saw that the outer airlock hatch was open, as well, and the access tube stretched beyond it. He politely thanked the two pilots and headed down the tube. Despite her insouciance, at least the copilot had the sense to bow properly. The tube was big enough for him to stand without stooping. The flooring felt slightly springy underfoot. It curved gently to the left; within a few paces he could no longer see the two pilots standing at the shuttle's hatch.

Then he saw the hatch to the base, which was closed. Someone had scrawled a graffito in blood-red above the curved top of the hatch: *Why, this is hell, nor am I out of it.*

Yamagata grunted at that. As he reached out his hand to tap the electronic panel that controlled the hatch, it swung open without his aid.

A lean, pale-skinned man with dark hair that curled over his ears stood on the other side of the hatch, wearing not the coveralls Yamagata expected, but a loose-fitting white shirt with flowing long sleeves that were fastened tightly at his wrists and a pair of dark baggy trousers stuffed into gleamingly polished calf-length boots. A wide leather belt cinched his narrow, flat middle.

He smiled politely and extended his hand to Yamagata. "Welcome to Goethe base, Mr. Yamagata. I can't tell you how pleased I am to have you here. I am Dante Alexios."

Yamagata accepted his hand. His grip was firm, his smile gracious. Yet there was something wrong with his face. The two sides of it seemed slightly mismatched, almost as if two separate halves had been grafted together by an incompetent surgeon. Even his smile was slightly lopsided; it made him appear almost mocking, rather than friendly.

And his eyes. Dante Alexios's dark brown eyes burned with some deep inner fury, Yamagata saw.

Dante's Inferno indeed, he thought.

SUNPOWER FOUNDATION

lexios showed Yamagata through the cramped, steamy base. It was small, built for efficiency, not human comfort. Little more than an oversized bubble of honeycomb metal covered with rubble from Mercury's surface to protect it from the heat and radiation, its inside was partitioned into cubicles and larger spaces. Goethe base was staffed with a mere two dozen engineers and technicians, yet it seemed as if hundreds of men and women had been packed into its crowded confines.

"We thought about establishing the base in orbit around the planet," Alexios explained as they walked down a row of humming consoles. Yamagata felt sweaty, almost disgusted at the closeness of all these strangers, their foreignness, their body odors. Most of them were Europeans or Americans, he saw; a few were obviously African or perhaps African-American. None of them paid the slightest attention to him. They were all bent over their consoles, intent on their tasks.

"My original plan was for the base to be in orbit," Yamagata said.

Alexios smiled diplomatically. "Economics. The great tyrant that dictates our every move."

Remembering the lessons in tolerance the lamas had pressed upon him, Yamagata was trying to keep the revulsion from showing on his face. He smelled stale food and something that reminded him of burned-out electrical insulation.

Continuing as if none of this bothered him in the slightest, Alexios explained, "We ran the numbers a half dozen times. If we'd kept the base in orbit we'd have to bring supplies to it constantly. Raised the costs too high. Here on the surface we have access to local water ice and plenty of silicon, metals, almost all the resources we need, including oxygen that we bake out of the rocks. Plenty of solar energy, of course. So I decided to plant the base here, on the ground."

"*You* decided?" Yamagata snapped.

"I'm an independent contractor, Mr. Yamagata. These people are my employees, not yours."

"Ah yes," Yamagata said, recovering his composure. "Of course."

"Naturally, I want to do the best job possible for you. That includes keeping the project's costs as low as I can."

"As I recall it, you were the lowest bidder of all the engineering firms that we considered, by a considerable margin."

"Frankly," Alexios said, smiling slightly, "I deliberately underbid the job. I'm losing money here."

Yamagata's brows rose in surprise.

"I'm fairly well off. I can afford a whim now and then."

"A whim? To come to Mercury?"

"To work with the great Saito Yamagata."

Yamagata searched Alexios's strangely asymmetrical face. The man seemed to be completely serious; not a trace of sarcasm. He dipped his chin slightly in acknowledgment of the compliment. They had come to the end of the row of consoles. Yamagata saw a metal door in the thin partition before them, with the name D. ALEXIOS stenciled on it. Beneath it was a smeared area where someone had tried to wipe out a graffito, but it was still faintly legible: *He who must be obeyed.*

It was somewhat cooler inside Alexios's office, and a good deal quieter. Acoustic insulation, Yamagata realized gratefully, kneading his throbbing temples as he sat in a stiff little chair. Alexios pulled up a similar chair and sat next to him, much closer than Yamagata would have preferred. The man's unbalanced face disturbed him.

"You need a drink," Alexios said, peering intently into Yamagata's perspiring face. "Tea, perhaps? Or something stronger?"

"Water would be quite welcome, especially if it's cold." Yamagata could feel his coveralls sticking to his sweaty ribs.

The office was tiny, barely big enough for a quartet of the spartan little chairs. There was no desk, no other furniture at all except for a small bare table and a squat cubicle refrigerator of brushed aluminum. Alexios went to it and pulled out an unmarked ceramic flask.

Handing it to Yamagata, he said, "Local product. Mercurian water, straight from the ice cache nearby."

Yamagata hesitated.

With a crooked grin, Alexios added, "We've run it through the purifiers, of course, although we left a certain amount of carbonation in it."

Yamagata took a cautious sip. It was cold, sparkling and delicious. He pulled in a longer swallow.

The room's only table was on Alexios's far side, so there was no place to set the bottle down except on the floor. Yamagata saw that it was tiled, but the plastic felt soft to his touch.

"Now then," he said as he deposited the bottle at his foot, "where we do we stand? What are your major problems?"

Alexios leaned back in his chair and took a palm-sized remote from the table. The partition on Yamagata's right immediately lit up with a flat screen display.

"There's Mercury," Alexios began, "the gray circle in the middle. The blue oblongs orbiting the planet are the first four solar power satellites, built at Selene and towed here."

Yamagata said, "With six more on their way here from the Moon."

"Correct," said Alexios. Six more blue oblongs appeared on the screen, clustered in the upper right corner.

"So it goes well. How soon can we be selling electrical power?"

"There is a problem with that."

Despite the fact that he knew, intellectually, that no project proceeds without problems, Yamagata still felt his insides twitch. "So? What problem?"

Alexios replied, "The point of setting up powersats in Mercury orbit is that they can generate power much more efficiently. Being almost two-thirds closer to the Sun than Earth is, we can take advantage of the higher power density to—"

"I know all that," Yamagata snapped impatiently. "That is why I started this project."

"Yes," Alexios said, his smile turning a trifle bitter. "But, as they say, the Lord giveth and the Lord taketh away."

"What do you mean by that?"

"The very intensity of sunlight that improves the solar panels' efficiency so beautifully also degrades the solar cells very quickly."

"Degrades them?"

The image on the wall screen changed to a graph that showed a set of curves.

"The blue curve, the one on the top, shows the predicted power output for a solar cell in Mercury orbit," Alexios explained.

Yamagata could see for himself. A yellow curve started out closely following the blue, then fell off disastrously. He looked along the bottom axis of the graph and gasped with dismay.

"It gets that bad after only six weeks?"

"I'm afraid so," Alexios said. "We're going to have to harden the cells, which will cut down on their efficiency."

"How much?"

"I have my people working on that now. I've also taken the liberty of transmitting this data back to your corporate headquarters on Earth so that your experts can double-check my people's calculations."

Yamagata sank back in the little chair. This could ruin everything, he thought. Everything!

As quickly as he gracefully could, Yamagata returned to *Himawari* riding in orbit around Mercury. He sat in gloomy silence in the little shuttle craft, mulling over the bad news that Alexios had given him. From his seat behind the two pilots, however, he couldn't help watching the European woman. It wouldn't do to pay any attention to her in front of her superior, he reasoned. Still, she was a fine-looking woman with strong features. The profile of her face showed a firm jawline, a chiseled nose, high cheekbones. Nordic, perhaps, Yamagata thought, although her hair was a dark brown, as were her eyes. Her coveralls were tight, almost form-fitting. Her form pleased Yamagata's discerning eye immensely.

Later, he thought, I'll dig her name out of the personnel files. Perhaps she would not be averse to joining me for an after-dinner drink this evening.

He had almost forgotten her, though, by the time he reached his stateroom aboard the fusion torch ship. His quarters were spacious and well-appointed, filled with little luxuries such as the single peony blossom in the delicate tall vase on the corner of his desk, and the faint aroma of a springtime garden that wafted in on the nearly silent air blowers.

Yamagata peeled off his sweaty coveralls, took a quick shower, then wrapped himself in a silk kimono of midnight blue. By then he had worked up the courage to call his son, back at corporate headquarters in New Kyoto.

Earth was on the other side of the Sun at the moment, and his call had to be relayed through one of the communications satellites in solar orbit. Transmission lag time, according to the data bar across the bottom of Yamagata's wall screen, would be eleven minutes.

A two-way conversation will be impossible, Yamagata realized as he put the call through on his private, scrambled channel. I'll talk and Nobu will listen; then we'll reverse the process.

It still startled him to see his son's image. Nobuhiko Yamagata was physically almost exactly the same age as his father, because of the years Saito had spent in cryonic suspension.

"Father," said Nobu, dipping his head in a respectful bow. "I trust you had a good journey and are safely in orbit at Mercury." Before Saito could reply, Nobu added jokingly, "And I hope you brought your sunblock lotion."

Saito rocked back with laughter in his contoured easy chair. "Sunblock lotion indeed! I didn't come out here for a tan, you know."

He knew it would take eleven minutes for his words to reach Nobu, and another eleven for his son's reply. So Saito immediately launched into a description of his visit to Goethe base on Mercury and the problem with the solar panels on the powersats.

He ended with, "This Alexios person claims he has sent the data to your experts. I am anxious to hear what they think about it."

And then he waited. Yamagata got up from his chair, went to the bar and poured himself a stiff Glenlivet, knocked it back and felt the smooth heat of the whisky spread through him. He paced around his compartment, admired the holograms of ancient landscapes that decorated the walls, and tried not to look at his wristwatch.

I know how to pass the time, he said to himself. Sliding into his desk chair, he opened a new window on the wall display and called up the ship's personnel files. Scanning through the names and pictures of the pilots aboard took several minutes. Ah! He smiled, pleased. There she is: Birgitta Sundsvall. I was right, she's Swedish. Unmarried. Good. Employee since . . .

He reviewed her entire dossier. There were several photographs of the woman in it, and Yamagata was staring at them when his son's voice broke into his reverie.

"Alexios has transmitted the data on the solar cells' degradation, Father," Nobuhiko replied at last.

Yamagata immediately wiped the personnel file from the screen, as if his son could see it all the way back on Earth.

Nobu went on, "This appears to be quite a serious problem. My analysts tell me that the decrease in power output efficiency almost completely wipes out any advantage of generating the power from Mercury orbit."

Yamagata knew it would be pointless to interrupt, and allowed his son to continue, "If this analysis stands up, your Mercury project will have to be written off, Father. The costs of operating from Mercury are simply too high. You might as well keep the sunsats in Earth orbit, all things considered."

"But have we considered all things?" Yamagata snapped. "I can't believe that this problem will stop us. We did analyses of cell degradation before we started this project. Why are the actual figures so much worse than our predictions?"

Yamagata realized he was getting angry. He took a deep breath, tried to remember a mantra that would calm him.

"Please call me," he said to his son, "when your people have more definite answers to my questions." Then he cut off the connection and the wall screen went blank.

Technically, the Mercury project was not being funded by Yamagata Corporation. Saito had officially retired from the corporation soon after he'd been revived from his long cryonic sleep. Instead, once he left the lamasery and returned to the world, he used his personal fortune to establish the Sunpower Foundation and began the Mercury project. As far as Nobu and the rest of the world were concerned, the Mercury project was devoted to generating inexpensive electrical power for the growing human habitations spreading through the solar system. Only Saito Yamagata knew that its true goal was to provide the power to send human explorers to the stars.

Saito—and one other person.

E ven after a dozen years of living with the lamas, Yamagata could not separate himself from his desire for creature comforts. He did not consider the accommodations aboard his ship *Himawari* to be particularly sumptuous, but he felt that he had a right to a certain amount of luxury. Sitting at the head of the small dining table in his private wardroom, he smiled as he recalled that the great fifteenth-century Chinese admiral Zheng He had included "pleasure women" among the crews of his great vessels of exploration and trade. At least I have not gone that far, Yamagata thought, although the memory of the Sundsvall woman still lingered in the back of his mind.

Seated at his right was Bishop Danvers, sipping abstemiously at a tiny stemmed glass of sherry. He was a big man, with heavy shoulders and considerable bulk. Yet he looked soft, round of face and body, although Yamagata noticed that his hands were big, heavy with horny calluses and prominent knuckles. The hands of a bricklayer, Yamagata thought, on the body of a churchman. On Yamagata's left sat Victor Molina, an astrobiologist from some Midwestern American university. The ship's captain, Chuichi Shibasaki, sat at the far end of the table.

Bishop Danvers had come along on *Himawari* because the New Morality had insisted that Mercury Base must have a chaplain, and the project manager had specifically asked for Danvers to take up the mission. Danvers, however, showed no inclination to leave the comforts of the ship and actually go down to the planet's surface. Hardly any of the ship's mainly Japanese crew paid the scantest attention to him, but the bishop did not seem to mind their secularist indifference in the slightest. Sooner or later he would go down to Goethe base and offer the men and women there his spiritual guidance. If anyone wanted some. What would the bishop think of pleasure women? Yamagata wondered, suppressing a grin.

Danvers put down his barely touched glass and asked in a sharp, cutting voice, "Victor, you don't actually expect to find living creatures on Mercury, do you?"

Victor Molina and Bishop Danvers knew each other, Yamagata had been told. They had been friends years earlier. The bishop had even performed Molina's wedding ceremony.

Molina was olive-skinned, with startling cobalt blue eyes and a pugnacious, pointed chin. His luxuriant, sandy hair was tied back in a ponytail, fastened by a clip of asteroidal silver that matched the studs in both his earlobes. He had already drained his sherry, and answered the bishop's question as one of the human waiters refilled his glass.

"Why not?" he replied, a trifle belligerently. "We've found living organisms on Mars and the moons of Jupiter, haven't we?"

"Yes, but—"

"And what about those enormous creatures in Jupiter's ocean? They might even be intelligent."

The bishop's pale eyes snapped angrily. "Intelligent? Nonsense! Surely you can't believe—"

"It isn't a matter of belief, Elliott, it's a question of fact. Science depends on observation and measurement, not some a priori fairytales."

"You're not a Believer," the bishop muttered.

"I'm an observer," Molina snapped. "I'm here to see what the facts are."

Yamagata thought that Dr. Molina could use some of the lamas' lessons in humility. He found himself fascinated by the differences between the two men. Bishop Danvers's round face was slightly flushed, whether from anger or embarrassment Yamagata could not tell. His hair was thinning, combed forward to hide a receding hairline. He refuses to take rejuvenation treatments, Yamagata guessed; it must be against his religious principles. Molina, on the other hand, looked like a young Lancelot: piercing eyes, flowing hair, strong shoulders. Yamagata pictured him on a prancing charger, seeking out dragons to slay.

Before the discussion became truly disagreeable Yamagata tried to intervene: "Everyone was quite surprised to find creatures living in the clouds of Venus, and even on that planet's surface," he said.

"Silicone snakes, with liquid sulfur for blood," Captain Shibasaki added, taking up on his employer's lead.

Bishop Danvers shuddered.

"Incredible organisms," Molina said. "What was that line of Blake's? 'Did He who made the lamb make thee?'" He stared across the table at the bishop, almost sneering.

"But none of those creatures have the intelligence that God gave us," Danvers countered.

"Those Jovian Leviathans just might," said Molina.

The table fell silent. At a nod from Yamagata, the two waiters began to serve the appetizers: smoked eel in a seaweed salad. Yamagata and the captain fell to with chopsticks. The two others used forks. Yamagata noted that neither of the gaijin did more than pick at the food. Ah well, he thought, they'll feel more at home with the steak that comes next.

Bishop Danvers wouldn't let the subject drop, however.

"But surely you don't expect to find anything living down on the surface of Mercury," he said to Molina.

"I'll grant you, it's not the most likely place to look for living organisms," Molina admitted. "The planet's been baked dry. Except for the ice caches near the poles there's not a drop of water anywhere, not even deep underground."

"Then what makes you think—"

"PAHs," said Molina.

"I beg your pardon?"

"PAHs," Molina repeated.

The bishop frowned. "Are you being deliberately rude to me, Victor?"

"I believe," Yamagata intervened, "that our noted astrobiologist is referring to a certain form of chemical compound."

"Polycyclic aromatic hydrocarbons," Molina agreed. "P-A-H. PAHs."

"Oh," said Bishop Danvers.

"You have found such compounds on the surface of Mercury?" Yamagata asked.

Nodding vigorously, Molina replied, "Traces of PAHs have been found in some of the rock samples sent for analysis by the people building your base down there."

"And you believe this indicates the presence of life?" Danvers challenged. "A trace of some chemicals?"

"PAHs are biomarkers," Molina said firmly. "They've been found on Earth, on other planets, on comets—even in interstellar clouds."

"And always in association with living creatures?" Yamagata asked.

Molina hesitated a fraction of a second. "Almost always. They can be created abiologically, under certain circumstances."

Danvers shook his head. "I can't believe anything could live on that godforsaken world."

"How do you know god's forsaken this planet?" Molina challenged.

"I didn't mean it literally," Danvers grumbled.

"How strong is this evidence?" Yamagata asked. "Does the presence of these compounds mean that life is certain to be found on Mercury?"

"Nothing's certain," Molina said. "As a matter of fact, the PAHs deteriorate very rapidly in the tremendous heat and totally arid conditions down there."

"Ah," said the bishop, smiling for the first time.

Molina's answering smile was bigger, and fiercer. "But don't you see? If the PAHs deteriorate quickly, yet we still find them present in the rocks, *then something must be producing them constantly*. Something down there must be continuously creating those complex, fragile compounds. Something that's alive."

The bishop's face blanched. Yamagata suddenly foresaw his sunpower project being invaded by armies of earnest environmentalists, each eager to prevent any activity that might contaminate the native life-forms.

GOETHE BASE

ante Alexios sat rigidly in his chair and tried not to let his satisfaction show on his face. The wall screen in his office clearly showed the earnest, intent expression on Molina's face.

He wants to come down to the base, Alexios said to himself, delighted. He's asking me for permission to come down here.

"My mission is sanctioned by the International Astronautical Authority," Molina was saying, "as well as the International Consortium of Universities and the science foundations of—"

"Of course," Alexios interrupted, "of course. I have no intention of interfering with your important research, Dr. Molina. I was merely trying to explain to you that conditions down here on the surface are rather difficult. Our base is still fairly rugged, you know."

Molina's intent expression softened into a smug smile. "I've been in rugged places before, Mr. Alexios. You should see the site on Europa, with all that radiation to protect against."

"I can imagine," Alexios replied dryly.

"Then you have no objection to my coming down to your base?"

"None whatsoever," said Alexios. "Our facility is at your disposal."

Molina's bright blue eyes sparkled. "Wonderful! I'll start the preparations immediately."

And with that, Molina ended the transmission. Alexios's wall screen went suddenly blank. He didn't bother to thank me, or even to say good-bye, Alexios thought. How like Victor, still as impetuous and self-centered as ever.

Alexios got up from his chair and stretched languidly, surprised at how tense his body had become during his brief conversation with the astrobiologist.

Victor didn't recognize me, Alexios said to himself. Not the slightest flicker of recall. Of course, it's been more than ten years and the nanosurgery has altered my face considerably. But he didn't even re-member my voice. I'm dead and gone, as far as he's concerned.

All to the good, Alexios told himself. Now he'll come down here on his fool's errand and destroy himself. I'll hardly have to lift a finger. He's eager to rush to his own annihilation.

Alexios dreamed troubling dreams that night. The steel-hard determi-nation that had brought him to Mercury and lured Victor Molina to this hellhole of a world softened as he slept, thawed slightly as he sank into the uncontrollable world of his inner thoughts, the world that he kept hidden and firmly locked away during his waking hours.

In his dream he was standing once again at the base of the sky-tower, craning his neck to follow its rigidly straight line as it rose be-yond the clouds, up, up, farther than the eye could follow, stretching up toward the stars.

Lara was standing beside him, her arm around his waist, her head resting on his strong shoulder. The diamond ring on her finger was his, not Victor's. She had chosen him and rejected Molina. Alexios turned to her, took her in his arms, kissed her with all the tenderness and love his soul could contain.

But she pulled away from him, suddenly terrified. Her lovely face contorted into a scream as the proud tower began to slowly collapse, writhing like an immense snake of man-made fibers, coiling languidly, uncontrollably, unstoppably, as it slowly but inexorably crashed to the ground. All in silence. In utter silence, as if he had suddenly gone completely deaf. Alexios wanted to scream, too, but his throat was frozen. He wanted to stop the tower's collapse with his bare hands, but he could not move, his feet were rooted to the spot.

The immense collapsing tower smashed into the workers' village and beyond, crushing houses and cinderblock work buildings, smashing the bodies of men, women, and children as it thundered to the ground, pulverizing dreams and plans and hopes beyond repair. The whole mountainside shook as dust rose to cover all the work, all the sweat and labor that had raised the tower to its full height. Alex-ios's mouth tasted of ashes and a bitterness that went beyond human endurance.

Lara had disappeared. All around him, as far as the eye could see, there was nothing but devastation and the mangled bodies of the dead.

My fault, he told himself. The sin of pride. My pride has ruined everything, killed all those millions of people. Covered with ashes, his soul crushed along with everything else, he screamed to the vacant sky, "My fault! It's all my fault!"

He awoke with a start, covered with cold sweat. In the years since the skytower's destruction, Alexios had learned that the catastrophe was not his fault, not at all. The soul-killing guilt he had once felt had long since evolved into an implacable, burning hatred. He thirsted not for forgiveness, nor even for the clearing of his name. He lived for vengeance.

THERMOPHILES

Victor Molina also dreamed that night as he slept on the airfoam bed in his stateroom aboard *Himawari*, in orbit around the planet Mercury.

He dreamed of the Nobel ceremony in Stockholm. He saw himself dressed in the severely formal attire of the ritual as the king of Sweden handed him the heavy gold award for biology. The discoverer of thermophiles on the planet Mercury, Molina heard the king announce. The courageous, intrepid man who found life where all others said it was impossible for life to exist. Lara sat in the front row of the vast audience, beaming happily. Victor reminded himself to add a line to his Nobel lecture, thanking his wife for her love and support through all the years of their marriage.

Then he began his lecture. The huge audience hall, crammed with the elite of every continent on Earth, fell into an expectant silence.

Thermophiles are organisms that live at temperatures far beyond those in which human beings can survive, he told the rapt and glittering audience. On Earth, microscopic thermophiles were discovered in the latter part of the twentieth century, existing deep underground at temperatures and pressures that were, up until then, considered impossible as habitats for living organisms. Yet these bacterial forms not only exist, they are so numerous that they actually outweigh all the living matter on the surface of the Earth! What is more, they survive without sunlight, shattering the firmly held belief that all life depends on sunlight as its basic source of energy. The thermophiles use the heat of Earth's hellish core to derive their metabolic energy.

A British cosmologist, Thomas Gold, had earlier predicted that a "deep, hot biosphere" existed far below the surface not only of Earth, but of Mars and any other planet or moon that had a molten core. Scornfully rejected at first, Gold's prediction turned out to be correct:

bacterial life forms have been found deep below the surface of Mars, together with the cryptoendoliths that have created an ecological niche for themselves inside Martian surface rocks.

While astrobiologists found various forms of life on the moons of Jupiter and even within the vast, planet-girdling ocean of that giant planet itself, the next discovery of true thermophiles did not occur until explorers reached the surface of Venus, where multicelled creatures of considerable size were found living on that hothouse planet's surface, their bodies consisting largely of silicones, with liquid sulfur as an energy-transfer medium, analogous to blood in terrestrial organisms.

Still, no one expected to find life on Mercury, not even thermophilic life. The planet had been baked dry from its very beginnings. There was no water to serve as a medium for biochemical reactions; not even molten sulfur. Mercury was nothing but a barren ball of rock, in the view of orthodox scientists.

Yet the surprising discovery of polycyclic aromatic hydrocarbons on the surface of Mercury challenged this orthodox view. PAHs are quickly broken down in the high-temperature environment of Mercury's surface. The fact that they existed on the surface meant that some ongoing process was generating them continuously. That ongoing process was life: thermophilic organisms living on the surface of Mercury at temperatures more than four times higher than the boiling point of water. Moreover, they are capable of surviving long periods of intense cold during the Mercurian night, when temperatures that sink down to -135° Celsius are not uncommon.

Now came the point in his lecture when Molina must describe the Mercurian organisms. He looked up from the podium's voice-activated display screen, where his notes were scrolling in cadence with his speaking, and smiled down at Lara. His smile turned awkward, embarrassed. He suddenly became aware that he had nothing to say. He didn't know what the creatures looked like! The display screen was blank. He stood there at the podium while his wife and the king and the huge audience waited in anticipation. He had no idea of what he should say. Then he realized that he was naked. He clutched the podium for protection, tried to hide behind it, but they saw him, they all saw he was naked and began to laugh at him. All but Lara, who looked alarmed, frightened. Do something! he silently begged her. Get out of your chair and do something to help me!

Suddenly he had to urinate. Urgently. But he couldn't move from behind the podium because he had no clothes on. Not a stitch. The audience was howling uproariously and Molina wanted, needed, desperately to piss.

He awoke with a start, disoriented in the darkness of the stateroom. "Lights!" he cried out, and the overhead panels began to glow softly. Molina stumbled out of bed and ran barefoot to the lavatory. After he had relieved himself and crawled back into bed he thought, I wish Lara were here. I shouldn't have made her stay at home.

TORCH SHIP *HIMAWARI*

The ship's name meant "sunflower." Yamagata had personally chosen the name, an appropriate one for a vessel involved in tapping the Sun's energy. Earlier generations would have said it was a fortunate name, a name that would bring good luck to his enterprise. Yamagata was not superstitious, yet he felt that *Himawari* was indeed the best possible name for his ship.

While all except the ship's night watch slept, Yamagata sat in the padded recliner in his stateroom, speaking to a dead man.

The three-dimensional image that stood before Yamagata was almost solid enough to seem real. Except for a slight sparkling, like distant fireflies winking on a summer's evening, the image was perfect in every detail. Yamagata saw a short, slightly chubby man with a shock of snow white hair smiling amiably at him. He was wearing a tweed jacket with leather patches on the elbows and blue jeans, with a soft turtleneck sweater of pale yellow and an incongruous velvet vest decorated with colorful flowers.

Robert Forward had died nearly a century earlier. He had been a maverick physicist, delving into areas that most academics avoided. Long before Duncan and his fusion propulsion drive, which made travel among the planets practical, Forward was examining the possibilities of antimatter rockets and laser propulsion for interstellar travel.

Yamagata had hired a team of clever computer engineers to bring together every public lecture that Forward had given, every seminar appearance, every journal paper he had written, and incorporate them into a digitized persona that could be projected as an interactive holographic image. Calling themselves "chip-monks," the young men and women had succeeded brilliantly. Yamagata could hold conversations with the long-dead Forward almost as if the man were actually present.

There were limits to the system, of course. Forward never sat down; he was always on his feet. He paced, but only a few steps in any direction, because the image had to stay within the cone of the hologram being projected from the ceiling of Yamagata's stateroom. And he always smiled. No matter what Yamagata said to him, Forward kept the same cheerful smile on his round, ruddy face. Sometimes that smile unnerved Yamagata.

As now. While Yamagata showed the disastrous efficiency curves to Forward's image, the physicist's hologram continued to smile even as he peered at the bad news.

"Degraded by solar radiation, huh?" Forward said, scratching at his plump double chin.

Yamagata nodded and tried not to scowl at the jaunty smile.

"The numbers check out?" Forward asked.

"My people back at New Kyoto are checking them."

"You didn't expect the degradation to be so severe, eh?"

"Obviously not."

Forward clasped his hands behind his back. "Wellll," he said, drawing the word out, "assuming the numbers check out and the degradation is a real effect, you'll simply have to build more power satellites. Or larger ones."

Yamagata said nothing.

Forward seemed to stand there, frozen, waiting for a cue. After a few seconds, however, he added, "If each individual powersat can produce only one-third the power you anticipated, then you'll need three times as many powersats. It's quite simple."

"That is impossible," said Yamagata.

"Why impossible? The technology is well in hand. If you can build ten powersats you can build thirty."

"The costs would be too high."

"Ah!" Forward nodded knowingly. "Economics. The dismal science."

"Dismal, perhaps, but inescapable. The Foundation cannot afford to triple its costs."

"Even if you built the powersats here at Mercury, instead of buying them from Selene and towing them here from the Moon?"

"Build them here?"

Forward's image seemed to freeze for an eyeblink's span, then he began ticking off on his chubby fingers, "Mercury has abundant metals. Silicon is rarer than on the Moon but there's still enough easily scooped from the planet's surface to build hundreds of powersats. You'd save on transportation costs, of course, and you'd cut out Selene's profits."

"But I would have to hire a sizeable construction crew," Yamagata objected. "And they will want premium pay to work here at Mercury."

Forward smile almost faded. But he quickly recovered. "I don't know much about nanotechnology; the field was in its infancy when I died. But couldn't you program nanomachines to build powersats?"

"Selene makes extensive use of nanomachines," Yamagata agreed.

"There you are," said Forward, with an offhand gesture.

Yamagata hesitated, thinking. Then, "But focusing thirty laser beams on a starship's lightsail . . . wouldn't that be difficult?"

Forward's smile returned in full wattage. "If you can focus ten lasers on a sail you can focus thirty. No problemo."

Yamagata smiled back. Until he realized that he was speaking to a man who had lived a century earlier and even then was known as a wild-eyed theoretician with no practical, hands-on experience.

NANOMACHINES

Nanomachines?" Alexios asked the image on his office wall.

"Yes," replied Yamagata with an unhappy sigh. "It may become necessary to use them."

"We have no nanotech specialists here," said Alexios, sitting up tensely in his office chair. It was a lie: he himself had experience with nanotechnology. But he had kept that information hidden from everyone.

"I am aware of that," Yamagata replied. "There are several in Selene who might be induced to come here."

"We're crowded down here already."

Yamagata's face tightened into a frown momentarily, then he regained control of himself and put on a perfunctory smile. "If it becomes necessary to build more power satellites than originally planned, your base will have to be enlarged considerably. We will need to build a mass launcher down there on the surface and hire entire teams of technicians to assemble the satellites in orbit."

Alexios nodded and tried to hide the elation he felt. It's working! he told himself. I'm going to bleed him dry.

Aloud, he said to Yamagata, "Many of my team are quite distressed by nanomachines. They feel that nanotechnology is dangerous."

Strangely, Yamagata grinned at him. "If you think *they* will be unhappy, imagine how Bishop Danvers will react."

Sure enough, Yamagata heard an earnest rap on his stateroom door within a half hour of his conversation with Alexios.

"Enter," he called out, rising from his comfortable chair.

Bishop Danvers slid the door open and stepped through, then carefully shut it again.

"How kind of you to visit me," said Yamagata pleasantly.

Danvers's usually bland face looked stern. "This is not a social call, I'm afraid."

"Ah so?" Yamagata gestured to one of the plush armchairs arranged around his recliner. "Let's at least be physically comfortable. Would you like a refreshment? Tea, perhaps?"

The bishop brushed off Yamagata's attempts to soften the meeting. "I understand you are considering bringing nanomachines here."

Yamagata's brows rose slightly. He must have spies in the communications center, he thought. Believers who report everything to him.

Coolly, he replied, "It may become necessary to use nanotechnology for certain aspects of the project."

"Nanotechnology is banned."

"On Earth. Not in Selene or anywhere else."

"It is dangerous. Nanomachines have killed people. They have been turned into monstrous weapons."

"They will be used here to construct a mass driver on Mercury's surface and to assemble components of power satellites. Nothing more."

"Nanotechnology is evil!"

Yamagata steepled his fingers, stalling for time to think. Do not antagonize this man, he warned himself. He can bring the full power of Earth's governments against you.

"Bishop Danvers," Yamagata said placatingly, "technology is neither evil nor good, in itself. It is men who are moral or not. It is the way we *use* technology that is good or evil. After all, a stone can be used to help build a temple or to bash someone's brains in. Is the stone evil?"

"Nanotechnology is banned on Earth for perfectly good reasons," Danvers insisted.

"On a planet crowded with ten billion people, including the mentally sick, the greedy, the fanatic, I understand perfectly why nanotechnology is banned. Here in space the situation is quite different."

Danvers shook his head stubbornly. "How do you know that there are no mentally sick people among your crew? No one who is greedy? No fanatics?"

A good point, Yamagata admitted silently. There could be fanatics here. Danvers himself might be one. If he knew this project's ultimate aim is to reach the stars, how would he react?

Aloud, Yamagata replied, "Bishop Danvers, every man and

woman here has been thoroughly screened by psychological tests. Most of them are engineers and technicians. They are quite stable, I assure you."

Danvers countered, "Do you truly believe that anyone who is willing to come to this hellhole for years at a time is mentally stable?"

Despite himself, Yamagata smiled. "A good point, sir. We must discuss the personality traits of adventurers over dinner some evening."

"Don't try to make light of this."

"I assure you, I am not. If we need nanomachines to make this project succeed, it will mean an additional investment that will strain the resources of the Sunpower Foundation to the utmost. Let me tell you, this decision will not be made lightly."

Danvers knew he was being dismissed. He got slowly to his feet, his fleshy face set in a determined scowl. "Think carefully, sir. What does it gain a man if he wins the whole world and suffers the loss of his immortal soul?"

Yamagata rose, too. "I am merely trying to provide electrical power for my fellow human beings. Surely that is a good thing."

"Not if you use evil methods."

"I can only assure you, Bishop, that if we use nanomachines, they will be kept under the strictest of controls."

Clearly unhappy, Bishop Danvers turned his back on Yamagata and left the stateroom.

Yamagata sank back into his recliner. I've made an enemy of him, he realized. Now he'll report back to his superiors on Earth and I'll get more static from the International Astronautical Authority and god knows what other government agencies.

Ordinarily he would have smiled at his unintentional pun about god. This time he did not.

Bishop Elliott Danvers strode back toward his own stateroom along the sloping corridor that ran the length of *Himawari*'s habitation module. He passed several crew personnel, all of whom nodded or muttered a word of greeting to him. He acknowledged their deference with a curt nod each time. His mind was churning with other thoughts.

Nanotechnology! My superiors in Atlanta will go ballistic when they learn that Yamagata plans to bring nanomachines here. Godless technology. How can God allow such a mockery of His will to exist?

Then Danvers realized that God would not allow it. God will stop them, just as he stopped the skytower, ten years ago. And he realized something even more important: I am God's agent here, sent to do His work. I haven't the power to stop Yamagata, not unless God sends a catastrophe to this wicked place. Only some disaster will bring Yamagata to his senses.

Despite his bland outward appearance, Elliott Danvers had led a far from dull life. Born in a Detroit slum, he was always physically big for his age. Other kids took one look at him and thought he was tough, strong. He wasn't. The real bullies in the 'hood enlarged their reputations by bloodying the big guy. The wiseguys who ran the local youth club made him play on the local semipro football team when he was barely fourteen. In his first game he got three ribs cracked; in the next contest they broke his leg. When he recovered from that the gamblers put him in the prizefight ring and quietly bet against him. They made money. Danvers's share was pain and blood and humiliation.

When he broke his hand slugging it out with a young black kid from a rival club, they tossed him out onto the street, his hand swollen monstrously, his face unrecognizable from the beating he'd taken.

One of the street missionaries from the storefront New Morality branch found Danvers huddled in the gutter, bleeding and sobbing. He took Danvers in, dressed his wounds, fed his body and spirit, and turned his gratitude into a life of service. At twenty he entered a New Morality seminary. By the time he was twenty-two, Elliott Danvers was an ordained minister, ready to be sent out into the world in service to God. He was never allowed to return to his old Detroit neighborhood. Instead he was sent overseas and saw that there were many wretched people around the globe who needed his help.

His rise through the hierarchy was slow, however. He was not especially brilliant. He had no family connections or well-connected friends to help push him upward. He worked hard and took the most difficult, least rewarding assignments in gratitude for the saving of his life.

His big chance came when he was assigned as spiritual counselor to the largely Latin-American crew building the skytower in Ecuador. The idea of a space elevator seemed little less than blasphemous to him, a modern-day equivalent to the ancient Tower of Babel. A tower that reached to the heavens. Clearly technological hubris, if nothing else. It was doomed to fail, Danvers felt from the beginning.

When it did fail, it was his duty to report to the authorities on who was responsible for the terrible tragedy. Millions of lives had been lost. Someone had to pay.

As a man of God, Danvers was respected by the Ecuadorian authorities. Even the godless secularists of the International Astronautical Authority respected his supposedly unbiased word.

Danvers phrased his report very carefully, but it was clear that he—like most of the accident investigators—put final blame on the leader of the project, the man who was in charge of the construction.

The project leader was disgraced and charged with multiple homicide. Because the international legal system did not permit capital punishment for inadvertent homicide, he was sentenced to be banished from Earth forever.

Danvers was promoted to bishop, and—after another decade of patient, uncomplaining labor—sent to be spiritual advisor to the small crew of engineers and technicians working for the Sunpower Foundation building solar power satellites at the planet Mercury.

He was puzzled about the assignment, until his superiors told him that the director of the project had personally asked for Danvers. This pleased and flattered him. He did not realize that the fiery-eyed Dante Alexios, running the actual construction work on the hell-hot surface of Mercury, was the young engineer who had been in charge of the skytower project, the man who had been banished from Earth in large part because of Danvers's testimony.

FIELD TRIP

Victor Molina licked his lips nervously. "I've never been out on the surface of another world before," he said.

Dante Alexios put on a surprised look. "But you told me you've been to Jupiter's moons, didn't you?"

The two men were being helped into the heavily insulated spacesuits that were used for excursions on Mercury's rocky, Sun-baked surface. Half a dozen technicians were assisting them, three for each man. The suits were brightly polished, almost to a mirror finish, and so bulky that they were more individual habitats than normal spacesuits.

Molina's usual cocky attitude had long since vanished, replaced by uncertainty. "I was at Europa, yeah," he maintained. "Most of the time, though, I was in the research station *Gold*, orbiting Jupiter. I spent a week in the smaller station in orbit around Europa itself but I never got down to the surface."

Alexios nodded as the technicians hung the life-support package to the back of his suit. Even in Mercury's light gravity it felt burdensome. Both men's suits were plugged into the base's power system, mainly to keep the cooling fans running. Otherwise they would already be uncomfortably hot and sweaty inside the massive suits.

He knew that Molina had never set foot on the surface of another world. Alexios had spent years accumulating a meticulous dossier on Victor Molina, the man who had once been his friend, his schoolmate, the buddy he had asked to be his best man when he married Lara. Molina had betrayed him and stolen Lara from him. Now he was going to pay.

It took two technicians to lift the thick-walled helmet over Molina's head and settle it onto the torso ring, like churchmen lowering a royal crown on an emperor. As they began sealing the helmet, two other techs lowered Alexios's helmet, muffling all the sounds outside. Strange, Alexios thought. We don't really notice the throbbing of the base's pumps and the hiss of the air vents until the sound stops. Through his thick quartz visor he could see the technicians fussing around Molina's suit, and the serious, almost grim expression on the astrobiologist's face. Once we pull down the sun visors I won't be able to see his face at all, Alexios knew.

He moved his arm with a whine of servomotors and pressed the stud on his left wrist that activated the suit's radio.

"Can you hear me, Dr. Molina?"

For a moment there was no reply, then, "I hear you." Molina's voice sounded strange, preoccupied.

The woman in charge of the technicians at last gave Alexios a thump on the shoulder and signaled a thumbs-up to him. He switched to the radio frequency for the base's control center:

"Molina and Alexios, ready for surface excursion."

"You are cleared for excursion," came the controller's voice. Alexios recognized it; a dour Russian whom he sometimes played chess with. Once in a while he even won.

"Cameras on?" Alexios asked, as he started clumping in the heavy boots toward the airlock hatch.

"Exterior cameras functioning. Relief crew standing by."

Two other members of the base's complement had suited up at the auxiliary airlock and were prepared to come out to rescue Alexios and Molina if they ran into trouble. Neither the main airlock nor the auxiliary was big enough to hold four suited people at the same time.

The inner airlock hatch swung open. Alexios gestured with a gloved hand. "After you, Dr. Molina."

Moving uncertainly, hesitantly, Molina stepped over the hatch's sill and planted his boots inside the airlock chamber. Alexios followed him, almost as slowly. One could not make sudden moves in the cumbersome suits.

Once the inner hatch closed again and the air was pumping out of the chamber, Molina said, "It's funny, but over this radio link your voice sounds kind of familiar."

Alexios's pulse thumped suddenly. "Familiar?"

"Like it's a voice I know. A voice I've heard before."

Will he recognize me? Alexios wondered. That would ruin everything.

He said nothing as the panel lights indicated the airlock chamber had been pumped down to vacuum. Alexios leaned a hand on the green-glowing plate that activated the outer hatch. It swung outward gradually, revealing the landscape of Mercury in leisurely slow motion. Molten sunlight spilled into the airlock chamber as both men automatically lowered their sun visors.

"Wow," said Molina. "Looks freaking hot out there."

Alexios got a vision of the astrobiologist licking his lips. Molina stayed rooted inside the chamber, actually backing away slightly from the sunshine.

"It's wintertime now," Alexios joked, stepping out onto the bare rocky surface. "The temperature's down below four hundred Celsius."

"Wintertime." Molina laughed shakily.

"When you step through the hatch, be careful of your radiator panels. They extend almost thirty centimeters higher than the top of your helmet."

"Yeah. Right."

Molina finally came out into the full fury of the Sun. All around him stretched a barren, broken plain of bare rock, strewn with pebbles, rocks, boulders. Even through the heavily tinted visor, the glare was enough to make his eyes tear. He wondered if the suit radio was picking up the thundering of his pulse, the awed gushing of his breath.

"This way," he heard Alexios's voice in his helmet earphones. "I'll show you where the crew found those rocks you're interested in."

Moving like an automaton, Molina followed the gleaming armored figure of Alexios out across the bare, uneven ground. He glanced up at the Sun, huge and menacing, glaring down at him.

"You did remember your tool kit and sample boxes, didn't you?" Alexios asked, almost teasingly.

"I've got them," said Molina, nodding inside his helmet. Something about that voice was familiar. Why should a voice transmitted by radio sound familiar when the man was a complete stranger?

They plodded across the desolate plain, steering around the rocks strewn haphazardly across the landscape. One of the boulders was as big as a house, massive and stolid in the glaring sunlight. The ground undulated slightly but they had no trouble negotiating the gentle rises and easy downslopes. Molina noticed a gully or chasm of some sort off to their right. Alexios kept them well clear of it.

It was hot inside the suit, Molina realized. Cooling system or not, he felt as if the juices were being baked out of him. If the radiators should fail, he said to himself, if the suit's electrical power shuts down—I'd be dead in a minute or two! He tried to push such thoughts out of his mind, but the sweat trickling down his brow and stinging his eyes made that impossible.

"You're nearing the edge of our camera range," came the voice of the controller back at the base. He sounded almost bored.

"Not to worry," Alexios replied. "We're almost there."

Less than a minute later Alexios stopped and turned slowly, like a mechanical giant with rusty bearings.

"Here we are," he said brightly.

"This is it?" Molina saw that they were in a shallow depression, most likely an ancient meteor crater, about a hundred and fifty meters across.

"This is where the construction team found the rocks you're interested in."

Molina stared at the rock-strewn ground. It wasn't as dusty as the Moon's surface was. They had walked all this way and their boots were barely tarnished. He saw their bootprints, though, looking new and bright against the dark ground.

"What was your construction crew doing all the way out here?" he heard himself ask.

Alexios did not reply for a moment. Then, "Scouting for locations for new sites. Our base is going to grow, sooner or later."

"And they found the rocks with biomarkers here, at this site?"

He sensed Alexios nodding solemnly inside his helmet. "You can tell which rocks contain the biomarkers," Alexios said. "They're the darker ones."

Molina saw that there were dozens of dark reddish rocks scattered around the shallow crater. He forgot all his other questions as he unclipped the scoop from his equipment belt and extended its handle so he could begin picking up the rocks—and the possible life-forms in them.

LARA

t was not easy for her to leave their eight-year-old son on Earth, but Lara Tierney Molina was a determined woman. Her husband's messages from the Japanese torch ship seemed so forlorn, so painful, that she couldn't possibly leave him alone any longer. When he suddenly departed for Mercury, he had told her that his work would absorb him totally and, besides, the rugged base out there was no place for her. But almost as soon as he'd left, he began sending pitifully despondent messages to her every night, almost breaking into tears in his loneliness and misery. That was so unlike Victor that Lara found herself sobbing as she watched her husband's despondent image.

She tried to cheer him with smiling responses, even getting Victor Jr. to send upbeat messages to his father. Still, Victor's one-way calls from Mercury were full of heartbreaking desolation.

So she made arrangements for her sister to take care of Victor Jr., flew from Earth to lunar orbit aboard a Masterson shuttlecraft, then boarded the freighter *Urania* that was carrying supplies to Mercury on a slow, economical Hohmann minimum energy trajectory. No high-acceleration fusion torch ship for her; she could not afford such a luxury and the Sunpower Foundation was unwilling to pay for it. So she coasted toward Mercury for four months, her living quarters a closet-sized compartment, her toilet facilities a scuffed and stained lavatory that she shared with the three men and two women of the freighter's crew.

She had worried, at first, about being penned up in such close quarters with strangers, but the crew turned out to be amiable enough. Within a few days of departure from Earth orbit, Lara learned that both the women were heterosexual and one of them was sleeping with the ship's communications officer. The other two males didn't come on to her, for which Lara was quite grateful. The entire crew treated her with a rough deference; they shared meals together and became friends the way traveling companions do, knowing that they would probably never see each other again once their voyage was over.

Lara Tierney had been born to considerable wealth. When the greenhouse floods forced her family from their Manhattan penthouse, they moved to their summer home in Colorado and found that it was now a lakeside property. Father made it their permanent domicile. Lara had been only a baby then, but she vaguely remembered the shooting out in the woods at night, the strangers who camped on Father's acreage and had to be rooted out by the National Guard soldiers, the angry shouts and sometimes a scream that silenced all the birds momentarily.

By and large, though, life was pleasant enough. Her father taught her how to shoot both rifles and pistols, and he always made certain that one of the guards accompanied Lara whenever she went out into the lovely green woods.

At school in Boulder, her friends said she led a charmed life. Nothing unhappy ever seemed to happen to her. She was bright, talented, and pleasant to everyone around her.

Lara knew that she was no beauty. Her eyes were nice enough, a warm gold-flecked amber, but her lips were painfully thin and she thought her teeth much too big for her slim jaw. She was gangly—her figure hardly had a curve to it. Yet she had no trouble dating young men; they seemed attracted to her like iron filings to a magnet. She thought it might have been her money, although her mother told her that as long as she smiled at young men they would feel at ease with her.

The most popular men on campus pursued her. Victor Molina, dashing and handsome, became her steady beau—until Molina introduced her to a friend of his, an intense, smoldering young engineer named Mance Bracknell.

"He's interesting," Lara said.

"Mance?" Molina scoffed. "He's a weirdo. Not interested in anything except engineering. I think I'm the only friend he has on campus."

Another student warned, "You know engineers. They're so narrow-minded they can look through a keyhole with both eyes."

Yet she found Bracknell fascinating. He was nowhere near handsome, she thought, and his social skills were minimal. He dressed carelessly; his meager wardrobe showed he had no money. Yet he was the only male in her classes who paid no attention to her: he was far too focused on his studies. Lara saw him as a challenge, at first. She was going to make him take his nose out of his computer screen and smell the roses.

That semester, she and Molina shared only one class with the young engineering student, a mandatory class in English literature. Bracknell was struggling through it. Lara decided to offer her help.

"I don't need help," Bracknell told her, matter-of-factly. "I'm just not interested in the material."

"Not interested in Keats? Or Shakespeare?" She was shocked.

With an annoyed little frown, Bracknell replied, "Are you interested in Bucky Fuller? Or Raymond Loewy?"

She had never heard of them. Lara made a deal with him. If he paid attention to the literature assignments, she would sign up for a basic science class.

Molina was not pleased. "You're wasting your time with Mance. For god's sake, Lara, the guy doesn't even wear socks!"

It took most of the semester for her to penetrate Bracknell's self-protective shell. Late one night after they had walked from one end of campus to the other as he flawlessly—if flatly—recited Keats's entire poem *The Eve of St. Agnes* to her, Bracknell finally told her what his dream was. It took her breath away.

"A tower that goes all the way up into space? Can it be built?"

"I can do it," he answered, without an eyeblink's hesitation.

He wanted to build a tower that rose up to the heavens, an elevator that could carry people and cargo into orbit for mere pennies per kilogram.

"I can do it," he told her, time and again. "I know I can! The big problem has always been the strength-to-weight ratio of the materials, but with buckyball fibers we can solve that problem and build the blasted thing!"

His enthusiasm sent Lara scurrying to her own computer, to learn what buckyball fibers might be and how a space elevator could be built.

Her friends twitted her about her fascination with "the geek." Molina fumed and sulked, angry that she was paying more attention to Bracknell than to him.

"How is he in bed?" Molina growled at her one afternoon as they walked to class together.

"Not as good as you, Victor dear," Lara replied sweetly. "I love him for his mind, not his body."

And she left him standing there in the autumn sunshine, amidst the yellow aspen leaves that littered the lawn.

It took months, but Lara realized at last that she was truly and hopelessly in love with Mance Bracknell and his dream of making spaceflight inexpensive enough so that everyone could afford it.

Even before they graduated, she used her father's connections to introduce Bracknell to industrialists and financiers who had the resources to back his dream. Most of them scoffed at the idea of a space elevator. They called it a "skyhook" and said it would never work. Bracknell displayed a volcanic temper, shouting at them, calling them idiots and blind know-nothings. Shocked at his eruptions, Lara did her best to calm him down, to soothe him, to show him how to deal with men and women who believed that because they were older and richer, they were also wiser.

It took years, years in which Bracknell supported himself with various engineering jobs, traveling constantly, a techno-vagabond moving from project to project. Lara met him now and then, while her parents prayed fervently that she would eventually get tired of him and his temper and find a young man more to their liking, someone like Victor Molina. Although she occasionally saw Molina as he worked toward his doctorate in biology, she found herself thinking about Bracknell constantly during the months they were separated. Despite her parents she flew to his side whenever she could.

Then he called from Ecuador, of all places, so excited she could barely understand what he was saying. An earlier attempt at building a space elevator in Ecuador had failed; probably it had been a fraud, a sham effort aimed at swindling money from the project's backers. But the government of Ecuador wanted to proceed with the project, and a consortium of European bankers had formed a corporation to do it, if they could find an engineering organization capable of tackling the job.

"They want me!" Bracknell fairly shouted, his image in Lara's phone screen so excited she thought he was going to hyperventilate. "They want me to head the project!"

"In Ecuador?" she asked, her heart pounding.

"Yes! It's on the equator. We've picked a mountaintop site."

"You're really going to do it?"

"You bet I am! Will you come down here?"

"Yes!" she answered immediately.

"Will you marry me?"

The breath gushed out of her. She had to gulp before she could reply, "Of course I will!"

But Bracknell's tower had collapsed, killing millions. He was disgraced, tried for mass homicide, exiled from Earth forever.

And now Lara Tierney Molina, married to Bracknell's best friend, mother of their eight-year-old son, rode a shabby freighter to Mercury to be with her husband.

Yet she still dreamed of Mance Bracknell.

GOETHE BASE

A s soon as the technicians peeled him out of the cumbersome spacesuit, Molina grabbed his sample box and rushed to the makeshift laboratory he had squeezed into the bare little compartment that served as his living quarters at Mercury base.

From the equipment box that blocked the compartment's built-in drawers he tugged out the miniature diamond-bladed saw. Sitting cross-legged on the floor, he wormed the safety goggles over his eyes, tugged on a pair of sterilized gloves, then grabbed one of the rocks out of his sample box and immediately began cutting microthin slices out of it.

He got to his knees and lifted out the portable mass spectrometer from his equipment box. Despite Mercury's low gravity it was so heavy he barely was able to raise it clear of the box. "Portable is a relative term," he muttered as he looked around for an electrical outlet. The spectrometer's laser drew a lot of power, he knew.

"So what if I black out the base?" he said to himself, almost giggling, as he plugged the thick power cord into a wall outlet. His quarters were hardly a sterile environment, but Molina was in too much of a hurry to care about that. I'll just work on a couple of the samples and save the rest for the lab up in *Himawari*, he told himself. Besides, he reasoned, these samples are fresh from the site; there hasn't been enough time for any terrestrial organisms to contaminate them.

Time meant nothing now. Hours flew by as Molina sawed sample microslices from the rocks and ran them through the spectrometer. When he got hungry or sleepy he popped cognitive enhancers and went back to work revitalized. Wish I had brought the scanning tunneling microscope here, he thought. For a moment he considered asking Alexios if there was one in the base, but he thought better of it. I've got one up in the ship, he told himself. Be patient.

But patience gave way to growing excitement. It was all there! he realized after nearly forty hours of work. Pushing a thick flop of his sandy hair back from his red-rimmed eyes, Molina tapped one-handed at his laptop. The sample contained PAHs in plenitude, in addition to magnetized bits of iron sulfides and carbonate globules, unmistakable markers of biological activity.

There's life on Mercury! Molina exulted. He wanted to leap to his feet and shout the news but he found that his legs were cramped and tingling from sitting cross-legged on the floor for so long. Instead, he bent over his laptop and dictated a terse report of his discovery to the astrobiology bulletin published electronically by the International Consortium of Universities. As an afterthought he fired off a copy to the International Astronautical Authority. And then a brief, triumphant message to Lara.

He realized that he hadn't called his wife since he'd left Earth, despite his promise to talk to her every day. Well, he grinned to himself, now I've got something to tell her.

I'll be famous! Molina exulted. I'll be able to take my pick of professorships. We can live anywhere we choose to: California, Edinburgh, New Melbourne, any of the best astrobiology schools on Earth!

He hauled himself slowly to his feet, his legs shooting pins and needles fiercely. Hobbling, laughing aloud, he staggered around his cluttered compartment, nearly tripping over the equipment he had scattered across the floor until his legs returned to normal. A glance at the digital clock above his bunk, which displayed the base's time, showed him that the galley had long since closed for the night. What matter? He was hungry, though, so he put in a call for Alexios. He's the head of this operation, Molina told himself. He ought to be able to get them to produce a meal for the discoverer of life on Mercury.

Alexios did better than that. He invited Molina to his own quarters to share a late-night repast, complete with a dust-covered bottle of celebratory champagne.

Alexios's living quarters were no larger than Molina's compartment, the astrobiologist saw, but the furnishings were much better. The bed looked more comfortable than Molina's bunk, and there was a real desk instead of a wobbly pullout tray, plus a pair of comfortably padded armchairs. Their supper—cold meats and a reasonably crisp salad—was augmented by a bowl of fruit and the champagne. It all tasted wonderful to Molina.

"Living organisms?" Alexios was asking. "You've found living organisms?"

"Not yet," said Molina, leaning back in the luxurious chair as he munched on a boneless pseudochicken wing.

Alexios raised his dark brows.

"As a point of fact," Molina said, gesturing with his plastic fork, "there might not be living organisms on Mercury."

"But I thought you said—"

Falling into his lecturer's mode of speech, Molina intoned, "What I've discovered here is evidence of biological activity. This shows conclusively that there was once life on Mercury. Whether life still exists here is another matter, calling for much more extensive exploration and study."

Alexios's slightly mismatched face showed comprehension. "I see. You're saying that life once existed here, but there's no guarantee that it is still extant."

"Precisely," said Molina, a trifle pompously. "We'll have to bring in teams to search the planet's surface extensively and bore deeply into the crust."

"Looking for organisms underground? Like the extremophiles that have been found on Earth?"

Nodding, Molina replied, "And Mars. And Venus. And even on Io."

Alexios smiled thinly. "I wonder what Bishop Danvers will think about this? The thought of extraterrestrial intelligence seems to bother him."

"Oh, I don't expect we'll find anything intelligent," said Molina, with a wave of one hand. "Microbes. Bacterial forms, that's what we're looking for."

"I see." Alexios hesitated, then asked, "But tell me, if you bring in teams to scour the surface and dig deep boreholes, how will that affect my operation? After all, we're planning to scoop ores from the surface and refine them with nanomachines so that we can—"

"All that will have to stop," Molina said flatly.

"Stop?"

"We can't risk contaminating possible biological evidence with your industrial operation. And nanomachines—they might gobble up the very evidence we're seeking."

Alexios sank back in his chair. "Mr. Yamagata is not going to be pleased by this. Not one bit." Yet he was smiling strangely as he spoke.

TORCH SHIP *HIMAWARI*

B ut that could ruin us!" Yamagata yowled, his usually smiling face knotted into an angry grimace.

Alexios had come up to the orbiting ship to present the troubling news personally to his boss. He shrugged helplessly. "The IAA regulations are quite specific, sir. *Nothing* is allowed to interfere with astrobiological studies."

The two men were standing in *Himawari*'s small observation blister, a darkened chamber fronted by a bubble of heavily tinted glasssteel. For several moments they watched in silence as the heat-blasted barren surface of Mercury slid past.

At last Yamagata muttered, "I can't believe that any kind of life could exist down there."

Alexios raised his brows slightly. "They found life on the surface of Venus, which is even hotter than Mercury."

"Venus has liquid sulfur and silicone compounds. Nothing like that has been found here."

"Not yet," Alexios said, in a barely voiced whisper.

Yamagata frowned at him.

"We won't have to stop all our work," Alexios said, trying to sound a little brighter. "We still have the power satellites coming in from Selene. Getting them up and running will be a considerable task."

"But how will we provide the life-support materials for the crew?" Yamagata growled. "I depended on your team on the surface for that."

Alexios clasped his hands behind his back and turned to stare at the planet's surface gliding past. He knew his base on Mercury was too small to be seen by the unaided eye from the distance of the *Himawari*'s orbit, yet he strained his eyes to see the mound of rubble anyway.

"Well?" Yamagata demanded. "What do you recommend?"

Turning back to look at his decidedly unhappy employer, Alexios shrugged. "We'll have to bring in the life-support materials from Selene, I suppose, if we can't scoop them from Mercury's regolith."

"That will bankrupt us," Yamagata muttered.

"Perhaps the suspension will only be for a short time," said Alexios. "The scientists will come, look around, and then simply declare certain regions to be off-limits to our work."

Even in the shadows of the darkened observation blister Alexios could see the grim expression on Yamagata's face.

"This will ruin everything," Yamagata said in a heavy whisper. "Everything."

Alexios agreed, but forced himself to present a worried, downcast appearance to his boss.

Fuming, trying to keep his considerable temper under control, Yamagata repaired to his private quarters and called up the computer program of Robert Forward. The long-dead genius appeared in the middle of the compartment, smiling self-assuredly, still wearing that garish vest beneath his conservative tweed jacket.

Between the smile and the vest, Yamagata felt too irritated to sit still. He paced around the three-dimensional image, explaining this intolerable situation. Forward's holographic image turned to follow him, that maddening smile never slipping by even one millimeter.

"But finding life on Mercury is very exciting news," the image said. "You should be proud that you helped to facilitate such a discovery."

"How can we continue our work if the IAA forces us to shut down all activities on the surface?" Yamagata demanded.

"That won't last forever. They'll lift the suspension sooner or later."

"After Sunpower Foundation has gone bankrupt."

"You have four powersats in orbit around Mercury and six more on the way. Can't you begin to sell energy from them? You'd have some income—"

"The solar cells degrade too quickly!" Yamagata snapped. "Their power output is too low to be profitable."

Forward seemed to think this over for a moment. "Then spend the time finding a solution for the cell degradation. Harden the cells; protect them from the harmful solar radiation."

"Protect them?"

"It's probably solar ultraviolet that's doing the damage," Forward mused. "Or perhaps particles from the solar wind."

Yamagata sank into his favorite chair. "Solar particles. You mean protons?"

Forward nodded, making his fleshy cheeks waddle slightly. "Proton energy density must be pretty high this close to the Sun. Have you measured it?"

"I don't believe so."

"If it's the protons doing the damage you can protect the powersats with superconducting radiation shields, just as spacecraft are shielded."

Yamagata's brows knit. "How do you know about radiation shielding? You died before interplanetary spacecraft needed shielding."

"I have access to all your files," Forward reminded him. "I know everything your computer knows."

Yamagata rubbed his chin thoughtfully. "If we could bring the powersats' energy output up to their theoretical maximum, or even close to it . . ."

"You'd be able to sell their energy at a profit," Forward finished his thought. "And go ahead with the starship."

Nodding, Yamagata closed the Forward program. The physicist winked out, leaving Yamagata alone in his quarters. He put in a call for Alexios, who had returned to the base on the planet's surface.

"I want to find out what's causing this degradation of the solar cells," Yamagata said sternly. "That must be our number one priority."

Alexios's mismatched image in the wall screen looked as if he had expected this decision. "I already have a small team working on it, sir. I'll put more people on the investigation."

"Good," said Yamagata. To himself he added silently, Let's hope we can solve this problem before the IAA drives me into bankruptcy.

EARTH

The International Consortium of Universities was less an organization than a collection of powerful fiefdoms. It consisted
of nearly a hundred universities around the world, no two of
which ever agreed completely on anything. Moreover, each
university was a collection of departments ranging from ancient literature to astrobiology, from psychodynamics to pale-
ontology, from genetic engineering to gymnastics. Each department
head tenaciously guarded her or his budget, assets, staff, and funding
sources.

It took a masterful administrator to manage that ever-shifting tan-
gle of alliances, feuds, jealousies, and sexual affairs.

Jacqueline Wexler was such an administrator. Gracious and
charming in public, accommodating and willing to compromise at
meetings, she nevertheless had the steel-hard will and sharp intellect
to drive the ICU's ramshackle collection of egos toward goals that she
herself selected. Widely known as "Attila the Honey," Wexler was all
sweetness and smiles on the outside and ruthless determination
within.

Today's meeting of the ICU's astrobiology committee was typical.
To Wexler it seemed patently clear that a top-flight team of investigators must be sent to Mercury to confirm Dr. Molina's discovery and or-
ganize a thorough study of the planet's possible biosphere. Indeed,
everyone around the long conference table agreed perfectly on that
point.

Beyond that point, however, all agreement ended. Who should
go? What would be their authority? How would they deal with the industrial operation already planted on Mercury's surface? All these
questions and more led to tedious hours of wrangling. Wexler let them
wrangle, knowing precisely what she wanted out of them, realizing

that sooner or later they would grow tired and let her make the effective decisions. So she smiled sweetly and waited for the self-important farts—women as well as men—to run out of gas.

The biggest issue, as far as they were concerned, was who would lead the team sent to Mercury. Rival universities vied with one another and there was much finger-pointing and cries of "You got the top spot last time!" and "That's not fair!"

Wexler thought it was relatively unimportant who was picked as the lead scientist for the team. She worried more about who the New Morality would send as their spiritual advisor to watch over the scientists. The spiritual advisor's ostensible task was to tend to the scientists' moral and religious needs. His real job, as far as Wexler was concerned, was to spy on the scientists and report what they were doing back to Atlanta.

There was already a New Morality representative on Mercury, she knew: somebody named Danvers. Would they let him remain in charge of the newcomers as well, or send in somebody over his head?

A similar meeting was going on in Atlanta, in the ornate headquarters building of the New Morality, but there were only four people seated at the much smaller conference table.

Archbishop Harold Carnaby sat at the head of the table, of course. Well into his twelfth decade of life, the archbishop was one of the few living souls who had witnessed the birth of the New Morality, back in those evil days of licentiousness and runaway secularism that had brought down the wrath of God in the form of the greenhouse floods. Although his deep religious faith prohibited Carnaby from accepting rejuvenation treatments such as telomerase injections or cellular regeneration, he still availed himself of every mechanical aid that medical science could provide. He saw nothing immoral about artificial booster hearts or kidney dialysis implants.

So he sat at the head of the square table in his powered wheelchair, totally bald, wrinkled and gnomelike, breathing oxygen through a plastic tube inserted in his nostrils. His brain still functioned perfectly well, especially since surgeons had inserted stents in both his carotid arteries.

"Bishop Danvers is a good man," said the deacon seated at Carnaby's left. "I believe he can handle the challenge, no matter how many godless scientists they send to Mercury."

Danvers's dossier was displayed on the wall screen for Carnaby to scan. Apparently someone in Yamagata's organization had specifically asked for Bishop Danvers to come to Mercury. Unusual, Carnaby thought, for those godless engineers and mechanics to ask for a chaplain at all, let alone a specific individual. Danvers must be well respected. But there was more at stake here than tending souls, he knew.

The deacon on Carnaby's right suggested, "Perhaps we could send someone to assist him. Two or three assistants, even. We can demand space for them on the vessel that the scientists ride to Mercury."

Carnaby nodded noncommittally and focused his rheumy eyes on the man sitting at the foot of the table, Bishop O'Malley. Physically, O'Malley was the opposite of Carnaby: big in the shoulders, wide in the middle, his face fleshy and always flushed, his nose bulbous and patterned with purple-red veins. O'Malley was a Catholic, and Carnaby did not completely trust him.

"What's your take on the situation, Bishop?" Carnaby flatly refused to use the medieval Catholic terms of address; "your grace" and "my lord" had no place in his vocabulary.

Without turning even to glance at the dossier displayed on the wall behind him, O'Malley said in his powerful, window-rattling voice, "Danvers showed his toughness years ago in Ecuador. Didn't let personal friendship stand in the way of doing his duty. Let him handle the scientists; he's up to it. Send him an assistant or two if you feel like it, but keep him in charge on Mercury."

"He's done good work since Ecuador, too," Carnaby agreed, his voice like a creaking hinge.

The two deacons immediately fell in line and agreed that Danvers should remain in charge.

"Remember this," Carnaby said, folding his fleshless, blue-veined hands on the table edge in front of him, "every time these secularists find another form of life on some other world, people lose a portion of their faith. There are even those who proclaim that extraterrestrial life proves the Bible to be wrong!"

"Blasphemy!" hissed the younger of the deacons.

"The scientists will send a delegation out to Mercury," Carnaby croaked on, "and they will confirm this man Molina's discovery. They'll trumpet the news that life has been found even where no one expected it to exist. More of the Faithful will fall away from their belief."

O'Malley hunched his bulky shoulders. "Not if Danvers can show that the scientists are wrong. Not if he can give them the lie."

"That's his real mission, then," Carnaby agreed. "To do whatever is necessary to disprove the scientists' claim."

The deacon on the left, young and still innocent, blinked uncertainly. "But how can he do that? If the scientists show proof that life exists on the planet—"

"Danvers must dispute their so-called proof," Carnaby snapped, with obvious irritation. "He must challenge their findings."

"I don't see how—"

O'Malley reached out and touched the younger man on his shoulder. "Danvers is a fighter. He tries to hide it, but inside his soul he's a fighter. He'll find a way to cast doubt on the scientists' findings, I'm sure."

The deacon on the right understood. "He doesn't have to disprove the scientists' findings, merely cast enough doubt on them so the Faithful will disregard them."

"At the very least," Carnaby said. "It would be best if he could show that those godless secularists are lying and have been lying all along."

"That's a tall order," said O'Malley, with a smile.

Carnaby did not smile back.

MERCURY ORBIT

Captain Shibasaki allowed himself a rare moment of irony in the presence of his employer.

"It's going to become crowded here," he said, perfectly straight-faced.

Yamagata did not catch his wry attempt at humor. Standing beside the captain on *Himawari*'s bridge, Yamagata unsmilingly watched the display screen that showed the two ships that had taken up orbits around Mercury almost simultaneously.

One was the freighter *Urania*, little more than a globular crew module and a set of nuclear ion propulsion units, with dozens of massive rectangular cargo containers clipped to its long spine. *Urania* carried equipment that would be useless if the scientists actually closed Mercury to further industrial operations. It also brought Molina's wife to him, a matrimonial event to which Yamagata was utterly indifferent.

The other vessel was a fusion torch ship, *Brudnoy*, which had blasted out from Earth on a half-*g* burn that brought its complement of ICU scientists and IAA bureaucrats to Mercury in a scant three days. Yamagata wished it would keep on accelerating and dive straight into the Sun. Instead, it braked expertly and took up an orbit matching *Himawari*'s. Yamagata could actually see through the bridge's main port the dumbbell-shaped vessel rotating slowly against the star-strewn blackness of space.

"*Urania* is requesting a shuttle to bring Mrs. Molina over to us," Captain Shibasaki said, his voice low and deferential. "They are also wondering when they will be allowed to offload their cargo containers."

Yamagata clasped his hands behind his back and muttered, "They might as well leave the containers in orbit. No sense bringing them down to the surface until we find out what the scientists are going to do to us."

"And Mrs. Molina?"

"Send a shuttle for her. I suppose Molina will be glad to see his wife."

Hesitantly, the captain added, "Two of the scientists from *Brudnoy* are asking permission to come aboard and meet you, as well."

"More mouths to feed," Yamagata grumbled.

"Plus two ministers from the New Morality. Assistants to Bishop Danvers."

Yamagata glowered at the captain. "Why didn't they send the Mormon Tabernacle Choir while they were at it?"

It took every ounce of Shibasaki's will power to keep from laughing.

Molina had rushed up to *Himawari* immediately after he had finished his preliminary examination of the rocks down at Mercury base. Once aboard the orbiting ship, he shut himself into the sterile laboratory facility that Yamagata had graciously allowed him to bring along and spent weeks on end studying his precious rocks.

The more he examined them, the more excited he became. Not only PAHs and carbonates and sulfides. Once he started looking at his samples in the scanning tunneling microscope he saw tiny structures that looked like fossils of once-living nanobacteria: ridged conical shapes and spiny spheroids. Life! Perhaps long extinct, but living organisms once existed on Mercury! Perhaps they still do!

He stopped his work only long enough to gulp a scant meal now and then, or to fire off a new set of data to the astrobiology journal. He stayed off the cognitive enhancers. Not that the pills were habit-forming or had serious side effects; he simply had run through almost his entire supply and decided to save the last few for an emergency. He slept when he could no longer stay awake, staggering to his quarters and collapsing on his bunk, then going back to his laboratory once his eyes popped open again and he showered and pulled on a clean set of coveralls.

It was only the announcement that his wife would be arriving aboard *Himawari* within the hour that pulled him away from his work. For weeks he had ignored all incoming messages except those from the International Consortium of Universities. He accepted their praise and answered their questions; personal messages from his wife he had no time for.

Dumbfounded with surprise, it took him several moments to register what the communications technician was telling him. "Lara? Here?" he asked the tech's image on his compartment's wall screen.

Once he was certain he had heard correctly, Molina finally, almost reluctantly, began to strip off his sweaty clothes and headed for the shower.

"What's Lara doing here?" he asked himself as the steamy water enveloped him. "Why did she come? What's wrong?"

To Molina's surprise, Yamagata himself was already waiting at the airlock when he got there, scant moments before his wife arrived.

"I should be very angry at you," Yamagata said, with a smile to show that he wasn't.

"Angry?" Molina was truly surprised. "Because there's life on Mercury?"

"Because your discovery may ruin my project."

Molina smiled back, a trifle smugly. "I'm afraid that momentous scientific discoveries take precedence over industrial profits. That's a well-established principle of the International Astronautical Authority."

"Yes," Yamagata replied thinly. "So it seems."

The speaker set into the metal overhead announced that the shuttle craft had successfully mated to *Himawari*'s airlock. Again Molina wondered worriedly why Lara had come. He saw the indicator lights on the panel set into the bulkhead beside the hatch turn slowly from red to amber, then finally to green. The hatch clicked, then swung inward toward them.

One of the shuttle's crew, a Valkyrie-sized woman in gunmetal gray coveralls, pushed the hatch all the way open and Lara Molina stepped daintily over the coaming, then, with a smile of recognition, rushed into her husband's waiting arms.

He held her tightly and whispered into her ear, "You're all right? Everything is okay back home?"

"I'm fine and so is Victor Jr.," she said, beaming happily.

"Then why didn't you tell me you were coming? What made you—"

She placed a silencing finger on his lips. "Later," she said, glancing toward Yamagata.

Molina understood. She wanted to speak to him in private.

Yamagata misunderstood her glance. "Come," he urged. "Dinner is waiting for us. You must be famished after having nothing but the freighter's food."

She's not truly beautiful, Yamagata thought as he sat at the head of the dinner table, but she is certainly lovely.

He had seated Mrs. Molina at his right, her husband on his left. Next to them, Bishop Danvers and Alexios sat opposite one another, and the two cochairmen of the ICU's scientific investigation team sat next to them. Captain Shibasaki was at the end of the table.

Yamagata saw that Lara Molina was slim as a colt; no, the picture that came to his mind was of a racing yacht, trim and sleek and pleasing to the eye. Her features were nothing extraordinary, but her amber-colored eyes were animated when she spoke. When she was silent, she kept her gaze on her husband, except for occasional glances in Alexios's direction. Alexios stared unabashedly at her, as if she were the first woman he'd seen in ages.

Molina was in his glory, with his wife hanging on his every word and two of the leading astrobiologists of Earth paying attention to him, as well. His obvious misgivings about his wife's unexpected arrival seemed far behind him now.

"Chance favors the prepared mind, of course," he was saying, wineglass in hand. "No one expected to find any trace of biological activity on Mercury, but I came out here anyway. Everybody said I was being foolish; even my lovely wife told me I was throwing away months that could be better spent back at Jupiter."

His wife lowered her eyes and smiled demurely.

"What brought you to Mercury, then?" Alexios asked. He had not touched his wine, Yamagata noted.

"A hunch. Call it intuition. Call it a belief that life is much tougher and more ubiquitous than even our most prestigious biologists can understand."

The elder of the ICU investigators, Ian McFergusen, russet-bearded and heavy-browed, rumbled in a thick Scottish accent: "When a distinguished but elderly scientist says something is possible, he is almost always right. When he says something is impossible, he is almost always wrong."

Everyone around the table laughed politely, Molina loudest of all.

"Clarke's Law," said the younger ICU scientist.

"Indeed," Yamagata agreed.

"But surely you must have had more than a hunch to bring you all the way out here," Alexios prodded, grinning crookedly.

Yamagata saw that Mrs. Molina stared at Alexios now. Is she angry at him for doubting her husband's word?

Molina seemed not to notice. He drained his wineglass and put it down on the tablecloth so carefully that Yamagata thought he must be getting drunk. One of the waiters swiftly refilled it with claret.

"More than a hunch?" Molina responded at last. "Yes. Of course. A man doesn't leave his loving wife and traipse out to a hellhole like this on a lark. It was more than a hunch, I assure you."

"What decided you?" Alexios smiled, rather like the smile on a cobra, Yamagata thought.

"Funny thing," Molina said, grinning. "I received a message. Said that the team working on the surface of Mercury was finding strange-looking rocks. It piqued my curiosity."

"A message? From whom?" asked Bishop Danvers.

"It was anonymous. No signature." Molina took another gulp of wine. "I kind of thought it was from you, Elliott."

"Me?" Danvers looked shocked. "I didn't send you any message."

Molina shrugged. "Somebody did. Prob'ly one of the work crew down on the surface."

"Strange-looking rocks?" Alexios mused. "And that was enough to send you packing for Mercury?"

"I had the summer off," Molina replied. "I was in line for an assistant professorship. I thought a poke around Mercury would look good on my curriculum vitae. Couldn't hurt."

"It has certainly helped!" Danvers said.

"I think it probably has," said Molina, reaching for his wineglass again.

"I'm sure it has," said Alexios.

Yamagata noticed that Alexios stared straight at Lara Molina as he spoke.

essages?" Molina blinked with surprise.

He and Lara were alone now in the stateroom that Yamagata had graciously supplied for them. It was larger than Molina's former quarters aboard the ship. The Japanese crewmen who had moved Molina's belongings to this new compartment laughingly referred to it as the Bridal Suite. In Japanese, of course, so neither of the gaijin would be embarrassed by their little joke.

"I couldn't leave you alone out here," Lara said as she unpacked the travel bag on the stateroom's double-sized bed. "You looked so sad, so lonely."

Molina knew he had never sent a single message to his wife until his triumphant announcement of his discovery. He also knew that he had promised to call her every day he was away from her.

"You got messages from me?" he asked again.

She turned from her unpacking and slid her arms around his neck. "Don't be shy, Victor. Of course I got your messages. They were wonderful. Some were so beautiful they made me cry."

Either I've gone insane or she has, Molina thought. Has she been hallucinating? Blurring the line between her dreams and reality?

"Lara, dearest, I—"

"Others were so sad, so poignant . . . they nearly broke my heart." She kissed him gently on the lips.

Molina felt his body stirring. One thing he had learned over nearly ten years of marriage was not to argue with success. Accept credit when it comes your way, no matter what. It had been a good guide for his scientific career, as well.

He kissed her more strongly and held her tightly. Wordlessly they sat on the edge of the bed. Molina pushed his wife's half-unpacked travel bag off the bed; it fell to the floor with a gentle thump in Mercury's low gravity. They lay side by side and he began undressing her.

I'll figure out what this message business is all about tomorrow, Molina told himself as the heat of passion rose in him. Tomorrow will be time enough.

Dante Alexios had returned to Goethe base on Mercury's surface after dinner aboard *Himawari*. Lara hasn't changed a bit, he thought. She's as beautiful as she was ten years ago. More beautiful, even.

Did she recognize me? he wondered as he undressed in his tiny compartment. Not my face, surely, but maybe she remembers my voice. The nanomachines didn't change my voice very much.

He stretched out on his bed and stared at the low ceiling. The room's sensors automatically turned the lights out, and the star patterns painted across the ceiling glowed faintly.

Victor looked puzzled that his wife had flown out here, Alexios said to himself. Wait until she tells him about the messages she got from him. That'll drive him crazy, trying to figure it out. Who would be nutty enough to send love letters to Lara and fake his image, his voice, for them?

It had been easy enough to do. Alexios had secretly recorded Molina's face and voice from his university dossier. It was simple to morph that imagery into the messages that Alexios composed. He had poured his heart into those messages, told her everything he wanted to say to her, everything he wanted her to know. Plagiarized from the best sources: Shakespeare, Browning, Rostand, Byron, and the rest.

He told Lara how much he loved her, had always loved her, would always love her. But he said it with her husband's image, with Victor's voice. He didn't dare use his own. Not yet.

Ian McFergusen was a burly man of delicate tastes. His fierce bushy beard and shaggy brows made him look like a Highland warrior of old, yet he had dedicated his career to the study of life. He was a biologist, not a claymore-swinging howling clansman.

Still, he was a fighter. Throughout academia he was known as a tough, independent thinker. A maverick, a burr under the saddle, often an inconvenient pain in the ass. He seldom followed the accepted wisdom on any subject. He asked the awkward questions, the questions that most people wished to shove under the rug.

McFergusen had studied all the data about the evidence for Mercurian biology that Molina had sent Earthward. Alone now in his compartment, as he sipped his usual nightcap of whisky, neat, he had to admit that the data were impressive. Molina may have made a real find here, McFergusen said to himself.

But something nagged at him. As he drained the whisky and set the empty glass on his night table, he fidgeted uneasily, scratched at his beard, knitted his heavy brows. It's all too convenient, he told himself, too convenient by far. He began pacing across his narrow compartment. Molina gets an anonymous tip. He's given a clutch of rocks that the construction workers have found. All in the same location.

The rocks contain PAHs and all the other biomarkers, that's sure enough. But it's all too easy. Too convenient. Nature doesn't hand you evidence on a platter.

He shook his shaggy head and sat heavily on the bunk. Maybe I'm getting too old and cranky, he said to himself. Then a new thought struck him. Maybe I'm just jealous of the young squirt.

So far," Alexios was saying, "the scientists have not discovered any other sites that contain biomarkers."

Yamagata had come down from *Himawari* to the surface base for this meeting, the first time he had been to Mercury's surface in more than a month. For nearly five weeks now the IAA scientists had been combing the planet's surface with automated tracked vehicles, searching for more rocks that contained signs of life.

"Yet still they prevent us from expanding this base," Yamagata grumbled. He was too troubled to sit in the chair Alexios had offered him. Instead he stood, hands clasped behind his back, and stared at the display screen that took up one whole wall of Alexios's modest office. It showed the barren, rock-strewn surface outside the base: the Sun was up and the hard-baked ground looked hot enough to melt.

The bleak landscape matched Yamagata's mood perfectly. If the scientists didn't lift their ban on industrial activities on Mercury's surface soon, Sunpower Foundation would go bankrupt. It angered Yamagata to be so frustrated. Despite all the teachings that the lamas had tried to instill in him, he found it impossible to accept what was happening, impossible to be patient. Yamagata wanted to round up McFergusen and his entire crew and send them packing back to Earth. Now. This day.

Standing respectfully beside him, Alexios said quietly, "At least we're putting the time to some good use. The preliminary tests on the shielded powersat look quite good."

Yamagata turned toward him. Alexios was slightly taller than he, a fact that added to his displeasure.

"Just as you suspected, the power degradation is caused by the solar proton influx," Alexios went on calmly.

"And the superconducting shields protect the cells?"

Alexios called out, "Computer: show results of shielding test."

The landscape disappeared from the wall screen, replaced by a set of graphs with curving lines in red, green, yellow, and blue. As Alexios explained them, Yamagata saw that the superconducting shields performed much as the Forward persona had predicted.

"The high positive potential of the structure around the cells deflects the protons," Alexios said, "and the magnetic field created by the superconducting wire keeps the electrons off."

"Otherwise the electrons would discharge the high positive potential," Yamagata muttered, showing his employee that he understood the physics involved.

"Exactly." Alexios nodded. "So we can shield the powersats and get them up close to their nominal power output, if . . ." His voice trailed off.

"If?" Yamagata snapped.

"If we can afford enough superconducting wire."

"It's expensive."

"Very. But most of the elements needed to make superconducting wire exist in Mercury's soil."

"You mean regolith," said Yamagata.

Alexios bowed slightly. "Excuse me. Of course, regolith. Soil would imply living creatures in the ground, wouldn't it?"

"We can manufacture the superconductors here, out of local materials?"

"I believe so. If we use nanomachines it should be relatively inexpensive."

"Once we are allowed to work on the surface again," Yamagata muttered.

Alexios stifled the satisfied little smile that began to form on his lips. Forcing his face into a sorrowful mask, he agreed, "Yes, we must get permission from the IAA before we can even begin to do anything."

Yamagata fumed. Instead of a mantra, he silently cursed the International Astronautical Authority, the International Consortium of Universities, all their members past and present, and all their members' mothers back to five generations.

Ian McFergusen looked around at the barren, sun-blasted rocky ground and shook his head. Nothing. Every site we've investigated has turned up nothing. Only that one site next to the base Yamagata's people have built.

Thanks to the virtual reality equipment that the ICU team had brought with them, McFergusen could sit in the laboratory they had set up aboard *Brudnoy* and still experience precisely what the tracked robot vehicle was doing down on the surface of Mercury. The first time he had used VR equipment, back when he was part of the third Mars expedition, it had seemed little less than a miracle to him. He could see, feel, hear what the robot machines were experiencing thousands of kilometers away, all while sitting in the comfort of a secure base. Now, so many years later, virtual reality was just another tool, no more wondrous than the fusion engines that propelled interplanetary torch ships or the tunneling microscopes that revealed individual atoms.

Sitting on a lab stool, his head and lower arms encased in the VR helmet and gloves, McFergusen picked up a rock in his clawlike pincers and brought it close to his sensors. A perfectly ordinary piece of volcanic ejecta, he thought. With the strength of the robot he broke the rock apart, then brought the broken edges to his sensor set and scanned their exposed interiors for several minutes.

Nothing. No PAHs, no sulfides, no iron nodules. If I bring it up to the ship's tunneling microscope, McFergusen thought, I won't find any nanometer-sized structures, either. He tossed the broken fragments of the rock back to the ground in disgust.

For long moments he simply sat there, his body aboard the torch ship *Brudnoy*, his eyes and hands and mind on the blazing hot surface of Mercury.

How can there be such rich specimens at one site and nothing anywhere else? Of course, he reminded himself, we have an entire planet to consider. In these few weeks we've barely tested a few dozen possible sites. Perhaps we're looking in the wrong places.

Yet, he reasoned, we concentrated our searches on sites that are similar to the one where Molina found his specimens. We should have found *something* by now.

Unless . . .

McFergusen did not want to consider the possibility that had arisen in his mind. We've got to widen our net, he told himself, search different kinds of sites.

That won't be easy, he knew. Not with Yamagata breathing down our necks. Lord, he's been sending messages to IAA headquarters daily, demanding to know when we'll allow him to start digging up the regolith again.

None of it is easy, McFergusen said to himself. It never is. Then that nagging suspicion surfaced in his mind again. How could Molina have been so lucky?

Luck plays its role in science, he knew. It's always better to be lucky than to be smart. But so damnably lucky? Is it possible?

Victor Molina was in his lab, flicking through the tunneling microscope's images of the latest rock samples brought up from the surface. Nothing. These samples were as dead and inert as rocks from the Moon. No hydrates, no organic molecules, no long-chain molecules of any sort. Baked dry and dead.

He leaned back in his chair and rubbed his eyes wearily. How can this be? Even the samples of dirt scraped off the ground showed no biomarkers of any kind.

Sitting up straight again, he reminded himself that the dirt samples from the surface of Mars tested by the old *Viking* landers a century ago showed no signs of biological activity, either. Not even a trace of organic molecules in the soil. And Mars not only bears life today but once bore intelligent life, before it was wiped out in an extinction-level meteor impact.

He turned and looked at the set of rocks he himself had tested when he'd first arrived at Mercury. They were carefully sealed in airtight transparent plastic containers. McFergusen wants me to let him send them back to Earth for further testing. Never! I'm not letting them out of my sight. They'll go back to Earth when I do, and they'll be tested by third parties only when I'm present.

Molina felt a fierce proprietary passion about those rocks. They were his key to a future of respect and accomplishment, his ticket to Stockholm and the Nobel Prize.

It took a few moments for him to realize that someone was knocking at his laboratory door, rapping hard enough to make the door shake. With some irritation he called out, "Enter."

Bishop Danvers slid the door back and stepped into the lab, a look of stern determination on his fleshy face. The door automatically slid shut.

"Hello, Elliott," Molina said evenly. "I'm pretty busy right now." It was a lie, but Molina was in no mood for his old friend's platitudes.

"This is an official visit," Danvers said, standing a bare two paces inside the doorway.

"Official?" Molina snapped. "What do you mean?"

Without moving from where he stood, Danvers said, "I'm here in my capacity as a bishop in the New Morality Church."

Despite himself, Molina grinned. "What are you going to do, Elliott, baptize me? Or maybe bless my rocks?"

"No," said Danvers, his cheeks flushing slightly. "I'm here to interrogate you."

Molina's brows shot up. "Interrogate? You mean like the Inquisition?"

Danvers's face darkened, his heavy hands knotted into fists. But he quickly regained control of himself and forced a thin smile.

"Victor, the New Morality has placed a heavy burden on my shoulders. I've been tasked with the responsibility of disproving your claim of finding life on Mercury."

Molina smiled and relaxed. "Oh, is that all."

"It's very serious!"

Nodding, Molina said, "I understand, Elliott." He gestured to the only other chair in the room. "Please, sit down. Make yourself comfortable."

The plastic seat of the tubular metal chair squeaked as Danvers settled his bulk into it. The bishop looked tense, wary.

"Elliott, how long have we known each other?" Molina asked.

Danvers thought a moment. "I first met you in Ecuador, more than twelve years ago."

"It's closer to fourteen years, actually."

"To be sure. But I haven't seen you since the trial at Quito, and that was about ten years ago."

Nodding again, Molina said, "But we were friends back in Ecuador. There's no reason why we shouldn't still be friends."

Danvers gestured to the analytical equipment lining the laboratory's walls. "We live in two different worlds, Victor."

"Different, maybe, but not entirely separate. There's no reason for us to be adversaries."

"I have my responsibilities," Danvers countered, somewhat stiffly. "My orders come straight from Atlanta, from the archbishop himself."

Molina let out a little sigh, then said, "All right, just what do they want you to do?"

"As I told you: they want me to disprove your claim that life exists on Mercury."

"I've never claimed that."

"Or once existed, ages ago," Danvers added.

"That seems irrefutable, Elliott."

"Because of the chemicals you've found in those rocks?" Danvers pointed to the clear plastic containers.

"That's right. The evidence is unmistakable."

"But as I understand it, McFergusen and his team haven't found any corroborating evidence."

"Corroborating evidence!" Molina smirked. "You're learning how to talk like a scientist, Elliott."

Danvers grimaced slightly. "Your fellow scientists seem terribly puzzled that they haven't been able to find anything similar to what you've discovered."

With a shrug, Molina replied, "Mercury may be a small planet, Elliott, but it's still a planet. A whole world. Its surface area must be similar to the continent of Eurasia, back on Earth. How thoroughly do you think a handful of scientists could explore all of Eurasia, from the coast of Portugal to the China Sea? In a few weeks, no less."

"Yet you found your rocks the first day you set foot on Mercury."

"So I did. I was lucky." Suddenly Molina came up with a new thought. "Perhaps, in your terms, God guided me to those rocks."

Danvers rocked back in his chair. "Don't make a joke of God. That's blasphemy."

"I didn't mean to offend you, Elliott," Molina said softly. "I was simply trying to put my good fortune in terms you'd understand."

"You should try praying, instead," said Danvers. "As far as your fellow scientists are concerned, they don't believe in your luck. Or God's grace."

TORCH SHIP *BRUDNOY*

want it clearly understood," McFergusen said, in his gravelly Highland brogue, "that this is strictly an informal meeting."

Informal, Molina repeated silently. Like a coroner's inquest or a session of the Spanish Inquisition.

The Scottish physicist sat at the head of the table, Molina at its foot. Along the table were ranked the other scientists that the IAA had sent, together with Bishop Danvers, who sat at Molina's right. They were using the captain's conference room; it felt crowded, tight, and stuffy. Too many people for a compartment this size, Molina thought.

"Although the ship's computer is taking a verbatim record of what we say," McFergusen went on, "no report of this meeting will be sent back to IAA headquarters until each person here has had a chance to read the record and add any comments he or she wishes to make. Is that clear?"

Heads nodded up and down the table.

McFergusen hesitated a moment, then plunged in. "Now then, our major problem is that we have been unable to find any specimens bearing biomarkers."

"Except for the ones I found," Molina added.

"Indeed."

"How do you account for that?" asked the woman on Molina's left.

He shrugged elaborately. "How do you account for the fact that, during some war back in the twentieth century, the first cannon shell fired into the city of Leningrad killed the zoo's only elephant?"

Everyone chuckled.

Except McFergusen. "We have been scouring the planet for some six weeks now—"

"Six weeks for a whole planet?" Molina countered. "Do you really believe you've covered everything?"

"No, of course not. But you found your specimens on your first day, didn't you?"

Feeling anger simmering inside him, Molina said, "You forget that I came here because of a tip from one of the construction workers. I didn't just blindly stumble onto those rocks."

"A tip from whom?" asked one of the younger men.

"I don't know. It was an anonymous message. I've questioned the workers down there on the surface and none of them admits to sending me the message."

"An anonymous tip that no one admits to sending," grumbled McFergusen. "It strains credulity a bit, doesn't it?"

The woman on Molina's left, young, slightly plump, very intense, asked, "Why you?"

"Why me what?"

"Why did he—or she—send that message to you? You're not a major figure in planetary studies. Why not to Professor McFergusen," she gestured toward the older man, "or the head of the IAA?"

"Yes," picked up one of the others. "Why wasn't the message sent to the head of the astrobiology department of a major university?"

"Why is the sky blue?" Molina snapped. "How the hell should I know?"

"We know why the sky is blue," McFergusen murmured, a slight smile on his bearded face.

"Rayleigh scattering," said the young woman on the other side of the table.

"The question remains," McFergusen said, in a voice loud enough to silence the others, "that you received an anonymous message that led you directly to the specimens you discovered, and no one else has been able to find anything similar."

"And no one else has tested your specimens," said the woman on Molina's left.

Seething, Molina hissed, "Are you suggesting that I *faked* my findings?"

"I am suggesting," she said, unfazed by his red-faced anger, "that you allow us to independently test your specimens."

"It's possible to make an honest mistake," Bishop Danvers said softly, laying a placating hand on Molina's arm.

"Look at Percival Lowell, spending his life seeing canals on Mars that didn't exist."

"Or the first announcement of pulsar planets."

McFergusen said gently, "No one is impugning your honesty, Dr. Molina. But we can't be certain of your results until they are checked by a third party. Surely you understand that."

Reluctantly, Molina nodded. "Yes. Of course. I'm sorry I got so excited."

Everyone around the table seemed to relax, ease back in their chairs.

"But," Molina added, pointing straight at McFergusen, "I want to be present when the tests are made."

"Certainly," McFergusen agreed. "I see no problem with that. Do any of you?"

No one objected.

"Very well, then. We can test the rocks tomorrow. Dr. Baines, here, is the best man for the job, don't you agree?"

Molina nodded.

"I will attend the procedure myself," McFergusen said, almost jovially. "With you, Dr. Molina."

Molina nodded again and muttered, "Thank you," through gritted teeth.

GOETHE BASE

"ou've got to help me," Victor Molina said, his voice trembling slightly. "You've *got* to!"

Dante Alexios sat stiffly in his straight-backed chair and struggled to keep any emotion from showing on his face. "*I* have to help you?"

"None of the others will. You're the only one who can."

The two men were in Alexios's bare little office. Molina was on his feet, pacing like a caged animal back and forth. Alexios sat unmoving, except for his eyes, which tracked Molina's movements like a predator sizing up its intended victim.

Molina paced to the wall, turned around, strode back to the opposite wall, turned again.

"I've got to find more samples!" he blurted. "They won't believe me if I don't. I've got to go out on the surface and find more rocks that contain biomarkers."

As evenly as he could manage, Alexios said, "But the IAA team is looking for samples all over the planet, aren't they? They've stopped us from doing any further activities—"

"The IAA team! McFergusen and his academics! A bunch of incompetent fools! They sit up there safe and comfortable in their ship and send teleoperated rovers to snoop around the surface for them."

"Virtual reality is a powerful tool," Alexios goaded.

Standing in front of him, bending over so that their noses nearly touched, Molina cried, "They won't allow me to use their VR system! I let them examine my rocks but they won't let me touch their equipment! It's not fair!"

Alexios slowly rose to his feet, forcing Molina to back off a few steps. "And that's why you've come to me."

"You have tractors sitting here at the base doing nothing. Let me borrow one. I've got to get out there and find more specimens."

Alexios's oddly irregular face slowly curled into a lopsided smile. "It's against safety regulations for anyone to go out on a tractor alone."

Molina's already-flushed face turned darker. Before he could say anything, though, Alexios added, "So I'll go out with you."

"You will?" Molina seemed about to jump for joy.

With a self-deprecating little shrug, Alexios said, "I have little else to do, thanks to the IAA."

He could have said, *Thanks to you*, but Molina never thought of that possibility.

Instead he asked, "When? How soon?"

"As soon as you're ready."

"I'm ready now!"

In truth, it took more than a day for Molina to be ready. He shuttled back up to *Himawari* to gather the equipment he wanted, and by then it was time for dinner. So he spent the night aboard Yamagata's torch ship with his wife. Alexios slept in his quarters alone, trying not to think of Molina in bed with Lara. He slept very little, and when he did his dreams were monstrous.

Molina arrived at the base early the next morning, with four crates of equipment. Alexios hid his amusement and walked him to the garage where the base's tractors were housed. A baggage cart trundled behind them on spongy little wheels, faithfully following the miniature beacon Alexios had clipped to his belt.

The garage was empty and quiet. "Mr. Yamagata came in here just once since the IAA embargoed us," Alexios said, his voice echoing off the steel ribs of the curving walls. "He wasn't happy to see all this equipment sitting idle."

Molina said nothing. The tractors were simple and rugged, with springy-looking oversized metal wheels and a glassteel bubble up front where the driver and passengers sat. The two men loaded Molina's equipment into the cargo deck in back, then closed the heavy cermet hatch.

"I'll get into my suit now," said Molina.

Alexios could see dark stains of perspiration on his coveralls. It couldn't be from the exertion of lifting those crates in this light gravity, he thought. Victor must be nervous. Or maybe he's afraid of going outside again.

He went with Molina and suited up also.

"But you won't have to leave the tractor," Molina objected as a team of technicians began to help them into the bulky suits.

"Unless you get into trouble," said Alexios.

"Oh."

"You wouldn't want to wait a half hour or more while I wiggled myself into this outfit."

"No, I imagine not."

At last they were both ready, the cumbersome, heavily insulated suits fully sealed and checked out by the technicians.

Alexios called base control with his suit radio. "Dr. Molina and I are going out on tractor number four. We will go beyond your camera range."

The controller's voice sounded bored. "Copy you'll go over the horizon. Sunup in one hour, seventeen minutes."

A flotilla of miniature surveillance satellites hugged the planet in low orbits, so every square meter of Mercury's surface was constantly covered by at least two of the minisats. They provided continuous communications links and precise location data.

"Sun in one seventeen," Alexios acknowledged.

"You are clear for excursion," said the controller.

It wasn't easy to climb up into the tractor's cab in the awkward suits, despite the low gravity. Alexios heard Molina grunt and puff until he finally settled in the right-hand seat.

"Comfortable?" Alexios asked.

"Are you kidding?"

Laughing lightly, Alexios engaged the tractor's electric engine and drove to the open inner airlock hatch.

"Do you have a specific route for us to follow or will we simply meander around out there?" Alexios asked as the inner hatch closed and the air was pumped out of the lock.

Molina struggled to fish a thumbnail-sized chip from his equipment belt and clicked it into the computer in the tractor's control panel. The display screen showed a geodetic map of the area with a route marked clearly by a red line.

Alexios studied the display for a moment, then tapped a gloved finger against it. "That's a pretty steep gully. We should avoid it."

Molina's voice in his earphones sounded irked. "That's the most likely spot to find what I'm looking for."

The outer hatch slid open. The barren landscape looked dark and foreboding, the horizon frighteningly near, thousands of stars gleaming steadily beyond it. Alexios saw the glowing band of the Milky Way stretching across the sky.

As he put the tractor in gear, he checked the status of the electrical power systems on the control panel displays. Fuel cells at max, backup batteries also. Once the Sun came up, he knew, the solar cells would take over.

They bounced over the hatch's edge and onto the rugged, uneven rocky surface.

"I'm afraid we can't take the tractor down into that gully," Alexios said.

Silence from Molina for a moment, although Alexios could hear his breathing in his helmet earphones. Then, "All right. Get as close to it as you can and I'll go down on foot."

Alexios felt his brows rise. Victor has guts, he said to himself. Or, more likely, he's driven by a demon.

Alexios knew all about being driven by demons.

SURFACE EXCURSION

Molina sat in silence inside the heavy pressurized suit, jouncing slightly as the tractor trundled along the route he had selected. They passed the shallow crater where he had found his specimens. In the tractor's headlights it looked gray and lifeless.

A relentless anger simmered through him, overwhelming the uneasiness he felt about being out on the surface of this deadly world, where a slight mistake could kill you.

Once he allowed McFergusen and his dilettantes to examine his samples, they wouldn't let go of them. Just one more test. Oh, yes, we thought of another way to probe the samples. You don't mind our keeping them another day or two, do you?

Molina saw that the results they were getting matched his own almost exactly. Within the margin of measurement error, at least. So why are they still sawing away at my rocks? What do they think they'll find that I haven't already found? They can't take the credit for discovering them away from me. What in hell are they trying to do?

He thought he knew the answer. They're trying to prove I'm wrong. They're doing their damnedest to discredit me. They'll keep poking and probing and studying until they find some error in my analysis, some mistake I've made.

Never! he told himself. There's no mistake. No error. The biomarkers are there and no matter what they do they can't make them go away.

But still they're hammering away at it, trying to show I'm wrong. Molina seethed with barely controlled fury. He tried to remember that age-old saw: *Extraordinary claims require extraordinary evidence.* Who said that originally? Fermi? Sagan?

What fucking difference does it make? he raged inwardly. The evidence is there. It's real, goddammit. They can't make it disappear.

But they won't be satisfied until more specimens with biomarkers are found. All right. They can't find them, sitting up there in orbit with their virtual reality thumbs up their asses. So I'll find them down here. I'll bring back more specimens and shove them under their noses and then they'll *have* to admit I'm right.

"We're coming up on that gully." Alexios's voice in his earphones startled him back to the here and now.

Blinking away his angry ruminations, Molina saw off to their right a long, fairly straight gorge paralleling their course, a split in the bare rocky surface. It didn't look very deep on the geodetic map, but now as he stared through the glassteel bubble of the tractor's cab, it seemed as yawning as the Grand Canyon.

It's just an illusion, he told himself. With no light except the stars, everything looks dark and deep and scary.

"Where do you want me to pull up?" Alexios asked.

Strange how familiar his voice sounded through the earphones, Molina thought. I couldn't have heard it before; I just met the man a few weeks ago. And yet—

"Where should I stop?" Alexios asked again.

"Get as close to the edge as you can," Molina said, feeling his insides fluttering with anticipation and more than a little fear.

Alexios drove the tractor up to the rim of the gully, so close that Molina was momentarily alarmed that they would topple into it. When he finally stopped the tractor, Molina could peer down into its shadowy depths.

"Better wait until the Sun comes up," Alexios suggested.

Nodding inside his helmet, Molina started to get up from his seat. "I'll get my equipment out of the back."

Alexios pressed the keypad on the control panel that popped the hatch on Molina's side of the bubble, then opened the hatch on his side. "I'll give you a hand."

They worked by starlight, hauling the cases of equipment out of the tractor's cargo bay. One of the metal boxes stuck to the tractor's deck.

"Frozen," Alexios muttered. "It must have had some moisture on its bottom when you put it in."

Molina realized that it was more than a hundred below zero in the nighttime darkness.

"It'll thaw quickly enough when the Sun comes up," said Alexios.

Impatient, Molina climbed up onto the deck and opened the crate there. He began hauling out the equipment it held: sample scoops, extensible arms, handheld radiation meters. One by one, he handed them to Alexios, who laid them in a neat row on the ground.

Alexios lifted his left arm so he could see the miniature display screen on his wrist. "Still another half hour to sunrise."

Molina was already setting up a winch and buckyball cable. Alexios saw a power drill among the equipment arrayed on the ground and helped the astrobiologist to firmly implant the steel-tubed frame into the hard, rocky ground. Then they fastened the winch to it and connected its power cable to the tractor's electrical outlet.

Worldlessly they lowered Molina's equipment to the bottom of the gully. It was a fair test of the winch, although none of the paraphernalia weighed as much as Molina and his suit.

Despite the coldness of the night, Alexios was sweating from his exertions. Good, he thought. The suit's well insulated. He straightened up and saw a pearly glow on the horizon.

"Look," he said to Molina, pointing.

For a moment Molina felt confused. Mercury has no atmosphere, he knew. There can't be a gradual dawn, like on Earth. Then he realized that what he was seeing was the Sun's zodiacal light, the sunlight scattered off billions of dust motes that orbited the Sun's equator, leftover bits of matter from the earliest times of the solar system's birth that hovered close to the star like two long oblate arms, too faint to see except when the overwhelming glare of the Sun itself was hidden, as it was now.

Molina grunted, then said, "I'd better get into the rig."

Inside his helmet, Alexios shook his head. You never were the poetic sort, Victor. Not a romantic neuron in your entire brain. But then a sardonic voice in his head reminded him, But he got Lara, didn't he?

By the time he had helped Molina into the climbing harness, the rim of the Sun was peeping above the horizon, sending a wave of heat washing across the desolate landscape. Alexios heard his suit ping and groan as its cermet expanded in the sudden roasting warmth. The air fans whirred like angry insects. The visor of his helmet automatically darkened.

"Ready?" he asked Molina.

He heard the man gulp and cough. Then he replied, "Yes, I'm ready.

The gully was filling with light as the Sun climbed higher against the black sky. Alexios stood by the winch as it unreeled its cable and Molina slowly, carefully, picked his way down the steep slope of the crevasse.

It's not all that deep, Alexios saw, peering down into the ravine. Ten meters, maybe twelve. Just deep enough. He watched as Molina reached the bottom and unhitched the cable from his climbing harness.

"Good hunting," Alexios called to him.

"Right," said Molina faintly. His voice was already breaking up slightly, relayed from the bottom of the crevasse to one of the comm-sats orbiting overhead and then to Alexios's suit radio.

In pace requiescat, Alexios added silently.

Once he'd removed the climbing cable from his suit, Molina took in a deep, steadying breath and looked up and down the gully. It was like a long, slightly irregular hallway without a roof. One steep wall was bathed in sunlight, the other in shadow. But enough light reflected off the bright side so that he could see the uneven floor and even the shadowed side fairly well.

This must be a fault line, he told himself. Maybe it cracked open when a meteor impacted. He attached his sampling scoop to the metal arm and extended it to its full length. Not much dust on the ground, he saw. The bottom here must be exposed ancient terrain. If I can get some ratio data from the radioactives I'll be able to come up with a rough date for its age.

It was all but impossible to kneel in the heavy, cumbersome suit, but slowly Molina lowered himself to his knees. Inside the suit he could hear its servomotors whine in complaint. He chipped out a small chunk of rock, then fumbled through the sets of equipment ly-ing on the ground until he found the radiation counter. No sense try-ing for argon ratios, he told himself. The heat's baked all the volatiles out of these rocks eons ago.

The radiation signature of uranium was there, however. Weak, but clearly discernable in the handheld's tiny readout screen. Then he tried the potassium signature. Stronger. Unmistakable. Molina weighed the sample, then did some rough calculating on the computer built into his suit's wrist. This sample is at least two and half billion years old, he concluded. If I can dig deeper, I should find older layers of rock.

He looked down the length of the slightly uneven corridor of rock. The floor seemed to drop away farther down. Maybe I can get to older strata without digging, he thought. I don't have a really powerful drill with me, anyway.

It took a mighty effort to get back on his feet again, even with the servomotors doing their best. Molina blinked sweat from his eyes and called up to Alexios:

"I'm going down the arroyo about a hundred meters or so."

It took a moment for the radio signal to bounce off the nearest commsat.

"Which direction?" Alexios asked.

Molina pointed, then realized it was foolish. He tapped at his wrist keyboard, then peered at the positioning data that came up on its display.

"North," he said into his helmet microphone. "To your left as you face the rim."

A silence longer than the time for the signal to be relayed off the satellite. Then, "Very well. If you go any farther, let me know and I'll bring the tractor and rig to your position."

"That won't be necessary," Molina answered immediately.

Again a delay. Finally, "Very well. I'll wait here."

Molina started slogging along the rock-walled chasm. That voice, he said to himself. Why should it sound so familiar?

Alexios climbed back into the tractor's bubble of a cab and sat awkwardly in the driver's seat. The chair was bare metal, designed to accommodate the bulky suits that the tractor crew had to wear.

No sense standing in the open, Alexios thought. The glassteel doesn't afford that much protection against radiation, but every little bit helps. He remembered an old adage he had heard from a mercenary soldier out in the Belt: "Never stand when you can sit. Never stay awake when you can sleep. And never pass a latrine without using it."

No latrines out here, Alexios knew. Nor out in the Belt, either. You piss into the relief tube built into your suit and you crap when you can find a toilet inside a pressurized vessel.

The Sun was halfway above the horizon now, already frighteningly large and glaring.

Alexios smiled. In another fifteen minutes or so it will dip back down and plunge this whole region into darkness again. What's Victor going to do when the light goes away and he's stuck down in that crevasse?

FALSE DAWN

ante Alexios sat in the cab of the tractor and watched the Sun drop toward the horizon, a twisted smile on his slightly mismatched face. Although Molina hadn't spoken to him since he announced he was heading farther up the gully, he could hear Victor's breathing through the open microphone in the astrobiologist's helmet.

Alexios turned off the suit-to-suit link and called in to the base on another frequency.

"Alexios to base control."

The reply was almost immediate. "Control here."

"Do you have our position?"

A slight delay. Alexios could picture the controller flicking his eyes to the geographic display.

"Yes, your beacon is coming through clearly."

"Good. Anything happening that I should know about?"

A slight chuckle. "Not unless you have a prurient interest in what the safety director and her assistant are up to."

Alexios laughed, too. "Not as long as they keep their recreations confined to the privacy of their quarters."

"So far. But there's a lot of heavy breathing going on at their workstations."

"I'll speak to her when I get back."

"Her? What about him?"

"Her," Alexios repeated. "The woman's always in control in situations like this."

"That's news to me," said the controller.

There was nothing else significant to report. One of the powersats was getting some experimental shielding; otherwise, the base was running in standby mode until the IAA gave them clearance to resume their work.

Alexios clicked off the link to the base and sat back as comfortably as he could manage inside the suit. How long will it take Yamagata to go bankrupt? he wondered. And when the Sunpower Foundation does go bust, will Yamagata simply siphon more money out of his corporation? Will his son allow that? A battle between father and son would be interesting.

The Sun was dipping lower. Turning, he could see bright stars spangling the blackness on the other side of the sky. Alone with the stars. And his thoughts.

Lara. She was Molina's wife. Had been for just about ten years now. They have a child, a son. Victor, Jr. His son, out of her body.

The pain Alexios felt was real, physical. He realized his jaws had clamped so tightly that he could hear his teeth grinding against one another.

With a physical effort, he forced himself to relax and tapped the keypad to reopen the suit-to-suit link.

"—dark down here," Molina was saying. "My helmet lamp isn't all that much help."

"The Sun's going down for a while," said Alexios.

"How long?"

Alexios had memorized the day's solar schedule. "Fifty-eight minutes, twelve seconds."

"A whole hour?" Molina's voice whined like a disappointed child's.

"Just about."

"What the hell am I supposed to do down in this hole in the dark for an hour? You should have told me about this!"

"I thought you knew."

"I can't see fucking shit down here!"

"You have the helmet lamp."

"Big help. It's like trying to find your way across the Rocky Mountains with a flashlight."

"Have you found anything?"

"No," Molina snapped. "And I won't, at this rate."

You won't at any rate, Alexios replied silently. Aloud, he asked, "Do you want to come back to the tractor?"

A long silence. Alexios could picture Molina angrily weighing the alternatives in his mind.

"No, dammit. I'll wait here until the frigging Sun comes up again."

"I'll move the tractor down to your location."

"Good. Do that."

With no atmosphere to dilute their brightness, the stars provided adequate light for Alexios to reel up the winch's cable, disassemble the rig and pack it all back onto the tractor's rear deck. Then he drove carefully along the rim of the crevasse to the spot where Molina sat, waiting and fuming, for enough sunlight to resume his search. A waste of time, Alexios knew. Victor won't find what he's looking for.

By the time he had drilled the holes in the ground for the rig's supporting frame and set the winch in place, the Sun was rising above the bare, too-near horizon once again. This time it would remain up for weeks. Even through the heavy tinting of his visor Alexios had to squint at its powerful glare. The Sun was tremendous, huge, a mighty presence looming above him.

The hours dragged on. Alexios listened to Molina panting and grumbling as he searched for rocks that might harbor biomarkers.

"Christ, it's hot," the astrobiologist complained.

Alexios flicked a glance at the outside temperature readout on the tractor's control panel. "It's only three-eighty Celsius. A cool morning on Mercury."

"I'm broiling inside this damned suit."

"You'd broil a lot faster outside the suit," Alexios bantered.

"There's nothing here. I'm going farther up the gully."

"Check your suit's coolant systems. If the levels are down in the yellow region of the display, you should come back."

"It's still in the green."

Alexios called up the suit monitoring program and saw that Molina's coolant systems were on the edge of the yellow warning region. He's got about an hour left before they'll dip into the red, he estimated.

Nearly an hour later, Alexios called, "Time to come back, Dr. Molina."

"Not yet. There's a bunch of rocks up ahead. I want to take a look at them."

"Safety regulations, sir," Alexios said firmly. "Your life-support systems are going critical."

"I can see the readouts as well as you can," Molina replied testily. "I've got a good hour or more before they reach the red line, and even then there's a considerable safety margin built in."

"Dr. Molina, the safety regulations must be followed. They were formulated for your protection."

"Yeah, yeah. Just let me take a look at—hey! Damn! Ow!"

"What happened?" Alexios snapped, genuinely alarmed. "What's wrong?"

"I'm okay. I fell down, that's all. Tripped over a crack in the ground."

"Oh."

Alexios heard grunting, then swearing, then quick, heavy breathing. The sound of panic.

"Christ, I can't get up!"

"What?"

"I can't lift myself up! I'm down on my left side and I can't get enough leverage in this goddamned suit to push myself up onto my feet again."

Alexios could picture his predicament. The suit's servomotors were designed to assist the wearer's normal arm and leg movements. Basically they were designed to allow a normal human being's muscle power to move the suit's heavy sleeves and leggings. Little more. Molina was down on the ground, trying to lift the combined weight of his body plus the suit back into a standing position. Even in Mercury's light gravity, the servos were unequal to the task.

"Can you sit up?" he asked into his helmet mike.

A grunt, then an exasperated sigh. "No. This damned iron maiden you've got me in doesn't bend much at the middle."

Alexios thought swiftly. He can last about two more hours in the suit, maybe three. I can leave him there and let him broil in his own juices. He left me when I needed him; why should I save his life? It's not my fault—he *wanted* to go down there. He insisted on it.

Base control wasn't on the suit-to-suit frequency. The suit radios could be picked up by the commsats, of course, but you had to plug into the commsat frequency and Victor didn't know that. He rushed out here without learning all the necessary procedures, Alexios thought. He depended on me to handle the details.

Just as I depended on him to help me when I needed it. And he walked away from me. He took Lara and left me to the wolves.

Inside his helmet, Alexios smiled grimly. He remembered Poe's old story, "The Cask of Amontillado." What were Fortunato's last words? *For the love of God, Montresor!* And Montresor replied, as he put the last brick in place and sealed his former friend into a lingering death, "Yes, for the love of God!"

"Hey!" Molina called. "I really need some help here."

"I'm sure you do," Alexios said calmly.

And he pictured himself bringing the sad news back to the base. Telling Yamagata how the noted astrobiologist had killed himself out on the surface of Mercury, nobly searching for evidence of life. I tried to help him, Alexios saw himself explaining, but by the time I reached him he was gone. He just pushed it too far. I warned him, but he paid no attention to the safety regs.

Then I'll have to tell his widow. Lara, your husband is dead. No, I couldn't say it like that. Not so abruptly, so brutally. Lara, I'm afraid I have very bad news for you . . .

He could see the shock in her soft gold-flecked eyes. The pain.

"I'm really stuck here," Molina called, a hint of desperation in his voice. "I need you to help me. What are you doing up there?"

Alexios heard himself say, "I'm coming down. It'll take a few minutes. Hang in there."

"Well for Christ's sake don't dawdle! I'm sloshing in my own sweat inside this frigging suit."

Alexios smiled again. You're not helping yourself, Victor. You're not making it easier for me to come to your aid.

But he pushed the door of the tractor's cab open and jumped to the ground, almost hoping that he'd snap an ankle or twist a knee and be unable to save Victor's self-centered butt. Angry with himself, furious with Victor, irritated at the world in general, Alexios marched to the winch and wrapped the cable around both his gloved hands. Slowly he began lowering himself down the steep side of the gully.

"What are you doing?" Molina demanded. "Are you coming?"

"I'll be there in a few minutes," Alexios said between gritted teeth.

I'll save your ass, Victor, he thought. I'll save your body. I won't let you die. I'll bring you back and let you destroy yourself. That's just as good as killing you. Better, even. Destroy yourself, Victor. With my help.

TORCH SHIP *BRUDNOY*

Had a bit of a scrape out there, eh?" asked Professor McFergusen as he poured a stiff whisky for himself.

Molina was sitting on the curved couch of the *Brudnoy*'s well-stocked lounge, his wife close beside him. Two tall glasses of fruit juice stood on the low table before them. No one else was in the lounge; McFergusen had seen to it that this meeting would be private.

McFergusen kept a fatherly smile on his weather-seamed face as he sat down in the plush faux-leather chair at the end of the cocktail table. He and the chair sighed in harmony.

"You're all right, I trust?" he asked Molina. "No broken bones, as far as I can see."

"I'm fine," Molina said. "It was just a little accident. Nothing to fuss over."

Mrs. Molina looked to McFergusen as if she thought otherwise, but she said nothing and hid her emotions by picking up her glass and sipping at it. Fruit juice. McFergusen suppressed a shudder of distaste.

"I think the entire affair has been exaggerated," said Lara. "From what Victor tells me, he was never in any real danger."

McFergusen nodded. "I suppose not. Good thing that Alexios fellow was there to help out, though."

"That's why the safety regulations require that no one goes out onto the surface alone," Molina said, a bit stiffly.

"Yes. Of course. The important thing, though—the vital question—is: did you find any more specimens while you were out there?"

Now Molina grabbed for his glass. "No," he admitted, then took a gulp of the juice.

McFergusen's bearded face settled into a worried frown. "You see, the problem is that we still have nothing but those specimens you collected your very first day on the planet."

"There must be more," Molina insisted. "We simply haven't found them yet."

"We've searched for weeks, lad."

"We'll have to search further. And more extensively."

The tumbler of whisky had never left McFergusen's hand. He took a deep draft from it, then finally put it down on the table. Shaking his head, he said firmly, "Yamagata's putting pressure on the IAA. And, frankly, I'm running out of excuses to send back to headquarters. Do you realize how much it costs to keep this ship here? And my committee?"

Molina looked obviously irritated. "How much is the discovery of life on Mercury worth? Can you put a dollar figure on new knowledge?"

"Is there life on Mercury?"

"That's the question, isn't it?"

"Some of my committee members think we're here on a fool's errand," McFergusen admitted.

"They're the fools, then," Molina snapped.

"Are they?"

Molina started to reply, but his wife put a hand on his arm. Just a feather-light touch, but it was enough to silence him.

"Wasn't it Sagan" she asked, in a soft voice, "who said that absence of proof is not proof of absence?"

McFergusen beamed at her. "Yes, Sagan. And I agree! I truly do! I'm not your enemy, lad. I want you to succeed."

Lara immediately understood what he had not said. "You want Victor to succeed, but you have doubts."

"Worse than that," McFergusen said, his tone sinking. "There's a consensus among my committee that your evidence, Dr. Molina, is not conclusive. It may not even be pertinent."

Molina nearly dropped his glass. "Not pertinent! What do you mean?"

Decidedly unhappy, McFergusen said, "I've called a meeting for tomorrow morning at ten. I intend to review all the evidence that we've uncovered."

"We've gone over the evidence time and again."

"There's something new," McFergusen said. "Something that's changed the entire situation here."

"What is it?" Lara asked.

"I prefer to wait until the entire committee is assembled," said McFergusen.

"Then why did you ask us to join you here this evening?"

Looking squarely at Molina, the professor said grimly, "I wanted to give you a chance to think about what you've done and consider its implications."

Molina's brow wrinkled in puzzlement. "I don't understand what you're talking about."

"All to the good, then," said McFergusen. "If you're telling the truth."

"Telling the truth! What the hell do you mean?"

Raising his hands almost defensively, McFergusen said, "Now, now, there's no sense losing your temper."

"Is somebody calling me a liar? Are any of those academic drones saying my evidence isn't valid?"

"Tomorrow," McFergusen said. "We'll thrash all this out tomorrow, when everyone's present." He gulped down the rest of his whisky and got to his feet.

Molina and his wife stood up, too.

"I don't understand any of this," Lara said.

McFergusen realized she was just as tall as he was. "Perhaps I shouldn't have met with you this evening. I merely wanted to give you a fair warning about what to expect tomorrow."

Molina's face was red with anger. His wife clutched at his arm and he choked back whatever he was going to say.

"I'll see you tomorrow at ten, in the conference room," McFergusen said, clearly embarrassed. "Good evening."

He hurried out of the lounge and ducked through the hatch into the ship's central passageway.

Lara turned to her husband. "At least he didn't have the effrontery to wish us pleasant dreams."

Molina was too furious to smile at her attempted humor.

TRIBUNAL

Molina could see from the expressions on their faces that this was going to be bad. McFergusen sat at the head of the conference table, his team of scientists along its sides. What bothered Molina most was that Danvers and his two young acolytes were also present, seated together toward the end of the table. The only empty chair, waiting for Molina, was at the absolute foot of the table.

They all looked up as Molina entered the conference room at precisely ten o'clock. A few of them smiled at him, but it was perfunctory, pasted on, phony. Obviously McFergusen had ordered them to come in earlier, most likely because he wanted to go over their testimony with them. *Testimony.* Molina grimaced at the word he had automatically used. This was going to be a trial, he knew. Like a court martial. Like a kangaroo court.

The conference room fell into complete silence as soon as he opened the door from the passageway and entered. In silence Molina took his chair and slipped his data chip into the slot built into the faux mahogany table.

"Dr. Molina," said McFergusen, "I presume you know everyone here."

Molina nodded. He had met most of the scientists and knew of their reputations. Danvers was an old friend, at least an old acquaintance. The two other ministers with him were nonentities, as far as Molina was concerned, but that didn't matter.

The conference room was stark. The narrow table that lined one of its walls was bare; no refreshments, not even an urn of coffee or a pitcher of water. The wall screens were blank. The room felt uncomfortably warm, stuffy, but Molina was ice-cold inside. This is going to be a battle, he told himself. They're all against me, for some reason. Why? Jealousy? Disbelief? Refusal to accept the facts? It doesn't matter. I have the evidence. They can't take that away from me. I've already published my findings on the nets. Maybe that's it. Maybe they're pissed off because I didn't send my findings through the regular academic channels to be refereed before putting them out for all the world to see.

McFergusen ostentatiously pressed the keypad on the board built into the head of the table. "I hereby call this meeting to order. It is being recorded, as is the usual practice."

Molina cleared his throat and spoke up. "I wish to submit my findings as proof that evidence of biological activity has been discovered on Mercury."

McFergusen nodded. "Your evidence is entered into the record of this meeting."

"Good."

"Any comments?"

A plump, grandmotherly woman with graying hair neatly pulled back off her roundish face spoke up. "I have a comment."

"Dr. Paula Kantrowitz," said McFergusen, for the benefit of the recording. "Geobiologist, Cornell University."

You're overdue for a regeneration treatment, Molina sneered silently at Dr. Kantrowitz. *And a month or two in an exercise center.*

She tapped at the keypad before her and Molina's data sprang up on the wall screens on both sides of the room.

"The evidence that Dr. Molina has found is incontrovertible," she said. "It clearly shows a range of signatures that are indicative of biological activity."

Molina felt his entire body relax. *Maybe this isn't going to be so bad after all,* he thought.

"There is no question that the rocks Dr. Molina tested bear high levels of biomarkers."

A few nods around the table.

"The question is," Kantrowitz went on, "did those rocks originate on Mercury?"

"What do you mean?" Molina snapped.

Avoiding his suddenly angry eyes, Kantrowitz went on, "When I tested the rock samples that Dr. Molina so kindly lent to us, I was bothered by the results I saw. They reminded me of something I had seen elsewhere."

"And what is that?" McFergusen asked, like the straight man in a well-rehearsed routine.

Kantrowitz touched another keypad and a new set of data curves sprang up on the wall screens alongside Molina's data. They looked so similar they were almost identical.

"This second data set is from Mars," she said. "Dr. Molina's rocks bear biomarkers that are indistinguishable from the Martian samples."

"What of it?" Molina challenged. "So the earliest biological activity on Mercury produces signatures similar to the earliest biological activity on Mars. That in itself is an important discovery."

"It would be," Kantrowitz replied, still not looking at Molina, "if your samples actually came from Mercury."

"Actually came from Mercury?" Molina was too stunned to be angry. "What do you mean?"

Kantrowitz looked sad, as if disappointed with the behavior of a child.

"Once I realized the similarity to Martian rocks, I tested the morphology of Dr. Molina's samples."

The data sets on the walls winked off, replaced by a new set of curves.

"The upper curves, in red, are from well-established data on Martian rocks. The lower curves, in yellow, are from Dr. Molina's samples. As you can see, they are so parallel as to be virtually identical."

Molina stared at the wall screen. No, he said to himself. Something is wrong here.

"The third set of curves, in red at the bottom, is from random samples of rocks I personally picked up from the surface of Mercury. They are very different in mineral content and in isotope ratios from the acknowledged Martian rocks. And from Dr. Molina's samples."

Molina sagged back in his chair, speechless.

Relentlessly, Kantrowitz went on, "I then used the tunneling microscope to search for inclusions in the samples."

Another graph appeared on the wall screen.

"I found several, which held gasses trapped within the rock. The ratio of noble gases in the inclusions match the composition of the

Martian atmosphere, down to the limits of the measurement capabilities. If these samples had been on the surface of Mercury for any reasonable length of time, the gases would have been baked out of the rock by the planet's high daytime temperatures."

"Are you saying," McFergusen asked, "that Dr. Molina's samples are actually rocks from Mars?"

"They're not from Mercury at all?" Danvers asked, unable to hide a delighted smile.

"That's right," Kantrowitz replied, nodding somberly. At last she turned to look directly at Molina. "I'm very sorry, Dr. Molina, but your samples are Martian in origin."

"But I found them here," Molina said, his voice a timid whine. "On Mercury."

McFergusen said coolly, "That raises the question of how they got to Mercury."

A deadly silence fell across the conference table. After several moments, one of the younger men sitting across from Kantrowitz, raised his hand. An Asian of some sort, Molina saw. Or perhaps an Asian-American.

"Dr. Abel Lee," pronounced McFergusen. "Astronomy department, Melbourne University."

Lee got to his feet. Molina was surprised to see that he was quite tall. "It's well known that some meteorites found on Earth originated from Mars. They were blasted off the planet by the impact of a much more energetic meteor, achieved escape velocity, and wandered through interplanetary space until they fell into Earth's gravity well."

"In fact," McFergusen added, "the first evidence that life existed on Mars was found in a meteorite that had landed in Antarctica—although the evidence was hotly debated for many years."

Lee made a little bow toward the professor, then continued, "So it is possible that a rock that originated on or even beneath the surface of Mars can be blasted free of the planet and eventually impact on another planet."

Molina nodded vigorously.

"But is it likely that such a rock would land on Mercury?" asked one of the other scientists. "After all, Mercury's gravity well is considerably smaller than Earth's."

"And with its being so close to the Sun," said another, "wouldn't the chances be overwhelming that the rock would fall into the Sun, instead?"

Lee replied, "I'd have to do the statistics, but I think both points are valid. The chances of a Martian rock landing on Mercury are vanishingly small, I would think."

"There's more to it than that," said McFergusen, his bearded face looking grim.

Molina felt as if he were the accused at a trial being run by Torquemada.

"First," said McFergusen, raising a long callused finger, "Dr. Molina did not find merely one Martian rock, but a total of eight, all at the same site."

"It might have been a single meteor that broke up when it hit the ground," Molina said.

McFergusen's frown showed what he thought of that possibility. "Second," he went on, "is the fact that although we have searched an admittedly small area of the planet's surface, no other such samples have been found."

"But you've only scratched the surface of the problem!" Molina cried, feeling more and more desperate.

McFergusen nodded like a judge about to pronounce a death sentence. "I agree that we have searched only a small fraction of the planet's surface. Still . . ." he sighed, then, staring squarely down the table at Molina, he went on, "There is such a thing as Occam's razor. When faced with several possible answers to a question, the simplest answer is generally the correct one."

"What do you mean?" Molina whispered, although he knew what the answer would be.

"The simplest answer," McFergusen said, his voice a low deadly rumble, "is that the site at which you discovered those rocks was deliberately seeded with samples brought to that location from Mars."

"No!" Molina shouted. "That's not true!"

"You worked on Mars, did you not?"

"Four years ago!"

"You had ample opportunity to collect rocks from Mars and eventually bring them to Mercury."

"No, they were already here! Some of the construction people found them! They sent a message to me!"

"That could all have been prearranged," McFergusen said.

"But it wasn't! I didn't—"

McFergusen sighed again, even more heavily. "This committee will make no judgment on how your samples arrived on Mercury, Dr. Molina. Nor will we accuse you or anyone else of wrongdoing. But we must conclude that the samples you claimed as evidence of biological activity on Mercury originated on Mars."

Molina wanted to cry. I'm ruined, he thought. My career as a scientist is finished. Ended. Absolutely ruined.

SCAPEGOAT

Bishop Danvers felt almost gleeful as he composed a message of triumph for New Morality headquarters in Atlanta.

The scientists themselves had disproved Molina's claim of finding life on Mercury! That was a victory for Believers everywhere. The entire thing was a sham, a hoax. It just shows how far these godless secularists will go in their efforts to destroy people's faith, Danvers said to himself.

He was saddened to see Molina's credibility shattered. Victor was a friend, an acquaintance of long standing. He could be boorish and overbearing at times, but now he was a broken man. He brought it on himself, though, Danvers thought. The sin of pride. Now he's going to pay the price for it.

Yet Danvers felt sorry for the man. They had known each other for almost a decade and a half, and although they were far removed from one another for most of that time, still he felt a bond with Victor Molina. Danvers had even performed the ceremony when Victor married Lara Tierney. It's wrong for me to rejoice in his mistake, he thought.

Deeper still, Danvers knew that the real bond between them had been forged in the destruction of another man, Mance Bracknell. Danvers and Victor had both played their part in the aftermath of that terrible tragedy in Ecuador. They had both helped to send Bracknell into exile. Well, Danvers said to himself, it could have been worse. After all, we saved the man from being torn apart by an angry mob.

With a heavy sigh, Danvers pushed those memories out of the forefront of his mind. Concentrate on the task at hand, he told himself. Send your report to Atlanta. The archbishop and his staff will be delighted to hear the good news. They can trumpet this tale as proof of how scientists try to undermine our faith in God. I'll probably be promoted higher up the hierarchy.

He finished dictating his report, then read it carefully as it scrolled on the wall screen in his quarters aboard the *Himawari*, adding a line here, changing an emphasis there, polishing his prose until it was fit to be seen by the archbishop. Yamagata must be pleased, he realized as he edited his words. He can resume his construction work, or whatever it is the engineers are supposed to be doing down on the planet's surface.

Nanomachines, he remembered. They want to begin using nanomachines on Mercury. What can I do to prevent that? If I could stop them, this mission to Mercury would become a double triumph for me.

When he was finally satisfied with his report, Danvers transmitted it to Earth. As an afterthought he sent courtesy copies to the two young ministers that Atlanta had sent to assist him. They'll be heading back to Earth now, he thought. He got to his feet and rubbed his tired eyes. In all probability I'll be heading back to Earth myself soon. He smiled at the prospects of a promotion and a better assignment as a reward for his work here. His smile turned wry. I hardly had to lift a finger, he thought. The scientists did all the work for me.

Then his thoughts returned to Molina. Poor Victor. He must be beside himself with grief. And anger, too, I suppose. Knowing Victor, the anger must be there. Perhaps suppressed right now, he's feeling so low. But sooner or later the anger will come out.

Bishop Danvers knew what he had to do. Squaring his shoulders, he left his quarters and marched down the ship's passageway toward the compartment that housed Victor Molina and his wife.

Molina was close to tears, Lara realized. He had burst into their compartment like a drunken man, staggering, wild-eyed. He frightened her, those first few moments.

Then he blubbered, "They think I falsified it! They think I'm a cheat, a liar!" And he nearly collapsed into her arms.

More than an hour had passed. Lara still held her husband in her arms as they sat on the couch. He was still shuddering, his face buried in her breast, his arms wrapped around her, mumbling incoherently.

Lara patted his disheveled hair soothingly. Haltingly, little by little, he had told her what had transpired at the meeting with McFergusen and the other scientists. She had murmured consoling words, but she knew that nothing she could say would help her husband. He had been accused of cheating, and even if he eventually proved he hadn't, the stigma would remain with him all his life.

"I'm ruined," he whimpered. "Destroyed."

"No, it's not that bad," she cooed.

"Yes it is."

"It will pass," she said, trying to ease his pain.

Abruptly, he pushed away from her. "You don't understand! You just don't understand!" His eyes were red, his hair wild and matted with perspiration. "I'm done! Finished! They've destroyed me. It would've been kinder if they'd blown my brains out."

Lara sat up straighter. "You are *not* finished, Victor," she said firmly. "Not if you fight back."

His expression went from despair to disgust. "Fight back," he growled. "You can't fight them."

"You can if you have the courage to do it," she snapped, feeling angry with her husband's self-pity, angry at the vicious fools who did this to him, angry at whoever caused this disaster. "You don't have to let them walk all over you. You can stand up and fight."

"You don't know—"

"Someone sent you a message, didn't they?"

"Yes, but—"

"You have a record of that message?"

"In my files, yes."

Lara said, "Whoever sent that message to you probably put those Martian rocks at the site you found."

Molina blinked several times. "Yes, but McFergusen and the others think that I set that up using a stooge."

"Prove that they're wrong."

"How in hell—"

"Find the man who set you up," Lara said. "He had to come to Mercury to plant those rocks at the site. He's probably still here."

"Do you think . . ." Molina fell silent. Lara studied his face. He wasn't bleating any more. She could see the change in his eyes.

"I don't think anybody's left Mercury since I arrived here. Certainly none of the team down at the base on the surface. None of Yamagata's people, I'm pretty sure."

"Then whoever set you up is probably still here."

"But how can we find him?"

Before Lara could think of an answer, they heard a soft rap at their door.

"I'll get it," she said, jumping to her feet. "You go wash up and comb your hair."

She slid the door open. Bishop Danvers's big, blocky body nearly filled the doorway.

"Hello, Lara," he said softly. "I've come to do what I can to solace Victor and help him in his hour of need."

Lara almost smiled. "Come right in, Elliott. We're going to need all the help we can get."

In his bare little office at Goethe base, Dante Alexios heard the news directly from Yamagata.

"It was all a hoax!" Yamagata was grinning from ear to ear. "The rocks were planted here. They actually came from Mars."

"Molina salted the site?" Alexios asked, trying to look astonished.

"Either he or a confederate."

"That's . . . shocking."

"Perhaps so, but it means that the blasted scientists have withdrawn their interdict on our operations."

"So soon?"

Yamagata shrugged. "They will, in a day or so. In the meantime, I want you to come up here to *Himawari* first thing tomorrow morning. We must plan the next phase of our operation."

"Building powersats here, out of materials from Mercury itself."

"Yes. Using nanomachines."

Alexios nodded. "We'll have to plan this very carefully."

"I realize that," Yamagata said, his grin fading only slightly. "That's why I want you here first thing in the morning."

"I'll be there."

"Good." Yamagata's image winked out.

Alexios leaned back in his chair and clasped his hands behind his head. Victor's finished, he said to himself. Now to get Danvers. And then my dear employer, Mr. Saito Yamagata, the murderer.

BOOK II
TEN YEARS EARLIER

And much of Madness, and more of Sin,
And Horror the soul of the plot.

THE SKYTOWER

ara Tierney couldn't catch her breath. It wasn't merely the altitude, although at more than three thousand meters the air was almost painfully thin. What really took her breath away, though, was the sight of the tower splitting the sky as the ancient Humvee rattled and jounced along the rutted, climbing road. Mance, sitting beside her, handed her a lightweight pair of electronic binoculars.

"They'll lock onto the tower," he shouted over the grinding roar of the Humvee's diesel engine. "Keep it in focus for you."

Lara put the binoculars to her eyes and found that they really did make up for some of the bumps in the Humvee's punishing ride. The skytower wavered briefly, then clicked into sharp focus, a thick dark column of what looked in the twin eyepieces like intertwined cables spiraling up, up, higher and higher, through the soft clouds and into the blue sky beyond, up into infinity.

"It's like a banyan tree," she gasped, resting the binoculars on her lap.

"What?" Mance Bracknell yelled from beside her. They were sitting together on the bench behind the driver, a short, stocky, dark-skinned mestizo who had inherited this rusting, dilapidated four-wheel-drive from his father, the senior taxi entrepreneur of the Quito airport.

Lara took several deep breaths, trying to get enough air into her lungs to raise her voice above the noise of the Humvee's clattering diesel engine.

"It's like a banyan tree," she shouted back, turning toward him. "All those strands . . . woven together . . . like a . . . banyan." She had to pull in more air.

"Right! That's exactly right!" Mance yelled, his dark brown eyes gleaming excitedly. "Like a banyan tree. It's organic! Nanotubes spun into filaments and then wrapped into coils; the coils are wound into those cables you're looking at."

She had never seen him so tanned, so athletically fit, so indestructibly cheerful. He looks more handsome than ever, she thought.

"Just like a banyan tree," he repeated, straining to make himself heard. "Damned near a hundred thousand individual buckyball fibers wound into those strands. Strongest structure on the face of the Earth."

"It's magnificent!"

Bracknell's smile grew wider. "We're still almost thirty kilometers away. Wait'll you get up close."

Like the beanstalk of the old fairy tale, the skytower rose up into the heavens. Lara spent the jouncing, dusty ride alternately staring at it and then glancing at Mance, sitting there as happy as a little boy on Christmas morning opening his presents. He's doing something that no one else has been able to do, she thought, and he's succeeding. He has what he wants. And that includes me.

All during the long flight from Denver to Quito she had wondered about her impulsive promise to marry Mance Bracknell. For the past three years all she'd seen of him was his quick visits back to the States and his occasional video messages. He had gone to Ecuador, asked her to marry him, and she had agreed. She had flown to Quito once before, when Mance was just starting on the project. He was so busy, so happily buried in his work that she had quietly returned home to Colorado. He didn't need her underfoot, and he barely raised more than a perfunctory objection when she told him she was going back home.

That was more than three years ago. I have a rival for his attentions, Lara realized. This tower he's building. She wondered if her rival would always stand between them. But when Mance called this latest time and asked her to come to Ecuador and stay with him, she had agreed immediately even though he hadn't mentioned a word about marriage.

Once she saw him, though, waiting for her at the airport terminal in Quito, the way his whole face lit up when he caught sight of her, the frenetic way he waved to her from the other side of the glass security partition as she went through the tiresome lines at customs, the way he smiled and took her in his arms and kissed her right there in the middle of the crowded airport terminal—she knew she loved him and she would follow him wherever he went, rival and marriage and everything else fading into trivia.

". . . if it works," he was hollering over the rumble of the truck's groaning engine, "we'll be able to provide electricity for the whole blinking country. Maybe for Colombia, Peru, parts of Brazil, the whole blasted northwestern bloc of South America!"

"If what works?" she asked.

"Tapping the ionosphere," he answered. Gesturing with both hands as he spoke, he shouted, "Enormous electrical energy up there, megawatts per cubic meter. At first we were worried that the tower would be like a big lightning rod, conducting down to the ground. Zap! Melt the bedrock, maybe."

"My god," Lara said.

"But we insulated the outer shell so that's not a problem."

Before Lara could think of something to say, Mance went on, "Then I started thinking about how we might tap some of that energy and use it to power the elevators."

"Tap the ionosphere?"

"Right. It's replenished by the solar wind. Earth's magnetic field traps solar protons and electrons."

"That's what causes the northern lights," Lara said, straining to raise her voice above the laboring diesel's growl.

"Yep. If we work it right, we can generate enough electricity to run the blinking tower and still have enough to sell to users on the ground. We can recoup all the costs of construction by selling electrical power!"

"How much electricity can you generate?" she asked.

"What?" he yelled.

She repeated her question, louder.

He waggled his right hand. "Theoretically, the numbers are staggering. Lots of gigawatts. I've got Mitchell working on it."

That's a benefit no one thought about, Lara said to herself. The original idea of the skytower was to build an elevator that could lift people and cargo into space cheaply, for the cost of the electrical energy it takes to carry them. Pennies per pound, instead of the hundreds of dollars per pound that rocket launchings cost. Now Mance is talking about using the tower to generate electricity, as well. How wonderful!

Then a new thought struck her. "Isn't this earthquake territory?" she shouted into Mance's ear.

His grin didn't fade even as much as a millimeter. He nodded vigorously. "You bet. We've had two pretty serious tremors already, Richter sixes. The world's highest active volcano is only a couple hundred kilometers or so from our site."

"Isn't that dangerous?"

"Not for us. That's one of the reasons we used the banyan tree design. The ground can sway or ripple all it wants to—the tower's not anchored to the ground, just tethered lightly. It won't move much."

Lara realized she looked unconvinced because Mance added, "Besides, we're not on a fault line. Nowhere near one. I got solid geological data before picking the site. The ground's not going to open up beneath us, and even if it did the tower would just stand there, solid as the Rock of Gibralter."

"But if it should fall . . . all that weight . . ."

Mance's smile turned almost smug. "It won't fall, honey. It can't. The laws of physics are on our side."

DATA BANK

kyhook. *Beanstalk. Space elevator. Skytower.* All these names and more have been applied to the idea of building an elevator that can carry people and cargo from the Earth's surface into orbital space.

Like many other basic concepts for space transportation, the idea of a skytower originated in the fertile mind of Konstantin Tsiolkovsky, the Russian pioneer who theorized about rocketry and astronautics in relative obscurity around the turn of the twentieth century. His idea for a "celestial castle" that could rise from the equator into orbital space, published in 1895, may have been inspired by the newly built Eiffel Tower, in Paris.

In 1960, the Russian engineer Yuri Artsutanov revived the concept of the space elevator. Six years later an American oceanographer, John Isaacs, became the first outside of Russia to write about the idea. In 1975, Jerome Pearson, of the U.S. Air Force Research Laboratory, brought the space elevator concept to the attention of the world's scientific community through a more detailed technical paper. The British author Arthur C. Clarke popularized the skyhook notion in several of his science fiction novels.

Although it sounds outlandish, the basic concept of a space elevator is well within the realm of physical possibility. As Clarke himself originally pointed out, a satellite in geostationary orbit, slightly more than thirty-five thousand kilometers above the equator, circles the Earth in precisely the same time it takes for the Earth to revolve about its axis. Thus such a satellite remains constantly above the same spot on the equator. Communications satellites are placed in geostationary *Clarke orbits* so that ground-based antennas may be permanently locked onto them.

To build a skytower, start at geostationary orbit. Drop a line down to the Earth's surface and unreel another line in the opposite direction, another thirty-five thousand kilometers into space. Simple tension will keep both lines in place. Make the line strong enough to carry freight and passenger elevators. *Voila!* A skyhook. A beanstalk. A skytower.

However, in the real world of practical engineering, the skytower concept lacked a suitable construction material. All known materials strong enough to serve were too heavy for the job. The tower would collapse of its own weight. A material with a much better strength-to-weight ratio was needed.

Buckyball fibers were the answer. Buckminsterfullerene is a molecule of sixty carbon atoms arranged in a sphere that reminded the chemists who first produced them of a geodesic dome, the type invented by the American designer R. Buckminster Fuller. Quickly dubbed buckyballs, it was found that fibers built of such molecules had the strength-to-weight ratio needed for a practical space elevator — with a considerable margin of error to spare. Where materials such as graphite, alumina, and quartz offer tensile strengths in the order of twenty gigapascals (a unit of measurement for tensile strength) the requirements for a space elevator are more than sixty gigapascals. Buckyball fibers have tensile strengths of more than one hundred gigapascals.

By the middle of the twenty-first century all the basic technical demands of a skytower could be met. What was needed was the capital and the engineering skill to build such a structure: a tower that rises more than seventy thousand kilometers from the equator, an elevator that can carry payloads into space for the price of the electricity used to lift them.

Backed by the nation of Ecuador and an international consortium of financiers, Skytower Corporation hired Mance Bracknell to head the engineering team that built the skytower a scant hundred kilometers from Quito. People in the streets of the Ecuadorian capital could see the tower rising to the heavens, growing thicker and stronger before their eyes.

Many glowed with pride as the tower project moved toward completion. Some shook their heads, however, speaking in worried whispers about the biblical Tower of Babel. Even in the university, philosophers spoke of man's hubris while engineers discussed moduli of elasticity. In Quito's high-rise business towers, men and women who dealt in international trade looked forward to the quantum leap that the tower would produce for the Ecuadorian economy. They saw their futures rising as high as the sky, and quietly began buying real estate rights to all the land between Quito and the base of the tower.

None of them realized that the skytower would be turned into a killing machine.

CIUDAD DE CIELO

t's *huge*," Lara said, as she stepped down from the Humvee. Inwardly she thought of all the phallic jokes the men must be making about this immense tower.

"A hundred meters across at the base," Bracknell said, heading for the back of the truck where her luggage was stored. "The size of a football field."

The driver stayed behind his wheel, anxious to get his pay and head back to the airport.

"It tapers outward slightly as it rises," Bracknell went on. "The station up at geosynch is a little more than a kilometer across."

The numbers were becoming meaningless to her. Everything was so huge. This close, she could see that each of the interwound cables making up the thick column must be a good five meters in diameter. And there were cables angling off to the sides, like the roots of a banyan, except that there were buildings where the cables reached the ground. They must be the tethers that Mance told me about, Lara thought.

"Well," he said, grinning proudly as he spread his arms, "this is it. Sky City. *Ciudad de Cielo*."

It was hard to take her eyes off the skytower, but Lara made the effort and looked around her. At Mance's instruction, the taxi had parked in front of a two-story building constructed of corrugated metal walls. It reminded her of an airplane hangar or an oversized work shed. Looking around, she saw rows of such buildings laid out along straight paved streets, a neat gridwork of almost identical structures, a prefabricated little city. Sky City. It was busy, she saw. Trucks and minivans bustled about the streets, men and women strode purposively along the concrete sidewalks. Very little noise, though, she realized. None of the banging and thumping that usually accompanied construction projects. Of course, Lara thought: all the vehicles are powered by electrical engines. This city was quietly intense, humming with energy and purpose.

Then she smiled. Somewhere down one of those streets someone was playing a guitar. Or perhaps it was a recording. A softly lyrical native folk song, she guessed. Its gentle notes drifted through the air almost languidly.

Bracknell pointed. "The music's coming from the restaurant. Some of our people have formed groups; they entertain in the evenings. Must be rehearsing now."

He picked up both her travel bags and led her from the parking lot up along the sidewalk toward the building's entrance.

"This is where my office is. And my living quarters, up on the second floor." He hesitated, his tanned face flushing slightly. "Uh, I could set you up in a separate apartment if you want . . ."

Both his hands were full with her luggage, so she stepped to him and wrapped her arms around his neck and kissed him soundly. "I didn't come all this way to sleep alone."

Bracknell's face went even redder. But he grinned like a schoolboy. "Well, okay," he said, hefting her travel bags. "Great."

Lara had brought only the two bags with her. They were close enough to Quito for her to buy whatever she lacked, she had reasoned.

Bracknell's apartment was small, utilitarian, and so gleamingly neat that she knew he had cleaned it for her. Through the screened windows she could see the streets of the little city and, beyond them, the green-clad mountains. The skytower was not in view from here.

"No air conditioning?" she asked as he plopped her bags onto the double-sized bed.

"Don't need it. Climate's very mild; it's always springtime here."

"But we're on the equator, aren't we?"

"And nearly four kilometers high."

She nodded. Like Santa Fe, she thought. Even Denver had a much milder climate than most people realized.

As she opened the larger of her two bags, Lara asked, "So the weather's not a problem for the skytower?"

"Even the rainy season isn't all that bad. That's one of the reasons

we picked this site," Bracknell said as he peered into the waist-high refrigerator in his kitchen alcove. He pulled out an odd-shaped bottle.
"Some wine? I've got this local stuff that's pretty bad, and a decent bottle of Chilean—"

"Just cold water, Mance," she said. "We can celebrate later."

He nearly dropped the bottle he was holding.

Bracknell had a surprise for her at dinner: Victor Molina, whom they
had both known at university.

"I had no idea you were part of this project," Lara said, as they sat
at a small square table in the corner of the city's only restaurant. A
quartet of musicians was tuning up across the way. Lara noticed that
their amplifiers were no bigger than tissue boxes, not the man-tall
monsters that could collapse your lungs when they were amped up
full blast.

The restaurant was hardly half filled, Lara saw. Either most of the
people eat at home or they come in much later than this, she reasoned. It was a bright, clean little establishment. No tablecloths, but
someone had painted cheerful outdoor scenes of jungle greenery and
colorful birds on the tabletops.

"Victor's the reason we're moving ahead so rapidly," Bracknell said.

Lara refocused her attention on the two men. "I thought you were
into biology back at school," she said.

"I still am," Molina replied, his striking blue eyes fastened on her.
He was as good-looking as ever, she thought, in an intense, urgent way.
Lara remembered how, at school, Molina had pursued the best-
looking women on campus. She had dated him a few times, until she
met Mance. Then she stopped dating anyone else.

Before she could ask another question, the robot waiter rolled up
to their table. Its flat top was a display screen that showed the evening's
menu and wine list.

"May I bring you a cocktail before you order dinner?" the robot
asked, in a mellow baritone voice that bore just a hint of an upper-class
British accent. "I am programmed for voice recognition. Simply state
the cocktail of your choice in a clear tone."

Lara asked for sparkling water and Bracknell did the same. Molina
said, "Dry vodka martini, please."

"Olives or a twist?" she asked the robot.

"Twist."

The little machine pivoted neatly and rolled off toward the service bar by the kitchen.

Lara leaned slightly toward Molina. "I still don't understand what a biologist is doing on this skytower project."

Before Molina could reply, Bracknell answered, "Victor's our secret weapon. He's the one who's allowed us to move ahead so rapidly."

"A biologist?"

Molina's eyes were still riveted on her. "You've heard of nanotechnology, haven't you?"

"Yes. It's banned, forbidden."

"True enough," he said. "But do you realize there's nanotechnology going on inside your body at this very instant?"

"Nanotech?"

"Inside the cells of your body. The ribosomes in your cells are building proteins. And what are they other than tiny little nanomachines?"

"Oh. But that's natural."

"Sure it is. So is the way we build buckyball fibers."

"With nanomachines?"

"Natural nanomachines," Bracknell said, trying to get back into the conversation. "Viruses."

The robot brought their drinks and, later, they selected their dinner choices from the machine's touch screen. Molina and Bracknell explained how Molina had used genetically engineered viruses to produce buckyball molecules and engineered microbial cells to put the buckyballs together into nanotubes.

"Once we have sets of nanotubes," Molina explained, "I turn them over to the regular engineers, and they string them together into the fibers that make up the tower."

"And you're allowed to do this in spite of the ban on nanotechnology?" Lara asked.

"There's nothing illegal about it," Molina said lightly.

"But we're not shouting the news from the rooftops," Bracknell added. "We want to keep this strictly under wraps."

"It's a new construction technique that'll be worth billions," Molina said, his eyes glowing. "Trillions!"

"Once we get it patented," Bracknell added.

Lara nodded, absently taking a forkful of salad and chewing contemplatively. Natural nanotechnology, she thought. Genetically engineered viruses. There are a lot of people who're going to get very upset when they hear about this.

"I can see why you want to keep it under wraps," she said.

PUBLISH OR PERISH

What I really want," Molina was saying, "is to get into astrobiology."

"Really?" Lara felt surprised. In all the weeks she had been at Ciudad de Cielo, this was the first time he'd broached the subject with her.

She was walking with the biologist along the base city's main street, wearing a colorful wool poncho that she'd bought from one of the street vendors that Mance allowed into town on the weekends. The wind off the mountains was cool, and it had drizzled for a half hour earlier in the morning. The thick wool poncho was just the right weight for this high-altitude weather. Molina had pulled a worn old leather jacket over his shirt and jeans.

"Astrobiology's the hot area in biology," he said. "That's where a man can make a name for himself."

"But you're doing such marvelous things here."

He looked over his shoulder at the skytower looming over them. Gray clouds scudded past it. With a discontented shrug, Molina said, "What I'm doing here is done. I've trained some bugs to make buckyball fibers for Mance. Big deal. I can't publish my work; he's keeping the whole process secret."

"Only until the patent comes through."

Molina frowned at her. "Do you have any idea of how long it takes to get an international patent? Years! And then the Skytower Corporation'll probably want to keep the process to themselves. I could waste the best years of my career sitting around here and getting no credit for my work."

Lara saw the impatience in his face, in his rigidly clenched fists, as they walked down the street. "So what do you intend to do?"

Molina hesitated for a heartbeat, then replied, "I've sent an application to several of the top astrobiology schools. It looks like Melbourne will accept me."

"Australia?"

"Yes. They've just gotten a grant to search for more Martian ruins and they're looking for people."

"To go to Mars?"

He made a bitter smile. "Australia first, then maybe Mars. If I do well enough for them here on Earth."

"I suppose that would be a good career move for you, Victor."

"Ought to be. Astrobiology. The field's wide open, with all the discoveries they're making on the moons of Jupiter and all."

"Then you'll be leaving us?"

"I've got to!" His voice took on a pained note. "I mean, Mance won't let me publish my work here until that fucking patent comes through. I'll be dead meat unless I can get into an area where I can make a name for myself."

"You and Mance work so well together, though," Lara said. "I know he'll be shocked when you tell him."

"He doesn't need me around here anymore. He's milked my brain and gotten what he wants."

Lara was surprised at the bitterness in his voice. "Mance will miss you," she said.

"Will *you?*"

"Of course I'll miss you, Victor."

He licked his lips, then blurted, "Then come to Melbourne with me, Lara! Let's get away from here together!"

Stunned, Lara staggered a few steps away from him.

"I'm in love with you, Lara. I really am. The past couple of months . . . it's been so . . ." He hesitated, as though gasping for breath. "I want to marry you."

He looked so forlorn, so despairing, yet at the same time so intense, so burning with urgency that Lara didn't know what to reply, how to react.

"I'm so sorry, Victor," she heard herself say gently. "I really am. I love Mance. You know that."

He hung his head, mumbling, "I know. I'm sorry, too. I shouldn't have told you."

"It's very sweet of you, Victor," she said, trying to soften his anguish. "I'm really very flattered that you feel this way. But it can't be."

"I know," he repeated. "I know." But what he heard in her words was, *If it weren't for Mance I could fall in love with you, Victor.*

Elliott Danvers knew that the elders of the New Morality were testing him. He had sweated and struggled through divinity school, accepting the snickers and snide jokes about a punch-drunk ex-prizefighter trying to become a minister of God. He had kept his temper, even when some of his fellow students' practical jokes turned vicious. *I can't get into a fight,* he would tell himself. *I'd be accused of attempted manslaughter if I hit one of them, and they know it. That's why they feel free to torment me. And I'm not clever enough to outwit them. Be silent. Be patient with those who persecute you. Turn the other cheek. This nonsense of theirs is a small price to pay for setting my life on a better path.*

He graduated near the bottom of his class, but he graduated. Danvers was a man who drove doggedly onward to complete whatever task he was burdened with. He had learned as a child in the filth-littered back alleys of Detroit that you took what came and you dealt with it, whether it was the punches of a faster, harder-hitting opponent or the thinly veiled contempt of a teacher who'd be happy to flunk you.

His reward for graduating without getting into any trouble was a ministry. He was now the Reverend Elliott Danvers, D.D. His faculty advisor congratulated him on bearing all the crosses that his playful classmates and vindictive teachers had hung on his broad shoulders.

"You've done well, Elliott," said his advisor, a pleased smile on his gray, sagging face. "There were times when I didn't think you'd make it, but you persevered and won the final victory."

Danvers knew that his academic grades had been marginal, at best. He bowed his head humbly and murmured, "I couldn't have made it without your help, sir. And God's."

His advisor laid a liver-spotted hand on Danvers's bowed head. "My blessings on you, my son. Wherever the New Morality sends you, remember that you are doing God's work. May He shower His grace upon you."

"Amen," said Danvers, with true conviction.

So they sent him to this strange, outlandish place in the mountains of Ecuador. It's a test, Danvers kept telling himself. The elders are testing my resolve, my dedication, my ability to win converts to God.

Ciudad de Cielo was a little prefab nest of unbelievers, scientists and engineers who were at best agnostics, together with local workers and clerks who practiced a Catholic faith underlain with native superstitions and idol worship.

Worst of all, though, they were all engaged in an enormous project that smacked of blasphemy. A tower that reached into the sky. A modern, high-technology Tower of Babel. Danvers was certain it was doomed to fail. God would not permit mortal men to succeed in such a work.

Then he remembered that he had been placed here to do God's work. If this tower is to fail, I must be the agent of its destruction. God wills it. That's why the New Morality sent me here.

Danvers knew that his ostensible task was to take care of people's souls. But hardly anyone wanted his help. The natives seemed quite content with their hodge-podge of tribal rituals and Catholic rites. Most of the scientists and engineers simply ignored him or regarded him as a spy sent by the New Morality to snoop on them. A few actively baited him, but their slings and barbs were nothing compared to the cruelty of his laughing classmates.

One man, though, seemed troubled enough to at least put up with him: Victor Molina, a close assistant of the chief of this tremendous project. Danvers watched him for weeks, certain that Molina was showing the classic signs of depression: moodiness, snapping at his coworkers, almost always taking his meals alone. He looked distinctly unhappy. The only time he seemed to smile was on those rare occasions when he had dinner in the restaurant with the project chief and the woman he was living with.

Living in sin, Danvers thought darkly. He himself had given up all thought of sex, except for the fiendish dreams that were sent to tempt him. No, he told himself during his waking hours. It was the desire for women and money that almost led you to your destruction in the ring. They broke your hand, they nearly destroyed your soul because of your indecent desires. Better to pluck out your eye if it offends you. Instead, Danvers used modern pharmacology to keep his libido stifled.

He approached Molina carefully, gradually, knowing that the man would reject or even ridicule an overt offer of help.

During lunchtime the city's only restaurant offered a buffet. After thinking about it for weeks, Danvers used it as an opening ploy with Molina.

"Do you mind if I sit with you?" he asked, holding his lunch-laden tray in both hands. "I hate to eat alone."

Molina looked up sourly, but then seemed to recognize the minister. Danvers did not use clerical garb; he wore no collar. But he always dressed in a black shirt and slacks.

"Yeah, why not?" Molina said. He was already halfway through his limp sandwich, Danvers saw.

Suppressing an urge to compliment the scientist on his gracious manners, Danvers sat down and silently, unobtrusively said grace as he began unloading his tray. They talked about inconsequential things, the weather, the status of the project, the sad plight of the refugees driven from coastal cities such as Boston by the greenhouse flooding.

"It's their own frigging fault. They had plenty of warning," Molina grumbled, finishing his sandwich. "Years of warning. Nobody listened."

Danvers nodded silently. No contradictions, he told himself. You're here to win his confidence, not to debate his convictions.

Over the next several weeks Danvers bumped into Molina often enough so that they started to be regular luncheon partners. Their conversations grew less guarded, more open.

"Astrobiology?" Danvers asked at one point. "That's what you want to do?"

Molina grinned wickedly at him. "Does that shock you?"

"Not at all," Danvers replied, trying to hide his uneasiness. "There's no denying that scientists have found living organisms on other worlds."

"Even intelligent creatures," Molina jabbed.

"If you mean those extinct beings on Mars, they might have been connected in some way with us, mightn't they?"

"At the cellular level, maybe. The DNA of the extant Martian microbial life is different from ours, though, even though it has a similar helical structure."

Danvers wasn't entirely sure of what his luncheon companion was saying, but that didn't matter. He said, "It doesn't seem likely that God would create an intelligent species and then destroy it."

"That's what happened."

"Don't you think that the Martians were a branch of ourselves? After all, the two planets are—"

"About sixty million kilometers apart, at their closest," Molina snapped.

"Yes, but Martian meteorites have been found on Earth."

"So?"

"So Mars and Earth have had exchanges in the past. Perhaps the human race began on Mars and moved to Earth."

Molina guffawed so loudly that people at other tables turned toward them. Danvers sat silently, trying to keep a pleasant face.

"Is that what you believe?" Molina asked at last, between chuckles.

"Isn't it possible?" Danvers asked softly.

"Possible for creatures with a stone age culture to build spacecraft to take them from Mars to Earth? No way!"

Molina was still chuckling when they left the restaurant. No matter, Danvers thought. Let him laugh. I'm winning his trust. Soon he'll be unburdening his soul to me.

As the weeks flowed into one another, Danvers began to understand that winning Molina's trust would not be that easy. Beneath his smug exterior Victor Molina was a desperately unhappy man. Despite his high standing in the skytower project, he was worried about his career, his future. And something else. Something he never spoke of. Danvers thought he knew what it was: Lara Tierney, the woman who was living with Bracknell.

Danvers felt truly sorry for Molina. By this time he regarded the biologist as a friend, the only friend he had in this den of idolaters and atheists. Their relationship was adversarial, to be sure, but he was certain that Molina enjoyed their barbed exchanges as much as he himself did. Sooner or later he'll break down and tell me what's truly troubling him.

Many, many weeks passed before Danvers realized there was something about Molina that was jarringly out of place. What's Victor doing here, on this damnable project? Why is a biologist involved in building the skytower?

NEW KYOTO

Nobuhiko Yamagata stood at his office window gazing out at the city spread out far below him. Lake Biwa glittered in the distance. A flock of large birds flapped by, so close that Nobu inadvertently twitched back, away from the window.

He was glad no one was in the office to see his momentary reaction. It might look like cowardice to someone; unworthy weakness, at least.

The birds were black gulls, returning from their summer grounds far to the north. A sign that winter is approaching, Nobuhiko knew. Winter. He grunted to himself. There hasn't been enough natural snow to ski on since my father died.

Nobu looked almost like a clone of his illustrious father: a few centimeters taller than Saito, but stocky, short-limbed, his face round and flat, his brown eyes hooded, unfathomable. The main difference between father and son was that while Saito's face was lined from frequent laughter, the lines on Nobu's face came from worry.

He hadn't heard from his father for more than a year now. The elder Yamagata had gone into a fit of regret over the killings out in the Asteroid Belt and become a true lama, full of holy remorse and repentance. It's as if he's died again, Nobu thought. He's cut off all contact with the world outside his lamasery, even with his only son.

The clock chimed once. No matter, Nobuhiko thought as he turned from the window. I can carry my burdens without Father's help. Squaring his shoulders, he said to the phone on his desk, "Call them in."

The double doors to his office swung inward and a half-dozen men in nearly identical dark business suits came in, each bearing a tiny gold flying crane pin in his lapel, each bowing respectfully to the head of Yamagata Corporation. They took their places at the long table abutting Nobu's desk like the stem of the letter T. No women served on this committee. There were several women on Yamagata's board of directors, but the executive committee was a completely male domain.

There was only one item on their agenda: the skytower.

Nobuhiko sat in his high-backed leather desk chair and called the meeting to order. They swiftly dispensed with formalities such as reading the minutes of the previous meeting. They all knew why they were here.

Swiveling slightly to his right, Nobu nodded to the committee's chairman. Officially, Nobuhiko was an ex-officio member of the executive committee, present at their meetings but without a vote in their deliberations. It was a necessary arrangement, to keep outsiders from accusing that Yamagata Corporation was a one-man dictatorship. Which it very nearly was. Nobu might not have had a vote on this committee, but the committee never voted against his known wishes.

"We are here to decide what to do about the skytower project," said the chairman, his eyes on Nobuhiko.

"It is progressing satisfactorily?" Nobu asked, knowing full well the answer.

"They are ahead of schedule," said the youngest member of the committee, down at the end of the conference table.

Nobuhiko let out a patient sigh.

"When that tower goes into operation," fumed one of the older men, "it will knock the bottom out of the launch services market."

One of Nobu's coups, once he took the reigns of the corporation from his father, had been to acquire the American firm Masterson Aerospace Corporation. Masterson had developed the Clippership launch vehicle, the rocket that reduced launch costs from thousands of dollars per pound to hundreds, the doughty little, completely reusable vehicle that not only opened up orbital space to industrial development, but also served—in a modified version—as a hypersonic transport that carried passengers to any destination on Earth in less than an hour.

By acquiring Masterson, Yamagata gained a major share not only of the world's space launching market, but of long-distance air travel, as well.

"One tower?" scoffed one of the other elder members from across the conference table. "How badly can one tower cut into the launch services market? How much capacity can it have?"

The other man closed his eyes briefly, as if seeking strength to deal with a fool. "It is not merely the one tower. It is the *first* skytower. If it succeeds, there will be others."

Nobu agreed. "And why pay for Clipperships to go into orbit when you can ride a skytower for a fraction of the cost?"

"Exactly so, sir."

"The skytower is a threat, then?"

"Not an immediate threat. But if it is successful, within a few years such towers will spring up all along the equator."

"Fortunate for us," said another, smiling, "that most of the equator is over deep ocean instead of land."

No one laughed.

"How much of our profit comes from Clippership operations?" Nobuhiko asked.

"Not as much from space launch services as from air transportation here on Earth," said the comptroller, seated on Yamagata's left.

Nobu said softly, "The numbers, please."

The comptroller tapped hurriedly on the palmcomp in his hand. "It's about eight percent. Eight point four, so far this year. Last fiscal year, eight point two."

"It's pretty constant."

"Rising slightly."

Nobu folded his hands across his vest, a gesture he remembered his father using often.

"Can we afford to lose eight percent of our profits?" asked the youngster.

"Not if we don't have to," said the comptroller.

"We own part of this skytower project, don't we?" Nobu asked.

"We bought into it, yes. We have a contract to supply engineers and other technical staff and services. But it's only a minor share of their operation, less than five percent. And the contract will terminate once they begin operations."

Nobu felt his brows rise. "We won't share in their operating profits?"

The comptroller hesitated. "Not unless we negotiate a new contract for maintenance or other services, of course."

"Of course," Nobuhiko muttered darkly. Sweat broke out on the comptroller's forehead.

The office fell silent. Then the director of the corporation's aerospace division cleared his throat and said, "May I point out that all of our discussion is based on the premise that the skytower will be successful? There is no guarantee of that."

Nobuhiko understood him perfectly. The skytower could be a failure if we take action to make certain it fails. Looking around the conference table, he saw that each and every member of the executive committee understood the unspoken decision.

CIUDAD DE CIELO

lliott Danvers was not brilliant, but he was not stupid, either. And he possessed a stubborn determination that allowed him to push doggedly onward toward a goal when others would find easier things to do.

Why is a biologist working on the skytower project? When he asked Molina directly, the man became reticent and evasive.

"What's a New Morality minister doing here, in Ecuador?" Molina would counter.

When Danvers frankly explained that his mission was to provide spiritual comfort to all who sought it, Molina cocked an eyebrow at him.

"Aren't you here to snoop on us, Elliott?" Molina asked, good-naturedly. "Aren't your superiors in Atlanta worried that this project is a modern Tower of Babel?"

"Nonsense," Danvers sputtered.

"Is it? My take on the New Morality is that they don't like change. They've arranged North America just the way they like it, with themselves in control of the government—"

"Control of the government!" Danvers was truly shocked at that. "We're a religious organization, not a secular one."

"So was the Spanish Inquisition," Molina murmured.

Despite their differences, they remained friends of a sort. Bantering, challenging friends. Danvers knew quite well that the only other man in Sky City that Molina regarded as a friend was the project director, Mance Bracknell. But something had come between them. No, not some*thing*, Danvers thought. Some*one*. Lara Tierney.

Molina invited Danvers to have dinner with him from time to time. Once, they joined Bracknell and Lara on a quick jaunt to Quito and dined in the best restaurant Danvers had ever seen. It didn't take long for Danvers to understand Molina's problem. Before the main courses were served he realized that Molina was in love with her, but she loved Bracknell. The eternal triangle, Danvers thought. It has caused the ruin of many a dream.

For himself, Danvers treasured Molina's company. Despite his atheistic barbs, Molina was the only close friend Danvers had made in this city of godless technicians and dark-skinned mestizos who worshipped their old blood-soaked gods in secret.

Yet the question nagged at him. Why is Molina here? What can a biologist do for this mammoth project?

After many weeks of asking everyone he knew, even men and women he had barely been introduced to, the path to understanding suddenly came to him, like a revelation from on high.

The woman. Lara Tierney. She is the key to Molina's presence here. To get him to tell the truth, Danvers realized, to open up his inner secrets, I must use his love for this woman. That's his vulnerable spot. Still, he wavered, reluctant to cause the pain that he knew Molina would feel. Danvers prayed long hours kneeling by his bedside, seeking guidance. Do I have the right to do this? he asked. The only answer he received was a memory of his mentor's words: *Remember that you are doing God's work.*

And then the revelation came to him. The way to promotion, the path to advancement within the New Morality, was by stopping this godless project. That's why they sent me here, he realized. To see if I can prevent these secularists from succeeding in their blasphemous project. That's how they're testing me.

Danvers rose from his knees, his heart filled with determination. The hour was late, but he told the phone to call Molina. He got the man's answering machine, of course, but made a date with him for dinner the following night. Not lunch. What he had to do would take more time than a lunch break. Better to do it after the working day is finished, in the dark of night. Be hard, he advised himself. Show no mercy. Drive out all doubts, all qualms. Be a man of steel.

Dinner wasn't much, and afterward Danvers and Molina walked slowly up the gently rising street toward the building where they both were quartered. The skytower was outlined by safety lights, flashing on and off like fireflies, trailing upward until they disappeared into the starry sky. A sliver of a Moon was riding over the mountains to the east. The sky was clear, hardly a cloud in sight, the night air crisp and chill.

All through dinner Danvers had avoided starting this probe into his friend's heart. But as they approached their building, he realized he could delay no longer.

"Victor," he began softly, "you and Bracknell and Ms. Tierney seem to be old friends."

"We all went to university together," Molina replied evenly.

The lamps along the street were spaced fairly widely, far apart enough for the two men to stroll through pools of shadow as they walked along. Danvers saw that Molina kept his eyes down, watching where he was stepping rather than gazing up at the skytower looming above them.

"You studied biology there?"

"Yes," said Molina. "Mance bounced around from one department to another in the school of engineering."

"And Ms. Tierney?"

Through the shadows he could hear Molina's sudden intake of breath. "Lara? She started out in sociology, I think. But then she switched to engineering. Aerospace engineering, can you believe it?"

"That was after she'd met Bracknell."

"Yeah, right. After she met Mance. She went so goofy over him that she switched her major just to be closer to him."

"You were attracted to her yourself, weren't you?"

"Fucking lot of good it did me once she met Mance."

Danvers walked on for a few steps in silence. He heard the bitterness in Molina's voice, and now that he had touched on the sore spot he had to open up that wound again.

"Did you love her then?" he asked.

Molina did not answer.

"You still love her, don't you?"

"That's none of your damned business, Elliott."

"I think it is, Victor. You're my friend, and I want to help you."

"How the hell can you help me? You want to pray for a miracle, maybe?"

"Prayer has its powers."

"Bullshit!"

Danvers nodded in the darkness. Victor's in pain, no doubt of it. My task is to use his pain, channel it into a productive course.

"Why did you come here, then? If you knew that Bracknell was heading this project, didn't you expect her to show up, sooner or later?"

"I suppose I did, subconsciously. Maybe I thought she wouldn't, that they were finished. I don't know!"

"But you came here, to this project. Did you volunteer or did Bracknell ask to come?"

"Mance called me when he got the go-ahead for the project. All excited. Said he needed me to make it work."

"He needed you?"

"Like an idiot I agreed to take a look at his plans. Next thing I knew I was on a plane to Quito."

"Why did he need you?"

"I didn't think Lara would come down here," Molina went on, ignoring the question. "I figured Mance would be so fucking busy with this crazy scheme of his that he wouldn't have time for her. Maybe he'd even forgotten her. Damned fool me."

"But why did he need you?" Danvers insisted.

"To make the buckyball fibers," Molina snapped, "what the fuck do you think?"

Ignoring Molina's deliberate crudities, Danvers pressed, "A biologist to build the fibers?"

"A biologist, yeah. Somebody who can engineer viruses to assemble buckyballs for you. You need a damned smart biologist to work down at the nanometer scale."

Danvers sucked in his breath. "Nanomachines?"

They were under a streetlamp now and Danvers could see the pain and anguish in Molina's face. For several long moments the biologist struggled for self-control. At last he said calmly, coldly:

"Not nanomachines, Elliott. Viruses. Living creatures. Is this what you're after? Trying to find out if we're using nanotech so you can turn us in to the authorities?"

"No, Victor, not at all," Danvers half-lied. "I'm trying to find out what's troubling you. I want to help you, I truly do."

"Great. You want to help me? Find some way to get Mance out of the picture. Get him away from Lara. That's the kind of help I need."

ATLANTA

The headquarters building of the New Morality was not as large as the capitol of a secular government, nor as ornate as a cathedral. But it was, in fact, the seat of a power that stretched across all of the North American continent north of the Rio Grande and extended its influence into Mexico and Central America.

In the days before the greenhouse floods, the New Morality was little more than a fundamentalist Christian sect, sterner than most others, that concentrated its work in the rundown cores of cities such as Atlanta, Philadelphia, Detroit, and other urban blights. It did good works: rescuing lost souls, driving drug dealers out of slum neighborhoods, rebuilding decaying houses, making certain that children learned to read and write in the schools it had installed in abandoned storefronts. In return for these good works, the New Morality insisted on iron discipline and obedience. Above all, obedience.

Then the Earth's climate tumbled over the greenhouse cliff. After half a century of warnings from climatologists that were ignored by temporizing politicians and ridiculed by disbelieving pundits, the global climate abruptly switched from postglacial to the kind of semitropical environment that had ruled the Earth in earlier eons. Icecaps melted. Sea levels rose by twenty meters over a few years. Coastal cities everywhere were flooded. The electrical power grid that sustained modern civilization collapsed. Killer storms raged while farmlands eroded into dust. Hundreds of millions of men, women, and children were driven from their homes, their jobs, their lives, all of them hungry, frightened, desperate.

The New Morality rejoiced. "This is the wrath of God that has been called down upon us!" thundered the Reverend Harold Carnaby. "This is our just punishment for generations of sinful licentiousness."

Governments across the world turned authoritarian, backed by fundamentalist organizations such as the Holy Disciples in Europe and the Flower Dragon in the Far East. Even the fractious Moslems came together under the banner of the Sword of Islam once Israel was obliterated.

After decades of authoritarian rule, however, people all across the Earth were growing restive. The climate had stabilized, although once again scientists were issuing dire warnings, this time of a coming Ice Age. They were ignored once again as the average family moved toward economic well-being and a better life. Prosperity was creeping across the world once more. Church attendance was slipping.

Carnaby, now a self-appointed archbishop, mulled these factors in his mind as he sat in his powered wheelchair and gazed out across the skyline of Atlanta's high-rise towers.

"We saved this city," he grumbled.

"Yes, sir," said one of the aides standing behind him respectfully. "We surely did."

"We saved the nation when it was sinking into crime and depravity," Carnaby added. "Now that the people are growing richer, they're turning away from God. They're more interested in buying the latest virtual reality games than in saving their souls."

"Too true," said the second aide.

Carnaby pivoted his wheelchair to face them. They were standing before his desk, arms at their sides, eyes focused on the archbishop.

"Sir, about the medical report . . ."

"I'm not interested in saving my mortal body," Carnaby said, frowning up at them through his dead-white eyebrows.

"But you must, sir! The Movement needs your guidance, your leadership!"

"I'm ready to meet my Maker whenever He calls me."

The one aide glanced at the other, obviously seeking support. The two of them were as alike as peas in a pod in their dark suits and starched white shirts. Carnaby wondered if they were twins.

"Sir," said the other one, his voice slightly deeper than his companion's, "the physicians are unanimous in their diagnosis. You must accept a heart implant. Otherwise . . ." He left the conclusion unspoken.

"Put a man-made pump into my chest and remove the heart that God gave me? Never!"

"No, sir, that isn't it at all. It's merely a booster pump, an auxiliary device to assist your heart. Your natural heart will be untouched," the deeper-voiced aide coaxed. "It's really rather minor surgery, sir. They insert it through an artery in the thigh."

"They won't open my chest?"

"No, sir," both aides said in chorus.

Carnaby huffed. He had accepted other medical devices. One day, he'd been told, he would have to get artificial kidneys. Ninety-two years old, he told himself, and I've never taken a rejuvenation treatment. Not many my age can say that. God is watching over me.

"An auxiliary pump, is it?"

"Yes, sir."

"You need it, sir. With all the burdens of work and the pressures you face every day, it's a miracle that your heart has lasted this long without assistance."

Carnaby huffed again to make sure that they understood that he didn't like the idea. But then he lowered his head and said humbly, "God's will be done."

The aides scampered out of his office, delighted that he had acquiesced, and more than a little awed at the archbishop's willingness to sacrifice his obvious distaste of medical procedures for the good of the Movement.

Alone at his desk, Carnaby called up the latest computer figures on church attendance. The New Morality was officially a nonsectarian organization. The bar graph that sprang up on his smart wall screen showed attendance reports for nearly every denomination in North and South America. The numbers were down—not by much, but the trend was clear. Even the Catholics were falling away from God.

His desktop intercom chimed. "Deacon Gillette calling, Archbishop," said the phone's angel-sweet voice. "Urgent."

"Urgent? What's so urgent?"

The phone remained silent for a moment, then repeated, "Deacon Gillette calling—"

"All right," Carnaby interrupted the synthesized voice, irked at its limited abilities. "Put him through."

Gillette's face replaced the attendance statistics. He was an African-American, his skin so dark it seemed to shine as if he were perspiring. His deepset brown eyes always looked wary, as if he expected some enemy to spring upon him.

"Deacon," said Carnaby, by way of greeting.

"Archbishop. I've received a disturbing report from our man in Ecuador."

"We have a man in Ecuador?"

"At the skytower project, sir," said Gillette.

"Ah, yes. A disturbing report, you say?"

"According to Rev. Danvers, the scientists of the skytower project are using a form of nanotechnology to build their structure."

"Nanotechnololgy!" Carnaby felt a pang of alarm. "Nanomachines are outlawed, even in South America."

Gillette closed his heavy-lidded eyes briefly, then explained, "They are not using nanomachines, exactly. Instead, they have developed genetically engineered viruses to work as nanomachines would, assembling the structural components of their tower."

Carnaby felt the cords at the back of his neck tense and knew he would soon be suffering a headache.

"Tell Danvers to notify the authorities down there."

"What they're doing is not illegal, Archbishop. They're using natural creatures, not artificial machines."

"But you said these creatures have been genetically engineered, didn't you?"

"Genetic engineering is not outlawed, sir," Gillette replied, then quickly added, "Unfortunately."

Carnaby sucked in a breath. "Then what can we do about it?"

With a sad shake of his head, Gillette answered, "I don't know, sir. I was hoping that you would think of a solution."

Fumbling for the oxygen mask in the compartment built into the wheelchair's side, Carnaby groused, "All right, let me think about it." He abruptly cut the phone connection and his wall returned to its underlying restful shade of pastel blue.

Carnaby held the plastic mask over his face for several silent moments. The flow of cool oxygen eased the tension that was racking his body.

Sudden thunder shook the building, startling Carnaby so badly that he dropped his oxygen mask. Then he realized it was another of those damnable rockets taking off from the old Hartsfield Airport.

He spun his chair to the window once again and craned his dewlapped neck, but there was nothing to see. No trail of smoke. No pillar of fire. The rockets used some kind of clean fuel: hydrogen, he'd been told. Doesn't hurt the environment.

He slumped back in his wheelchair, feeling old and tired. I've spent my life trying to save their souls. I've rescued them from sin and the palpable wrath of God. And what do they do as soon as things begin to go smoothly again? They complain about our strict laws. They want more freedom, more license to grow fat and prosperous and sinful.

Then he looked out at the empty sky again. They're getting richer because those rockets are bringing in metals and stuff from the asteroids. And they've built those infernal solar satellites up in orbit to beam electrical power to the ground.

Those space people. Scientists and engineers. Godless secularists, all of 'em. Poking around on other worlds. Claiming they've found living creatures. Contradicting Genesis every chance they get.

And now, Carnaby thought, those space people are building a high-tech Tower of Babel. They're going to make it *easier* to get into space, easier to make money out there. And using nanotechnology to do it. Devil's tools. Evil, through and through.

They're building their blasphemous tower in South America someplace, right in the middle of all those Catholics.

They've got to be stopped, Carnaby told himself, clenching his blue-veined hands into bony fists. But how? How?

RIDING THE ELEVATOR

How high are we?" Lara asked, her eyes wide with excitement.

Bracknell glanced at the readout screen set next to the elevator's double doors, where Victor Molina was standing. "Eighty-two kilometers, no, now it's eighty-three."

"I don't feel anything," she said. "No sense of motion at all."

For nearly a month Bracknell had resisted Lara's pleas for a ride in the space elevator. The instant he had told her the first elevator tube had completed all its tests and was officially operational, she had begged him for a ride. Bracknell had temporized, delayed, tried to put her off. To his surprise, he found that he was worried about the elevator's safety. *All these years I've drafted the plans, laid out the schematics, overseen the construction,* he castigated himself, *and when we get right down to it, I don't trust my own work. Not with Lara's life. I'm afraid to let her ride the elevator.*

That realization stunned him. *All the number crunching, all the tests, and I don't trust my own work. I'm willing to let others ride the elevator, I'm even willing to ride it myself, but when it comes to Lara—I'm afraid. Superstition, pure and simple,* he told himself. Yet he found excuses to keep her from his skytower.

The elevator worked fine, day after day, week after week, hauling technicians and cargo up to the stations at the various levels of the tower. Bracknell's confidence in the system grew, and Lara's importunings did not abate. If anything, she became even more insistent.

"You've been up and down a dozen times," she whispered to him as they lay together in the shadows of their darkened bedroom, her head on his naked chest. "It's not fair for you to keep me from going with you. Just once, at least."

Despite his inner tension, he grinned in the darkness. "It's not fair? You're starting to sound like a kid arguing with his parents."

"Was I whining?" she asked.

"No," he had to admit. "I've never heard you whine."

She lay silent for several moments. He could feel her breathing slowly, rhythmically, as she lay against him.

"Okay," he heard himself say. "We'll go up to the LEO deck," he conceded.

Lara knew the Low Earth Orbit station was five hundred kilometers up. Her elation was immediately tinged with disappointment.

"Not all the way?" she asked. "Not to the geostationary level?"

Bracknell shook his head. "That's up on the edge of the Van Allen Belt radiation. The crew hasn't installed the shielding yet. They work up there in armored suits."

"But if they—"

"No," he said firmly, grasping her bare shoulders. "Some day we're going to have children. I'm not exposing you to a high-radiation environment, even in a shielded spacesuit."

He sensed her smiling at him. "The ultimate argument," she said. "It's for the good of our unborn children."

"Well, it is."

"Yes dear," she teased. Then she kissed him.

They made love slowly, languorously. Afterward, as they lay spent and sticky in their sweaty sheets, Bracknell thought: This is the real test. Do you trust your work enough to risk her life on it?

And Lara understood: He worries about me so. He lets others ride the elevator but he's worried about me.

The next day was a Sunday, and although a full team of technicians was at work, as usual, Bracknell walked over to the operations office and told the woman on duty there that he and Lara would be riding up to the LEO platform.

The operations chief that Sunday morning was a portly woman who wore her ash-blonde hair pulled back in a tight bun, and a square gold ring on her left middle finger.

"I'll tell Jakosky," she said, grinning. "He's won the lottery."

"What lottery?" Bracknell asked, surprised.

"We've been making book about when you'd let your lady take a ride up," said the operations chief. "Jackpot's up to damn near a thousand Yankee dollars."

Bracknell grinned weakly to cover his surprise and a pang of embarrassment. As he left the building and started back up toward his quarters, he saw Molina coming down the street, heading toward him. Victor's going to be leaving, Bracknell knew. Going to Australia to start a new career in astrobiology. And he's sore at me for not letting him publish the work he's done here.

"Hello, Victor," he called as the biologist neared. He knew that Molina despised being called Vic.

"Hi, Mance," Molina replied, without slowing his pace.

Bracknell grasped his arm, stopping him. "Lara and I are riding up to the LEO deck. Want to come with us?"

Molina's eyes widened. "You're taking her up?"

"Just to the lowest level."

"But the safety certification . . ."

"Came through a week ago. For the LEO platform."

"Oh."

"Come with us," Bracknell urged. "You're not doing anything vital this morning, are you?"

Molina stiffened. "I'm finishing up my final report."

"You can do that later. You don't want to head off to Australia without riding in the tower you helped to build, do you? Come on with us."

With a shake of his head, Molina said, "No, I've got so much to do before I leave . . ."

Bracknell teased, "You're not scared, are you?"

"Scared? Hell no!"

"Then come on along. The three of us. Like old times."

"Like old times," Molina echoed, his face grim.

Bracknell knew that he himself was frightened, a little. If we bring Victor along I'll have him to talk to, to keep me from worrying about Lara's safety. But he knew that was an excuse. Superstition again: nothing bad will happen if it isn't just Lara and me riding the tube.

Molina, who hadn't been alone with Lara since he'd confessed that he was in love with her, allowed Bracknell to turn him around and lead him back to their apartment building. What the fuck, he said to himself. This may be the last time I see her.

"It's like we're standing still," Lara said as the elevator rose smoothly past the hundred-kilometer mark.

"Like Einstein's old thought experiment about the equivalence of gravity and acceleration," Bracknell said.

The elevator cab was big enough to handle freight and new enough to still look sparkling and shiny. An upholstered bench ran along its rear wall, but Lara and the two men remained standing. The walls and floor of the cab were buckyball sheets, hard as diamond but not as brittle, coated with scuff-resistant epoxy. The ceiling was a grillwork through which Lara could see the shining inner walls of the tube speeding smoothly by.

No cables, she knew. No pulleys or reels like an ordinary elevator. The entire tube was a vertical electric rail gun; the elevator cab was being lifted by electromagnetic forces, like a particle in a physics lab's accelerator or a payload launched off the Moon by an electric mass driver. Pretty slow for a bullet, Lara thought, but they were accelerating all the way up to the halfway point, where they would start decelerating until the cab braked to a stop at the LEO level.

Molina stayed tensely silent. He hadn't said more than two words to either of them since Lara had joined them for this brief trip into space.

LEO PLATFORM

Y ou should have windows," Lara said as she walked to the bench along the cab's rear wall and sat down. "It's boring without a view."

Bracknell sat beside her and glanced at his wristwatch. "Another twenty minutes."

Molina had not spoken a word since they'd boarded the elevator, more than a half hour earlier. He remained standing, pecking away at his palmcomp.

"You need a window," Lara repeated. "The view would be spectacular."

"If you didn't get nauseous watching the Earth fall away from you. Some people are afraid of glass elevators in hotels, you know."

"They wouldn't have to look," Lara replied primly. "I think the view would be a marvelous attraction, especially for tourists."

Conceding her point with a nod, Bracknell said, "We'll be adding several more elevator tubes. I'll look into the possibilities of glassing in at least one of them."

"Are we slowing down?" Lara asked.

"Should be."

"I get no sensation of movement at all."

"That's because we've kept the cab's acceleration down to a minimum. We could go a lot faster if we need to."

"No," she said, with a slight shake of her head. "This is fine. I'm not complaining."

As he sat next to Lara, Bracknell got a sudden urge to take her in his arms and kiss her. But there was Molina standing a few meters away, like a dour-faced duenna, his nose almost touching his handheld's screen.

"Victor," he called, "come and sit down. You don't have to work *all* the time."

"Yes, I do," Molina snapped.

Turning back to Lara, "Tell him to put away that digital taskmaster of his and come over here and join us."

To his surprise, Lara responded, "Leave Victor alone. He's doing what he feels he has to do."

Feeling a little puzzled, Bracknell clasped his hands behind his head and leaned back against the cab's rear wall. It felt cool and very hard. We ought to put some cushioning along here, he thought, making a mental note to suggest it to the people who were handling interior design. And look into glassing in one of the outer tubes, he added silently.

When the cab finally stopped, a chime sounded and a synthesized female voice announced, "Level one: Low Earth Orbit."

Bracknell got to his feet, Lara beside him. She looked puzzled.

"I thought we'd be in zero gravity," Lara said.

With a shake of his head, Bracknell said, "We're five hundred klicks up, but the tower isn't moving at orbital velocity. It's moving at the same rate as the Earth."

"Oh." Lara looked slightly disappointed, he thought.

The elevator doors slid open and the din of work teams immediately assailed their ears as they stepped out of the elevator cab. Lara saw a wide expanse of bare decking topped by a dome that looked hazy in the dust-filled air. A drill was screeching annoyingly off somewhere and the high-pitched whine of an electrical power generator made her teeth ache. Sparks from welding torches hissed off to her right. The dust-laden air smelled of burnt insulation and stranger odors she could not place. Men and women in coveralls were putting up partitions, most of them working in small groups along the deck; she spotted several cambering along the scaffolding, high above. An electrically-powered cart scurried past on a rail fastened to the deck plates, its cargo bed piled high with bouncing sheets of what looked like honeycomb metal. Everyone seemed to be yelling at everyone else:

"Hold it there! That's it!"

"I need more light up here; it's darker than a five-star restaurant, fer chrissakes!"

"When the hell were you ever in a five-star restaurant, bozo?"

"I've got it. Ease up on your line."

Bracknell made a sweeping gesture and hollered over the din, "Welcome to level one."

Moline scowled out at the noisy activity. Lara clapped her hands over her ears. Bracknell grinned at them.

Pointing off to their left, Bracknell led them carefully past a gaggle of workers gathered around a small table that held a large stainless steel urn of coffee. At least, Lara assumed it was coffee. Several of the workers raised their covered plastic mugs to Bracknell as he led them past. Mance nodded and grinned at them in return.

"Sippy cups," Lara said, with a giggle. "Like babies use."

"Keeps the dust out of the coffee," Bracknell said.

There were curved partitions in place here, and the noise abated a little. As they walked onward, the partitions became roofed over like an arched tunnel and the din diminished considerably.

"As you can see—and hear," Bracknell said, "level one is still very much under construction."

"My ears are ringing," Lara said.

"They're a noisy bunch, all right," Bracknell conceded. "But if they were quiet they wouldn't be getting any work done."

Moline gave a half-hearted nod.

Pointing to the curved metal overhead, Bracknell said with a hint of pride in his voice, "These partitions were scavenged from the heavy-lift boosters that brought most of the materials up here."

Lara grinned at him. "Waste not, want not."

"In spades. Nothing of the boosters was returned to Earth except their rocket engines."

She pointed to the open gridwork of the floor. "There aren't any floor tiles."

With a nod, Bracknell said, "The crew hasn't gotten this far yet. We got to gandydance the rest of the way."

"Gandydance?"

"Just step along the girders and don't get your foot caught in the open space. Be careful." Then Bracknell saw Molina's grim expression. "Victor, will you be okay?"

"I think so," Molina said, without much conviction.

As they inched along the bare gridwork of the corridor, holding their arms out for balance, Bracknell explained, "Back there where we came in, the biggest area will be a preparation center for launching satellites."

Lara said, "You'll carry them up here on the elevators and then launch them at this altitude."

"It'll be a lot cheaper than launching them from the ground with rockets," Bracknell said, "even though we'll still a kick booster to place the satellite in the orbit its owners want."

"You'll launch geostationary satellites from the platform up at that level, right?" Lara asked.

"Right. Up at that level all we'll need is a little maneuvering thrust to place them in their proper slots."

"Masterson Aerospace and the other rocket companies aren't going to like you," she said.

"I guess not. The buggywhip makers must have hated Henry Ford."

Lara laughed.

The noise was far behind them now, still discernable, but down to a background level. They came to a heavy-looking hatch set into a wall. Bracknell tapped out the proper code on the keypad set into the wall and the hatch sighed open. Lara felt a slight whisper of air brush past her from behind.

"You wanted a window?" Bracknell said to her. "Here's a window for you."

They stepped through and Lara's breath caught in her throat. They were in a narrow darkened compartment. One entire wall was transparent. Beyond it curved the gigantic bulk of Earth, sparkling blue oceans gleaming in the sunlight, brilliant white clouds hugging the surface, wrinkles of brown mountains.

"Oh my god," Lara gasped, gliding to the long window.

Molina hung back.

Bracknell rapped his knuckles against the window. "Glassteel," he said. "Imported from Selene."

"It's so *beautiful!*" Lara exclaimed. "Look! I think I can see the Panama Canal."

"That's Central America, all right," Bracknell said. Pointing to a wide swirl of clouds, "And that looks like a tropical storm off in the Pacific."

Molina pushed up behind him and peered at the curling swath of clouds. "Will it affect the tower?"

"Not likely. Tropical storms don't come down to the equator, and we're well away from the coast anyway."

"But still . . ."

"The tower can take winds of a thousand kilometers per hour, Victor. More than three times the most powerful hurricane on record."

"I can't see straight down," Lara said, almost like a disappointed child. "I can't see the base of the tower."

"Look out to the horizon," said Bracknell. "That's the Yucatan peninsula, where the ancient Mayas built their temples."

"And those mountains to our right, they must be the Andes," she said. The peaks were bare, gray granite, snowless since the greenhouse warming had struck.

"Mance," said Lara, "you could use glassteel to build a transparent elevator tube."

He snorted. "Not at the prices Selene charges for the stuff."

Molina glided back toward the open hatch. "This door is an airtight seal, isn't it?"

"That's right," Bracknell answered. "If the outside wall of this compartment is punctured and there's a loss of air pressure, that hatch automatically closes and seals off the leak."

"And traps anybody in this compartment," Molina said.

"That's right," Bracknell replied gravely.

Lara said, "But you have spacesuits in here so they can save themselves. Don't you?"

Bracknell shook his head. "It would take too long to get into the suits. Even the new nanofiber soft suits would take too long."

"What you're telling us," Molina said, "is that we're in danger in here."

"Only if the outer shell is penetrated."

"How likely is that?" said Lara.

Smiling tightly, Bracknell said, "The tower's been dinged by micrometeorites thousands of times. Mostly up at higher altitudes. No penetrations, though."

"Wasn't there a satellite collision?" Molina asked.

"Every satellite launch is planned so that the bird's orbit doesn't come closer than a hundred kilometers of the tower. The IAA's been very strict about that."

"But a satellite actually hit the tower?" Lara looked more curious than afraid.

With a nod, Bracknell replied, "Some damnfool paramilitary outfit launched a spy satellite without clearing it with the IAA. It smacked into the tower on its second orbit."

"And?"

"Hardly scratched the buckyball cables, but it wrecked the spysat completely. Most of the junk fell down and burned up in the atmosphere. We had to send a team outside to clean off the remaining debris and inspect the area where it hit. The damage was very superficial."

"When you stop to think about it," Lara said, "the impact of even a big satellite hitting this tower would be like a mosquito ramming an elephant."

Bracknell laughed as he turned back toward the open hatch.

"The only way to hurt this beanstalk," said Molina, "would be to somehow disconnect it up at the geostationary level."

Bracknell looked over his shoulder at the biologist. "That's right, Victor. Do that, and the lower half of the tower collapses to the ground, while the upper half goes spinning off into deep space."

"The tower would collapse?" Lara asked. "It would fall down to the ground?"

Bracknell nodded. "Only if it's disconnected from the geostationary platform."

"That would destroy everything?" Lara asked.

"Quite completely," said Bracknell. "But don't worry, we've built that section with a two-hundred-percent overload capacity. It can't happen."

YAMAGATA ESTATE

Nobuhiko Yamagata's knees ached as he sat on the tatami mat facing this, this . . . fanatic. There was no other way to describe the leader of the Flower Dragon movement. Like a ninja of old, he thought, this man is a fanatic.

Yoshijiro Umetzu was named after a shamed ancestor, a general who had surrendered his army rather than fight to the death. From earliest childhood his stern father and uncles had drilled into him their expectation that he would grow up to erase this century-old stain on the family's honor. While upstarts like Saito Yamagata made vast fortunes in business and Japanese scientists earned world recognition for their research work, Umetzu knew that only blood could bring true respect. Respect is based on fear, he was told endlessly. Nothing less.

By the time he was a teenager, the world was racked with terrorism. The poor peoples of the world struck almost blindly against the rich, attempting to destroy the wealth that they themselves could never attain. Japan was the target of many terrorist attacks: poison gas killed thousands in Tokyo; biological weapons slaughtered tens of thousands in Osaka. The nanomachine plague that nearly destroyed the entire island of Kyushu, killing millions, led directly to the international treaty banning nanotechnology everywhere on Earth.

When the greenhouse cliff toppled the world's climate, coastal cities everywhere were drowned by the suddenly rising seas. But an even worse fate befell Japan: in addition to the devastating floods, earthquakes demolished the home islands.

Out of the ashes, though, rose a new Japan. The century-long experiment in democracy was swept aside and a new government, strong and unyielding, came to power. The true strength of that government was the Flower Dragon movement, a strange mix of religion and zeal, of Buddhist acceptance and disciplined political action. Like other fundamentalist movements elsewhere in the world, the Flower Dragon movement spread beyond its place of origin: Korea, China, Thailand, Indochina. On the vast and miserable Indian subcontinent, decimated by biowar and decades-long droughts brought on by the collapse of the monsoons, followers of the Flower Dragon clashed bloodily with the Sword of Islam.

Now the leader of the Flower Dragon movement sat on the other side of the exquisite tea set from Nobuhiko. Umetzu wore a modern business suit, as did Yamagata. The leader of the Flower Dragon movement had the lean, parched face of an ascetic, his head shaved bald, a thin dark moustache drooping down the corners of his mouth almost to his jawline. The expression on his face was severe, disapproving. Nobuhiko felt distinctly uneasy in his presence, almost ashamed of his well-fed girth.

Yet Nobu understood that Umetzu had come to him. I called and he came, Yamagata told himself. I'm not without power here. The fact that Umetzu was apparently a few years younger than he should have made Nobu feel even more in command of this meeting. But it didn't.

Umetzu had arrived at the Yamagata family estate in an unmarked helicopter, accompanied by four younger men. Nobu had chosen his family's home for this meeting so that they would be safe from the prying eyes and news media snoops that were unavoidable in the corporate offices in New Kyoto. Here, on his spacious estate up in the hills, surrounded by servants who had been with the family for generations, he could have airtight security.

They sat in a small room paneled in polished oak, the tea set between them. The wall to Nobu's right was a sliding shoji screen; to his left a window looked out on a small, enclosed courtyard and raked stone garden. The kimono-clad women who had served the tea had left the room. Umetzu's aides were being fed in another room, far enough away so that they could not overhear their master's discussion with Yamagata, close enough so that they could reach him quickly if they had to. Nobu understood without being told that those young men were bodyguards.

"What do you want of me?" Umetzu asked, dropping all pretense of polite conversation. He had not touched the lacquered cup before him.

Nobu took a sip of the hot, soothing tea before answering. "There is a task that must be done in complete secrecy."

Umetzu said nothing.

"I had thought of negotiating with one of the Islamic groups," Nobu went on. "They are accustomed to the concept of martyrdom."

"Yet you have asked to speak with me. In private."

"It is a very delicate matter."

Umetzu took in a long, slow breath. "A matter that involves death."

"Many deaths, most likely."

"The followers of the Flower Dragon's way do not fear death. Many of them believe in reincarnation."

"You do not?" Nobuhiko asked.

"My beliefs are not the subject of this meeting."

Nobu bowed his head a centimeter or so.

"Just what is it that you require?" asked Umetzu.

Now Nobuhiko hesitated, trying to fathom what lay behind his guest's hooded eyes. Can I trust him? Is this the best way for me to go? He wished he had his father here to advise him, but the elder Yamagata was still locked away in the Himalayas, playing at being a lama.

"What I require," Nobu said at last, "must never be traced back to me or to Yamagata Corporation. Is that clear? Never."

Umetzu almost smiled. "It must be truly horrible, for you to be so afraid."

"Horrible enough," said Nobu. "Horrible enough."

"Then what is it?"

"The skytower. It must be destroyed."

Umetzu drew in a breath. "I have been informed that the skytower is being built by nanomachines."

Surprised, Nobuhiko blurted, "Where did you hear that?"

Allowing himself a thin smile, Umetzu replied, "Flower Dragon has contacts in many places, including the New Morality."

"I did not realize that they are using nanomachines."

"Of a sort. They are within the law, apparently, but just barely."

"Perhaps we could stop them legally, through the international courts."

Umetzu shook his head the barest fraction of a centimeter. "Do not put your faith in the courts. Direct action is better."

"Then you are willing to help me?" Nobuhiko asked.

"Of course. The skytower must be destroyed."

"Yes. And it must be destroyed in a manner that will discredit the very idea of building such towers. It must be brought down in a disaster so stunning that no one will ever dare to bring up the idea of building another."

Nobuhiko felt his cheeks flushing and realized that he was squeezing his miniature teacup so hard its edge was cutting into the flesh of his palm.

Umetzu seemed unmoved. "How do you intend to accomplish this tremendous feat?"

Regaining his self-control, Nobuhiko put the lacquered cup back on its tray as he answered, "My technical people know how to bring it down. They have all the information we require. What I need is men who will do the task."

"Men who will become martyrs."

Nobuhiko bowed his head once again.

"That is not terribly difficult," said Umetzu. "There are those who welcome death, especially if they believe they will accomplish something of worth in their dying."

"But it must be kept absolutely secret," Nobuhiko repeated in an urgent hiss. "It must never be traced back to Yamagata Corporation."

Umetzu closed his eyes briefly. "We can recruit martyrs from elsewhere: even the fat Americans have fanatics among their New Morality groups."

"Truly?" Nobuhiko asked.

"But what of your own technicians? Will they be martyred also?"

"That will not be necessary."

"Yet they will have the knowledge that you wish kept secret. Once the tower falls, they will know that you have done it."

"They will be far from Earth when that happens," Nobuhiko said. "I have already had them transferred to Yamagata operations in the Asteroid Belt."

Umetzu considered this for a moment. "I have heard that the Asteroid Belt is a very dangerous place."

"It can be."

"Wars have been fought there. Many were killed."

"I have heard that the Flower Dragon has followers even in the Belt. Loyal followers."

Umetzu understood Nobu's unspoken request. This time he did smile thinly. "So your people will not be martyrs. Instead they will fall victims to accidents."

"As you said," Nobu replied, "the Belt is a very dangerous place."

CIUDAD DE CIELO

Elliott Danvers was lonely after Molina left for Australia. He missed their meals together, their adversarial chats, the verbal cut and parry that kept his mind stimulated.

Over the weeks that followed Molina's departure, Danvers tried to forget his own needs and buried himself in his work. No, he reminded himself time and again. Not my work. God's work.

He felt puzzled that Atlanta had shown no visible reaction to his report that nanotechnology was being used to build the skytower. He had expected some action, or at least an acknowledgement of his intelligence. Nothing. Not a word of thanks or congratulations on a job well done. Well, he told himself, a good conscience is our only sure reward. And he plunged himself deeper into his work. Still, he felt nettled, disappointed, ignored.

He went to Bracknell and asked permission to convert one of the warehouse buildings into a nondenominational chapel. As the skytower neared completion, some of the buildings fell into disuse, some of the workers departed for their homes. Danvers noted that there seemed to be fewer Yankee and Latino construction workers in the streets, and more Asian computer and electronics technicians.

"A chapel?" Bracknell looked surprised when Danvers raised the question.

Standing in front of Bracknell's desk, Danvers nodded. "You have several empty buildings available. I won't need much in way of—"

"You mean you've been working here all this time without a church building?" Bracknell looked genuinely surprised. "Where do you hold your services?"

"Outdoors, mostly. Sometimes in my quarters, for smaller groups."

Bracknell's office was far from imposing. Nothing more than a corner room in the corrugated-metal operations building. He sat at a scuffed and dented steel desk. One wall held a smart screen that nearly reached the low ceiling. Another had photos of the tower at various stages of its construction pasted to it. Two windows looked out on the streets and, beyond one of them, the dark trunk of the tower, rising above the distant green hills and into the heavens.

Gesturing to the plain plastic chair in front of his desk, Bracknell said, "I thought we already had a church here, someplace."

Danvers smiled bitterly as he settled his bulk in the creaking little chair. "You're not a churchgoer."

With an almost sheepish grin, Bracknell admitted, "You've got me there."

"Are you a Believer?"

Bracknell thought it over for a moment, his head cocked slightly. "Yes, I think I can truthfully say that I am. Not in any organized religion, understand. But—well, the universe is so blasted *orderly*. I guess I do believe there's some kind of presence overseeing everything. Childhood upbringing, I suppose. It's hard to overcome."

"You don't have to apologize about it," Danvers said, a little testily. He was thinking, Not in any organized religion, the man says. He's one of those intellectual esthetes who rationalizes everything and thinks that that's religion. Nothing more than a damnable Deist, at best.

Bracknell called up a map of the city and told his computer to highlight the unused buildings. The wall screen showed four of them in red.

"Take your pick," he said to Danvers, gesturing to the screen.

Danvers stood up and walked to the map, studying it for several moments. "This one," he said at last, rapping his knuckles against the screen.

"That's the smallest one," said Bracknell.

"My congregations have not been overwhelming. Besides, the location is good, close to the city's center. More people will see their friends and associates going to services. It's a proven fact that people tend to follow a crowd."

"It's the curious monkey in our genes," Bracknell said easily.

Danvers tried to erase the frown that immediately came over him. "Was that too Darwinian for you?"

"We are far more than monkeys," Danvers said tightly.

"I suppose we are. But we're mammals; we enjoy the companionship of others. We need it."

"That's true enough, I suppose."

"So why don't you join Lara and me at dinner tonight? We can talk over the details of your new chapel."

Danvers was surprised at the invitation. He knew, in his mind, that a man could be a non-Believer and still be a decent human being. But this man Bracknell, he's leading this nearly blasphemous skytower project. I mustn't let him lull me into friendship, Danvers told himself. He may be a pleasant enough fellow, but he is the enemy. You either do God's work or the devil's. There is no neutrality in the struggle between good and evil.

The restaurant was only half full, Bracknell saw as he came through the wide-open double doors with Lara. A lot of the construction people had already left. Once the geostationary platform was finished, they would shift entirely to operational status.

He saw that Rev. Danvers was already seated at a table, chatting with the restaurant's owner and host, a tall suave Albanian who towered over his mestizo kitchen staff. As soon as the host saw Bracknell and Lara enter, he left Danvers in midsentence and rushed to them.

"Slow night tonight," he said by way of greeting.

Bracknell said, "Not for much longer. Lots of people heading here. By this time next year you'll have to double the size of this place."

The host smiled and pointed out new paintings, all by local artists, hanging on the corrugated metal walls. Village scenes. Cityscapes of Quito. One showed the mountains and the skytower in Dayglo orange. Bracknell thought they were pretty ordinary and said nothing, while Lara commented cheerfully on their bright colors.

The dinner with Rev. Danvers started off rather awkwardly. For some reason the minister seemed guarded, tight-lipped. But then Lara got him to talking about his childhood, his early days in the slums of Detroit.

"You have no idea of what it was like growing up in that cesspool of sin and violence. If it weren't for the New Morality, Lord knows where I'd be," Danvers said over a good-sized ribeye steak. "They worked hard to clean up the streets, get rid of the crooks and drug pushers. They worked hard to clean *me* up."

Lara asked lightly, "Were you all that dirty?"

Danvers paled slightly. "I was a prizefighter back then," he said, his voice sinking low. "People actually paid money to see two men try to hurt each other, try to pound one another into unconsciousness."

"Really?"

"Women, too. Women fought in the ring and the crowds cheered and screamed, like animals."

Bracknell saw that Danvers's hands were trembling. But Lara pushed further, asking, "And the New Morality changed all that?"

"Yes, praise God. Thanks to their workers, cities like Detroit became safer, more orderly. Criminals were jailed."

"And their lawyers, too, from what I hear," Bracknell said. He meant it as a joke, but Danvers did not laugh and Lara shot him a disapproving glance.

"Many lawyers went to jail," Danvers said, totally serious, "or to retraining centers. They were protecting the criminals instead of the innocent victims! They deserved whatever they got."

"With your size," Lara said, "I'll bet you were a very good prizefighter."

Danvers smiled ruefully. "They could always find someone bigger."

"But you beat them, didn't you?"

"No," he answered truthfully. "Not very many of them."

"And now you fight for people's souls," Lara said.

"Yes."

"That's much better, isn't it?"

"Yes."

Bracknell looked around the restaurant. Only about half the tables were taken. "Looks like a slow night," he said, trying to change the subject.

"Mondays are always slow," said Lara.

"Not for us," Bracknell said. "We topped off the LEO platform today. It's all finished and ready to open for business."

"Really!" Lara beamed at him. "That's ahead of schedule, isn't it?"

Bracknell nodded happily. "Skytower Corporation's going to make a public announcement about it at their board meeting next month. Big news push. I'm going to be on the nets."

"That's wonderful!"

Danvers was less enthusiastic. "Does this mean that you're ready to launch satellites from the LEO platform?"

"We already have contracts for four launches."

"But the geostationary platform isn't finished yet, is it?"

"We're ahead of schedule there, too."

"But it's not finished."

"Not for another six months," Bracknell said, feeling almost as if he were admitting a wrongdoing. Somehow Danvers had let the air out of his balloon.

By the time they finished their desserts and coffee, theirs was the only occupied table in the restaurant. The robot waiter was already sweeping the floor and two of the guys from the kitchen were stacking chairs atop tables to give the robot leeway for its chore.

Danvers bade them good night out on the sidewalk and headed for his quarters. Bracknell walked with Lara, arm in arm.

As they passed through the pools of light and shadow cast by the streetlamps, Lara said, "Rev. Danvers seems a little uncomfortable with the idea that we're living in sin."

Bracknell grinned down at her. "Best place to live, all things considered."

"Really? Is that what you think?"

Looking up at the glowing lights of the tower that split the night in half, Bracknell murmured, "Um . . . Paris is probably better."

"That's where the board meeting's going to be, isn't it?"

"Right," said Bracknell. "That's where Skytower Corporation turns me into a news media star."

"My handsome hero."

"Want to come with me?" he asked.

"To Paris?"

"Sure. You can do some clothes shopping there."

"Are you saying I need new clothes?"

He stopped in the darkness between streetlamps and slipped his arms around her waist. "You'll need a new dress for the wedding, won't you?"

"Wedding?" Even in the shadows he could see her eyes go wide with surprise.

Bracknell said, "With the tower almost finished and all this publicity the corporation's going to generate, I figure I ought to make an honest woman of you."

"You chauvinist pig!"

"Besides," he went on, "it'll make Danvers feel better."

"You're serious?" Lara asked. "This isn't a joke?"

He kissed her lightly. "Dead serious, darling. Will you marry me?"

"In Paris?"

"If that's what you want."

Lara flung her arms around his neck and kissed him as hard as she could.

GEOSTATIONARY PLATFORM

L ook on my works, ye mighty," quoted Ralph Waldo Emerson, the chief engineer, "and despair."

In a moment of whimsy brought on by their joy at his birth, his parents had named him after the poet. Emerson suspected their euphoria was helped along by the recreational drugs they used; certainly he saw enough evidence of that while he was growing up in the caravan city that trundled through the drought-dessicated former wheat belt of Midwestern America.

His father was a mechanic, his mother a nurse: both highly prized skills in the nomadic community. And both of them loved poetry. Hence his name.

Everybody called him Waldo. He learned to love things mechanical from his father and studied mechanical engineering through the computer webs and satellite links that sometimes worked and sometimes didn't. Once he grew into manhood Emerson left the caravan and entered a real, bricks-and-mortar engineering college. All he wanted was a genuine degree so that he would have real credentials to show prospective employers. No caravan life for Waldo. He wanted to settle down, get rich (or at least moderately prosperous), be respectable, and build new things for people.

His life didn't quite work out that way. There was plenty of work for a bright young engineer, rebuilding the shattered electrical power grid, erecting whole new cities to house the refugees driven from their homes by the greenhouse floods, designing solar power farms in the clear desert skies of the Southwest. But the various jobs took him from one place to another. He was still a nomad; he just stayed in one place a bit longer than his gypsying parents did.

He never got rich, or even very prosperous. Much of the work he did was commissioned by the federal or state government at minimum wage. Often enough he was conscripted by local chapters of the New Morality and he was paid nothing more than room, board, and a pious sermon or two about doing God's work. He married twice, divorced twice, and then gave up the idea of marriage.

Until a guy named Bracknell came to him with a wild idea and a gleam in his eye. Ralph Waldo Emerson fell in love with the skytower project.

Now that it was nearly finished he almost felt sad. He had spent more years in Ecuador than anywhere else in his whole life. He was becoming fond of Spanish poetry. He no longer got nauseous in zero gravity. He gloried in this monumental piece of architecture, this tower stretching toward heaven. He had even emblazoned his name into one of the outside panels that sheathed the tower up here at the geostationary level, insulating the tower from the tremendous electrical flux of the Van Allen belt. Working in an armored spacesuit and using an electron gun, he laboriously wrote his full name on one of the buckyball panels.

He laughed at his private joke. Someday some maintenance dweeb is going to see it, he thought, and wonder who the hell wrote the name of a poet on this tower's insulation skin.

Now he stood at the control board in the compact oval chamber that would soon be the geosynch level's operations center. His feet were ensconced in plastic floor loops so that he wouldn't float off weightlessly in the zero gravity of the station. Surrounding him were display screens that lined the walls like the multifaceted eyes of some giant insect. Technicians in gray coveralls bobbed in midair as they labored to connect the screens and get them running. One by one, the colored lights on the control board winked on and a new screen lit up. Emerson could see a dozen different sections of the mammoth geostationary structure. There was still a considerable amount of work to do, of course, but it was mostly just a matter of bringing in equipment and setting it up. Furnishing the hotel built into the platform's upper level. Checking out the radiation shielding and the electrical insulation and the airlocks. Making certain the zero-g toilets worked. Monkey work. Not creative. Not challenging.

There was talk of starting a new skytower in Borneo or central Africa.

"'Tis not too late to seek a newer world," he muttered to himself. "To sail beyond the sunset."

"Hey, Waldo," the voice of one of his assistants grated annoyingly in the communication plug in his right ear, "the supply ship is coming in."

"It's early," Emerson said, without needing to look at the digital clock set into the control board.

"Early or late, they're here and they want a docking port."

Emerson glanced up at the working screens, then played his fingers across the keyboard on the panel. One of the screens flicked from an interior view of the bare and empty hotel level upstairs to an outside camera view of a conical Masterson Clippership hovering in co-orbit a few hundred meters from the platform. He frowned at the image.

"We were expecting an uncrewed supply module," he said into his lip mike.

"And we got a nice shiny Clippership," his assistant replied. "They got our cargo and they want to offload it and go home."

Shaking his head slightly, Emerson checked the manifest that the Clippership automatically relayed to the platform's logistics program. It matched what they were expecting.

"Why'd they use a Clipper?" he wondered aloud.

"They said the freight booster had a malf and they swapped out the supply module with the Clippership's passenger module."

It didn't make sense to Emerson, but there was the Clippership waiting to dock and offload its cargo, and the manifest was exactly what they expected.

"Ours not to reason why," Emerson misquoted. "Hook 'em to docking port three; it's closest to them."

"Will do."

Franklin Zachariah hummed a cheerful tune to himself as he sat shoe-horned into the cramped cockpit of the Clippership. The pilot, a Japanese or Vietnamese or some kind of Asian gook, shot an annoyed glance over his shoulder. Hard to tell his nationality, Zach thought, with those black shades he's wearing. Like a mask or some macho android out of a banned terminator flick.

Zachariah stopped his humming but continued to play the tune in his head. It helped to pass the boring time. He had expected to get spacesick when the rocket went into orbit, but the medication they'd given him was working fine. Zero gravity didn't bother him at all. No upchucks, not even dizziness.

Zachariah was an American. He did not belong to the New Morality or the Flower Dragon or any other fundamentalist movement. He did not even follow the religion of his forefathers. He found that he couldn't believe in a god who made so many mistakes. He himself was a very clever young man—everyone who had ever met him said so. What they didn't know was that he was also a very destructive fellow.

Although he'd been born in Brooklyn, when he was six years old and the rising sea level caused by the greenhouse warming finally overwhelmed the city's flood control dams, Zachariah's family fled to distant cousins in the mountains near Charleston, West Virginia. There young Zach, as everyone called him, learned what it meant to be a Jew. At school, the other young boys alternately beat him up and demanded help with their classwork from him. His father, a professor in New York, had to settle for a job as a bookkeeper for his younger cousin, a jeweler in downtown Charleston who was ultimately shot to death in a holdup.

Zach learned how to avoid beatings by hiring the toughest thugs in school to be his bodyguards. He paid them with money he made from selling illicit drugs that he cooked up in the moldy basement of the house they shared with four other families.

By the time Zach was a teenager he had become a very accomplished computer hacker. Unlike his acne-ridden friends, who delved into illegal pornographic sites or shut down the entire public school system with a computer virus, Zach used his computer finesse in more secretive and lucrative ways. He pilfered bank accounts. He jiggered police records. He even got the oafish schoolmate who'd been his worst tormentor years earlier arrested by the state police for abetting an abortion. The kid went to jail protesting his innocence, but his own computer files proved his guilt. Cool, Zach said to himself as the bewildered lout was hauled off to a New Morality work camp.

Zach disdained college. He was having too much fun tweaking the rest of the world. He was the lone genius behind the smallpox scare that forced the head of the Center for Disease Control to resign. He even reached into the files of a careless White House speechwriter and leaked the contents of a whole sheaf of confidential memos, causing mad panic among the president's closest advisors. Way cool.

Then he discovered the thrill of true destruction. It happened while he was watching a pirated video of the as-yet-unreleased Hollywood re-re-remake of *Phantom of the Opera*. Zach sat in openmouthed awe as the Phantom sawed through the chain supporting the opera house's massive chandelier. Cooler than cool! he thought as the ornate collection of crystal crashed into the audience, splattering fat old ladies in their gowns and jewels and fatter old men in black tuxes.

Franklin Zachariah learned the sheer beauty, the sexual rush, of real destruction. Using acid to weaken a highway bridge so that it collapsed when the morning's traffic of overloaded semis rolled over it. Shorting out an airport's electrical power supply—and its backup emergency generator—in the midst of the evening's busiest hour. Quietly disconnecting the motors that moved the floodgates along a stretch of the lower Potomac so that the storm surge from the approaching hurricane flooded the capital's streets and sent those self-important politicians screaming to pin the blame on someone. Coolissimo.

Most of the time he worked alone, living off bank accounts here and there that he nibbled at, electronically. For some of the bigger jobs, like the Potomac floodgates, he needed accomplices, of course. But he always kept his identity a secret, meeting his accomplices only through carefully buffered computer links that could not, he was sure, be traced back to him.

It was a shock, then, when a representative of the Flower Dragon movement contacted him about the skytower. But Zach got over his shock when they described to him the coolest project of them all. He quickly asked for the detailed schematics of the skytower and began to study hard.

ara and Bracknell were driving one of the project's electric-powered minivans to the Quito airport. Bracknell planned to attend Skytower Corporation's board meeting and the news conference at which they would make the announcement that the tower was ready for operations. Then they would stay for a weekend of interviews and publicity events and return to Quito the following Monday.

"You sure you don't want to get married in Paris?" he asked her, grinning happily as he drove the quiet minivan down the steep, gravel-surfaced road. "We could have the ceremony at the top of the Eiffel Tower. Be kind of symbolic."

Trucks and buses ground by in the opposite direction, raising clouds of gritty gray dust as they headed uphill toward Sky City.

Lara shook her head. "I tried to get through all the red tape on the computer link, Mance, but it's hopeless. We'd have to stay two weeks, at least."

"The French want our tourist dollars."

"And they want to do their own blood tests, their own searches of our citizenship data. I think they even check Interpol for criminal records."

"So we'll get married when we come back," he said easily.

"And we can invite our families and friends."

"I'll ask Victor if he can come back for the occasion and be my best man."

Lara made no reply.

"Hey! Why don't we ask Rev. Danvers to perform the ceremony?"

"At his new chapel?"

"Unless you'd rather do it in the cathedral in Quito."

"No," Lara said. "Let's do it at the base of the tower. Rev. Danvers will be fine."

He wanted to kiss her; he even considered pulling off on the shoulder of the road to do it. Instead, he drove in silence for a while, grinning happily. The road became paved as they neared Quito's airport. Traffic built up. Lara turned in her seat and looked out the rear window.

"It's going to feel strange not seeing the tower in the sky," she said.

"It'll be there when we get back," Bracknell said easily. "For the next few days you'll just have to settle for the Eiffel Tower."

"Docking confirmed," said the Clippership's copilot. He was wearing dark glasses, too, like the pilot. Zach thought he looked kind of like an Asian, but his accent sounded California or some other part of the States.

"Tell the tower crew they can begin unloading," the pilot replied.

Zach knew what that meant. The Clipper was attached to the skytower now by a docking adaptor, a short piece of insulated tunnel that linked the tower's airlock to the Clipper's cargo hatch. A team of technicians from the skytower would come through the adaptor and begin unloading the Clipper's cargo bay. Zach thought of them as chimps doing stupid monkey tasks.

Unseen by the tower personnel, a dozen men and women recruited from god knows where would exit one of the Clippership's other airlocks, in spacesuits, of course, carrying the Clipper's *real* cargo: fifty tiny capsules of nanomachines, gobblers programmed to tear apart carbon molecules such as buckyballs. Zach had spent months studying the schematics of the skytower that the Flower Dragon people had supplied him, calculating just how to bring the tower down. They had balked at first when he suggested gobblers; nanotechnology was anathema to them. But someone higher up in the organization had overridden their objections and provided the highly dangerous gobblers for Zach's project of destruction.

Now twelve religious fanatics were out there playing with nanomachines that could kill them if they weren't careful. Each of the EVA team bore a minicam attached to his or her helmet, so Zach could direct their actions from the safety of the cockpit, securely linked to the outside crew by hair-thin optical fibers that carried his radio commands with no chance that they'd be overheard by the guys in the tower.

Now comes the fun part, Zach thought as he powered up the laptop he would use for communicating with the EVA team.

Ralph Waldo Emerson was also remotely watching the unloading, still wondering why the supply contractor had gone to the expense of hiring a shiny new Clippership instead of sending up another automated freighter.

"In faith, 'twas strange," he murmured as he stood in the control center, " 'twas passing strange."

"You spouting poetry again?" his assistant asked.

Emerson considered yanking the comm plug out of his ear, but knew that would be the wrong thing to do. Instead he asked, "How's it going?"

"It's going. Riley and his guys are pushin' the packages through the hatch and I'm checkin' 'em off as they come in. Nothing much to it. Just a lot of muscle work. Trained chimps could do this."

Emerson could see the bored team on one of the working screens, gliding the weightless big crates along through the adaptor tunnel.

"Well just be careful in there," he said. "Just because we're in zero-g doesn't mean those packages don't have mass. Get caught between a crate and a wall and you'll get your ribs caved in, just like on Earth."

"I know that." His assistant sounded impatient, waspish.

"Just make sure your chimpanzees know it."

"What? No poetry for the occasion?"

Emerson immediately snapped, "A fool and his ribcage are soon parted."

Zach was humming tunelessly to himself as he called up the schematics and matched them with the camera views from his EVA team. The connection between the geostationary platform and the tower's main cables was the crucial point. Sever that link and some thirty-five thousand kilometers of skytower go crashing down to Earth. And the other thirty-five thou, on the other side of the platform, goes spinning off into space, carrying the platform with it.

He suppressed the urge to giggle, knowing it would annoy the sour-faced pilots sitting as immobile as statues an arm's reach in front of him. I'm going to wipe out the biggest structure anybody's ever built! *Wham!* And down it goes.

It'll probably fall onto Quito, Zach reasoned. Kill a million people, maybe. Like the hammer of god slamming them flat. Like a big boot squishing bugs.

The culmination of my career, Zach thought. But nobody will know that I did it. Nobody really knows who I am. Not anybody who counts. But they will after this. I'm going to stand up and tell the world that *I* did this. Me. Franklin Zachariah. The terror of terrors. Dr. Destruction.

Lara was wearing open-weave huaraches instead of regular shoes, Bracknell realized as they inched along the line at the airport's security site. He frowned as he thought that they'd probably want him to take off his boots before going through the metal detector.

Damned foolishness, he said to himself. There hasn't been a terrorist threat at an airport in more than twenty years but they still go through this goddamned nonsense.

Sure enough, the stocky, stern-faced security guard pointed silently to Bracknell's boots as Lara sailed unbothered through the metal detector's arch. Grumbling, Bracknell tugged the boots off and thumped them down on the conveyor belt that ran through the X-ray machine.

He set off the metal detector's alarm anyway and had to be searched by a pair of grim-looking guards. He had forgotten the hand-held computer/phone he was carrying in his shirt pocket.

"No, no," Zach said sharply into his laptop's microphone. "Just open the capsule and wedge it into the cable. That's all you have to do, the nanobugs'll do the rest."

The job was taking much longer than he'd expected. Fifty cables, that's all we have to break, Zach grumbled silently, and these chimps are taking all fucking day to do it.

The underside of the geostationary platform looked like an immense spiderweb to Zach as he peered at it through the cameras of his EVA team. It matched the specs in his files almost exactly; there were always slight deviations between the blueprints and the actual construction. Nobody can build anything this big without straying from the plans here and there, at least a little bit.

Zach knew that the tower's main support came from these cables, stretched taught by centrifugal force as the whole gigantic assembly swung through space in synchrony with the Earth's daily spin. Break that connection here at the geostationary level and the stretching force disappears. The tower will collapse to the ground while the equally-long upper section goes spinning out into space.

Fifty cables, he repeated to himself. Let those nanobugs eat through fifty cables and the others won't have the strength to hold the rig together. Fifty cables.

Emerson's ear plug chimed softly with the tone he knew came from the safety officer.

"Go ahead," he said into his lip mike.

"Got something strange goin' on here."

"What?"

"That Clipper you've got docked. It's venting gases."

"Venting?"

"Hydrogen and oxygen, from what the laser spectrometer tells me."

Emerson thought a moment. "Bleeding a nearly-empty tank, maybe?"

The safety officer's voice sounded troubled. "This isn't a bleed. They're pumpin' out a lot of gas. Like the propellant they'd be using for their return trip."

"Curiouser and curiouser," Emerson quoted.

Zach licked his lips. The fifty cables were now being eaten away by the gobblers. He had calculated that blowing thirty of the cables would be enough to do the job, but he'd gone for fifty as an extra precaution. Okay, we've got fifty and we're all set.

He looked up at the two Asian pilots, still wearing those cool dark shades. "The nanomachines are in place."

"Good."

"All the EVA guys are back inside?"

"That is not your responsibility."

Zach felt the pilot was being snotty. "Okay," he said, "if any of them get eaten by the bugs, you write the condolence letters."

"Start the nanomachines working," the pilot said, without turning to look at Zach.

"They are working."

"Very well."

"Shouldn't we disconnect from the dock now?"

"No. Not yet."

THE COLLAPSE

Zach thought it was a little weird to stay connected to the tower's geostationary docking tunnel while the nanomachines were chewing away at the cables, but he figured the pilot knew what he was doing. The bugs won't get the chance to damage the Clippership; we'll disconnect before we're in any danger, he was pretty certain.

Besides, these two black-goggled pilots aren't going to kill themselves, Zach further assured himself. Not knowingly.

Outside the ship there was no sound. No vibration. Nothing.

For the first time, the pilot turned in his seat and lifted his glasses to glare directly at Zach. "Well? Have you done it?"

"Yeah," Zach replied, feeling nettled. "It's done. Now get us the hell out of here before the upper half of the tower starts spinning off to Alpha Centauri."

"That won't be necessary," said the pilot.

In the geostationary operations center, Emerson felt a slight tremor, a barely sensed vibration, as if a subway train had passed below the floor he stood on.

"What was that?" he wondered aloud.

His assistant's voice responded, "Yeah, I felt it too."

Tremors and vibrations were not good. In all the hours he'd spent in the tower at its various levels, it had always been as solid and unmoving as a mountain. What the hell could cause it to shake?

"Whatever it was," his assistant said, "it stopped."

But Emerson was busy flicking his fingers along his keyboard, checking the safety program. No leaks, no loss of air pressure. Electrical systems in the green. Power systems functioning normally. Structural integrity—

His eyes goggled at the screen. Red lights cluttered the screen. Forty, no fifty of the one hundred and twenty main cables had been severed. For long moments he could not speak, could hardly breathe. His brain refused to function. Fifty cables. We're going to die.

As he stared at the screen's display, another cable tore loose. And another. He could fell the deck beneath his feet shuddering.

"Hey, what's going on?" one of the technicians yelled from across the chamber.

"Let's to it, pell mell," Emerson whispered, more to himself than anyone who might hear him. "If not to heaven, then hand in hand to hell."

Bracknell was standing by the ceiling-high window at the Quito airport terminal gate, waiting for the Clippership for Paris to begin boarding. It sat out on its blast-scarred concrete pad, a squat cone constructed of diamond panels, manufactured by lunar nanomachines at Selene. They can use nanomachines up there but we can't here, Bracknell thought. Well, we've gotten around that stupid law. Once we get the patent—

A flash of light caught his eye. It was bright, brilliant even, but so quick that he wasn't certain if he'd actually seen anything real. Like a bolt of lightning. It seemed to come from the skytower, standing straight and slim, rising from the mountains and through the white clouds that swept over their peaks.

Lara came up beside him, complaining, "They can fly from Quito to Paris in less than an hour, but it takes longer than that to board the Clipper."

Bracknell smiled at her. "Patience is a virtue, as Rev. Danvers would say."

"I don't care. I'm getting—" Her words broke off. She was staring at the skytower. "Mance . . . look!"

He saw it, too. The tower was no longer a straight line bisecting the sky. It seemed to be rippling, like a rope that is flicked back and forth at one end.

His mind racing, Bracknell stared at the tower. It can't fall! It can't! But if it does . . .

He grabbed Lara around the shoulders and began running, dragging her, away from the big windows. "Get away from the windows!" he bellowed. "*Quitarse las ventanas!* Run! *Vamos!*"

•   •   •

"Nothing is happening," said the pilot accusingly.

"Yes it is," Zach answered. He was getting tired of the Asian's stupidity. These guys are supposed to be patient; didn't anybody ever give them Zen lessons? "Give it a few minutes. Those cables are popping, one by one. The more that snap, the faster the rest of 'em go."

"I see nothing," insisted the pilot, pointing toward the cockpit window.

Maybe if you took off those flicking glasses you could see better, creep, Zach grumbled silently. Aloud, he snapped, "You're gonna see plenty in two-three minutes. Now get us the flick outta here or else we're gonna go flipping out into deep space!"

"So you say."

A blinding flash of light seared Zach's eyes. He heard both pilots shriek. What the fuck was that? Zach wondered, pawing at his eyes. Through burning tears he saw the Clippership's cockpit, blurred, darkened, everything tinged in red. Rubbing his eyes again Zach squinted down at his laptop. The screen was dark, dead.

Then he realized that both pilots were jabbering in their Asian language.

"What happened?" he screeched.

"Electrical discharge." The pilot's voice sounded edgy for the first time. "An enormous electrical discharge."

"Even though we expected it," said the copilot, "it was a helluva jolt."

"Are we okay?" Zach demanded.

"Checking . . ."

"Get us out of here!" Zach screamed.

"All systems are down," the copilot said. "Complete power failure."

"Do something!"

"There is nothing to be done."

"But we'll die!"

"Of course."

Zach began blubbering, babbling incoherently at these two lunatics.

Removing his glasses and rubbing at his burning eyes, the pilot turned to his copilot and said in Japanese, "The American genius doesn't want to be a martyr."

The copilot's lean face was sheened with perspiration. "No one told him he would be."

"Will that affect his next life, I wonder? Will he be reborn as another human being or something less? A cockroach, perhaps."

"He doesn't believe in reincarnation. He doesn't believe in anything except destruction and his own ego."

The pilot said, "In that case, he has succeeded admirably. He has destroyed his own ego."

Neither man laughed. They sat strapped into their seats awaiting their fate with tense resignation while Zach screamed at them to no avail.

The massive electrical discharge released when some of the skytower's insulating panels were eaten away completed the destruction of the connectors that held the tower's two segments together at the geostationary level.

Although buckyball fibers are lighter in weight than any material that is even half their tensile strength, a structure of more than thirty-five thousand kilometers' length weighs millions of metric tons.

The skytower wavered as it tore loose from the geostationary platform, disconnected from the centrifugal force that had pulled it taut. One end suddenly free of its mooring, its other end still tethered to the ground, the lower half of the tower staggered like a prizefighter suddenly struck by a knockout blow, then began its long, slow-motion catastrophic collapse.

The upper end of the tower, equally as long as the lower, was also suddenly released from the force that held it taut. It reacted to the inertia that made it spin around the Earth each twenty-four hours. It continued to spin, but now free of its anchor it swung slowly, inexorably, unstoppably, away from Earth and into the black silent depths of space.

In the geostationary ops center Emerson saw every damned screen suddenly go dark; his control panel went dead. He felt himself sliding out of his foot restraints and sailing in slow motion across the operations center while the technicians who had been working on installing the new equipment were yanked to the ends of their tethers, hanging in midair, more shocked and surprised than frightened.

"What the shit is going on, Waldo?" one of them hollered.

He banged his shoulder painfully against the wall and slid to the floor. Soon enough, he knew, the immense structure would swing around and we'll all be slung in the opposite direction.

"Waldo, what the fuck's happening?" He heard panic creeping into their voices now.

We're dead, he knew. There's not a thing that anybody can do. Nor all thy tears wash out a word of it.

"Waldo! What's goin' on?"

They were screaming now, horror-struck, aware now that something had gone terribly wrong. Emerson tried to blank out their yammering, demanding, terrified screams.

"Fear death?" he quoted Browning:

> "To feel the fog in my throat,
>   The mist in my face,
> When the snows begin, and the blasts denote
>   I am nearing the place . . .
>   The post of the foe;
> Where he stands, the Arch Fear in a visible form,
>   Yet the strong man must go . . ."

And the upper half of the skytower spun out and away from the Earth forever.

The lower half of the skytower slowly, slowly tumbled like a majestic tree suddenly turned to putty. Its base, attached to the rotating Earth, was moving more than a thousand kilometers per hour from west to east. Its enormous length, unsupported now, collapsed westward in a long, long, *long* plunge to Earth.

The operations crew on duty at Sky City saw their screens glare with baleful red lights. Some of them rushed out into the open, unwilling to believe what their sensors were telling them unless they saw it with their own fear-widened eyes. The skytower was collapsing. They could see it! It was wavering and toppling over like a reed blown by the wind.

People on the streets in Quito looked up and screamed. Villagers in the mountains stared and crossed themselves.

At the Quito airport, Mance Bracknell dragged Lara by the arm as he ran down the terminal's central corridor, screaming, "Keep away from the windows! *Quitarse las ventanas!*"

He pulled Lara into the first restroom he saw, a men's room. Two men, an elderly maintenance worker in wrinkled coveralls and a businessman in a linen suit, stood side by side at urinals. They both looked shocked at the sight of a wild-eyed gringo dragging a woman into this place. They began to object but Mance yelled at them, "Down on the floor! Get down on the floor! There's going to an explosion! An eruption!"

"*Erupción?*" asked the old man, hastily zipping his fly.

"*Erupción grande!*" Mance said "*Temblor de tierra!* Earthquake!"

The businessman rushed for the exit while the older man stood there, petrified with sudden fear.

Mance pushed Lara onto the cold tiles and dropped down beside her, his arm wrapped protectively around her.

"Mance, how can—"

"There's no place to run to," he hissed in her ear. "If it hits here we're pulverized."

Slowly at first, but then with ever-increasing speed, the skytower's lower half collapsed to the Earth. Its immense bulk smashed into Ciudad de Cielo, the tethers at its base snapping like strings, the shock wave from its impact blowing down those buildings it did not hit directly. The thunder of its fall shattered the air like the blast of every volcano on Earth exploding at once. Seconds later the falling tower smashed down on the northern suburbs of Quito like a gigantic tree crushing an ant hill. The city's modern high-rise glass and steel towers, built to withstand earthquakes, wavered and shuddered. Their safety-glass facades blew out in showers of pellets. Ordinary windows shattered into razor-sharp shards that slashed to bloody ribbons the people who crowded the streets, screaming in terror. Older buildings were torn from their foundations as if a nuclear explosion had ripped through the city. The old cathedral's thick masonry walls cracked and its stained glass windows shattered, each and every one of them. Water pipes ruptured and gas mains broke. Fire and flood took up their deadly work where the sheer explosive impact of the collapse left off.

And still the tower fell.

Down the slope that led to the sea, villages and roads and farms and open fields and trees were smashed flat, pulverized, while the shock wave from the impact blew down woodlands and buildings for a hundred kilometers and more in either direction, as if a giant meteor had struck out of the sky. A fishing village fell under the shadow of sudden doom, its inhabitants looking up to see this immense arm of God swinging down on them like the mighty bludgeon of the angel of death.

And still the tower fell.

Its length splashed into the Pacific Ocean with a roar that broke eardrums and ruptured the innards of men, beasts, birds, and fish. Across the coastal shelf it plunged and out beyond into the abyssal depths. Whales migrating hundreds of kilometers out to sea were pulped to jelly by the shock wave that raced through the water. The tsunami it raised washed away shoreline settlements up and down the coast and rushed across the Pacific, flooding the Galapagos Islands, already half-drowned by the greenhouse warming. The Pacific coast of Central America was devastated. Hawaii and Japan were struck before their warning systems could get people to move inland. Samoa and Tahiti were hit by a wall of water nearly fifteen meters high that tore away villages and whole cities. People in Los Angeles and Sydney heard the mighty thunderclap and wondered if it was a sonic boom.

And still the tower fell, splashing all the way across the Pacific, groaning as part of its globe-girdling length sank slowly into the dark abyssal depths. When it hit the spiny tree-covered mountain backbone of Borneo it snapped in two, one part sliding down the rugged slopes, tearing away forests and villages and plantations as it slithered snake-like across the island.

The other part plunged across Sumatra and into the Indian Ocean, narrowly missing the long green finger of Malaysia but sending a tsunami washing across the drowned ruins of Singapore. Along the breadth of equatorial Africa it fell, smashing across Kenya, ploughed into the northern reaches of Lake Victoria, drowning the city of Kampala with a tidal wave, and continued westward, crushing cities and forests alike, igniting mammoth forest fires, driving vast herds of animals into panicked, screaming stampedes. Its upper end, still smoking from the titanic electrical discharge that had severed it, plunged hissing into the Atlantic, sinking deep down into the jagged rift where hot magma from the Earth's core embraced the man-made structure that had, mere minutes earlier, stood among the stars.

Across the world the once-proud skytower lay amidst a swath of death and desolation and smoking ruin, crushing the life from people, animals, plants, crushing human ambition, human dreams, crushing hope itself.

Lying flat on the tiles of the airport men's room, Bracknell felt the floor jump as a roll of thunder boomed over them, so loud that his ears rang. Even so, he heard screams and terrified cries.

"Are you all right?" he asked Lara, his voice sounding strange, muffled, inside his head.

She nodded weakly. He saw that her nose was bleeding slightly. Bracknell climbed slowly to his feet. The old man was still lying on the floor, facedown. Bracknell called to him, then nudged his shoulder. The man did not move. Rolling him over, Bracknell saw his soft brown eyes staring out sightlessly.

"He's dead," Lara said. Bracknell could barely hear her over the buzzing in his head.

Feeling stunned, thick-witted, Bracknell gazed around the windowless men's room. One of the tiled walls had cracked. Or had it been that way when they had rushed in here?

"Dead?" he echoed numbly.

"A heart attack, maybe," Lara said. She clung close to Bracknell. He could feel her trembling.

"He's lucky," said Bracknell.

THE RUINS

t took three days before they arrested Bracknell. He had made his
way back to the shattered ruins of the Sky City, fighting through the
panicked crowd at the airport, holding Lara close to him. The vast
parking lot outside the airport seemed undamaged, except for the
gritty dust that covered everything and crunched under their feet as
they walked, tottering, for what seemed like hours until they found
the minivan sitting there where they'd left it. Other people were
milling around the parking lot, looking dazed, shocked.

A pall of smoke was rising from the city. Soon enough the looting
would begin, Bracknell realized. *For the moment they're too stunned
to do much of anything, but that'll pass and they'll start looting and
stealing. And raping.*

The minivan looked as if it had gone a thousand klicks without
being washed. Bracknell helped Lara into the right-hand seat, then
went around and got in himself. The car started smoothly enough. He
used the windshield wipers to clear away enough of the dust so he
could see to drive, then started slowly out toward the road that led back
up into the hills. A few people waved pathetically to him, seeking a
ride. *To where?* Bracknell asked himself silently as he drove past them,
accelerating now. A couple of young men trotted toward the minivan
and he pushed the accelerator harder. The toll gate at the exit was unoccupied, its arm raised, so he drove right through. In the rear mirror
he saw a uniformed guard or policeman or something waving angrily
at him. He drove on.

When they finally reached Ciudad de Cielo, they saw that most of
it was flattened. Buildings were crushed beneath the skytower's fallen
bulk or blown flat by the shock wave of its collapse. Trucks overturned,
lampposts bent and twisted. Dust hung in the air and the stench of
death was everywhere, inescapable.

For three days Bracknell and Lara did nothing but dig bodies out of the collapsed buildings of the base city. The tower lay across the ruins like an immense black worm, dead and still, strangely warm to the touch. It had ripped out of all but one of its base tethers. In a distant corner of his mind Bracknell thought that they had designed the tethers pretty well to stand up even partially to the stress.

He worked blindly, numbly, side by side with the few surviving technicians, clerks, maintenance people, cooks, and others who had once been a proud team of builders. Lara worked alongside him, never complaining, like Bracknell and all the others too tired and shocked and disheartened to do much of anything except scrabble in the debris, eat whatever meager rations they could find, and sleep when they were too tired to stand any longer. Grimy, her face smeared with soot, her fingers bloody from digging, her clothes sodden with perspiration, Lara still worked doggedly at rescuing the few who were still alive and dragging out the mangled bodies of the dead.

The third night they saw torches lining the road from Quito, heading toward them.

"Volunteers?" Lara asked, her voice ragged with exhaustion.

"More likely a lynch mob," said Bracknell, getting up from the rubble he'd been digging in.

"Can you blame them?" said Danvers who was working beside them. "They're coming to kill everyone here."

"No," Bracknell replied, standing up straighter. "It's me they want. I'm the one responsible for this."

Lara, her weariness suddenly forgotten, turned her smudged face to Danvers. "You're a man of god! Do something! Talk to them! Stop them!"

Danvers looked terrified. "Me?"

"There's no one else," Lara insisted.

"I'll go," Bracknell said grimly. "I'm the one they want."

"I'll . . . I'll go with you," Danvers stammered.

"You stay here," Bracknell said to Lara.

"The hell I will!"

"This is going to be ugly."

"I'm going where you go, Mance."

The three of them walked—tottered, really—down the rubble-strewn street to the main road, where the torch-waving mob was marching toward them. Farther down the road, Bracknell could see the headlights of approaching trucks.

The crowd was mainly young men, all of them looking tired and grimy, clothes torn, faces blackened with soot and dirt. They carried shovels, picks, planks of wood. Christ, they look like us, Bracknell said to himself. They've been digging for survivors, too.

Danvers fished a small silver crucifix out of his pocket and held it up. In the flickering torchlight it gleamed fitfully. The mob stopped uncertainly.

"My sons," he began.

One of the men, taller than the others, his eyes glittering with anger and hatred, spat out a string of rapid Spanish. Bracknell caught his drift: We want the men who killed our families. We want justice.

Danvers raised his voice, "Do any of you speak English?"

"We want justice!" a voice yelled from the crowd.

"Justice is the Lord's," Danvers bellowed. "God will avenge."

The crowd surged forward dangerously. Danvers backed up several steps. Bracknell saw that it was going to be no use. The trucks were inching through the rear of the mob now. Bringing reinforcements, he thought. He stepped forward. "I'm the one you want," he said in Spanish. "I'm the man responsible."

An older man scurried up to Bracknell and peered at him. Turning back to the others, he shouted, "This is he! This is the chief of the skytower!"

The mob flowed forward, surrounding Bracknell. Lara screamed as Danvers dragged her back into the shadows, toward safety. The leader of the mob spat in Bracknell's face and raised his shovel high in the air.

A shot cracked through the night. Everyone froze into immobility. Bracknell could feel his heart pounding against his ribs. Then he saw soldiers pouring out of the trucks, each of them armed with assault rifles. An officer waved a pistol angrily and told the men of the mob to back away.

"This man is under arrest," the officer announced loudly. "He is going to jail."

Bracknell's knees nearly gave way. Jail seemed much better than having his brains splattered with a shovel.

THE TRIAL

As the crisply uniformed soldiers with their polished helmets and loaded guns bundled Bracknell into one of the trucks, he thought, Of course. They need to blame someone for this catastrophe. Who else? I'm the one in charge. I'm the one at fault.

He was treated with careful respect, as if he were a vial of nitroglycerine that might explode if mishandled. They placed him in the prison hospital, where a team of physicians and psychologists diagnosed Bracknell as suffering from physical exhaustion and severe emotional depression. He was dosed with psychotropic drugs for five of the six months between his arrest and his trial. During those five months, he was allowed no visitors, no television, nor any contact with the outside world, although police investigators questioned him for hours each day.

Skytower Corporation declared bankruptcy. Its board of directors issued a statement blaming the tower's collapse on the technical director who headed the construction project in Ecuador, the American engineer Mance Bracknell. Several of the board members fled to the lunar city of Selene, where Earthly legal jurisdiction could not reach them.

After five months of imprisonment Bracknell's interrogators flushed his body of the drugs they had used on him and showed him the written record of his confession. He signed it without argument. Only then was he allowed to speak to an attorney whom the government of Ecuador had appointed to represent him. When Lara was at last allowed to visit him, he had only the haziest of notions about what had happened to him since his arrest. Physically he was in good condition, except that he had lost more than five kilos in weight, his deep tan had faded, and his voice had withered to a whisper. Emotionally he was a wreck.

"I'll get you the best lawyers on Earth," Lara told him urgently.

Bracknell shrugged listlessly. "What difference does it make?"

The whole world watched his trial, in the high court in what was left of Quito. The court building had escaped major damage, although there were still engineers who had been brought in from Brazil poking around the building's foundations; most of the court's high stately windows, blown out by the shock of the tower's collapse, had been replaced by sheets of clear plastic.

Skytower Corporation dissolved itself in the face of trillions of dollars of damage claims. Bracknell was too guilt-ridden even to attempt to find himself a lawyer other than the government-appointed lackey. Lara coaxed a family friend to help represent him. The old man came out of retirement reluctantly and told Bracknell at their first meeting that his highest hope was to avoid the death penalty.

Lara was shocked. "I thought international law forbids the death penalty."

"More than four million deaths are being blamed on you," the old man said, frowning disapprovingly at Bracknell. "Mass murder, they're calling it. They want to make an example of you."

"Why not?" Bracknell whispered.

Although the trial took place in Quito, it was held under the international legal regime. Years earlier, Lara's lawyer had helped to write the international legal regime's guiding rules. That did not help much. Nor did Bracknell do much to help himself.

"It's my fault," he kept repeating. "My fault."

"No, it isn't," Lara insisted.

"The structure failed," he told Lara and her lawyer, time and again. "I was in charge of the project, so it's my responsibility."

"But you're not to blame," Lara insisted each time. "You didn't deliberately destroy the tower."

"I'm the only one left to blame," Bracknell pointed out morosely. "All the others were killed in the collapse."

"No, that's not true," said Lara. "Victor is in Melbourne. He'll help you."

At Lara's importuning Molina flew in from Melbourne. Sitting between his two lawyers on the opening day of the trial, dressed in a state-provided suit and a stiffly starched shirt that smelled of detergent,

Bracknell felt a flicker of hope when he saw his old friend enter the courtroom and sit directly behind him, beside Lara. But once the trial began, it became clear that nothing on Earth could save him.

The first witness called by the three-judge panel was the Reverend Elliott Danvers.

The prosecuting attorney was a slim, dark-haired Ecuadorian of smoldering intensity, dressed in a white three-piece suit that fit him without a wrinkle. The video cameras loved his handsome face with its dark moustache, and he knew how to play to the vast global audience watching this trial. To Bracknell he looked like a mustachioed avenging angel. He started by establishing Danvers's position as spiritual advisor to the people of Ciudad de Cielo.

"Most of them are dead now, are they not?" asked the prosecutor. Since the trial was being held under the international legal regime, and being broadcast even to Selene and the mining center at Ceres, it was conducted in English.

Danvers answered with a low "Yes."

The prosecutor smoothed his moustache as he gazed up at the cracks in the courtroom's coffered ceiling, preparing dramatically for his next question. "You were troubled by what you learned about this construction projection, were you not?"

Bit by bit, the prosecutor got Danvers to tell the judges that Bracknell had been using genetically engineered microbes as nanomachines to produce the tower's structural elements.

The state-appointed defense attorney said nothing, but the lawyer that Lara had hired rose slowly to his feet and called in a tired, aged voice, "Objection. There is nothing illegal about employing genetically engineered microbes. And referring to them as 'nanomachines' is prejudicial."

The judges conferred in hurried whispers, then upheld the objection.

The prosecutor smiled thinly and bowed his head, accepting their decision, knowing that the dreaded term would be remembered by everyone.

"Have such genetically engineered microbes been used in any other construction projects?"

Danvers shrugged his heavy shoulders. "I'm not an engineer . . ."

"To the best of your knowledge."

"To the best of my knowledge: no, they have not. The project's biologist, Dr. Molina, seemed quite proud of the originality of his work. He had applied for a patent."

The prosecutor turned toward Bracknell with a thin smile. "Thank you, Rev. Danvers."

Bracknell's defense attorney got to his feet, glanced at the state-appointed attorney, then said, "I have no questions for this witness at this time."

Lara, sitting behind Bracknell, touched his shoulder. He turned to her, saw the worried look on her face. And said nothing. Molina, sitting beside her, looked impatient, uncomfortable.

"I call Dr. Victor Molina to the stand," said the prosecutor, with the air of a magician pulling a rabbit out of his hat.

Molina got to his feet and walked slowly to the witness chair; he tried to make a smile for Bracknell but grimaced instead.

Once again, the prosecutor spent several minutes establishing Molina's credentials and his position on the project. Then he asked:

"You left the skytower project before it was completed, did you not?"

"Yes, I did," said Molina.

"Why is that?"

Molina hesitated a moment, his eyes flicking toward Bracknell and Lara, sitting behind him.

"Personal reasons," he answered.

"Could you be more specific?"

Again Molina hesitated. Then, drawing in a breath, he replied, "I wasn't certain that the structures produced by my gengineered microbes were sufficiently strong to stand the stresses imposed by the tower."

Bracknell blinked and stirred like a man coming out of a coma. "That's not true," he whispered, more to himself than to his lawyers.

But Molina was going on, "I wanted more testing, more checking to make sure that the structure would be safe. But the project director wouldn't do it."

"The project director was Mr. Mance Bracknell," asked the prosecuting attorney needlessly. "The accused?"

"Yes," said Molina. "He insisted that we push ahead before the necessary tests could be done."

Bracknell said to his attorney, "That's not true!" Turning to Lara, he said, "That isn't what happened!"

The chief judge, sitting flanked by his two robed associates at the high banc of polished mahogany, tapped his stylus on the desktop. "The accused will remain silent," he said sternly. "I will tolerate no disruptions in this court."

"Thank you, Your Honor," said the prosecutor. Then he turned back to Molina, in the witness chair.

"So the accused disregarded your warnings about the safety problems of the tower?"

Molina glanced toward Bracknell, then looked away. "Yes, he did."

"He's lying!" Bracknell said to his lawyer. Jumping to his feet, he shouted to Molina, "Victor, why are you lying?"

His lawyer pulled him back down onto his chair while the chief judge leveled an accusatory stare at Bracknell. "I warn you, sir: another such outburst and you will be removed from this courtroom."

"What difference would that make?" Bracknell snapped. "You've convicted me already."

The judge nodded to the pair of burly soldiers standing to one side of the banc. They pushed past the attorney on Bracknell's left and grabbed him by his arms, hauling him to his feet.

He turned to glance back at Lara as they dragged him out of the courtroom. She was smiling. Smiling! Bracknell felt his guts churn with sudden hatred.

Lara watched them hustle Mance out of the courtroom, smiling as she thought, At least he's waking up. He's not just sitting there and accepting all the blame. He's starting to defend himself. Or trying to.

THE VERDICT

The trial proceeded swiftly. With Bracknell watching the proceedings on video from a locked and guarded room on the other side of the courthouse, the prosecuting attorney called in a long line of engineers and other technical experts who testified that the skytower was inherently dangerous.

"No matter what safety precautions may or may not have been taken," declared the somber, gray-haired dean of the technology ethics department of Heidelberg University, "such a structure poses an unacceptable danger to the global environment, as we can all see from this terrible tragedy. Its very existence is a menace to the world."

Bracknell's attorney called in technical witnesses, also, who testified that all the specifications and engineering details of the skytower showed that the structure had been built well within tolerable limits.

"I personally reviewed the plans before construction ever started," said the grizzled, square-faced professor of engineering from Caltech. "The plan for that tower was sound."

"Yet it fell!" snapped the prosecutor, on cross-examination. "It collapsed and killed millions."

"That shouldn't have happened," said the Caltech professor.

"It shouldn't have happened," the prosecutor repeated, "*if* the actual construction followed the plans."

"I'm sure it did," the professor replied.

"Did the plans call for nanotechnology to be employed in manufacturing the structural elements?"

"No, but—"

"Thank you. I have no further questions."

As Bracknell sat and seethed in his locked room, the prosecution built its case swiftly and surely. There were hardly any of the skytower crew left alive to testify to the soundness of the tower's construction. And when they did the prosecutor harped back to the use of nanotechnology.

"Call Victor back to the stand," Bracknell urged his attorney with white-hot fury. "Cross-examine him. Make him tell the truth!"

"That wouldn't be wise," the old man said. "There's no sense reminding the judges that you used nanomachines."

"I didn't! They were natural organisms!"

"Genetically modified."

"But that doesn't make any difference!"

The attorney shook his head sadly. "If I put Molina back in the witness stand and he sticks to his story, it will destroy you."

"If you don't, I'm destroyed anyway."

The hardest part of the trial, for Bracknell, was the fact that the judges would not let him see anyone except his attorneys. Every day he sat in that stuffy little isolation room and watched Lara in the courtroom, with Molina now at her side. She would leave with Victor. On the morning that the verdict was to be announced she arrived with Victor.

On that morning, before the proceedings began, the chief judge stepped into Bracknell's isolation room, flanked by two soldiers armed with heavy black pistols at their hips. After weeks of viewing him only in his black robe up on his high banc, Bracknell was mildly surprised to see that the man was very short and stocky. His skin was light, but he was built like a typical mestizo. His face bore the heavy, sad features of a man about to do something unpleasant.

Bracknell got to his feet as the judge entered the little room.

Without preamble, the judge said in barely accented English, "I am to pass sentence on you this morning. Can you restrain yourself if I allow you back into the courtroom?"

"Yes," said Bracknell.

"I have your word of honor on that?"

Almost smiling, Bracknell replied, "If you believe that I have any honor, yes, you have my word."

The judge did not smile back. He nodded wearily. "Very well, then." Turning, he told the soldiers in rapid Spanish to escort the prisoner into the courtroom.

The courtroom was jammed, Bracknell saw as he came in, escorted by the soldiers. From the video screen in his isolation room he'd been unable to see how many people attended the trial. Now he realized there were reporters and camerapersons from all over the world wedged along both side walls. The benches were packed with people, most of them dour, dark Ecuadorians who stared at him with loathing. Looking for my blood, Bracknell realized.

Lara jumped to her feet as he entered; Molina rose more slowly. Both of Bracknell's attorneys stood up, too, looking as if they were attending a funeral. They are, Bracknell thought. Once he got to his chair Lara leaned across the mahogany railing separating them and threw her arms around his neck.

"I'm with you, darling," she whispered into his ear. "No matter what happens, I'm with you."

Bracknell drank in the warmth of her body, the scent of her. But his eyes bore into Molina's, who glared back angrily at him.

Why is Victor sore at me? Bracknell asked himself. What's he got to be pissed about? *He* betrayed *me*; I haven't done anything to *him*.

"Everyone stand," called the court announcer.

The judges filed in, their robes looking newer and darker than Bracknell remembered them. Their faces were dark, too.

Once everyone was properly seated, the chief judge picked up a single sheet of paper from the desk before him. Bracknell noted that his hand trembled slightly.

"The prisoner will stand."

Bracknell got to his feet, feeling as if he were about to face a firing squad.

"It is the judgment of this court that you, Mance Bracknell, are responsible for the deaths of more than four million human souls, and the destruction of many hundreds of billions of dollars in property."

Bracknell felt nothing. It was as if he were outside his own body, watching this foreordained drama from a far distance.

"Since your crime was not willful murder, the death sentence will not be considered."

A stir rippled through the packed courtroom. "He killed my whole family!" a woman's voice screeched in Spanish.

"Silence!" roared the judge, with a power in his voice that stilled the crowd. "This is a court of justice. The law will prevail."

The courtroom went absolutely silent.

"Mance Bracknell, you have been found guilty of more than four million counts of negligent homicide. It is the decision of this court that you be exiled from this planet Earth forever, so that you can never again threaten the lives of innocent men, women, and children."

Bracknell's knees sagged beneath him. He leaned on the tabletop for support.

"This case is closed," said the judge.

BOOK III
EXILED

Beware the fury of a patient man.

BOOK IX
EXILED

LEAVING EARTH

They wasted no time hustling Bracknell off the planet. Within two days of his trial's inevitable conclusion, a squad of hard-faced soldiers took him from his prison cell to a van and out to the Quito airport, where a Clippership was waiting to carry him into orbit.

The airport looked relatively undamaged, Bracknell saw from the window of the van, except for the big plywood sheets where the sweeping windows had been. It's a wonder the crash didn't trigger earthquakes, he thought.

The soldiers marched him through the terminal building, people turning to stare at him as they strode to the Clippership gate. Bracknell was not shackled, not even handcuffed, but everyone recognized him. He saw the look in their eyes, the expressions on their faces: hatred, anger, even fear—as if he were a monster that terrified their nightmares.

Lara was waiting at the terminal gate, wearing black, as if she were attending a funeral. She is, Bracknell thought. Mine.

She rushed to him and leaned her head against his chest. Bracknell felt awkward, with the grim-faced soldiers flanking him. He slid his arms around her waist hesitantly, tentatively, then suddenly clung to her like a drowning man clutching a life preserver.

"Darling, I'll go out to the Belt with you," Lara said, all in a gush. "Wherever they send you, I'll go there too."

He pushed her back away from him. "No! You can't throw away your life. They're putting me in some sort of a penal colony; you won't be allowed there."

"But I—"

"Go back home. Live your life. Forget about me. I'm a dead man. Dead and gone. Don't throw away your life on a corpse."

"No, Mance, I won't let you—"

He shoved her roughly and turned to the soldier on his left. "Let's go. *Andale!*"

Lara looked shocked, her eyes wide, her mouth open in protest.

"*Andale!*" he repeated to the soldiers, louder, and started walking toward the gate. They rushed to catch up with him. He did not dare look back at Lara as the soldiers marched him into the access tunnel that led to the Clippership's hatch. His last sight of her was the stunned look on her face. He didn't want to see the tears filling her eyes, the hopelessness. He felt wretched enough for both of them.

The access tunnel was smooth windowless plastic. A birth canal, Bracknell thought. I'm being born into another life. Everything I had, everything and everyone I knew, is behind me now. I'm leaving my life behind me and entering hell.

And then he saw the bulky form of Rev. Danvers standing at the end of the tunnel, blocking the Clippership hatch. The minister was also in black, he looked downcast, sorrowful, almost guilty.

Bracknell felt a wave of fury burn through his guts. Damned ignorant viper. Frightened of anything new, anything different. He's happy that the tower failed, but he's trying to put on a sympathetic face.

Bracknell walked right up to Danvers. "Don't tell me you're going out to the Belt with me."

Danver's face reddened. "No, I hadn't intended to. But if you feel the need for spiritual consolation, perhaps I—"

With a bitter laugh, Bracknell said, "Don't worry, I was only joking."

"I can contact the New Morality office at Ceres on your behalf," Danvers suggested.

Bracknell wanted to spit out, "Go to hell," but he bit his lip and said nothing.

"You'll need spiritual comfort out there," Danvers said, his voice low, almost trembling. "You don't have to be alone in your time of tribulation."

"Is that what you came here to tell me? That I can have some pious psalm singer drone in my ear? Some consolation!"

"No," Danvers said, his heavy head sinking slightly. "I came to . . . to tell you how sorry I am that things have worked out the way they have."

"Sure you are."

"I am. Truly I am. When I reported to my superiors about your using nanotechnology, I was merely doing my duty. I had no personal
animosity toward you. Quite the opposite."

Despite his anger Bracknell could see the distress in Danvers's
flushed face. Some of the fury leached out of him.

"I had no idea it would lead to this," Danvers was going on, almost
blubbering. "You must believe me, I never wanted to cause harm to
you or anyone else."

"Of course not," Bracknell said tightly.

"I was merely doing my duty."

"Sure."

One of the soldiers prodded Bracknell's back.

"I've got to get aboard," he said to Danvers.

"I'll pray for you."

"Yeah. Do that."

They left Danvers at the hatch and entered the Clippership. Its
circular passenger compartment was empty: twenty rows of seats
arranged two by two with an aisle down the middle. Instead of flight at-
tendants, two marshals with stun wands strapped to their hips were
standing just inside the hatch.

"Take any seat you like, Mr. Bracknell," said the taller of the two
men.

"This flight is exclusively for you," said the other, with a smirk.
"Courtesy of Masterson Aerospace Corporation and the International
Court of Justice."

Bracknell fought down an urge to punch him in his smug face.
He looked around the circular compartment, then chose one of the
few seats that was next to a window. One of the soldiers sat next to him,
the other directly behind him.

It took nearly half an hour before the Clippership was ready for
launch. Bracknell saw there was a video screen on the seat back in
front of him. He ignored its bland presentation of a Masterson Aerospace documentary and peered out the little window at the workers
moving around the blast-blackened concrete pad on which the rocket
vehicle stood. He heard thumps and clangs, the gurgling of what he
took to be rocket propellant, then the screen showed a brief video
about safety and takeoff procedures.

Bracknell braced himself for the rocket engines' ignition. They lit off with a demon's roar and he felt an invisible hand pressing him down into the thickly cushioned seat. The ground fell away and he could see the whole airport, then the towers and squares of Quito, and finally the long black snake of the fallen skytower lying across the hilly land like a dead and blasted dream.

It was only then that he burst into tears.

Although Bracknell's Clippership ride from Quito to orbit was exclusively for him, the vehicle they transferred him to held many other convicts.

It was not a torch ship, the kind of fusion-driven vessel that could accelerate all the way out to the Belt and make it to Ceres in less than a week. Bracknell was put aboard a freighter named *Alhambra*, an old, slow bucket that spent months coasting from Earth out to the Belt.

His fellow prisoners were mostly men exiled for one crime or another, heading for a life of mining the asteroids. Bracknell counted three murderers (one of them a sullen, drug-raddled woman), four thieves of various accomplishments, six embezzlers and other white-collar crooks, and an even dozen others who had been convicted of sexual crimes or violations of religious authority.

The captain of the freighter obviously did not like ferrying convicts to the Belt, but it paid more than going out empty to pick up ores. The prisoners were marched into the unused cargo hold, which had been fitted out with old, rusting cots and a row of portable toilets. It was big, bare metal womb with walls scuffed and scratched by years worth of heavy wear. The narrow, sagging metal-framed cots were bolted to the floor, the row of toilet cubicles lined one wall. As soon as the *Alhambra* broke orbit and started on its long, coasting journey to the Belt, the captain addressed his "passengers" over the ship's video intercom.

"I am Captain Farad," he announced. In the lone screen fixed high overhead in the hold, Bracknell and the others could see that the captain's lean, sallow face was set in a sour, stubbly scowl that clearly showed his contempt for his "passengers."

"I give the orders aboard this vessel and you obey them," he went on. "If you don't give me any trouble I won't give you any trouble. But if you start any trouble, if you're part of any trouble, if you're just only *near* trouble when it happens, I'll have you jammed into a spacesuit and put outside on the end of a tether and that's the way you'll ride out to Ceres."

The convicts mumbled and glowered up at the screen. Bracknell thought that the captain meant every word of what he'd said quite literally.

Even with that warning, the journey was not entirely peaceful. There were no private accommodations for the convicts aboard the freighter; they were simply locked into the empty cargo hold. Within a day, the hold stank of urine and vomit.

Alhambra's living module rotated slowly at the end of a five-kilometer tether, with its logistics and smelting modules on the other end, so that there was a feeling of nearly Earth-level gravity inside. Meals were served by simple-minded robots that could neither be bribed nor coerced. Bracknell did his best to stay apart from all the others, including the women convicted of prostitution, who went unashamedly from cot to cot once the overhead lights had been turned down for the night.

Still, it was impossible to live in peace. His mind buzzed constantly with the memory of all he'd lost: Lara, especially. His dreams were filled with visions of the skytower collapsing, of the millions who had been killed, all of them rising from their graves and pointing accusing skeletal fingers at him. Where did it go wrong? Bracknell asked himself, over and over and over again. The questions tortured him. The structure was sound, he knew it was. Yet it had failed. Why? Had some unusually powerful electrical current in the ionosphere snapped the connector links at the geostationary level? Should I have put more insulation up at that level? What did I do wrong? What did I do?

It was his dreams—nightmares, really—that got him into trouble. More than once he was awakened roughly by one of the other convicts, angry that his moaning was keeping all those around his cot from sleeping.

"You sound like a fuckin' baby," snarled one of the angry men, "cryin' and yellin'."

"Yeah," said another. "Shut your mouth or we'll shut it for you."

For several nights Bracknell tried to force himself to stay awake, but eventually he fell asleep and once he did his haunting dreams returned.

Suddenly he was being yanked off his cot, punched and kicked by a trio of angry men. Bracknell tried to defend himself, he fought back and unexpectedly found himself enjoying the pain and the blood and the fury as he smashed their snarling faces, grabbed a man by the hair and banged his head off the metal rail of his cot, kneed another in the groin and pounded him in the kidneys. More men swarmed over him and he went down, but he was hitting, kicking, biting, until he blacked out.

When he awoke he was strapped down in a bunk. Through swollen, blood-encrusted eyes he realized that this must be the ship's infirmary. It smelled like a hospital: disinfectant and crisply clean sheets. No one else was in sight. Medical monitors beeped softly above his head. Every part of his body ached miserably. When he tried to lift his head a shock of pain ran the length of his spine.

"You've got a couple of broken ribs," said a rough voice from behind him.

The captain stepped into his view. "You're Bracknell, eh? You put up a good fight, I'll say that much for you." He was a small man, lean and lithe, his skin an ashen light tan, the stubble on his unshaved face mostly gray. A scar marred his upper lip, making him look as if he were perpetually snarling. His hair was pulled back off his face and tied into a little queue.

Bracknell tried to ask what happened, but his lips were so swollen his words were terribly slurred.

"I reviewed the fight on the video monitor," the captain said, frowning down at him. "Infrared images. Not as clear as visible light, but good enough for the likes of you scum."

"I'm not scum," Bracknell said thickly.

"No? You killed more people than the guys who were pounding you ever did."

Bracknell turned his head away from the captain's accusing eyes.

"I was an investor in Skytower Corporation," the captain went on. "I was going to retire and live off my profits. Now I'm broke. A lifetime's savings wiped out because you screwed up the engineering. What'd you do, shave a few megabucks on the structure so you could skim the money for yourself?"

It was all Bracknell could do to murmur, "No."

"Not much, I'll bet." The captain stared down at Bracknell, unconcealed loathing in his eyes. "The guys who jumped you are riding outside, just as I promised troublemakers would. You'd be out there, too, except I don't have enough suits."

Bracknell said nothing.

"You'll spend the rest of the flight here, in the infirmary," said the captain. "Think of it as solitary confinement."

"Thanks," Bracknell muttered.

"I'm not doing this for you," the captain snapped. "Long as you're in the hold with the rest of those savages you're going to be a lightning rod. It'll be a quieter ride with you in here."

"You could have let them kill me."

"Yeah, I could have. But I get paid for every live body I deliver at Ceres. Corpses don't make money for me."

With that, the captain left. Bracknell lay alone, strapped into the bunk. When his nightmares came there was no one to be bothered by his screams.

CERES

As the weeks dragged by, Bracknell's ribs and other injuries slowly healed. The ship's physician—an exotic-looking, dark-skinned young Hindu woman—allowed him to get up from the bunk and walk stiffly around the narrow confines of the infirmary. She brought him his meals, staring at him through lowered lashes with her big liquid eyes.

Once, when he woke up screaming in the middle of the night, the physician and the captain both burst into the tiny infirmary and sedated him with a hypospray. He slept dreamlessly for a day and a half.

After weeks of being tended by this silent physician with her almond eyes and subtle perfume, Bracknell realized, My god, even in a wrinkled, faded set of sloppy coveralls she looks sexy. He thought of Lara and wondered what she was doing now, how she was putting together the shattered pieces of her life. The physician never spoke a word to him and Bracknell said nothing to her beyond a half-whispered "Thank you" when she'd bring in a tray of food. The young woman was obviously wary of him, almost frightened. If I touch her and she screams I'll end up outside in a spacesuit, trying to stay alive on liquids and canned air, he told himself.

At last one day, when he was walking normally again, he blurted, "May I ask you something?"

She looked startled for a moment, then nodded wordlessly.

"Why put the troublemakers outside?" Bracknell asked. "Wouldn't it be easier to dope them with psychotropics?"

The young woman hesitated a heartbeat, then said, "Such drugs are very expensive."

"But I should think the government would provide them for security purposes, to keep the prisoners quiet."

A longer hesitation this time, then, "Yes, they do. My father sells the drugs at Ceres. They fetch a good price there."

"Your father?"

"The captain. He is my father."

Holy lord! Bracknell thought. *Good thing I haven't touched her. I'd arrive in Ceres in a body bag.*

The next morning the captain himself carried in his food tray and stayed to talk.

"She told you I'm her father," he said, standing by the bunk as Bracknell picked at the tray on his lap.

"She reports everything to you, doesn't she?" Bracknell replied.

"She doesn't have to. I watch you on the monitor when she's in here."

"Oh. I see."

"So do I. Every breath you draw. Remember that."

"She doesn't look like you."

The captain's scarred lip curled into a cold sneer. "Her mother was a Hindu. Met her in Delhi when I was running Clipperships there from the States. Once her parents found out she had married a Muslim they threw her out of their home."

"You're a Muslim?"

"All my life. My father and his father, too."

"And you married a Hindu."

"In India. Very tight situation. I wanted to take her back to the States but she was trying to get her parents to approve of our marriage. They wouldn't budge. I knew that, but she kept on trying."

"Is your wife on the ship, too?"

Without even an eyeblink's hesitation the captain answered, "She was killed in the food riots back in 'sixty-four. That's where I got this lip."

Bracknell didn't know what to say. He stared down at his tray.

"My daughter says I shouldn't be so hard on you."

Looking up into the captain's cold stone gray eyes, Bracknell said, "I think you've been treating me pretty well."

"Do you."

"You could have let them kill me, back in the hold."

"And lost the money I get when I deliver you? No way."

There didn't seem to be anything else to say. Bracknell picked up his plastic fork. Then a question arose in his mind.

"How did you break up the fight? I mean, how'd you stop them from killing me?"

With a sardonic huff, the captain said, "Soon's the automated alarm woke me up and I looked at the monitor, I turned down the air pressure in the hold until you all passed out. Brought it down to about four thousand meters' equivalent, Earth value."

Bracknell couldn't help grinning at him. "Good thing none of those guys were from the Andes."

"I'd've just lowered the pressure until everybody dropped," the captain evenly. "Might cause some brain damage, but I get paid to deliver live bodies, regardless of their mental capacities."

Alhambra arrived at Ceres at last and Bracknell was marched with the other convicts through the ship's airlock and into the *Chrysalis II* habitat.

The mining community that had grown at Ceres had built the habitat that orbited the asteroid. It was a mammoth ring-shaped structure that rotated so that there was a feeling of gravity inside: the same level as the Moon's, one-sixth of Earth normal.

Stumbling, walking haltingly in the unaccustomedly low gravity, the twenty-six men and women were led by a quartet of guards in coral-red coveralls into what looked to Bracknell like an auditorium. There was a raised platform at one end and rows of seats along the carpeted floor. The guards motioned with their stun wands for the prisoners to sit down. Most of them took seats toward the rear of the auditorium while the guards stationed themselves at the exits. Bracknell went down to the third row; no one else had chosen to sit so close to the stage.

For a few minutes nothing happened. Bracknell could hear half-whispered conversations behind him. The auditorium looked clean, sparkling, even though its walls and ceiling were bare tile. It even smelled new and fresh, although he realized the scent could be piped in through the air circulation system.

Just as the pitch of the chatter behind started to rise to the level of impatience, a huge mountain of a shaggy, red-haired man strode out onto the stage. Bracknell expected to see the stage's floorboards sag under his weight, even in the lunar-level gravity.

"My name's George Ambrose," he said, in a surprisingly sweet tenor voice. "For some obscure reason folks 'round here call me Big George."

A few wary laughs from the convicts.

"For my sins I've been elected chief administrator of this habitat. It's like bein' the mayor or the governor. Top dog. Which means everybody drops their fookin' problems in my lap."

Like the guards, George Ambrose wore coral-red coveralls, although his looked old and more than slightly faded. His brick-red hair was a wild thatch that merged with an equally thick beard.

Pointing at his audience, Ambrose continued, "You blokes've been sent here because you were found guilty of crimes. Each of you has been sentenced to a certain length of what they call penal servitude. That means you work for peanuts or less. Okay. I don't like havin' my home serve as a penal colony, but the powers-that-be back Earthside don't know what else to do with you. They sure don't want you anywhere near them!"

No one laughed.

"Okay. Here's the way we work it here in the Belt. We don't give a shit about your past. What's done is done. You're here and you're gonna work for the length of your sentence. Some of you got life, so you're gonna stay here in the Belt. The rest of you, if you work hard and keep your arses clean, you'll be able to go home with a clear file once you've served your time. You can't get rejuvenation treatments while you're serving time, of course, but we can rejuve you soon's your time's been served, if you can afford it. Fair enough?"

Bracknell heard muttering behind him. Then someone called out, "Do we get any choice in the jobs we get?"

Ambrose's shaggy brows rose slightly. "Some. We've got miners and other employers all across the Belt reviewin' your files. Some of 'em will make requests for you. If you get more'n one request you can take your choice. Only one, then you're stuck with it."

A deep, heavy voice asked, "Suppose I don't get any?"

"Then *I'll* have to deal with you," Ambrose replied. "Don't worry, there's plenty of work to be done out here. You won't sit around doin' nothing."

I'm here for life, Bracknell said to himself. I'll have to make a life for myself out here in the Belt. Maybe it's a good thing that I won't be allowed any rejuvenation treatments. I'll just get old and die out here.

JOB OFFER

The rest of the day, the convicts were led through medical exams and psychological interviews, then shown to the quarters they would live in until assigned to a job. Bracknell noted that each of the prisoners obeyed the guards' instructions without objection. *This is all new to them, and they don't know what to make of it,* he thought. *There's no sense making trouble and there's no place for them to run to. We're millions of klicks from Earth now; tens of millions of kilometers.*

They were served a decent meal in a cafeteria that had been cleared of all its regular customers. *No mixing with the local population,* Bracknell realized. *Not yet, at least.*

At the end of the long, strangely tense day, the guards led them down a long corridor faced with blank doors and assigned them to their sleeping quarters, two to a compartment. Bracknell was paired with a frail-looking older man, white haired and with skin that looked like creased and crumpled parchment.

The door closed behind them. He heard the lock click. Surveying the compartment, Bracknell saw a pair of bunks, a built-in desk and bureau, a folding door that opened onto the lavatory.

"Not bad," said his companion. He went to the lower bunk and sat on it possessively. "Kinda plush, after that bucket we rode here in."

Bracknell nodded tightly. "I'll take the upper bunk."

"Good. I got a fear of heights." The older man got up and went to the bureau. Opening the top drawer he exclaimed, "Look! They even got jammies for us!"

Trying to place the man's accent, Bracknell asked, "You're British?"

Frowning, the man replied, "Boston Irish. My name's Fennelly."

Bracknell extended his hand. "I'm—"

"I know who you are. You're the screamer."

Feeling embarrassed, Bracknell admitted, "I have nightmares."

"I'm a pretty heavy sleeper. Maybe that's why they put us in together."

"Maybe," Bracknell said.

"You're the guy from the skytower, ain'tcha."

"That's right."

"They arrested me for lewd and lascivious behavior," said Fennelly, with an exaggerated wink. "I'm gay."

"Homosexual?"

"That's right, kiddo. Watch your ass!" And Fennelly cackled as he walked to the lavatory, nearly stumbling in the light gravity.

In the top bunk with the lights out and the faintly glowing ceiling a bare meter above his head, Bracknell suddenly realized the ludicrousness of it all. Fennelly's down there wondering if I'm going to keep him up all night with my nightmares and I'm up here worried that he might try to make a pass at me. It was almost laughable.

If he did dream, Bracknell remembered nothing of it in the morning. They were awakened by a synthesized voice calling through the intercom, "Breakfast in thirty minutes in the cafeteria. Directions are posted on the display screens in the corridor."

The scrambled eggs were mediocre, but better than the fare they had gotten on the *Alhambra*. After breakfast the same quartet of guards took the convicts, one by one, to job interviews. Bracknell watched them leave the cafeteria until he was the only person left sitting at the long tables.

No one wants to take me on, he thought. I'm a pariah. Sitting alone with nothing to do, his mind drifted back to the skytower and its collapse, and the mockery of a trial that had condemned him to a life of exile. And Victor's betrayal. It was Victor's testimony that convicted me, he thought. Then he told himself, No, you were judged and sentenced before the first minute of the trial. But Victor did betray you, insisted a voice in his mind. He sat there and lied. Deliberately.

Why? Why? He was my friend. Why did he turn on me?

And Danvers. He reported to his New Morality superiors that we were using nanotechnology. In league with the devil, as far as he's concerned. Did the New Morality have something to do with the tower's collapse? Did they sabotage the skytower? No, they couldn't have. They wouldn't have. But somebody did. Suddenly Bracknell was convinced of it. Somebody deliberately sabotaged the tower! It couldn't have collapsed by itself. The construction was sound. Somebody sabotaged it.

One of the guards reappeared at the cafeteria's double doors and crooked a finger at him. Bracknell got to his feet and followed the guard down another corridor—or maybe it was merely an extension of the passageway he'd gone through earlier. It was impossible to get a feeling for the size or scope of this habitat from the inside, and he and his fellow convicts had not been allowed an outside view.

There were other people moving along this corridor, men in shirts and trousers, women wearing skirted dresses or blouses and slacks. He saw only a few in coveralls. They all looked as if they had someplace to go, some task to accomplish. That's what I must have looked like, back before the accident, Bracknell thought. Back when I had a life.

But it wasn't an accident, whispered a voice in his head. It wasn't your fault. The tower was deliberately destroyed.

He saw names on the doors lining both sides of the corridors. Some of the doors were open, revealing offices or conference rooms. This is where they run this habitat, he realized. Why is this guard bringing me here?

They stopped at a door marked CHIEF ADMINISTRATOR. The guard opened it without knocking. Inside was a sizable office: several desks with young men and women busily whispering into lip mikes. Their display screens showed charts and graphs in vivid colors. They glanced up at him and the guard, then quickly returned their attention to their work.

Gesturing for him to follow, the guard led Bracknell past their desks and to an inner door. No name on it. Again the guard opened it without knocking. It was obviously an anteroom. A matronly looking woman with short-cropped silver hair sat at the only desk, holding a conversation in low tones with another woman's image in her display screen. Beyond her desk was still another door, also unmarked.

She looked up and, without missing a beat of her conversation, touched a button on her phone console. The inner door popped open a few centimeters. The guard shooed Bracknell to it.

Pushing the door all the way open, Bracknell saw George Ambrose sitting behind a desk that looked too small for his bulk, like a man sitting at a child's play desk. He was speaking to his desktop screen.

"Come on in and sit down," Ambrose said. "Be with you in a sec." Turning his gaze to his desktop screen he said, "Save file. Clear screen."

The display went dark as Bracknell took the contoured chair in front of the desk. It gave slightly under his weight. Ambrose swiveled his high-backed chair to face Bracknell squarely.

"I've got a message for you," Ambrose said.

"From Lara?"

Shaking his shaggy head, Ambrose said, "Convicts aren't allowed messages from Earthside, normally. But this one is from some New Morality bloke, the Reverend Elliott Danvers."

"Oh." The surge of hope that Bracknell felt faded away.

"D'you want to see it in privacy?"

"No, it doesn't matter."

Pointing to the wall on Bracknell's right, Ambrose said, "Okay, then, here it is."

Danvers' slightly bloated, slightly flushed face appeared on the wall screen. Bracknell felt his innards tighten.

"Mance—if you don't mind me calling you by your first name—I hope this message finds you well and healthy after your long journey to Ceres. I know this is a time of turmoil and anguish for you, but I want you to realize that you are not alone, not forgotten. In your hour of need, you may call on me. Whenever you feel the need of council, or prayer, or even just the need to hear a familiar voice, call me. The New Morality will pay the charges. Call me whenever you wish."

Danvers's image disappeared, replaced by the cross-and-scroll logo of the New Morality.

Bracknell stared at the screen for a few heartbeats, then turned back to Ambrose. "That's the entire message?"

Nodding, "Looks it. I di'n't open it till you got here."

Bracknell said nothing.

"D'you want to send an answer? It'll take about an hour to reach Earth."

"No. No answer."

"You sure?"

"That man's testimony helped convict me."

Ambrose shook his red-maned head. "Way it looks to me, you were convicted before the trial even started. They needed a scapegoat. Can't have four million deaths and chalk it up as an act of god."

Bracknell stared at the man. It was difficult to tell the color of his eyes beneath those bushy red brows.

"Well, anyway," Ambrose said more cheerfully, "I got a job offer for you."

"A job offer?"

"Only one. You're not a really popular fella, y'know."

"That means I'll have to take the job whether I want to or not."

"'Fraid so."

Taking in a breath, Bracknell asked, "What is it?"

"Skipper of the ship you came in on. Says he needs a new third mate."

Blinking with surprise, Bracknell said, "I don't know much about spacecraft."

"You'll learn on the job. It's a good offer, a lot better than spendin' half your life in a suit runnin' nanobugs on some chunk o' rock."

"The captain of the *Alhambra* asked for me? Me, specifically?"

"That he did."

"Why on Earth would he do that?" Bracknell wondered.

"You're not on Earth, mate. Take the job and be glad of it. You got no choice."

THE BELT

A t first Bracknell half-thought, half-feared, that he'd been brought to the *Alhambra* to become a husband for the captain's daughter. His first day aboard the ship disabused him of that notion.

Bracknell was taken from the habitat by one of the coraluniformed guards to an airlock, where he retraced his steps of a few days earlier and returned to the *Alhambra*. The captain was standing at the other end of the connector tunnel with his hands clasped behind his back, waiting for him with a sour expression on his lean, pallid face.

"I'm taking you on against my better judgment," said the captain as he walked with Bracknell toward the ship's bridge. Bracknell saw that he gripped a stun wand in his right hand. "Only the fact that my third man jumped his contract and took off for Earthside has made me desperate enough to do this."

Bracknell began, "I appreciate—"

"You will address me as Sir or Captain," the captain interrupted. "The computers do most of the brainwork aboard ship, but you will still have to learn astrogation, logistics, communications, propulsion, and life support. If you goof off or prove too stupid to master these subjects I'll sell you off to the first work gang on the first rock we rendezvous with. Is that clear?"

"Perfectly clear," said Bracknell. Then, seeing the captain's eyes flare, he hastily added, "Sir."

Captain Farad stopped at a door in the corridor. "This is your quarters. You will maintain it in shipshape condition at all times. You'll find clothing in there. It should fit you; if it doesn't, alter it. I'll expect you on the bridge, ready to begin your duties, in half an hour."

"Yes, sir," said Bracknell.

Alhambra departed Ceres that day, heading deeper into the Belt to begin picking up metals and minerals from mining crews at various asteroids. For the next several weeks Bracknell studied the computer's files on all he was supposed to learn, and took regular stints of duty on the bridge, always under the sternly watchful eyes of Captain Farad. He saw nothing of the captain's daughter.

He spent virtually all of his spare time learning about the ship and its systems. Like most deep-space vessels, *Alhambra* consisted of two modules balanced on either side of a five-kilometer-long buckyball tether, rotating to produce an artificial gravity inside them. One module held the crew's quarters and the cargo hold that was often used to hold convicts outward bound to the Belt. The other module contained supplies and what had once been a smelter facility. The smelter had become useless since the introduction of nanomachines to reduce asteroids to purified metals and minerals.

The captain assigned Bracknell to the communications console at first. It was highly automated; all Bracknell had to do was watch the screens and make certain that there was always a steaming mug of coffee in the receptacle built into the left arm of the captain's command chair.

Through the round ports set into the bridge's bulkhead Bracknell could see outside: nothing but dark emptiness out there. The deeply tinted quartz windows cut out all but the brightest stars. There were plenty of them to see, but somehow they seemed to accentuate the cold darkness out there rather than alleviate it. No Moon in that empty sky. No warmth or comfort. For days on end he didn't even see an asteroid, despite being in the thick of the so-called Belt.

Bracknell didn't see the captain's daughter either until the day one of the crew's family got injured.

He was gazing morosely through the port at the endless emptiness out there when an alarm started hooting, startling him like a sudden electric shock.

"What's going on there, Number Three?" the captain growled.

Bracknell saw that one of the keys on his console was blinking red. He leaned a thumb on it and his center screen showed two women kneeling beside the unconscious body of what appeared to be a teenaged boy. His face was covered with blood.

"We've had an accident!" one of the women was shouting, looking up into the camera set far above her. "Emergency! We need help down here!"

"What the hell's going on over there?" the captain growled. Pointing at Bracknell, he commanded, "Get into a suit and go across to them."

"Me?" he piped.

"No, Jesus Christ and the twelve apostles. You, dammit! Get moving! Take a medical kit and a VR rig. Addie will handle whatever medical aid the kid needs."

That was how Bracknell learned the name of the captain's daughter: Addie.

He jumped from his comm console chair and loped to the main airlock. It took several minutes for him to wriggle into one of the nanofabric spacesuits stored in the lockers there, and minutes more for him to locate the medical kit and virtual reality rig stored nearby. Through the ship's intercom the captain swore and yelled at him every microsecond of the time.

"The kid could bleed to death by the time you get your dumb ass there!"

It was scary riding the trolley along the five-kilometer-long tether that connected the ship's two rotating units. The trolley was nothing more than a platform with a minuscule electric motor propelling it. With nothing protecting him except the flimsy nanofiber suit, Bracknell felt like a turkey wrapped in a plastic bag inside a microwave oven. He knew that high-energy radiation was sleeting down on him from the pale, distant Sun and the still-more-distant stars. He hoped that the suit's radiation protection was as good as its manufacturer claimed.

At last he reached the smelter unit and clambered through its airlock hatch. He felt much safer inside.

Despite its being unused for several years, the smelter bay was still gritty and smeared with dark swaths of sooty dust. As Bracknell pulled down the hood of his monomolecular-thin suit, a heavy, pungent odor filled his nostrils. The boy was semiconscious by the time Bracknell reached him. The two women were still kneeling by him. They had cleaned most of the blood from his face.

Clamping the VR rig around his head so that its camera was positioned just above his eyes, Bracknell asked, "What happened?"

One of the women pointed to the catwalk that circled high above the smelting ovens. "He fell."

"How in the world could he fall from up there?"

The woman snapped, "He's a teenaged boy. He was playing a game with his brother."

"Thank the Lord we're running at one-sixth g," said the other woman.

Then Bracknell heard the captain's daughter's voice in his earplug. "The bleeding seems stopped. We must test to see if he has a concussion."

For the better part of an hour Bracknell followed Addie's instructions. The boy had a concussion, all right, and a bad laceration on his scalp. Probably not a fractured skull, but they would X-ray him once they had him safely in the infirmary. No other bones seemed to be broken, although his right knee was badly swollen.

At Addie's direction he sprayed a bandage over the laceration and inflated a temporary splint onto the leg. With the women's help he got the still-groggy kid into a nanosuit. All three of them carried him to the airlock and strapped him onto the trolley.

Clinging to the trolley by a handhold, Bracknell again rode the length of the ship's connecting tether, surrounded by swarms of stars that gazed unblinkingly down at him. And invisible radiation that could kill him in an instant if his suit's protection failed. He tried not to think about that. He gazed at the stars and wished he could appreciate their beauty. One of them was Earth, he knew, but he couldn't tell which one it was.

Addie and the captain were waiting for him at the airlock on the other end of the tether. Together they carried the boy to the infirmary that had once been Bracknell's isolation cell and left him in Addie's care.

"What's a teenaged boy doing aboard the ship, captain?" Bracknell asked as he peeled himself out of the nanosuit, back at the airlock.

"My number one sails with his family. They make their quarters in the old smelter. Cheaper for him than paying rent at Ceres, and his wife's aboard to keep him company."

A cozy arrangement, Bracknell thought. But boys can get themselves into trouble. I'll bet they don't sail with us on the next trip from Ceres.

"Your shift on the bridge is just about finished," the captain said gruffly, as they headed back toward the bridge. "You might as well go back to your quarters. I can get along on the bridge without you."

It wasn't until he was back in his quarters, after a quick stop at the galley for some hot soup, that Bracknell realized his duty shift still had more than two hours to run.

Was the captain being kind to me? he wondered.

PURGATORY

His life had no purpose, Bracknell realized. He breathed, he ate, he slept, he worked on the bridge of *Alhambra* under the baleful scrutiny of Captain Farad. But why? What was the point of it? He lived for no reason, no goal, drifting through the cold dark emptiness of the Belt, sailing from one nameless chunk of rock to another, meaninglessly. He was like an automaton, working his brain-numbingly dull tasks as if under remote control while his mind churned the same agonizing visions over and over again: the tower, the collapse, the crushed and bleeding bodies.

Sometimes he thought of Lara and wondered what she was doing. Then he would tell himself that he wanted her to forget him, to build a new life for herself. One of the terms of his exile was that neither Lara nor anyone else he'd known on Earth would be told where he was. He was cut off from all communication with his former friends and associates; he was totally banished. For all those who once knew him on Earth, Mance Bracknell was dead and gone forever.

Except for Rev. Danvers. *He got a message through to me; maybe he'll accept a message from me.* Bracknell tried to put that out of his mind. What good would it do to talk to the minister? Besides, Danvers had helped to convict him. Maybe his call was in response to a guilty conscience, Bracknell thought. *Damn the man!* Better to be totally cut off than to have this slim hope of some communication, some link with his old life. Danvers was torturing him, holding out that meaningless thread of hope.

Now and then, between duty shifts and always with the captain's permission, Bracknell would pull on one of the nanofabric spacesuits and go outside the ship. Hanging at the end of a tether he would gaze out at the stars, an infinite universe of stars and worlds beyond counting. It made him feel small, insignificant, a meaningless mote in the vast spinning galaxy. He learned to find the blue dot that was Earth. It made him feel worse than ever. It reminded him of how alone he was, how far from warmth and love and hope. In time, he stopped his outside excursions. He feared that one day he would open his suit and let the universe end his existence.

The only glimmer of sunshine in his new life was the captain's daughter, Addie. Although *Alhambra* was a sizable ship, most of its volume was taken up by cargo holds and the smelting facility where the first mate's family lived. The crew numbered only twelve, at most, and often Farad sailed without a full complement of crew. The habitation module was small, almost intimate. Bracknell knew there were liaisons between crew members; he himself had been propositioned more than once, by men as well as women. He had always refused. None of them tempted him at all. He saw relationships form among crew members, both hetero and homosexual. He saw them break apart, too, sometimes in bitterness and sorrow, more than once in violence that the captain had to suppress with force.

Once in a while he bumped into Addie, quite literally, as they squeezed past one another in the ship's narrow passageways or happened to be in the galley at the same time. She always had a bright smile for him on her dark, almond-eyed face. Her figure was enticingly full and supple. Yet he never spoke more than a few words of polite conversation to her, never let himself react to the urgings of his glands.

One day, as he left the bridge after another tediously boring stint of duty, Bracknell ducked into the galley for a cup of coffee. Addie was sitting at the little square table, sipping from a steaming mug.

"How's the coffee today?" Bracknell asked.

"It's tea."

"Oh." He picked out a mug and poured from the ceramic urn, then pulled a chair out and sat next to her. Addie's eyes flicked to the open hatch and for an instant Bracknell thought she was going to jump to her feet and flee.

Instead, she seemed to relax, at least a little.

"Life on this ship isn't terribly exciting, is it?" he said.

"No, I suppose it isn't."

For long moments neither one of them knew what to say. At last Bracknell asked, "Your name—Addie. Is it short for Adelaide?"

She broke into an amused smile. "No, certainly not. My full name is Aditi."

"Aditi?"

"It is a Hindu name. It means 'free and unbounded.' It is the name of the mother of the gods."

Hindu, Bracknell thought. Of course. The captain told me she's from India. That explains the lilt in her accent.

"Free and unbounded," he echoed. "Kind of ironic, here on this nutshell of a ship."

"Yes," she agreed forlornly. Then she brightened. "But my father is making arrangements for me to marry. He has amassed a large dowry for me. In another few years I will be wed to a wealthy man and live in comfort back on Earth."

"You're engaged?"

"Oh, no, not yet. My father hasn't found the proper man for me. But he is seeking one out."

"And you'll marry whoever he picks?"

"Yes, of course."

"Don't you want to pick your husband for yourself?"

Her smile turned slightly remorseful. "What chance do I have for that, aboard this ship?"

Bracknell had to admit she was right.

He went back to his quarters, but before he could close the door, the captain pushed against it, glowering at him.

"I told you to keep away from my daughter."

"She was in the galley," Bracknell explained. "We spoke a few words together."

"About marriage."

"Yes." Bracknell felt his temper rising. "She's waiting for you to find her a husband."

"She'll have to wait a few more years. Fifteen's too young for marriage. Maybe it's old enough in India, but where I come from—"

"Fifteen? She's only fifteen?"

"That's right."

"How can she be a doctor . . . ?"

The captain's twisted lip sneered at him. "She's smart enough to run the computer's medical diagnostics. Like most doctors, she lets the computer program make the decisions."

"But—"

"You keep your distance from her."

"Yes, *sir*," Bracknell said fervently. Fifteen, he was thinking. That voluptuous body is only fifteen years old.

"Remember, I watch everything you do," the captain said. "Stay away from her."

He left Bracknell's quarters as abruptly as he'd entered. Bracknell stood there alone, shaking inside at the thought that a fifteen-year-old could look so alluring.

He was the family's oldest retainer, a wizened, wrinkled man with a flowing white mane that swept past the shoulders of his modest sky-blue kimono. Nobuhiko remembered riding on those shoulders when he'd been a tot. The man had never accepted rejuvenation treatments, but his shoulders were still broad and only slightly sagging.

They walked together along the gravel path that wound through the carefully tended rock garden just inside the high wall that sheltered the Yamagata estate in the hills above New Kyoto. A cutting, clammy wind was blowing low gray clouds across the sky; Nobuhiko suppressed the urge to shiver beneath his light gray business suit. He had never shown such a weakness before his servant and he never willingly would.

Never show a weakness to anyone, he reminded himself. Not even yourself. He had been shocked when he learned that four million had been killed by the skytower's collapse. Four million! Nobu had known there would be deaths, that was unavoidable. It was what the military called "collateral damage." But four million! It had taken years to overcome the sense of guilt that had risen inside him like a tidal wave, threatening to engulf him. What difference does it make? he argued against his own conscience. Four hundred or four thousand or four million? They would have died anyway, sooner or later. The world goes on. I did what I had to do. For the good of the family, for the good of the corporation. For the good of Japan, even. What's done is done.

It hadn't been finished easily, he knew. There were still more lives that had to be snuffed out, loyal men and women whose only offense had been to carry out Nobuhiko's wishes. They were repaid with death, the ultimate silencer. But now it's done, Nobuhiko thought. It's finished at last. That's what this old man has come to tell me.

Once they were too far from the house to be overheard, Nobu said politely, "The years have been very kind to you."

The old man dipped his chin slightly. "You are very gracious, sir."

With a wry grin, Nobu patted his belly. "I wish I could be as fit as you are."

The man said nothing. They both knew that Yamagata's tastes in food and wine, and his distaste for exercise, caused the difference between their figures.

Delicately changing the subject, the old man asked, "May I inquire as to your father's well-being?"

Nobu looked up at the sky. This man had served his father since he'd been a teenager. He still regards Saito as the head of the family, Nobu thought, no matter that Father has been retired in that lamasery for so many years.

"My father is well," he said at last. It was not a lie, although Nobu had not heard from his father for many months.

"I am pleased to hear it. He has great strength of character to abandon this world and take the hard path toward enlightenment."

And I do not have strength of character? Nobu snarled inwardly. Is this old assassin throwing an insult into my teeth?

Aloud, however, he said merely, "Yet some of us must remain in this world and carry its burdens."

"Most true, sir."

"How many years has it been since the skytower fell?" Nobuhiko asked.

"Not enough for anyone to dare suggest building another."

"So. That is good."

The old man dipped his chin again in acknowledgement.

"Have all the people who participated in the event been properly disposed of?"

"They have been tracked down and accounted for." Both men knew what that meant.

"All of them?"

The old man hesitated only a fraction of a second. "All but one."

"One?" Nobu snapped, suddenly angry. "After all this time, one of them still lives?"

"He is either very clever or very lucky."

"Who is he? Where is he?"

"He is the nanotechnology expert that we recruited from Selene."

Nobu could feel his pulse thundering in his ears. Before he could respond to his servant's words the old man added:

"He has changed his identity and his appearance several times. Even his retinal patterns have been altered, my agents report. The man is something of a genius."

"He must be found," Nobu said firmly. "And dealt with."

"He will be, I assure you."

"I don't want assurances. I want results!"

"Sir, please do not alarm yourself. The man is neutralized. He cannot tell anyone of his part in the skytower project without revealing his true identity. If he should dare to do that, we would locate him and deal with him. He is intelligent enough to understand that, so he maintains his silence."

"Not good enough," said Nobu. "I will not be held dependent on this fugitive's decisions."

"So I understand, sir. We are tracking him down."

"No one must know *why* are tracking him!"

"No one does, sir, except you and me."

Nobuhiko took a deep breath, trying to calm himself.

The old man added, "And once he is found and disposed of, I too will leave this world. Then only you will have the knowledge of the skytower program."

"You?"

"I have lived long enough. Once this obligation to you is filled, my master, I will join my honorable ancestors."

Nobu stood on the gravel path and stared at this relic from the ancient past. The chill wind blew the man's long white hair across his face, hiding his expression from Nobu. Still, Yamagata could see the implacable determination in those unblinking eyes.

BETRAYAL

Months slipped into years. *Alhambra* plied its slow, silent way through the Belt and then back toward Earth at least once a year. Bracknell saw the blue and white splendor of his home world, close enough almost to touch, bright clouds and sparkling seas and land covered with green. All his life was there, all his hopes and love and dreams. But he never reached it. The captain and other crew members shuttled down to the surface for a few days each time they visited Earth, but Bracknell stayed aboard the ship, knowing that no port of entry would accept an exile, not even for a day or two of ship's liberty. Nor would Selene or any of the other lunar settlements.

Each time, once *Alhambra*'s crew unloaded the refined metals it had carried in its hold and taken a few days' liberty, Captain Farad headed back to the dark silence of the Belt once more.

Like a vision of heaven, Bracknell said to himself as the glowing blue and white sphere dwindled in the distance. It grew blurry as his eyes teared.

He grew a beard, then shaved it off. He had a brief affair with a woman who signed aboard as a crew member to pay for her passage on a one-way trip from Earth to Ceres, feeling almost ashamed of himself whenever he saw Addie. By the time his erstwhile lover left the ship he was glad to be rid of her.

The captain never relaxed his vigilance over his daughter, although he seemed to grow more tolerant of Bracknell holding casual conversations with her. He even invited Bracknell to have dinner with himself and his daughter, at rare intervals. The captain was sensitive enough never to talk about Earth nor to ask Bracknell about his former life.

Addie began to explain Buddhism to him, trying to help him accept the life that had been forced upon him.

"It is only temporary," she would tell him. "This life will wither away and a new life will begin. The great wheel turns slowly, but it does turn. You must be patient."

Bracknell listened and watched her animated face as she earnestly explained the path toward enlightenment. He never believed a word of it, but it helped to pass the time.

On some visits to Earth, *Alhambra* picked up other groups of convicts exiled to the Belt. The captain forbade Bracknell and the other crew members to have anything to do with them beyond what was absolutely necessary.

When fights broke out among the prisoners in the hold, the captain lowered their air pressure until everyone passed out. Then Bracknell and other crew members crammed the troublemakers into old-fashioned hard-shell spacesuits and tethered them outside the ship until they learned their lesson. It had happened many times, but Bracknell never became inured to it. Always he thought, There but for the grace of god go I.

Then he would ask himself, God? If there is a god he must be as callous and capricious as the most sadistic tyrant in history. At least the Buddha that Addie tells me about doesn't pretend to control the world; he just sought a way to get out of it.

There is a way, Bracknell would remind himself late at night as he lay in his bunk, afraid to close his eyes and see again in his nightmares the skytower toppling, crushing the life out of so many millions, crushing the life he had once known. I can get out of this, he thought. Slice my wrists, swallow a bottle of pills from Addie's infirmary, seal myself in an airlock and pop the outer hatch. There are lots of ways to end this existence.

Yet he kept on living. Like a man on an endless treadmill he kept going through the paces of a pointless life, condemning himself for a coward because he lacked the guts to get off the wheel of life and find oblivion.

Except for Addie he had no friends, no companions. The captain tolerated him, even socialized with him now and then, but always kept a clear line of separation between them. The women that occasionally joined the crew hardly appealed to him, except when his needs overcame his reluctance. And even in the throes of sexual passion he thought of Lara.

If I could only see her, he thought. Talk to her. Even if it's only a few words.

In the midst of his tortured fantasies he remembered the old message from Rev. Danvers, back when he'd just started this miserable banishment. Call me, the minister had said. Despite the fact that he was supposed to be held incommunicado with everyone back on Earth, Danvers had held out that slim hope.

Bracknell was wise enough in the ways of his captain to ask Farad's permission before attempting to contact Danvers.

The captain snorted disdainfully. "Call somebody Earthside? Won't do you any good, they won't put the call through."

Desperate enough to overcome his fears, Bracknell replied, "You could put the call through for me, sir."

The captain scowled at him and said nothing. Bracknell returned to his duties, defeated.

Yet the next day, as Bracknell took up his station on the bridge, the captain said, "Take the comm console, Mr. Bracknell."

Feeling more curiosity than hope, Bracknell relieved the communications officer. The captain told him to put through a call for him to the Reverend Danvers, routing it through New Morality headquarters in Atlanta. His fingers trembling, Bracknell wormed the speaker plug into his ear and got to work.

With more than an hour's transit time for messages, there was no hope of a normal conversation. It took half his duty shift for Bracknell to get through to the communications program at Atlanta and learn that Danvers was now a bishop serving in Gabon, on Africa's west coast.

When Danvers's ruddy face finally came up on Bracknell's screen, the captain called from his command chair, "Go ahead and see if he'll talk to you."

Danvers was sitting at a polished ebony desk, wearing an open-necked black shirt with some sort of insignia pinned to the points of his collar. Behind him a window looked down on the busy streets and buildings of Libreville and, beyond, the blue Atlantic's white-frothed combers rolling up on a beach. A dark cylindrical form snaked through the greenery beyond the city and disappeared in the frothing surf. Bracknell's heart clutched inside him: it was the remains of the fallen skytower, still lying there after all these years.

It took more hours of one-way messages and long waits between them before Danvers realized who was calling him.

"Mance!" Surprise opened his eyes wide. "After so many years! I'm delighted to hear from you." The bishop turned slightly in his high-backed chair. "You can probably see the remains of the skytower. It's a tourist attraction here. People come from all over Africa to see it."

Bracknell's insides smoldered. A tourist attraction.

"The locals have stripped a lot from it. Filthy scavengers. We've had to post guards to protect the ruins, but still they sneak in and rip off parts."

Bracknell closed his eyes, trying to keep his temper under control. No sense getting angry with Danvers; he can't help the situation. Get to the point, tell him why you've contacted him.

He took a breath, then plunged in. "I was wondering, hoping, that you might get a message to Lara Tierney for me," he said, embarrassed at how much it sounded like begging. "I don't know where she is now, but I thought perhaps you could find her and give her a message for me."

Then he waited. His shift on the bridge ended and his replacement arrived at the comm console but the captain silently waved the woman away. Bracknell sat there attending to the ship's normal communications while his eyes constantly flicked back to the screen where Bishop Danvers's image sat frozen.

At last the attention light beneath that screen went from orange to green. The bishop's image shimmered slightly and became animated. But his expression looked doubtful, uncertain.

"Mance, she's Lara Molina now. She and Victor married more than eighteen months ago. I performed the ceremony."

Bracknell felt his face redden with sudden anger.

"Under the circumstances," Bishop Danvers continued, "I don't think it would be wise for you to contact her. After all, it would be illegal, wouldn't it? And there's no sense bringing up old heartaches, opening old wounds. After all, it's taken her all this time to get you out of her mind and begin her life again. Don't you agree that it would be better if you—"

Bracknell cut the connection with a vicious stab of his thumb on the keyboard.

Married, his mind echoed. She married Victor. The man who betrayed me. And that pompous idiot performed the ceremony. He betrayed me, too. They've all betrayed me!

REVELATION

For weeks Bracknell stormed through his duties aboard *Alhambra*, raging inwardly at Molina and Danvers. He wanted to be angry with Lara, too; he wanted to be furious with her. Yet he found he couldn't be. He couldn't expect her to live out the rest of her life alone. But with Victor? She married that lying, back-stabbing son of a bitch?

She doesn't realize that Victor betrayed me, Bracknell told himself; Lara doesn't know that Victor lied in his testimony at the trial. But Victor knew, and so did Danvers. Of that Bracknell was certain. They had combined to put him out of the way so that Victor could have Lara for himself.

Bracknell understood it all now. Victor betrayed him because he wanted Lara for himself. Once the skytower collapsed, Victor had the perfect opportunity to get me out of his way forever. And Danvers helped him, of that Bracknell was certain.

Once the skytower collapsed, he repeated to himself. Could they have *made* the tower collapse? Caused it? Sabotaged it? Bracknell wrestled with that idea for weeks on end. No. How could they? Victor didn't know enough about the tower's construction to bring it down. He's a biologist, not a structural engineer. It would take a team of trained saboteurs, demolition experts. It would take money and planning and a ruthless cold-bloodedness that was frighteningly beyond Victor's capability. Or Danvers's. He doubted that even the New Morality at its most fanatical had the viciousness to deliberately bring the tower down. Or the competence.

No, Bracknell concluded. Victor simply took advantage of his opportunity. Took advantage of me. And Danvers helped him.

Still, his rage boiled inside him, made him morose and curt with everyone around him, even Addie. The captain watched his new attitude and said nothing, except once, when Bracknell was assigned to escorting a new group of convicts into their makeshift quarters down in the hold. One of the prisoners started a scuffle with another one. Bracknell dove into them swinging his stun wand like a club and beat them both unconscious.

"You're starting to come back to life," the captain said after a pair of husky crewmen had pulled him off the bleeding prisoners. He made a strange, twisted smile. "You're starting to feel pain again."

"I've felt pain before," Bracknell muttered as they trudged up the passageway toward the bridge.

"Maybe," said the captain. "But now you can feel the demon gnawing at your guts. Now you know how I felt when they killed my wife. How I still feel."

Bracknell stared at him with new understanding.

Back and forth through the Belt sailed *Alhambra*, and then set out on the long, tedious journey to Earth to deliver refined metals and pick up convicts. It seemed to Bracknell, when he thought about it, that there were always more convicts waiting to be sent out to the Belt, always more men and women who'd run afoul of the law. Teenagers, too. The governments of Earth had found a convenient way to get rid of troublemakers: dump them out in the Asteroid Belt. They must be making the laws tighter all the time, more restrictive, he thought. Or maybe they're just using banishment to the Belt instead of other punishments.

On one of *Alhambra*'s stops at Earth, still another set of convicts was herded into the empty cargo hold—sixteen men and eleven women, most of them looking too frightened to cause any trouble. Only two of the bunch had been guilty of violent crimes: a strong-arm mugger and a murderer who had stabbed her boyfriend to death.

Bracknell was surprised, then, when the alarm hooted shortly after they had locked the prisoners in the hold. From his duty station on the bridge he looked over at the intercom screen. Two men were beating up a third, a tall, skinny scarecrow of a man. He saw their hapless victim trying to defend himself by wrapping his long arms around his head, but his two attackers knocked him to the metal deck with a rain of vicious body blows, then began kicking him.

"Get down there!" the captain snapped to Bracknell as he tapped on the controls set into the armrest of his command chair. Bracknell jumped up from his own seat, ducked through the hatch and sprinted toward the hold. He knew that the captain was dropping the air pressure in there hard enough to pop eardrums. They'll all be unconscious by the time I get to the hold, he thought.

He could hear the footfalls of two other crewmen following him down the passageway. Stopping at the hatch only long enough to slip on the oxygen masks hanging on the wall, the three of them opened the hatch and pulled out three of the unconscious bodies: the bloodied scarecrow and his two attackers. Leaving the other crewmen to deal with the attackers, Bracknell picked up the victim and started running toward the infirmary. The man was as light as a bird, nothing but skin and bones.

Addie was waiting at the infirmary. She allowed Bracknell to lay the unconscious man on one of the two beds there as she powered up the diagnostic sensors built into the bulkhead.

"You should get back to the bridge," she said to Bracknell as she began strapping the man down.

"As soon as he's secure," Bracknell said, fastening a strap across the man's frail chest. "He's a prisoner, after all."

The man moaned wretchedly but did not open his eyes. Bracknell saw that they were both swollen shut, and his nose appeared to be broken. Blood covered most of his face and was spattered over his gray prison-issue coveralls.

"Go!" Addie said in an urgent whisper. "I can take care of him now."

Bracknell headed back to the bridge. By the time he slid back into the chair before his console, he could see that the other convicts were stirring in the hold, regaining consciousness as the air pressure returned to normal. The two attackers were already sealed into hardshell space-suits and being dragged to an airlock.

"What started the fight?" he wondered aloud.

"What difference does it make?" the captain retorted. "It wasn't much of a fight, anyway. Looked to me like those two gorillas wanted to beat the scarecrow to death. He probably tried to proposition them."

Half an hour later Bracknell punched up the outside camera view. One of the spacesuited figures was floating inertly at the end of a buckyball tether. The other had crawled along the length of his tether and was pounding at the airlock hatch with a gloved fist.

"Too bad there's no radio in his suit," the captain remarked sourly. "I imagine we'd pick up some choice vocabulary."

Once his shift was finished, Bracknell headed for his quarters. As he passed the open door of the infirmary, though, Addie called to him.

He stopped at the doorway and saw that she was at the minuscule desk in the infirmary's anteroom, the glow from the desktop screen casting an eerie greenish light on her face.

"You were the chief of the skytower project, weren't you," Addie said. It was not a question.

His insides twitched, but Bracknell answered evenly, "Yes. And this is where it got me."

"Permanently exiled from Earth."

He nodded wordlessly.

Glancing over her shoulder at the open doorway to the infirmary's beds, Addie said, "The man you brought in, he keeps mumbling something about the skytower."

"Lots of people remember the skytower," Bracknell said bitterly. "It was the biggest disaster in history."

She shook her head. "But this man is not who he claims to be in his prison file."

"What do you mean?"

"The patient in the infirmary," she said, "keeps babbling about the skytower. He says they want to kill him because he knows about the skytower."

"Knows what?"

Addie's almond eyes were steady, somber. "I don't know. But I thought that you would want to speak with him."

"You're damned right I do."

She got up from the desk and Bracknell followed her into the infirmary. Her patient was asleep or unconscious as they squeezed into the cramped compartment. The other bed was unoccupied. Medical monitors beeped softly. The place had that sterile smell of antiseptics overlaying the metallic tang of blood.

Bracknell saw a tall, very slim, long-limbed man stretched out on the narrow infirmary bed. He was still in the clothes he'd been wearing when he'd been hurt: a pair of gray coveralls, wrinkled and dark with perspiration, spattered with his own blood. His face was battered, swollen, a bandage sprayed over one lacerated brow, another along the length of his broken nose. His body was immobilized by the restraining straps, and a slim plastic intravenous tube was inserted in his left forearm.

Addie called up the diagnostic computer and scans of the man's body sprang up on the wall beside his bed.

"He has severe internal injuries," she said, in a whisper. "They did a thorough job of beating him. A few more minutes and he would have died."

"Will he make it?"

"The computer's prognosis is not favorable. I have called back to Selene to ask for a medevac flight, but I doubt that they will go to the trouble for a prisoner."

Bracknell asked, "What's his name?"

"That's just it," she said, with a tiny frown that creased the bridge of her nose. "I'm not certain. His prison file shows him as Jorge Quintana, but when I ran a scan of his DNA profile the Earthside records came up with the name Toshikazu Koga."

"Japanese?"

"Japanese descent, third generation American. Raised in Selene, where he graduated with honors in molecular engineering."

Bracknell gaped at her. "Nanotechnology?"

"I believe so."

Bracknell stared down at the unconscious convict. He did not look Asian, there were no epicanthic folds in his closed eyes. Yet there was an odd, unsettling quality about his face. The skin was stretched tight over prominent cheekbones and a square jaw that somehow looked subtly wrong for the rest of his face, as if someone had roughed it out and pasted it onto him. The color of his skin was strange, too, a mottled gray. Bracknell had never seen a skin tone like it.

He looked back at Addie. "Can you wake him up?"

THE PRISONER'S TALE

They'll kill me sooner or later," said Toshikazu Koga, his voice little more than a painfully labored whisper. "There's no place left that I can run to."

Bracknell was bending over his infirmary bed to hear him better. Addie sat on the other, unused bed.

"Who wants to kill you?" she asked. "Why?"

"The skytower—"

"What do you know about the skytower?" Bracknell demanded.

"I was a loyal follower, a Believer . . ."

"What about the skytower?"

"I didn't know. I should have guessed." Toshikazu coughed. "Truth is, I didn't want to know."

It took all of Bracknell's self-control to keep from grabbing the man by the shoulders and shaking his story out of him.

"What was it that you didn't want to know?" Addie asked gently.

"All that money. They wouldn't pay all that money for something legitimate. I should have refused. I should have . . ." His voice faded away.

"Damn!" Bracknell snapped. "He's passed out again."

Addie's eyes flicked to the monitors on the wall. "We must let him rest."

"But he knows something about the skytower! Something to do with nanotechnology and the tower."

Getting up from the bed and looking him squarely in the eyes, Addie said, "We'll learn nothing from him if he dies. Let him rest. Let me try to save his life."

Knowing she was right despite his desperate desire to wring the truth out of the unconscious patient, Bracknell nodded tightly. "Let me know when he comes to."

He got as far as the doorway to the anteroom, then turned. "And don't let anyone else near him. No one!"

She looked alarmed at the vehemence of his command.

Little by little, in bits and pieces over the next two days, they wormed Toshikazu's story out of him while Addie repeatedly called to Selene to beg for a medevac mission before *Alhambra* coasted too far from the Moon.

"The best I can do is stabilize him. He'll die unless he gets proper medical help."

Bracknell hoped he'd stay alive long enough to reveal what he knew about the skytower.

Toshikazu Koga had been an engineer in Selene's nanotechnology laboratory, working mainly on nanomachines designed to separate pure metals out of the ores in asteroids. Instead of the rock rats digging out the ores and smelting them the old-fashioned way, nanomachines could pull out individual atoms of a selected metal while the human miners waited and watched from the comforts of their spacecraft.

Toshikazu was also a Believer, a devout, churchgoing member of the New Morality. Although his fellow churchgoers disapproved of nanotechnology, he saw nothing wrong with its practice on the Moon or elsewhere in space.

"It's not like we're on Earth, with ten billion people jammed in cheek by jowl," he would tell those who scowled at his profession. "Here on the Moon nanomachines produce the air we breathe and the water we drink. They separate helium three from the regolith sands to power the fusion generators. And now I'm helping the miners in the Asteroid Belt, making their lives safer and more profitable."

But there was another side to his nanotech work. His brother Takeo ran a lucrative clinic at the Hell Crater complex, where he used Toshikazu's knowledge of nanotechnology for medical purposes. Because of his religious beliefs, Toshikazu felt uneasy about his brother's using nanomachines to help rejuvenate aging men and women. Or for the trivial purposes of cosmetic surgery.

"Why use a scalpel or liposuction," his brother would ask him, "when you can produce nanobugs that will tighten a sagging jawline or trim a bulging belly?"

Toshikazu knew that his brother was doing more than lifting breasts and buttocks. Men would come to him furtively, asking to have their faces completely changed. Takeo accepted their money and never asked why they wanted to alter their appearance. Toshikazu knew they were criminals trying to escape the law.

He was surprised, then, when a pair of churchmen visited him in his laboratory in Selene.

"At first I thought they wanted me to give them evidence against my brother," he whispered painfully to Bracknell from his infirmary bed. "But no . . . it was worse than that . . ."

One of the churchmen was a high official of the New Morality. The other was a Chinese member of the Flower Dragon movement. What they wanted was a set of nanomachines that could destroy buckyball fibers.

Bracknell clutched at the injured man's arm when he heard that, making him yowl so loud that Addie rushed in to see what had happened.

"You'll kill him!" she screamed at Bracknell.

"I . . . I'm sorry," he stammered. "I didn't mean to hurt him."

Toshikazu lay on the bed, his eyes glazed with pain. Addie demanded that Bracknell leave the infirmary.

"I'll tell you when you can come back," she said.

For a moment he thought he'd push her out of his way and get the rest of the story from the injured man. Then he took a deep breath and wordlessly left the infirmary.

All that night his mind seethed with what Toshikazu was telling him. He checked in at the infirmary on his way to the bridge the next morning, but Addie would not let him past the anteroom. "Let him rest," she said. "He'll be no use to you dead."

Bracknell could hardly keep his attention on his duties. The captain snarled at him several times for his mental lapses. Then a message came in from another vessel, a Yamagata torch ship named *Hiryu*. Bracknell saw on the comm console's main screen an aged Japanese man with long snow-white hair flowing past his shoulders.

"We have heard your call for a medical evacuation," said the white-haired man. "We can reach you in six hours and evacuate your injured prisoner."

Bracknell was tempted to tell the man not to bother; he didn't want Toshikazu removed from *Alhambra* until he'd gotten his full story out of him. But, feeling the captain's eyes on his back, he dutifully switched the call to the captain's screen. In two minutes they had agreed for *Hiryu* to pick up the convict and ferry him back to Selene's medical center.

"*Hiryu*," the captain muttered after the call was terminated. "That means 'flying dragon' in Japanese, I think."

As soon as his shift was finished, Bracknell hurried down the passageway to the infirmary. Addie wasn't in the anteroom; he saw her bending over Toshikazu's bed. He could see from the tortured look on her face that something was very wrong.

"He's dying," she said.

"A ship is on its way to pick him up," Bracknell said, torn between his need to hear Toshikazu's full story and a humanitarian instinct to get proper medical care for the man. "It'll be here in less than four hours."

"Thank the gods," breathed Addie.

"Is he awake?"

She nodded. Bracknell pushed past her to the injured man's bedside. Toshikazu's eyes were open, but they looked unfocused, dazed from the analgesics Addie had been pumping into him.

"I've got to know," Bracknell said, bending over him. "What did those church people want from you? What did you do for them?"

"Gobblers," Toshikazu whispered.

Bracknell heard Addie, behind him, draw in her breath. She knew what gobblers were. Nanomachines that disassembled molecules, tore them apart atom by atom. Gobblers had been used as murder weapons, ripping apart protein molecules.

"To break up the buckyball fibers of the skytower?" Bracknell asked urgently.

Toshikazu nodded and closed his eyes.

"Gobblers are illegal," said Addie. "Even in Selene . . ."

"But you made them, didn't you?" Bracknell said to Toshikazu.

He understood it all now. Gobblers tore apart the skytower's structure at the geostationary level. That's why the lower half of the tower collapsed while the upper half went spinning off into deep space. And the evidence was at the bottom of the Atlantic's midocean ridge, being melted away by the hot magma boiling into the ocean water.

"I made . . . gobblers . . . for them," Toshikazu admitted, his eyes still closed.

"You made the gobblers for the Flower Dragon people?" Bracknell asked. "Or for the New Morality?"

With a weary shake of his head, Toshikazu replied, "Neither. They were . . . merely the agents . . . for . . ."

"For who?"

"Yamagata."

Bracknell gaped at the dying man. Yamagata Corporation. Of course! It would take a powerful interplanetary corporation to plan and execute the destruction of the skytower.

"Yamagata," Toshikazu repeated. "I was the last . . . the last one to know . . ."

Addie looked up at Bracknell. "Now we know."

"No!" said Toshikazu. "I've told you . . . nothing. Nothing. I died . . . without telling you . . . anything. If they thought you knew . . ."

His eyes closed. His head slumped to one side.

And Bracknell said, "Yamagata."

CRIME AND PUNISHMENT

Bracknell was still in the infirmary with Addie and the unconscious Toshikazu when the rescue team from *Hiryu* came in, led by Captain Farad. The elderly Japanese man was accompanied by two young muscular types, also Asian, who gently lifted Toshikazu onto a stretcher and carried him away.

The old man stayed and asked Addie for Toshikazu's medical file. She popped the chip from the computer storage and handed it to him.

With a sibilant hiss of thanks, the old man pushed his long hair back away from his face and asked her, "Does this chip include audio data, perhaps?"

"Audio data?" asked Addie.

"You must have spoken to him extensively while he was under your care," said the old man. "Are your conversations included in this chip?"

She glanced at Bracknell, who said, "He was unconscious most of the time. When he did talk, it was mostly rambling, incomprehensible."

"I see." The old man looked from Bracknell's face to Addie's and then back again. "I see," he repeated.

Captain Farad, impatient as usual, asked, "Is there anything else you need?"

The old man stroked his chin for a moment, as though thinking it over. "No," he said at last. "I believe I have everything I need."

He left with the captain.

Addie broke into a pleased smile. "I think we saved his life, Mance."

"Maybe," Bracknell said, still gazing at the open hatch where the captain and the Japanese elder had left.

"There's nothing more to do here," said Addie. "I'm going to my quarters and take a good long shower."

Bracknell nodded.

"Will you walk me home?" she asked, smiling up at him.

Her quarters were down the passageway; his own a dozen meters farther. When they got to her door, Addie clutched at his arm and tugged him into her compartment.

He began to protest, "Your father—"

"—Is busy seeing off the rescue team," Addie interrupted. "And there are no cameras in my quarters; I've made certain of that."

"But I shouldn't be in here alone with you."

"Are you afraid?" She grinned impishly.

"Damned right!"

The compartment was much like his own quarters: a bunk, a built-in desk and dresser, accordion-pleat doors for the closet and lavatory.

Addie touched the control panel on the wall and the overhead lights turned off, leaving only the lamp on the bedside table.

"Addie, this is wrong." But he heard the blood pulsing through his body, felt his heart pounding.

She stood before him, smiling knowingly. "Don't you like me, Mance? Not even a little?"

"It's not that—"

"Today is my seventeenth birthday, Mance. I am legally an adult now. And rather wealthy, you know. I can control my own dowry now. I can make my own decisions."

She reached up to the tab at the throat of her coveralls and slid the zipper all the way down to her crotch. She wasn't wearing a bra, he saw. Her body was young and full and beckoning.

"I love you, Mance," Addie murmured, stepping up to him and sliding her arms around his neck.

He clutched her and pulled her close and kissed her upturned face.

And heard the door behind him burst open with a furious roar from Captain Farad. Before Bracknell could turn to face her father, he felt the searing pain of a stun wand at full charge and blacked out as he slumped to the floor.

•   •   •

Aboard *Hiryu* the elderly Japanese assassin composed a final message to Nobuhiko Yamagata. He encrypted the video himself, a task which took no little time, even with the aid of the ship's computer:

"Most illustrious master: The last individual is now in our care. He will be treated as required. Unfortunately, he has probably contaminated the vessel in which we found him. Therefore that vessel will be dealt with. This will be my last transmission to you or anyone in this life. Sayonara."

When Bracknell came back to consciousness he was already in a hardshell suit, its helmet sealed to the neck ring. The captain was glaring at him, his eyes raging with fury.

"I told you to keep away from her!" he screamed at Bracknell, loud enough to penetrate the helmet's thick insulation. "I *warned* you!"

"Where is she? What have you done—"

"She's in her quarters, crying. She'll get over it. I'll have to marry her off sooner than I planned, but it'll be better than having her throw herself at scum like you."

Bracknell felt himself being hauled to his feet and realized there were at least two other crewmen behind him. His legs wouldn't function properly; the stun wand's charge was still scrambling his nervous system.

"Drag him down to the auxiliary airlock," the captain snarled. "That goddamn *Hiryu* is still connected to the main lock."

"But I didn't do anything!" Bracknell protested.

"The hell you didn't!"

Like a sack of limp laundry Bracknell was hauled along the passageway and into the airlock. The captain clipped a tether to the waist of his spacesuit and handed him the loose end.

"You can find a cleat for yourself and clip onto it. Otherwise you can float out to infinity, for all I care."

Bracknell tottered uncertainly in the hard-shell suit. His legs tingled as if they'd been asleep. He's going to kill me! he thought. I'm going to die out there! There's no way I can survive in a suit all the way out to the Belt. Even if he sends out more air and food how can I—

The inner airlock hatch slammed shut and Bracknell felt through the thick soles of his boots the pump starting to chug the air out of the darkened metal chamber. In less than a minute the pump stopped and the outer hatch swung open silently.

Bracknell saw the cold distant stars staring at him. On unsteady legs still twitching from the stun charge, he clumped to the lip of the hatch. Peering out along the ship's skin, he saw a set of cleats within arm's reach. For a moment he thought of refusing to go outside. I'll just stay here in the airlock, he told himself. Then he realized that the captain would simply have a few men suit up and throw him out, maybe without even the tether. So, like a man going through the motions of a nightmare, he attached the end of his tether to the nearest cleat and then stepped out into nothingness. The airlock hatch slid shut behind him.

He glided silently as the tether unreeled, then was pulled up short. A sardonic voice in his head mocked, You're at the end of your tether. A helluva way to die. He realized that despite his contemplation of suicide, despite Addie's tutoring him in the desirelessness of the Buddhist path, he very much wanted to live.

Why? Why not just open the seal of this helmet and end it all here and now? The answer rose in his mind like the fireball of a nuclear explosion: Vengeance. Victor and Danvers had betrayed him. And Yamagata was the biggest bastard of them all. Yamagata had brought down the skytower, and that had given Victor the opportunity to steal Lara from him.

Molina. Danvers. Yamagata. He would live to work his vengeance on them. But you won't live long enough to succeed, that mocking inner voice told him.

Looking around as he floated in the emptiness he saw, on the far side of *Alhambra*'s curving hull, that the other ship was still linked. What was its name? *Hiryu*, the captain had said. Flying dragon. Why would it still be connected? If they intend to bring Toshikazu back to Selene they ought to light off as quickly as they can.

Then Bracknell remembered that *Hiryu* was a Yamagata vessel. And Yamagata certainly wasn't here to help Toshikazu recover from his wounds.

The silent explosion blinded him, but it did not surprise him.

DEATH AND TRANSFUGURATION

Whirling blindly through space, Bracknell knew for certain that he was a dead man now.

He could feel himself spinning giddily. The explosion must have torn my tether free of *Alhambra*, he thought. I'll twirl like this forever. I'll probably be the first man to reach Alpha Centauri, even though I'll be too dead to know it.

Then the realization hit him. Addie! The captain. All the people on *Alhambra*. Did the bastards kill everybody? Madly he tried to paw at his tear-filled eyes; his gloved hands bumped into the thick quartz visor of his helmet. Blinking furiously, he tried to force his vision to return. All he saw was the searing after-image of the explosion's fireball.

They wouldn't have blown up the whole ship, he said to himself. Why would they? They wanted Toshikazu and they got him. Why the explosion? An accident?

No, he realized. They suspected that Toshikazu had been talking to us. They wanted no witnesses, nobody left alive. Dead men tell no tales. Neither do dead women, even if they're only seventeen years old. His eyes filled with tears again, but now he was sobbing for Addie, killed because of me. The final casualty of the skytower. They killed her and everybody else because of me.

Then he thought of Yamagata. I didn't kill them, Bracknell reminded himself. He did. Yamagata. He's back on Earth, living in luxury, with the blood of millions on his hands.

Slowly his vision returned. Eventually he could see the wreckage of *Alhambra* spreading outward like dandelion seeds puffed by the wind. It was dwindling, dwindling as he himself spiraled away through space.

Yamagata did this. Bracknell kept the image of Saito Yamagata in the forefront of his mind. It kept him alive, gave him a reason to keep on breathing. He had never met the mighty founder of Yamagata Corporation, but he had seen vids of the man on the news net. Yamagata was supposed to have retreated to some monastery in Tibet, Bracknell remembered, but the newscasters smugly reported that this was just a ruse. The old man was still running his interplanetary corporate maneuvers, they assured their watchers.

Saito Yamagata, Bracknell told himself as he tumbled endlessly through space. Saito Yamagata. When he finally lapsed into unconsciousness he was still burning with hatred of Saito Yamagata.

He opened his eyes and almost smiled. Bracknell found himself lying on an infirmary bed, safe and warm, with a crisp sheet over his naked body. It was all a dream, he thought. A nightmare.

But the dark-skinned, slightly plump nurse who stepped into his view was a stranger. And she wore a white uniform with the crescent logo of Selene on her left breast, just above a name tag that identified her as NORRIS, G.

Bracknell blinked at her, then croaked, "Where am I?"

She smiled pleasantly at him, white teeth gleaming in her dark face. "A classic question."

"But where—"

"You're in the hospital at Selene. A salvage team picked you up when they went out to claim the wreck of *Alhambra*."

"*Alhambra*?"

The nurse fussed over the intravenous drip inserted in Bracknell's arm as she replied, "From what I hear, *Alhambra* collided with some Yamagata ship and they both blew up. You're lucky to be alive."

Raising his head anxiously, Bracknell asked, "Did anybody else . . . are there are any other . . ."

"No, you're the only one who survived. What were you doing outside in a spacesuit?" Without waiting for an answer the nurse went on, "Whatever, it saved your life. Were you outside doing some repairs, or what?"

He sank back onto the pillow. "I don't remember," he lied.

The nurse cast him a doubtful glance. "There wasn't any ID on you when they brought you in. What's your name?"

Bracknell started to reply, then caught himself. "I . . . I don't remember," he said.

"You don't remember your own name?"

Trying to look upset about it, Bracknell said, "I can't remember *anything*. It's all a blank."

"Posttraumatic shock," muttered the nurse. "We'll have to run some scans on you, then, and check them against the files."

She left Bracknell's bedside. He raised himself up on his elbows and looked around. He was in a cubicle created by portable plastic partitions. His clothes were nowhere in sight. And he knew he had to get out of this hospital before the computer scans identified him as Mance Bracknell, the criminal who'd been sentenced to lifelong exile.

In his office in New Kyoto, Nobuhiko Yamagata watched the image of the white-haired servant as he delivered his final message. It's finished, then, he said to himself. At last it's finished. I can breathe freely again.

Within an hour the news came that a corporation ship named *Hiryu* had been destroyed in an accident that also wiped out the freighter *Alhambra*. No survivors were reported.

Nobu's first instinct was to uncork a bottle of champagne, but he knew that would be incorrect. Besides, he found that he didn't feel like celebrating. Instead, a profound sense of gloom settled upon him like a massive weight.

It's finished, he repeated to himself. This terrible business is finished at last.

BOOK IV
VENGEANCE

Vengeance is in my heart, death in my hand,
Blood and revenge are hammering in my head.

After a bland meal, Bracknell pushed his tray aside and got out of the hospital bed. The floor tiles felt comfortably warm to his bare feet. He seemed strong enough, no wobbles or shakes. The cubicle was barely large enough to hold his bed. Portable plastic partitions, he saw. No closet. Not even a lavatory. And this damned IV hooked into my arm.

He cracked the accordion door a centimeter and peeped out. The same nurse was striding down the corridor in his direction.

Bracknell hopped back into the bed and pulled the sheet over his naked body.

She pushed the door back and gave him an accusing look. "I saw you peeking out the door. Feeling better, huh?"

"Yes," said Bracknell.

"Long as you're taking solid food we can disconnect this drip," she said, gripping his arm and gently pulling the IV tube out of him. Even so, Bracknell winced.

As she sprayed a bandage over his punctured arm, Nurse Norris said happily, "You're going to have a pair of visitors, Mr. X."

"Visitors?" He felt immediately alarmed.

"Yep. Psychotechnician to talk to you about your amnesia, and some suit from the corporate world. Don't know what he wants."

"Can I get some clothes?" Bracknell asked. "It's kind of awkward like this."

Norris looked at one of the monitors on the wall behind the bed and fiddled with her handheld remote. "The coveralls you came in with were pretty raw. I sent 'em to the laundry. I'll see if I can find them for you. Otherwise it's hospital issue."

"Before the visitors arrive?"

She gave him that unhappy look again. "For a charity case you make a lot of demands."

Before he could answer, though, she ducked back outside and slid the partition closed.

Once I get my clothes back I can make a run for it, Bracknell said to himself. I can't let them scan me; I've got to get out of here before they find out who I am.

And go where? I'm in Selene, on the Moon. As soon as they find out who I am they'll slap me into another ship and send me back to the Belt. Where can I hide?

He thought about escaping back to Earth, to Lara. But he knew that was ridiculous. How can I get to Earth from here? Besides, she's Victor's wife now. Even if she wanted to hide me, she wouldn't be able to. Then he realized that he hadn't the faintest idea of where on Earth Lara might be. Shaking his head morosely, he decided that going back to Earth would be impossible.

Toshikazu said he had a brother, he remembered. What was his name? Takeo. Takeo Koga. And he's here, on the Moon. Somewhere in the Hell Crater complex. Maybe I can get to him. Maybe—

The partition slid open again and somebody, he couldn't see who, tossed a flapping pair of gray coveralls at him. In the soft lunar gravity they arched languidly through the air and landed softly on his bed. By then the door had slid shut again. A new set of underwear was tucked into one of his coverall sleeves.

He was sealing the Velcro seam up his torso when someone rapped politely on his door frame. They can see me, Bracknell realized, looking up toward the ceiling. They must have a camera in here somewhere.

He sat on the bed and swung his legs up onto the sheet. "Come in," he called. Then he realized that his feet were bare. They hadn't brought any shoes.

Two men entered his cubicle as Bracknell touched the control stud that raised the bed to a sitting position. One of the men wore a white hospital smock over what looked like a sports shirt and corduroy slacks. He was round-faced and a little pudgy, but his eyes seemed aware and alert. The other was in a gray business suit and white turtleneck, hawk-nosed, his baggy-eyed expression morose.

"I'm Dr. DaSilva," said the medic. "I understand you're having a little trouble remembering things."

Bracknell nodded warily.

"My name is Pratt," said the suit. "I represent United Life and Accident Assurance, Limited." His accent sounded vaguely British.

"Insurance?" Bracknell asked.

DaSilva grinned. "Well, you remember insurance, at least."

Bracknell fell back on a pretense of confusion. "I don't understand . . ."

Pratt said, "We have an awkward situation here. Like many ship's crews, the crew of *Alhambra* was covered by a shared-beneficiary accident policy."

"Shared beneficiary?"

"It's rather like an old-fashioned tontine. In case of a fatal accident, the policy's principal is paid to the survivors among the crew— after the deceaseds' beneficiaries have been paid, of course."

"What does that mean?" Bracknell asked, feeling nervous at being under DaSilva's penetrating gaze.

"It means, sir," said Pratt, "that as the sole survivor of *Alhambra*'s fatal accident, you are the secondary beneficiary of each member of the crew; you stand to gain in excess of ten million New International Dollars."

Bracknell gasped. "Ten million?"

"Yes," Pratt replied, quite matter-of-factly. "Of course, we must pay out to the families of the deceased; they *are* the primary beneficiaries. But there will still be some ten million or so remaining in the policy's fund."

"And it goes to me?"

Pratt cleared his throat before answering, "It goes to you, providing you can identify yourself. The company has a regulation against paying to anonymous persons or John Does. International laws are involved, you know."

"I . . . don't remember . . . very much," Bracknell temporized.

"Perhaps I can help," said DaSilva.

"I hope so," Bracknell said.

"Before we start scanning your brain to see if there's any physical trauma, let me try a simple test."

"What is it?"

DaSilva pulled a handheld from the breast pocket of his smock. Smiling cheerfully, he said, "This is what I call the ring-a-bell test. I'm going to read off the names of *Alhambra*'s crew and you tell me if any of them ring a bell."

Bracknell nodded, thinking furiously. Ten million dollars! If I can get my hands on that money—

"Wallace Farad," DaSilva called out.

Bracknell blinked at him. "The captain's name was Farad."

"Good! Your memory isn't a total blank."

"You couldn't forget the captain," said Bracknell fervently. Then he remembered that the captain was dead. And Addie. And all the rest of them. Dead. Killed by Yamagata.

"I'll skip the women's names," DaSilva was saying. "I don't think you had a sex-change procedure before they picked you up."

Pratt chuckled politely. Bracknell thought of Addie and said nothing.

DaSilva read off several more names of the crew while Bracknell tried to figure out what he should do.

Finally DaSilva said, ". . . and Dante Alexios. That's the last of them."

Dante Alexios had been the vessel's second mate, Bracknell knew. He didn't know much about him except that he wasn't a convict and he didn't have a wife or children.

"Dante Alexios," he repeated. "Dante Alexios."

"Ring a bell?" DaSilva asked hopefully.

Bracknell looked up at the psychotechnician. "Dante Alexios! That's who I am!"

Pratt looked less than pleased. "All well and good. But I'm afraid you're going to have to prove your identity before I can allow the release of the policy's payout."

HELL CRATER

Catch-22, Bracknell thought as he sat on his bed. I can get ten million dollars if I can prove I'm Dante Alexios, so I need to let them scan my body. But as soon as they do they'll find out I'm Mance Bracknell and ship me back out to the Belt as a convict.

A different nurse breezed into his cubicle and shoved a data tablet onto his lap. "Press your right thumb on the square at the bottom," she said.

Bracknell looked up at her. She was young, with frizzy red hair, rather pretty.

"What's this?" he asked, almost growling.

"Standard permission form for a full-spectrum body scan. We need your thumbprint."

I don't want a scan, Bracknell said to himself, and I don't want to give them a thumbprint; they could compare it with Alexios's real print.

He handed the tablet back to the nurse. "No."

She looked stunned. "Whattaya mean, no? You've got to do it or we can't do the scan on you."

"I don't want a scan. Not yet."

"You've got to have a body scan," the nurse said, somewhere between confused and angry at his refusal. "It says so in your chart."

"Not now," Bracknell said. "Maybe tomorrow."

"They can *make* you take a scan, whether you want to or not."

"The hell they can!" Bracknell snapped. The nurse flinched back half a step. "I'm not some criminal or lunatic. I'm a free citizen and I won't be coerced into doing something I don't want to do."

She stared at him, bewildered. "But it's for your own good."

"I'll decide what's good for me, thank you." And Bracknell felt a surge of satisfaction well up in him. He hadn't asserted himself for years, he realized. I used to be an important man, he told himself. I gave orders and people hopped to follow them. I'm not some convict or pervert. I didn't kill all those people. Yamagata did.

The redheaded nurse was fidgeting uncertainly by his bed, shifting the tablet from one hand to the other.

"Listen," Bracknell said, more gently, "I've been through a lot. I'm not up to getting poked and prodded—"

"The scan is completely nonintrusive," the nurse said hopefully.

"Okay, tell you what. Find me a pair of shoes and let me walk around a bit, stretch my legs. Then tomorrow morning I'll sign for the scan. Okay?"

She seemed relieved, but doubtful. "I'll hafta ask my supervisor."

"Do that. But first, get some shoes for me."

Less than half an hour later Mance Bracknell walked out of Selene Hospital's busy lobby, wearing his old gray coveralls and a crinkled pair of hospital-issue paper shoes. No one tried to stop him. No one even noticed him. There was only one guard in the lobby, and when Bracknell brazenly waved at him the guard gave him a halfhearted wave in return. He wasn't in hospital-issue clothes; as far as the guard was concerned, Bracknell was a visitor leaving the hospital. Or maybe one of the maintenance crew going home.

Most of Selene was underground, and the hospital was two levels down. Bracknell's first move was to call up a map on the information screen across the corridor from the hospital's entrance. He found the transportation center, up in the Main Plaza, and headed for it.

I'm free! he marveled as he strode along the spacious corridor, passing people walking the other way. Not a thing in my pockets and the hospital authorities might call Selene's security people to search for me, but for the moment I'm free to go where I want to.

The place he wanted to go to was Hell Crater.

He located a powered stairway and rode it up to Selene's Main Plaza, built on the surface of the great crater Alphonsus. Its concrete dome projected out from the ringwall mountains and onto the crater floor. Bracknell saw that the Plaza was green with grass and shrubbery; there were even trees planted along the winding walkways. An Olympic-sized swimming pool. A bandshell and stage for performances. Shops and little bistros where people sat and chatted and sipped drinks. Music and laughter floated through the air. Tourists flitted overhead, flying on their own muscle power with colorful rented plastic wings. Bracknell smelled flowers and the aroma of sizzling food.

It's marvelous, he thought as he headed for the transportation center. This is what they cut me off from: real life, real people enjoying themselves. Freedom. Then he realized that he had neither cash nor credit. How can I get to Hell Crater? Freedom doesn't mean much when you are penniless.

As he approached the transportation center, an eager-looking young man in a splashy sports shirt and a sparkling smile fell in step beside him. "Going to Hell?" he asked brightly.

Bracknell looked him over. Blond crew cut, smile plastered in place, perfect teeth. A glad-handing salesman, he realized.

"I'm thinking about it," Bracknell said.

"Don't miss Sam Gunn's Inferno Casino," said the smiling young man. "It's got the best action."

"Action?" Bracknell played naïve.

"Roulette, blackjack, low-grav craps tables, championship karate competition." The smile grew even wider. "Beautiful women and free champagne. Dirty minds in clean bodies. What more could you ask for?"

Bracknell looked up at the transportation center's huge display of departures and arrivals.

The young pitchman gripped his arm. "Don't worry about that! There's an Inferno Special leaving in fifteen minutes. Direct to the casino! You'll be there in less than two hours and they'll even serve you a meal in transit!"

"The fare must be—"

"It's free!" the blond proclaimed. "And your first hundred dollars' worth of chips is on the house!"

"Really?"

"As long as you buy a thousand dollars' worth. That's a ten percent discount, right off the bat."

Bracknell allowed himself to be chivvied into a cable car painted with lurid red flames across its silver body. Fourteen other men and women were already sitting inside, most of them middle-aged and looking impatient.

As he took the empty seat up front, by the forward window, one of the dowdyish women called out, "When are we leaving? We've been waiting here almost an hour!"

The blond gave her the full wattage of his smile. "I'm supposed to fill up the bus before I let it go, but since you've been so patient, I'll send you off just as soon as I get one more passenger."

It took another quarter hour, but at last the car was sealed up. It rode on an overhead cable to the massive airlock built into the side of the Main Plaza's dome. Within minutes they were climbing across Alphonsus's worn old ringwall mountains and then down onto the plain of Mare Nubium. The cable car rocked slightly as it whizzed twenty meters above the bleak, pockmarked regolith. It smelled old and used; too many bodies have been riding in this bucket for too long, Bracknell thought. But he smiled to himself as the car raced along and the overhead speakers gave an automated lecture about the scenic wonders they were rushing past.

There was no pilot or crew in the cable car; everything was automated. The free meal consisted of a thin sandwich and a bottle of "genuine lunar water" obtained from the vending machine at the rear of the car. Bracknell chewed contentedly and watched the Straight Wall flash by.

True to the blond pitchman's word, the cable car went directly inside the Inferno Casino. The other passengers hurried out, eager to spend their money. Bracknell left the car last, looking for the nearest exit from the casino. It wasn't easy to find; all he could see was an ocean of people lapping up against islands of gaming tables, looking either frenzied or grim as they gambled away their money. Raucous music poured from overhead speakers, drowning out any laughter or conversation. No exits in sight; the casino management wanted their customers to stay at the gaming tables or restaurants. There were plenty of sexy young women sauntering around, too, many in spray-paint costumes, but none of them gave Bracknell more than a cursory glance: in his gray coveralls he looked more like a maintenance man than a high roller.

When he finally found the casino's main entrance, Bracknell saw that the entire Hell Crater complex of casinos, hotels, restaurants, and shops was built inside one massive dome. Like Selene, the complex's living quarters and offices were tunneled underground. Bracknell studied a map display, then headed on foot to the rejuvenation clinic of Takeo Koga. It was one of six such clinics in the complex.

Down two levels and then a ten-minute walk along the softly lit, thickly carpeted corridor to Koga's clinic. It was blessedly quiet down here, and there were only a few other people in sight. No one paid attention to Bracknell, for which he was thankful. It meant that there was no alarm yet from the hospital about his absence.

The sign on the door was tastefully small, yet Bracknell found it almost ludicrously boastful: IDEAL RENEWAL CENTER. KOGA TAKEO, M.D., D.C.S.

Hoping he didn't look too disreputable, Bracknell opened the door and stepped into the small waiting room. Two brittle-looking women sitting in comfortable armchairs looked up at him briefly, then turned their attention back to the screen on the far wall, which was showing some sort of documentary about wild animals. Silky music purred from hidden speakers. There were two empty armchairs and a low table with another screen built into its surface. The table's screen glowed softly.

Bracknell went to the table and bent over it slightly.

"Welcome to Ideal Renewal Center," said a woman's pleasant voice. "How may I help you?"

"I need to see Dr. Koga."

"Do you have an appointment?"

"This is about his brother, Toshikazu," Bracknell replied.

A moment's hesitation, then a different voice said, "Please take a seat. Someone will be with you in a moment."

KOGA CLINIC

A young Asian woman opened the door on the far end of the waiting room and crooked a finger at Bracknell. Wordlessly she led him to a small examination room, gestured to the chair next to the examination table, and softly closed the door behind her as she left.

Bracknell suddenly felt uncomfortable. What if they're calling security? But no, how would they know who I am? Still, he felt trapped in this tiny, utterly quiet room.

He stood up and reached for the door just as it swung open and a stocky, grim-faced Asian stepped in. He looked young, but his handsome face did not seem to go with his chunky build. His cheekbones were sculptured, his jawline firm, his throat slim and unlined. He wore a trim, dark moustache, and his hair was cut short and combed straight back off his forehead.

"I am Toshikazu's brother, Takeo," he said as he firmly closed the door behind him. Takeo looked suspicious, almost angry. He took in Bracknell's unimpressive coveralls and paper shoes at a glance. He must be a good diagnostician, Bracknell thought.

"Well, what's he done now?"

Bracknell took in a breath, then said, "I'm afraid he's dead."

Takeo's eyes widened. He tottered to the examination couch and sagged against it. "Dead? How did it happen?"

"He died in an explosion aboard the freighter *Alhambra*. He was a convict, being shipped out to the Belt."

"They finally got him, then."

"You know about it," Bracknell said.

Rubbing at his eyes, Takeo replied, "Only that he was running from something, someone. He was frightened for his life. He wouldn't tell me what it was about; he said then I'd be marked for murder, too."

Bracknell sat in the chair in the corner. "Did he ever mention Yamagata to you?"

"No," Takeo answered, so sharply that Bracknell knew it was a lie. "He never told me anything about why he was being pursued. I only knew that he was in desperate trouble. I changed his appearance, his whole identity, twice."

"And they still found him."

"Poor Toshi." Takeo's chin sank to his chest.

"He told me about your ability to change people's identities," said Bracknell.

Takeo's head snapped up. He glared at Bracknell.

"I need my identity changed."

"You said Toshi was a convict? You're one also, eh?"

Bracknell almost smiled. "The less you know, the safer you are."

Shaking his head, Takeo said, "I helped my brother because he's my brother. I'm not going to stick my neck out for you."

"You've helped other people who wanted to start new lives. Toshikazu told me about your work."

"Those people could afford my fees. Can you?"

With a rueful grin, Bracknell admitted, "I don't have a penny."

"Then why should I help you?"

"Because if you don't, I'll tell you your brother's whole story. Who was after him, and why. Then you'll know, and then I'll let Yamagata's people know that you know. The people who killed him will come here to kill you."

Takeo was silent for several long moments. He stared into Bracknell's eyes, obviously trying to calculate just how desperate or determined this stranger was.

At last he said, "You want a complete makeover, then?"

"I want to become a certain individual, a man named Dante Alexios."

"I presume this Alexios is dead. It would be embarrassing if he showed up after you claim his identity."

"He died in the same explosion your brother did."

Takeo nodded. "I'll need his complete medical records."

"They should be available from the International Astronautical Authority. They keep duplicates of all ship's crews."

"And they keep those records private."

"You've done this sort of thing before," said Bracknell.

"For people who provided me with what I needed."

"You're a doctor. Tell the IAA you've got to identify a body for United Life and Accident Assurance, Limited. They carried the policy for *Alhambra*."

Takeo said, "I don't like getting involved in this."

"You've done worse, from what Toshikazu told me. Besides, you don't have much of a choice."

"You're blackmailing me!"

Bracknell sighed theatrically. "I'm afraid I am."

The makeover took weeks, and it wasn't anything like what Bracknell had expected. Takeo obtained Alexios's medical files from the IAA easily enough; a little money was transferred electronically and he received the dead man's body scans in less than a day. Then began the hard, painful work.

Takeo kept Bracknell in one of the small but luxuriously appointed suites behind his medical offices. For the first ten days he didn't see Takeo, except through the intercom phone. Bracknell grew increasingly impatient, increasingly fearful. Any moment he expected security guards to burst into the little suite and drag him back to a ship headed outward to the Belt.

He paced the suite: sitting room, bedroom, a closet-sized kitchen in which he prepared bland microwaved meals from the fully stocked pantry. No liquor, no drugs, no visitors. His only entertainment was video, and he constantly scanned the news nets from Selene and Earth for any hint that he was being hunted. Nothing. He wanted to phone the Selene hospital to see what their files showed about him, but found that he could not place outgoing calls. He was a prisoner again. His jail cell was comfortable, even plush, but still he felt penned in.

When he complained to Takeo, the physician's artificially handsome image on the phone screen smiled at him. "You're free to leave whenever you want."

"You haven't even started my treatment yet!"

"Yes I have."

Bracknell stared at the face on the screen.

"The most difficult part of this process," Takeo explained, with ill-concealed annoyance, "is programming the nanomachines. They've got to alter your face, your skin, your bone structure. Once I've got them programmed, the rest is easy."

It wasn't easy.

One ordinary morning, as Bracknell flicked from one news channel to another, thinking that even being arrested again would be better than this utter boredom, a young Asian nurse entered his sitting room bearing a silver tray with a single glass of what looked like orange juice.

"This is your first treatment, sir."

"This?" Bracknell asked dubiously as he picked up the glass.

"You should go to bed for a nap as soon as you drink it," the nurse said. "It contains a sedative."

"And nanomachines?"

She nodded solemnly. "Oh, yes, sir. Many nanomachines. Hundreds of millions of them."

"Good," said Bracknell. He drained the glass, then put it back on her tray with a clink.

"You should go to bed now, sir."

Bracknell thought of asking her if she would accompany him, but decided against it. She left the suite and he walked into his bedroom. The bed was still unmade from the previous night's sleep.

This is ridiculous, he thought. I'm not sleepy and there's no—

A wave of giddiness made his knees sag. He plopped onto the bed, heart thumping. His face tingled, itched. He felt as if something was crawling under his skin. It's only psychosomatic, he told himself. But as he stretched out on the rumpled bed he felt as if some alien parasites had invaded his body. He wanted to scratch his face, his ribs, everywhere. He writhed on the bed, filled with blind dread, moaning in his terror. He squeezed his eyes shut and hoped that sleep would come before he began screaming like a lunatic.

Each morning for six days, the same nurse brought him a glass filled with fruit juice. And nanomachines. For six mornings Bracknell took it with a trembling hand, then went to bed and waited for the sedative to knock him out while his body twitched and writhed. Each day the pain grew sharper, deeper. It was as if his bones were being sawn apart, the flesh of his face and body flayed by a sadistic torturer. He thought of insects infected with the eggs of parasitic wasps that ate out their host's insides. He lived in writhing agony and horror as the nanomachines did their work inside his body.

But he saw no difference in his face. Every morning he staggered to the lavatory and studied himself in the mirror above the sink. He looked the same, except that his beard did not grow. After three days of the nanotherapy he stopped shaving altogether. There was no need. Besides, his frightened hands shook too much.

He phoned Takeo every day, and received only a computer's synthesized, "Dr. Koga will return your call at the appropriate time."

Maybe he's killing me, Bracknell thought. Using nanomachines to eat out my guts and get rid of me. Still, despite his fears each morning he swallowed down the juice and the invisible devices swarming in it. And suffered the agonies of hell until he passed thankfully into unconsciousness.

One week to the day after Bracknell had started taking the nanotherapy, Koga showed up in his suite.

"How do you feel?" the physician asked, peering at Bracknell intently.

"Like I'm being eaten inside," Bracknell snapped.

Takeo tilted his head slightly. "Can't be helped. Normally we go more slowly, but both of us are in a hurry so I've given you some pretty heavy dosages."

"I don't see any change," said Bracknell.

"Don't you?" Takeo smiled condescendingly. "I do."

"My face is the same."

Walking over to the desktop phone, Takeo said, "The day-to-day change is minuscule, true enough." He spoke a command in Japanese to the phone. "But a week's worth of change is significant."

Bracknell saw his own image on the phone's display.

"Take a look in the mirror," said Takeo.

Bracknell went to the bathroom. He stared, then ducked back into the living room. The difference was subtle, but clear.

Takeo smiled at his handiwork. "In another week not even United Life and Accident Assurance will be able to tell you from the original Dante Alexios."

"It's painful," Bracknell said.

"Having your bones remolded involves some discomfort," Takeo replied, unconcerned. "But you're getting a side benefit: you'll never have to shave again. I've eliminated the hair follicles on your face."

"It still hurts like hell."

Takeo shrugged. "That's the price you must pay."

Another week, thought Bracknell. I can put up with this for another week.

DANTE ALEXIOS

arvin Pratt frowned at the dark-haired man sitting in front of his desk. The expression on the stranger's face was utterly serious, determined.

"You're not the man I saw in the hospital," he said.

"I am Dante Alexios," said Bracknell. "I've come to claim my money as the sole beneficiary of the *Alhambra*'s accident policy."

"Then who was the man in the hospital?" Pratt demanded.

Alexios shrugged his shoulders. They were slimmer than Bracknell's had been. "Some derelict, I suppose."

"He disappeared," Pratt said, suspicion etched onto his face. "Walked out of the hospital and disappeared."

"As I said, a derelict. I understand there's an underground community of sorts here in Selene. Criminals, homeless people, all sorts of oddballs hiding away in the tunnels."

Pratt leaned back in his swivel chair and let air whistle softly between his teeth as he compared the face of the man sitting before him with the image of Dante Alexios on his desktop screen. Both had pale skin and dark hair; the image on the screen had a shadow of stubble along his jaw while the man facing him was perfectly clean-shaven. His face seemed just a trifle out of kilter, as if the two halves of it did not quite match. His smile seemed forced, twisted. But the retinal patterns of his dark brown eyes matched those on file in the computer. So did his fingerprints and the convolutions of his ears.

"How did you survive the explosion?" Pratt asked, trying to keep his tone neutral, nonaccusative.

Smoothly, Alexios replied, "I was outside doing routine maintenance on the attitude thrusters when the two ships blew up. I went spinning off into space for several days. I nearly died."

"Someone picked you up?"

"Another freighter, the *Dubai*, outbound for the Belt. After eight days they transferred me to an inbound ship, the *Seitz*, and I arrived here in Selene yesterday. That's when I called your office."

Pratt looked as if he didn't believe a word of it, but he went through the motions of checking Alexios's story. Alexios had paid the captains of the two vessels handsomely for their little lies, using Takeo's money on the promise that he'd repay the physician once he got the insurance payout into his hands.

"This other man, the amnesiac," said Pratt warily. "He was rescued from the *Alhambra* also."

Smoothly, Bracknell answered, "Then he must have been a convict. Captain Farad had the pleasant little trick of putting troublemakers outside, in spacesuits, until they learned to behave themselves."

"I see." At last Pratt said, "You're a very fortunate man, Mr. Alexios."

"Don't I know it!"

With a look of utter distaste, Pratt commanded his phone to authorize payment to Dante Alexios.

Alexios asked, "May I ask, how much is the, uh, benefit?"

Pratt glanced at his display screen. "Twelve point seven million New International Dollars."

Alexios's brows lifted. "That much?"

"What do you intend to do with your money?"

Taking a deep breath, Alexios said, "Well, there are some debts I have to pay. After that . . . I don't know . . . I just might start my own engineering firm."

He surprised Takeo by paying the physician's normal fee for a cosmetic remake. Then Dante Alexios opened a small consulting engineering office in Selene. He started by taking on charity work and performing community services, such as designing a new water processing plant for Selene's growing population of retirees from Earth. His first paying assignment was as a consultant on the new mass driver being built out on Mare Nubium to catapult cargos of lunar helium three to the hungry fusion power plants on Earth. He began to learn how to use nanotechnology. With a derisive grin he would tell himself, *Damned useful, these little nanomachines.*

In two years he was well known in Selene for his community services. In four he was wealthy in his own right, with enough contracts to hire a small but growing staff of engineers and office personnel. Often he thought about returning to Earth and looking up Lara, but he resisted the temptation. That part of his life was finished. Even his hatred of Victor and Danvers had abated. There was nothing to be done. The desire for vengeance cooled, although he still felt angry whenever he thought of their betrayal.

Instead of traveling to Earth, Dante Alexios won a contract to build a complete research station on Mars, a new base in the giant circular basin in the southern hemisphere called Hellas. He flew to Mars to personally supervise the construction.

He lived at the construction site, surrounded by nanotech engineers and some of the scientists who would live and work at the base once it was finished. He walked the iron sands of the red planet and watched the distant, pale Sun set in the cloudless caramel-colored sky. He felt the peace and harmony of this empty world, with its craggy mountains and rugged canyons and winding ancient river beds.

We haven't corrupted this world, Alexios told himself. There are only a handful of humans here, not enough to tear the place apart and rebuild it the way we've done to Earth, the way we're doing to the Moon.

Yet he knew he was a part of that process; he had helped to extend human habitation across the dead and battered face of the Moon. Mars was different, though. Life dwelled here. Once, a race of intelligent creatures built their homes and temples into the high crevasses in the cliffs. Alexios got permission from the scientists running the exploration effort to visit the ruins of their cliff dwellings.

Gone. Whoever built these villages, whoever farmed those valleys, they were all wiped out by an impersonal planetwide catastrophe that snuffed out virtually all life on the red planet, blew away most of its atmosphere, flash-froze this world into a dusty, dry global desert. The scientists thought the plain of Hellas held the key to the disaster that sterilized Mars sixty-five million years ago, the same disaster that wiped out the dinosaurs and half of all living species on Earth.

Alexios felt very humble when he stared through his spacesuit visor at the crumbling ruins of a Martian cliff dwelling. Life can be snuffed out so easily. Like a skytower falling, crushing the life out of millions, ending a lifetime of hope and work with a snap of destiny's fingers.

He was mulling his own destiny when he returned to the base nearing completion at Hellas. As the rocket glider that carried him soared over the vast circular depression, Alexios looked through the thick quartz window with some pride. The base spread across several square kilometers of the immense crater's floor, domes and tunnels and the tangled tracks of many vehicles. The work of my mind, he said to himself. The base is almost finished, and I did it. I created it. With a little help from my nanofriends. Like the skytower, taunted a voice in his mind.

That night, he lay in his bunk and watched the Earthside news broadcasts while the Martian wind moaned softly past the plastic dome that housed the construction crew. Then he saw an item that made him sit straight up in bed.

Saito Yamagata was going to start a project to build solar power satellites in orbit around the planet Mercury.

Yamagata! He's come out of his so-called retreat in Tibet and he's heading for Mercury.

Without a moment's hesitation, without a heartbeat of reflection, Alexios decided he would go to Mercury, too. He owed Yamagata a death. And as he sat in his darkened bedroom, the flickering light from the video screen playing across his transformed features, he realized that he could pay back both Victor and Danvers, too.

All the old hatred, all the old fury, all the old seething acid boiled up anew in his guts. Alexios felt his teeth grinding together. I'll make them pay, he promised himself. I had almost forgotten about them, about what they did to me and all those millions of others. Almost forgotten Addie and her father and the others aboard *Alhambra*. How easy it is to let a comfortable life swallow you up. How easy to let the blade's edge go dull.

He threw back the bed covers and strode naked to his desktop phone. Yamagata. Molina. Danvers. I'll get all three of them on that hellhole of a world, Mercury.

GOETHE BASE

S itting in his bare little office, Dante Alexios smiled bitterly to himself as the memories of his ten lost years came flooding back to him. He finished reading the report issued by McFergusen and his ICU committee and leaned back in his desk chair. They've worded it very diplomatically, Alexios thought as he read the final paragraph, but their meaning is clear.

The aforementioned tests unequivocally show that the rocks in question originated on Mars. While there is a vanishingly small chance that they were deposited on Mercury's surface by natural processes, the overwhelming likelihood is that they were transported to Mercury by human hands. The discovery of biomarkers in these samples by V. Molina is not, therefore, indicative of biological activity on the planet Mercury.

Victor is wiped out, Alexios said to himself, with satisfaction. McFergusen won't come right out and say it, but the implication is crystal clear: either Victor planted those rocks here himself, or he fell dupe to some prankster who did it. Either way, Victor's reputation as a scientist is permanently demolished.

Laughing out loud, Alexios thought, Now it's your turn, Danvers.

He put in a call to Molina, to start the process of destroying Bishop Elliott Danvers.

As he strode down the central corridor of the orbiting *Himawari*, heading toward Molina's quarters, Alexios began to feel nervous. Lara will be there, he knew. She lives with him. Sleeps with him. They have an eight-year-old son. He worried that sooner or later she would see through his nanotherapy and recognize Mance Bracknell. Then he realized that even if she did it wouldn't change anything.

Still, he hesitated once he arrived at the door to their stateroom, his fist in midair poised to knock. What will I do if she does recognize me? he asked himself. What will you do if she doesn't? replied the scornful voice in his head.

He took a breath, then knocked. Lara opened the door immediately, as if she had been standing behind it waiting anxiously for him.

He had to swallow before he could say, "Hello, Mrs. Molina."

"Mr. Alexios." Her voice was hushed, apprehensive. "Won't you come in?"

Feeling every fiber of his body quivering nervously, Alexios stepped into their compartment. Victor was sitting on the two-place sofa set against the far bulkhead, his head in his hands. The bed was neatly made up; everything in the stateroom seemed in fastidious order. Except for Molina: he looked a wreck, hair mussed, face ashen, a two-day stubble on his jaw, dark rings under his eyes.

Alexios relaxed somewhat. This isn't going to be difficult at all. He's ready to clutch at any straw I can offer.

Lara asked, "Can I get you something, Mr. Alexios?"

"Dante," he said. "Please call me Dante."

With a nod, she said, "Very well, Dante. A drink, maybe?"

His memory flashed a picture of all the times he and Lara had drunk together. She'd been partial to margaritas in the old days; Mance Bracknell had a taste for wine.

"Just some water, please," he said.

"Fruit juice?" she suggested.

He almost shuddered with the recollection of the nanomachine-laden juice he had drunk in Koga's clinic. "Water will be fine, thank you."

Lara went to the kitchenette built behind a short bar next to the sofa. Alexios pulled up one of the plush chairs and sat across the coffee table from Molina.

"As I said on the phone, Dr. Molina, I'm here to help you in any way I can."

Molina shook his head. "There isn't anything you can do," he said in a hoarse whisper.

"Someone set you up for this," Alexios said gently. "If we can find out who did it, that would show everyone that you're not at fault."

Lara placed a tray of glasses on the coffee table and sat next to her husband. "That's what I've been telling him. We can't just take this lying down. We've got to find out who's responsible for this."

"What can you do?" Molina asked morosely.

Alexios tilted his head slightly, as if thinking about the problem. "Well . . . you said you received an anonymous call about the rocks."

"Yes. Somebody left a message for me at my office on campus. No name. No return address."

"And on the strength of that one call you came out here to Mercury?"

Anger flared in Molina's eyes. "Don't you start, too! Yes, I came here on the strength of that one call. It sounded too good to be ignored."

Lara laid a placating hand on his knee. "Victor, he's trying to help you," she said soothingly.

Molina visibly choked back his anger. "I figured that if it's a blind alley I could be back home in a couple of weeks. But if it is was real, it would be a terrific discovery."

"But it was a deliberate hoax," Alexios said, as sympathetically as he could manage.

"That's right. And they all think I did it. They think I'm a fraud, a cheat, a—"

"The thing to do," Alexios said, cutting through Molina's rising bitterness, "is to track down who made that call."

"I don't see how—"

"Whoever it was had access to Martian rocks," Alexios went on. "And he probably knew you."

"What makes you think that?" Lara asked, surprise showing clearly in her amber eyes.

With a small shrug, Alexios replied, "He called you, no one else. He wanted you, specifically you, to come here and be his victim."

"Who would do such a thing?" Lara wondered. "And why?"

"That's what we've got to find out."

EVIDENCE

lexios knew he had to work fast, because Lara and Victor were due to leave Mercury in a few days. Yet he couldn't be too swift; that might show his hand to them. Besides, now that the IAA's interdict on his work on the planet's surface was lifted, he had plenty of tasks to accomplish: resume scooping raw materials from the regolith, hire a nanotech team and bring them to Mercury, lay out plans for building a mass driver and the components for solar power satellites that would be catapulted into orbit and assembled in space.

He waited for two days. Then he rode the shuttle back to *Himawari* with the evidence in his tunic pocket.

Lara and Victor eagerly greeted him at the airlock. They hurried down the passageway together toward the Molinas' stateroom, Victor in a sweat to see what Alexios had uncovered, Lara just as eager but more controlled.

As soon as the stateroom door closed Molina demanded, "Well? What did you find?"

"Quite a bit," said Alexios. "Is McFergusen still here? He should see—"

"He left two days ago," Molina snapped. "What did you find out?"

Alexios pulled two thin sheets of plastic from his tunic and unfolded them on the coffee table as Molina and his wife sat together on the little sofa. He tapped the one on top.

"Is this the anonymous message you received?" he asked Molina.

The astrobiologist scanned it. "Yes, that's it."

Alexios knew it was. He had sent it. He turned that sheet over to show the one beneath it.

"What's this?" Lara asked.

"A copy of a requisition from the International Consortium of

Universities, selling eleven Martian rocks to a private research facility on Earth."

"My rocks!" Molina blurted.

"How did they get from Earth to Mercury?" Lara asked.

Alexios knew perfectly well, but he said, "That part of it we'll have to deduce from the available evidence."

"Who sent this message to me?" Molina demanded, tapping the first sheet.

"It wasn't easy tracking down the sender. He was very careful to cover his tracks."

"Who was it?"

"And he had a large, well-financed organization behind him, as well," Alexios added.

"*Who was it?*" Molina fairly screamed.

Alexios glanced at Lara. She was obviously on tenterhooks, her lips parted slightly, her eyes wide with anticipation.

"Bishop Danvers," said Alexios.

"Elliott?" Molina gasped.

"I can't believe it," said Lara. "He's a man of god—he wouldn't stoop to such chicanery."

"He's my friend," Molina said, looking bewildered. "At least, I thought he was."

Alexios said, "The New Morality hates the discoveries you astrobiologists have made, you know that. What better way to discredit the entire field than by showing a prominent astrobiologist to be a fraud, a liar?"

Molina sank back in the sofa. "Elliott did this? To me?"

"What proof do you have?" Lara asked.

Alexios looked into her gold-flecked eyes. "The people who traced this message used highly irregular methods—"

"Illegal, you mean," she said flatly.

"Extralegal," Alexios countered.

"Then this so-called evidence won't hold up in a court of law."

"No, but there must be a record of this message in Danvers's computer files. Even if he erased the message, a scan of his memory core might find a trace of it."

Lara stared hard at him. "The bishop could claim that someone planted the message in his computer."

Alexios knew she was perfectly correct. But he said, "And why would anyone do that?"

Impatiently, Molina argued, "We can't examine Elliott's computer files without his permission. And if he really did this he won't give permission. So where are we?"

"You're forgetting this invoice," said Alexios. "It can be traced to the New Morality school in Gabon, in west Africa."

Lara looked at her husband. "Elliott was stationed in Libreville."

"For almost ten years," Molina said.

She turned back to Alexios. "You're certain of all this?"

He nodded and lied, "Absolutely. I paid a good deal of money to obtain this information."

"Elliott?" Molina was still finding it difficult to accept the idea. "Elliott deliberately tried to destroy me?"

"I'm afraid he *has* destroyed you," Alexios said grimly. "Your reputation is permanently tainted."

Molina nodded ruefully. Then his expression changed, hardened. "Then I'm taking that pompous sonofabitch down with me!"

CONFRONTATION

t's utterly ridiculous!" cried Bishop Danvers.

Molina was standing in Danvers's stateroom, too furious to sit down. He paced the little room like a prowling animal. Lara sat on one of the upholstered chairs, Alexios on the other one. Danvers was on the sofa between them, staring bewilderedly at the two flimsy sheets that Alexios had brought.

"We have the proof," Molina said, jabbing a finger toward the message and the invoice.

"It's not true, Victor," said Danvers. "Believe me, it's not true."

"You deliberately ruined me, Elliott."

"No, I—"

"Why?" Molina shouted. "Why did you do this to me?"

"I didn't!" Danvers howled back, his face reddening. "It's a pack of lies." Desperately, he turned to Lara. "Lara, you believe me, don't you? You know I wouldn't have done this. I couldn't have!"

Lara's eyes flicked from her husband to the bishop and back again.

"Someone has deliberately ruined Victor's reputation," she said evenly, fixing her gaze on Alexios. "No matter who did this, Victor's career is destroyed."

"But it wasn't me!" Danvers pleaded.

"Wasn't it?" Molina snapped. "When I think of all the talks we've had, over the years, all the arguments—"

"Discussions!" Danvers corrected. "Philosophical discussions."

"You've had it in for me ever since you found out that I was using those gengineered viruses to help build the skytower," Molina accused. "You and your kind hate everything that science stands for, don't you?"

"No, it's not true." Danvers seemed almost in tears.

Molina stopped his pacing to face the bishop. "When I told you about what I was doing at the skytower, you reported it to your New Morality superiors, didn't you?"

"Of course. It was important information."

"You were a spy back in Ecuador. You were sent to the skytower project to snoop, not to pray for people's souls."

"Victor, please believe me—"

"And now they've sent you here to Mercury to destroy my work, my career. You've ruined my life, Elliott! You might as well have taken a knife and stabbed me through the heart!"

Danvers sank his face in his hands and started blubbering. Lara stared at him, her own eyes growing misty. Then she looked up at her husband.

"Victor, I don't think he did this," she said calmly.

"Then who did?" Molina demanded. "Who would have any reason to?"

Lara focused again squarely on Alexios. "Are you certain of this information?" she asked. "Absolutely certain?"

Alexios fought down the urge to squirm uncomfortably under her gaze. As smoothly as he could, he replied, "As your husband said, who else would have a motive for doing this to him? The New Morality must have marked Victor years ago, when they learned what he was doing for the skytower."

"And they'd wait all this time to get back at him?"

Shrugging, Alexios said, "Apparently so. That's what the evidence suggests."

Abruptly, Molina bent over the coffee table and snatched the two flimsy sheets. "I'm calling McFergusen. I've been the victim of a hoax, a scam. And then I'm calling the news nets. The New Morality is going to pay for this! I'll expose them for the psalm-singing hypocrites that they are!"

Exactly what I thought you'd do, Alexios said to himself. Aloud, however, he tried to sound more reasonable. "I agree that a call to McFergusen is in order. But a news conference? Do you really want to attack the New Morality?"

"Why not?" Molina snapped. "What do I have to lose?"

Lara got to her feet. "Victor, Mr. Alexios is right. Don't be too hasty. Talk with McFergusen first. He might be able to salvage something out of this situation."

"Salvage what? Even if I can prove that I've been scammed, I still look like an idiot. Nobody will ever believe me again. My career is finished!"

"But perhaps—"

"Perhaps nothing! They've destroyed me; I'm going to do my damnedest to destroy them. And you in particular, Elliott, you goddamned lying bastard!"

Danvers looked up at the astrobiologist, his face white with shock, his eyes filled with tears.

Molina took his wife by the wrist and slammed out of the stateroom, leaving Alexios alone with the bishop.

"I didn't do it," Danvers mewed, bewildered. "As God is my witness, I never did any of this."

Alexios scratched his chin, trying to prevent himself from gloating. "Would you allow me to check your computer? I presume you brought your memory core with you when you came to Mercury."

Danvers nodded glumly and gestured toward the desk, where the palm-sized computer rested. Alexios spent a half hour fiddling with it while the bishop sat on the sofa in miserable silence. Alexios found the trace of the message he had paid to have planted in the computer's core. It looked as if it had been erased from the active memory, but still existed deep in the core.

Getting up from the desk at last, Alexios lied, "Well, if it's in your machine's memory it would take a better expert than me to find it."

"It doesn't matter," Danvers said, his heavy head drooping.

"I should think it would be important."

His voice deep and low with despair, Danvers said, "You don't understand. A scandal like this will ruin me. The New Morality doesn't permit even a suspicion of wrongdoing among its hierarchy. We must all be above evil, above even accusations of evil. This . . . once Victor tells people about this . . . I'll be finished in the New Morality. Finished."

Alexios took a breath, then replied, "Maybe you can get a position as chaplain on a prison ship, or out in the Asteroid Belt. They could use your consolations there."

Danvers looked up at him, blinking. He seemed to have aged ten years in the past half hour.

Alexios smiled, thinking, You wouldn't last a month out there, you fat old fraud. Somebody would strangle you in the middle of your hymns.

OBSERVATION LOUNGE

Alexios fidgeted nervously as he stood in *Himawari*'s dimmed observation lounge, gazing through the glassteel blister as the starflecked depths of infinite space spun slowly, inexorably past his altered eyes. The eyes of heaven, he said to himself, halfremembering a poem from his school days. The army of unalterable law, that's what the poet called the stars.

I should feel triumphant, he thought. Victor's career is in tatters, and Danvers is in disgrace. All that's left is Yamagata and I'll be taking care of him shortly. Yet he felt no delight in his victory over them. No triumph. He was dead inside, cold and numb. Ten years I've waited to get even with them and now that I have . . . so what? So Victor will spend the rest of his life in some obscure university trying to live down his mistake here on Mercury. And Danvers will be defrocked, or whatever they do in the New Morality. What of it? How does that change my life?

Lara, he said to himself. It all depends on Lara. She's the one I did this for. She's the one who kept me alive through all those long years out in the Belt. My only glimmer of hope when I was a prisoner, a miserable exile.

As the torch ship rotated, the surface of Mercury slid into view, barren, heat-blasted, pitted with craters and seamed with cracks and fault lines. Like the face of an old, old man, Alexios thought, a man who's lived too long. He saw a line of cliffs and the worn, tired mountains ringing an ancient crater. He knew where Goethe base was, but he could not see the modest mound of rubble covering its dome from the distance of the ship's orbit, nor the tracks of the vehicles that churned up the thin layer of dust on the ground down there.

Once we've built the mass driver you'll be able to see it from orbit, he thought. Five kilometers long. We'll see it, all right.

The door behind him slid open, spilling light from the passageway into the darkened compartment. Alexios's heart constricted in his chest. He did not dare to turn around, but in the reflection off the glassteel bubble he saw that it was Lara.

He slowly turned toward her as she slid the door shut. The compartment became dim and shadowed again, but he could see her lovely face, see the curiosity in her eyes.

"You asked me to meet you here?" she said, her voice soft and low.

He realized he'd been holding his breath. He nodded, then managed to get out, "It's one of the few places aboard ship where we can meet privately."

"You have some further information about my husband?"

"No . . . not really . . ." It took all his self-control to keep from reaching out and clasping her in his arms. Surely she could hear his heart thundering.

"I don't understand," Lara said with a little frown. "You asked me to see you, to come alone, without Victor."

"Lara, it's me," he blurted. "Mance."

Her mouth dropped open.

"I know I look different," he said, the words coming in a rush now. "I had to change my appearance, my background, I came here to Mercury but I had no idea you'd come out here too and now that you're here I can't keep up the masquerade any longer, I want to—"

"Mance?" she whispered, unbelieving.

"Yes, it's me, darling."

She staggered back several steps, dropped onto the bench running along the compartment's rear bulkhead. "It can't be," she said, her voice hollow.

He went to her, knelt before her, grasped both her hands in his own. "Lara, I've gone through hell to find you again. I love you. I've always loved you."

She was staring at him, searching for the Mance Bracknell she had known. He could see the play of starlight in her eyes and then the harsh glare reflected from Mercury casting her face into stark light and shadow.

"I know I don't look the same, Lara. But it really is me, Mance. I have a new identity. I'm a free man now. The old Mance Bracknell is dead, as far as the officials are concerned. But we can begin our lives again, Lara, we can take up where we left off."

She shuddered, like a woman coming out of a trance. "Begin our lives again?"

"Yes! I love you, dearest. I want to marry you and—"

"I'm already married. I have an eight-year-old son. Victor's son."

"You can divorce Victor. Nobody will blame you for leaving him."

Recognition lit her eyes. "*You* did this to Victor! It wasn't Elliott, it was you!"

"I did it for you," he said.

"You destroyed my husband's career and ruined Elliott."

"Because I love you."

"What kind of love is that?"

Alexios saw the disgust in her eyes. "You don't understand," he said. "They destroyed me. Victor deliberately lied at my trial. He wanted me out of the way so he could have you. He stole you from me. He stole my entire life!"

"And now you've stolen his."

"Yes! And I want you back. You're the reason I've done all this."

"Oh, my god," she moaned.

"You loved me, you know you did. You said you wanted to be with me. Well, now we can—"

"And Elliott, too? What do you have against him?"

Anger rising inside him, Alexios said, "He's the one who started the scheme to destroy the skytower. Him and his New Morality hatred for nanotechnology or anything else that they can't find in the Old Testament."

"Destroy the skytower?"

"It was sabotaged. Deliberately knocked down. They didn't care how many people they killed, they just wanted the tower destroyed. And me with it."

She stared at him. "You're saying that Victor helped to bring the tower down?"

"No, I don't think so. I don't know. But he lied at my trial. He was perfectly willing to lie so that the blame would all be dumped on me. So that I'd be sent off Earth and he'd have you to himself."

Lara shook her head, just the slightest of movements, as she said, "I can't believe that. I don't believe any of this!"

"But it's true! It's all true! Victor is a lying thief and Danvers helped him."

She sagged back on the padded bulkhead. Alexios climbed to his feet and sat beside her.

"I know it's a lot to accept all at once. But I really am Mance Bracknell. At least I was, once. Now I'm Dante Alexios. I'm fairly prosperous; I can offer you a fine life back on Earth. Victor stole you from me. I want you back."

"He's my husband," Lara repeated weakly.

He looked directly into her eyes. In the dim lighting of the compartment he could not see any tears in them.

"Lara, you can't tell me that you love Victor the way you loved me."

She said nothing.

"We were perfect for each other," he said. "The minute I first saw you, back in that dull statistics class with the Chinese T.A. who could barely speak English, I fell hopelessly in love with you."

For long moments she remained silent. Then, "You certainly didn't show it."

"I was too shy. It didn't seem possible that anyone as wonderful as you would have the slightest interest in me."

Lara smiled faintly.

"We belong together, Lara. They've separated us for so many years, but we can be together again now."

Again that slight shake of her head. "So many years have gone by."

"But we can start again," he urged.

"It's not that simple."

"It can be, if you want it to be. Victor got what's coming to him. He's finished, out of the picture."

"He's my husband," she said, still again.

"He stole you from me!"

She looked away for a moment, then turned back to him. "Look, Mance or Alexios or whoever you are. I am married to Victor Molina. He's the father of my child. You've tried to ruin him—"

"Nothing less than he deserves," Alexios growled, feeling his anger simmering inside him again. "In fact, he deserves a lot worse."

"What you've told me might save him," Lara said.

Alexios was thunderstruck. He felt a wave of nausea wash over him. "You'd take him over me?"

"Mance Bracknell is dead," Lara said, her voice flat and cold. "So be it. We could never recapture what we had all those years ago. Do you think I could leave Victor and go with you, knowing what you've done to him?"

"But he *deserves* it!"

"No, he doesn't. And even if he did, his wife should be by his side, protecting and supporting him. For the sake of our child, if for no other reason."

"You belong with me!"

"No. My place is with my husband and son, no matter what happened in the past."

"That's . . ." Alexios ran out of words. This has gone all wrong, he said to himself. All wrong.

Lara got to her feet. "I'm going to tell Victor about this, and then McFergusen. I won't mention Mance Bracknell. I'll simply tell them that you confessed to me that you planted the false evidence."

"They'll find out who I am!" Alexios pleaded. "They'll send me back to the Belt!"

"Not if you can prove that the skytower was sabotaged. Not if you can lead the authorities to the people who are really responsible for all those deaths."

He stood up beside her, his knees unsteady, and watched as she abruptly turned away from him and left the observation lounge. He stood frozen, watching as the door slid closed. Then he felt the glare from Mercury's surface blaze through the heavily tinted blister of glassteel. It felt like the hot breath of doom.

GOETHE BASE

t's all gone wrong, Alexios said to himself as he sat miserably alone in his sparely furnished office at the construction base. Horribly wrong.

Lara, Victor, and Danvers had left for Earth on the ship that had shepherded the six new power satellites from Selene. She must be telling Victor everything, Alexios thought. It's only a matter of time before the IAA or some other group sends investigators here to check me out. If they suspect I'm not who I say I am, they'll want to do DNA scans on me. If I refuse they'll get a court order.

It's finished, he told himself. Over. She's not the same Lara I knew. The years have changed her.

He stood up and studied his reflection in the blank wall screen. They've changed me, too, he realized. He paced across the little office, thinking that he was still all alone in the universe. Lara doesn't love me anymore. No one in the entire solar system cares about me. There's only one thing left to do. Get Yamagata down here and finish the job. Make him pay before they come after me. After that, it doesn't matter what happens.

Yet he hesitated. When the investigators come I could tell them the whole story, tell them how Yamagata sabotaged the skytower, how *he's* the one who's really responsible for all those deaths.

But the mocking voice in his head sneered, And they'll believe you? Against Yamagata? Where's your evidence? He's murdered everyone connected with the sabotage. Toshikazu was the last one, and his assassins even killed themselves so there'd be no possible witnesses remaining.

Alexios knew the severed end of the skytower lay more than four thousand meters beneath the surface of the Atlantic, near the fracture zone where hot magma wells up from deep beneath the Earth's crust.

No one would send an expedition to search for the remains of nanomachines that had probably been dissolved by now, he knew.

He also knew that Saito Yamagata maintained the convenient fiction that his son ran Yamagata Corporation. He was in a lamasery in Tibet when the skytower went down, Alexios remembered. Yes, of course, the voice in his mind taunted. He pulled all the strings for this vast murderous conspiracy from his retreat in the Himalayas. Try getting the authorities to buy that.

Alexios shook his head slowly. No, I'm not going to try to get the authorities to do anything. I'm going to take care of Yamagata myself. I'm going to end this thing once and for all.

He told the phone to call Saito Yamagata.

Yamagata was clearly uncomfortable about being out on the surface; Alexios could see the unhappy frown on his face through the visor of his helmet. Don't worry, he said silently, you won't be out here long. Only for the rest of your life.

The two men were riding a slow, bumping tractor across the bleak surface of Mercury, dipping down into shallow craters and then laboring up the other side, moving farther and farther from the base. It was night; the Sun would not rise for another hour, but the glow of starlight and the pale glitter of the zodiacal light bathed the bleak landscape in a cold, silvery radiance.

Despite all the months he'd been on Mercury, Alexios still could not get accustomed to the little planet's short horizon. It was like the brink of a cliff looming too close; the edge of the world. In the airless vacuum the horizon was sharp and clear, no blurring or softening with distance, a knife edge: the solid world ended and the black infinity of space lay beyond.

"You'll be out of camera range in two more minutes," the base controller's calm flat voice said in Alexios's helmet earphones.

"You have a satellite track on us, don't you?" he asked.

"Affirmative. Two of 'em, as a matter of fact."

"Our beacon's coming through all right?"

"Loud and clear."

"Good enough."

Even though the tractor's glassteel cabin was pressurized, both Yamagata and Alexios were wearing full spacesuits, their helmet visors closed and sealed. Safety regulations, Alexios had told Yamagata when the older man had grumbled about getting into the uncomfortable suit.

"How far are we going to go?" Yamagata asked as the tractor slewed around a house-sized boulder.

Taking one gloved hand off the steering controls to point out toward the horizon, Alexios said, "We've got to get to the other side of that fault line. Then we'll double back."

Yamagata grunted, and the frown on his face relaxed, but only slightly.

It had been easy enough to get him down to the planet's surface.

"I'd like to show you the site we're considering for the mass driver," Alexios had told Yamagata. "Naturally, we can't make the final decision. That's up to you."

Yamagata's image in Alexios's wall screen had turned thoughtful. "Is it necessary for me to inspect this location personally?"

Choosing his words carefully, Alexios had replied, "I understand, sir, that it's inconvenient and uncomfortable to come down here to the surface. Even a little dangerous, to be truthful."

Yamagata had stiffened at that. Drawing himself up to his full height, he'd told Alexios, "I will come to the base tomorrow. My transportation coordinator will inform you of when you may expect me."

Alexios had smiled. Touch the man on his Japanese brand of machismo and you've got him. The old samurai tradition. He doesn't want to lose face in front of his employees.

"I received a report from my son's technical experts in Japan," Yamagata said, staring straight ahead as he sat alongside Alexios in the lumbering tractor. "They believe your numbers on the solar cell degradation problem are exaggerated."

Alexios knew perfectly well that they were. "Exaggerated?" he asked.

"Overstated," said Yamagata, his voice muffled slightly by the spacesuit helmet.

It was impossible to shrug inside the heavy suit. Alexios said smoothly, "I admit that I showed you the worst-case numbers. I thought it best that way."

Yamagata grunted. "We may not have to harden the power satellites after all."

"That's good news, then," Alexios replied. It didn't matter now, he thought. None of it mattered any more.

Yamagata was silent for several kilometers. Then, "What makes you think this is the best site for the catapult launcher?" he demanded. "If it takes this long to get there, why is this site so preferable?"

Alexios smiled behind his visor. "It's that blasted fault line. If you approve the site, we'll bridge over it. But right now we have to go all the way around it. Won't be long now, though."

Yamagata nodded and seemed to settle down inside his suit.

It won't be long now, Alexios repeated silently.

Lara Tierney Molina could not sleep. Victor lay beside her, dead to the world on the sedatives and tranquilizers he'd been taking ever since boarding the creaking old freighter, coasting now on a four-month trajectory back to Selene.

The clock's digits glowing in the darkness read 12:53. She slipped out of bed, groped in the shadows of the darkened stateroom for the first dress she could find in her travel bag, and pulled it on. Victor would sleep for hours more, she knew. She tiptoed to the door, opened it as softly as she could, and stepped out into the passageway. As she slid the door closed and heard the faint click of its lock, she wondered which way led to the galley.

I have to think, she told herself as she walked slowly along the passageway. Its plastic walls were scuffed and dulled from long use, the floor tiles even worse. *Xenobia* had ferried a set of solar power satellites to Mercury for Yamagata's project; now its only cargo was a disgraced New Morality bishop, a humiliated astrobiologist, and herself. The IAA was paying Victor's fare and her own. The New Morality had refused to pay for Danvers's return; Saito Yamagata had graciously taken care of it.

Victor had demanded a hearing before the IAA's disciplinary board. McFergusen will chair that meeting, Lara thought. I'll have to tell them what Mance confessed to me. No, not Mance. He's a different man, this Dante Alexios. He's no longer Mance Bracknell.

Deep inside her she wondered why she hadn't told Victor about Alexios's confession. Victor was dazed and thick-witted from the tranquilizers that Yamagata's medical people had dosed him with, but she knew that wasn't the reason. Could she believe this Alexios person? Is he really Mance? How else would he know about how we met? He must be Mance. But that makes it even worse, even more complicated. Mance deliberately ruined Victor, revenged himself on poor Victor like some savage out of the dark ages. I'll *have* to tell Victor, I can't keep this from him. It might save his career, save his life.

Yet she hesitated, wondering, uncertain of herself or anything. Victor had lied at Mance's trial? Perjured himself to get rid of Mance? For me? How can I believe that? How can I believe any of this?

She saw a phone screen on the passageway wall and called up a schematic of the ship's interior layout. She'd been heading in the wrong direction, she saw. Turning, she started more confidently toward the galley. No one else was in the passageway at this time of night. There's probably a crew on duty in the bridge, Lara thought. Otherwise they're all sleeping.

All but me. I can save Victor. I'll go to the meeting and tell them that he was deliberately duped by false evidence planted by Dante Alexios. I can clear Victor's name. Elliott's, too.

And what happens to Dante Alexios? she asked herself. She thought she knew. McFergusen and his committee would not take her unsupported word. They'd want corroboration. They would send investigators to Mercury to question Mance—Alexios. And what if he claims innocence? What if he tells them my story is a total fabrication, a desperate attempt to save my husband?

The galley was empty. Nothing more than a small metal table and four swivel chairs bolted to the deck, with a row of food and drink dispensers lining one wall. Lara poured herself a mug of tepid coffee and sat wearily in one of the chairs.

I'll have to tell them that Alexios is really Mance Bracknell, she realized. They'll run tests on him to settle his identity. Once they find that he's Mance they'll send him back to the Belt, back to exile.

Can I do that to him? He said Victor stole me from him, said that he still loves me and wants me. Can I reward him by sending him back into exile? She wanted to cry. It would be such a relief to simply dissolve into tears and wait for someone else to solve this problem for her.

But there is no one else, she told herself. Except Victor, Jr. That made her sit up straighter. Her son. Hers and Victor's. He has a stake in this, too. I can't allow McFergusen or Mance or anyone else to ruin little Victor's future. He needs my protection.

A shadow fell across her and she turned to see Elliott Danvers's hulking form filling the hatchway.

"You couldn't sleep either?" Danvers said, going to the coffee dispenser.

"No."

Danvers settled his bulk in the chair opposite Lara. It groaned as he sat on it, and the bishop sighed heavily.

"I've sent half a dozen messages to my superiors in Atlanta and they haven't seen fit to reply to any of them."

Lara saw that his fleshy face was pale, creased with lines she'd never noticed before. "What will happen to you once we get back to Earth?" she asked.

Danvers shrugged his massive shoulders. "I wish I knew. A reassignment, at least. They'll want to strip me of my title, I'm sure. Perhaps they'll throw me out altogether."

"I know you didn't do it," Lara said.

Danvers's eyes flared briefly. Then he murmured, "Thank you."

"I'm not merely being kind, Elliott. I know who actually duped Victor and planted the evidence that puts the blame on you."

Now his eyes stayed wide. "You . . . you do?"

"But if I tell who it really is, it will ruin his life."

"But he's trying to ruin my life!"

"I don't know what I should do," Lara said plaintively.

"Yes, you do," said the bishop. "You must do what is right. You can't cover up a lie. Forget about me—your husband's career is at stake."

"I know," said Lara.

"And what about your son? This affects him, too."

"I know," she repeated.

Danvers stared at her as if trying to pry the information out of her by sheer willpower. At last he asked, "Why wouldn't you name the wrongdoer?"

"Because it will hurt him. Because he's been terribly hurt already and I'm not sure that I can do this to him, hurt him again."

"But . . . your husband! Your son! Me!"

Lara gripped her cup with both hands and stared down into it. "Maybe if I simply tell the committee that the man told me he did it, that he cleared you entirely, maybe that would be enough."

"Without naming him, so they can check? They'd think you're nothing but a wife who's willing to lie to protect her husband."

She nodded dejectedly. "I can't help one without hurting the other."

The bishop waited a heartbeat, then reached across the table to take her hands in his massive paws. "Lara, morality doesn't come in shades of gray. It's black and white. You either do the right thing or you do the wrong thing. There's no middle ground."

She looked into his soft gray eyes, red with sleeplessness, and thought that morality was simple when doing the right thing would save your own neck.

"It's more complicated than that," she said quietly.

"Then think of this," Danvers said, almost gently. "What is the greatest good for the greatest number of people? You have your husband and son to think of, as opposed to this mysterious wrongdoer."

She nodded. "My husband and son—and you."

BOREALIS PLANITIA

Wrapped in their cumbersome spacesuits, Alexios and Yamagata sat side by side in the tractor's transparent cab as it slowly trundled along the pitted, rock-strewn landscape.

"Borealis Planitia," Yamagata muttered. "The northern plain."

He sounded slightly nervous to Alexios, a little edgy. Inside the pressurized glassteel cabin they could hear one another without using the suits' radios, although their voices were muffled by the heavy helmets.

"This region is an ancient lava flow," Yamagata went on, as much to himself as to his companion. "Planetologists claim that this entire area was once a lake of molten lava, billions of years ago."

Alexios contented himself with steering the tractor through the maze of boulders that lay scattered across the ground. Now and again he rolled right over a smaller rock, making the tractor pitch and sway. To their right, the yawning crack of the fault line was narrowing. They would reach the end of it soon, Alexios knew.

Yamagata continued, "From orbit you can see the outlines of even older craters, ghost craters, drowned by the lava when it flowed across this region."

Alexios nodded inside his helmet. The man's talking just to hear himself talk, he thought. Trying to hide his fear at being out here. Grimly, Alexios added, He has a lot to be afraid of.

They drove on in silence. The time stretched. Alexios could feel in his bones the vibrating hum of the tractor's electric motors, hear his own breathing inside the helmet. He drove like an automaton; there seemed to be no emotion left inside him.

"You are very quiet," Yamagata said at last.

"Yes," replied Alexios.

"What are you thinking about?"

Alexios turned his head inside the fishbowl helmet to look squarely at the older man. "I've been thinking," he said, "about the skytower."

"The skytower?" Yamagata looked surprised. "That was years ago."

"Many years. Many lives."

"Technological hubris," said Yamagata. "The people who built it paid no attention to the danger it might pose."

"Part of it is still spinning outward, in deep space."

"Carrying the bodies of dozens of dead men and women."

"Murdered men and women," said Alexios.

Yamagata grunted. "That's one way to look at it, I suppose."

"The tower was sabotaged. All those who died were murdered."

"Sabotaged?"

"By agents of Yamagata Corporation."

Yamagata's jaw dropped open. "That's not true! It's impossible!"

Without taking his gloved hands from the steering controls, Alexios said, "We both know that it *is* possible and it did happen."

"Paranoid fantasy," Yamagata snapped.

"Is it? I was told the full story by the last surviving member of the plot. Just before your hired killers closed his mouth forever."

"My hired killers?" Yamagata scoffed. "I was in Chota Lamasery in the Himalayas when the skytower fell. We didn't even hear about it until a week or more after the tragedy."

"Yes, I know. That's your cover story."

Yamagata stared at this coldly intent man sitting beside him. He's insane, he thought. Alexios's eyes glittered with something beyond anger, beyond fury. For the first time since he'd been diagnosed with brain cancer, back in his first life, Yamagata felt fear gripping his innards.

"I was the director of the skytower project," Alexios told him, all the while wondering at the glacial calm that had settled upon him, as if he were sheathed in ice.

"The director of the skytower project was exiled," said Yamagata.

Alexios made a wan smile. "Like you, I've led more than one life."

"I had nothing to do with the skytower," Yamagata insisted.

"It was sabotaged by Yamagata Corporation people, using nano-machines to snap the tower at its most vulnerable point. The man who produced the nanobugs for you told me the entire story just before your assassins caught up with him."

"And you believed him?"

"He was terrified for his life," said Alexios. "Your assassins got him. They also blew up the ship we were in, to make sure that anyone he talked to would be killed, too."

"But you survived."

"I survived. To seek justice for all those you killed. To gain vengeance for having my own life destroyed."

"But I—" Yamagata caught himself and shut his mouth. He's a madman, he told himself. I had nothing to do with this; I was in the lamasery. Nobuhiko was running the corporation, just as he is now.

Suddenly his pulse began thudding in his ears. Nobu! If Yamagata Corporation was involved in destroying the skytower, it was under Nobu's direction!

No, that couldn't be, Yamagata said to himself. Shaking his head, he thought, Nobu wouldn't do such a thing. He couldn't be that ruthless, that . . . murderous.

Or could he? Yamagata recalled those years when his advice to his son had led to the slaughters of the second Asteroid War, the massacre of the *Chrysalis* habitat. Nobu learned to be ruthless from me, he realized. The blood drained from his face. I have turned my son into a monster.

Alexios misread the ashen expression on Yamagata's face. "You admit it, then? You admit that the skytower was destroyed on your orders. Four million men, women, and children murdered—by you."

Yamagata realized there was nothing else to do. If I tell him that it was Nobuhiko's doing this madman will want to kill Nobu. Better to let him think it was me. Nobu is my son, my responsibility. Whatever he has done is my fault as much as his. Better for me to take the blame and the punishment. Let my son live.

"Well?" Alexios demanded.

Yamagata seemed to draw himself up straighter inside the bulky spacesuit. "I accept full responsibility," he said, his voice flat, lifeless.

"Good," said Alexios. He turned the steering wheel and the tractor veered slowly toward the yawning fault line, grinding slowly but inexorably toward the rift in Mercury's bleak ground as the first blazing edge of the Sun peeped above the horizon.

Bishop Danvers's mind was churning as he made his way back to his compartment. Is Lara telling the truth? he asked himself. She must be. She *must* be! She wouldn't make up a story like that, she couldn't. But the other side of his mind argued, Why wouldn't she? She's desperate to save her husband and protect her son. She might say anything if she thought it would help Victor.

As he slid back the door to his compartment he saw that the phone's yellow message light was blinking in the darkness. A message! His heart began thumping. From Atlanta. It must be an answer to my calls to Atlanta. Flicking on the ceiling lights, Danvers rushed to the compartment's flimsy little desk and told the phone to display the message.

It was indeed from Atlanta. From the archbishop himself!

Carnaby's wrinkled, bald, gnomish features took form in the phone's small display screen. He was unsmiling, his eyes flinty.

"Bishop Danvers, I am replying to your messages personally because your case is one of extreme importance to the New Morality movement."

Danvers felt immensely grateful. The archbishop is replying to me personally! Even though he knew it would take half an hour, at least, to get a reply back to Earth he automatically started to frame his message of gratitude to the archbishop.

Carnaby was going on, however, "A great American once said that extremism in the defense of our values is no vice. I can appreciate the extreme measures you took to discredit the godless scientists you've been battling against. But in our battle against these secularists, the movement must be seen by the general public as being beyond reproach, above suspicion. Your methods, once exposed to the public, will bring suspicion and discredit upon us all."

But I didn't do it! Danvers screamed silently at Carnaby's implacable image. I haven't done anything discreditable! Lara can prove it!

"Therefore," the archbishop continued, "I have no choice but to ask you for your resignation from the New Morality. One man must not be allowed to throw doubt upon our entire movement. I know this seems harsh to you, but it is for the higher good. Remember that a man may serve God in many ways, and your way will be to resign your office and your ordination in the movement. If you refuse you will be put on public trial as soon as you return to Earth and found guilty. I'm truly sorry it has to be this way, but you have become a liability to the New Morality and no individual, no matter who he is, can be allowed to threaten our work. May God be merciful to you."

The screen went blank.

Danvers stared at it for long, wordless minutes. His mind seemed unable to function. His chest felt constricted; it was an effort just to breathe.

At last, blinking with disbelief, lungs rasping painfully, Danvers realized that he had been drummed out of the New Morality movement. Thrown out into the gutter, just as the gamblers had done to him all those long years ago. All my work, all my years of service, they mean nothing, he thought. Lara's claim to know who actually planted the false evidence won't move them. I've been tainted, and they will be merciless with me.

I'm ruined. Destroyed. I have nowhere to go! No one to turn to. Even if I could prove my innocence they wouldn't take me back. I'm tainted! Unclean!

My life is over, he told himself.

Lara returned to her compartment, where Victor was still tossing fitfully in their bed. She sat at the desk and sent a message to Victor, Jr., smiling reassuringly for her son and telling him she and his father would be back home in a few weeks.

Then she sat, wide awake, until Victor rose groggily from the roiled bedclothes and blinked sleep-fogged eyes at her.

"You're up?" he asked dully.

"I couldn't sleep."

He padded barefoot to the lavatory. She heard him urinate, then wash his face. He came back, hair still tousled, but looking reasonably alert.

"Victor," Lara heard herself ask him, "at Mance's trial, did you tell the truth about the skytower's construction?"

He looked instantly wary. "Why do you ask that?"

"Did you tell the truth?"

"It was so many years ago . . ."

"Did you deliberately lie to put the blame on Mance?"

Molina stood next to the lavatory doorway, wearing nothing but his wrinkled underpants, staring at his wife.

"I've got to know, Victor," said Lara. "You've got to tell me the truth now."

He shuffled to the bed and sat wearily on it. "The tower collapsed," Molina said. "There was nothing any of us could do about that. They were going to blame it on Mance anyway—he didn't have a chance in hell of getting out of that trial alive. I wanted you, Lara! I've always wanted you! But as long as Mance was around you wouldn't even look at me!"

Lara said nothing. She didn't know what she could say.

"I wanted Mance out of the way," he admitted, his voice so low she could barely hear him. "I was so crazy in love with you. I still am."

He burst into tears.

Lara got up from the desk chair and went to the bed. Cradling her husband's head in her arms she crooned soothingly, "I understand, darling. I understand."

"I shouldn't have done it, I know," Molina blubbered. "I ruined Mance's life. But I did it for you. For you."

Lara was quite dry-eyed. "What's done is done," she said. "Mance is dead now. We've got to live the rest of our lives."

As she held him, Lara did not think of Mance Bracknell, nor of the strangely vicious man who called himself Dante Alexios. She did not think of Bishop Danvers or her husband, really, or even of herself. She thought of their son. Only Victor, Jr. He was the only one who mattered now.

SUNRISE

T he rim of the slowly rising Sun was like molten lava pouring heat into the tractor's little bubble of a cab. Yamagata saw that Alexios was steering directly toward the sunrise and the yawning rift.

"What are you doing?" he demanded.

Turning the lumbering vehicle just before it reached the edge of the fault line, Alexios leaned on the brakes. The tractor ground to a halt.

"We get off here," he said.

"I thought—"

"Let's stretch our legs a little," said Alexios, popping the hatch on his side of the glassteel bubble.

Although he felt nothing inside his spacesuit, Yamagata realized that all the air in the cabin immediately rushed into the vacuum outside. Alexios turned back toward him and tapped the keypad on the wrist of his spacesuit. Yamagata heard the man's voice in his helmet earphones, "We'll have to use the suit radios to speak to one another now."

"You intend to kill me, then?" Yamagata asked as he opened the hatch on his side.

"You murdered four million people," Alexios said, his voice strangely soft, almost amused. "I think executing you is a simple act of justice."

"I see." Yamagata clambered slowly down from his seat to the hard, rock-strewn, airless ground. I'm in the hands of a madman, he thought.

"In case you're wondering," Alexios said as he walked around the tractor toward Yamagata, "your suit radio won't reach the base. Not without the tractor's relay, and I've disabled the tractor's outgoing frequency."

"I can't call for help, then," said Yamagata.

"Neither can I." With that, Alexios touched a control stud on his suit and the tractor started up again, silently churning up puffs of dust from the ground, and started trundling away from them.

"You're not going with it?" Yamagata asked, surprised.

"No, I'll stay here with you. We'll die together. Back at the base they'll see the tractor's beacon and think everything is normal. Until it's too late."

Yamagata almost laughed. "This is a simple act of justice?"

"Maybe not so simple, after all," Alexios agreed. "I've been dispensing justice for several days, but I don't quite seem to have the proper knack for it."

Alexios stepped closer to him. Yamagata backed away a few steps, then realized the edge of the fault rift was close behind him.

"Dispensing justice?" he asked, stalling for time to think. "What do you mean?"

"Molina and Danvers," Alexios answered easily. "I'm the one who brought those Martian rocks here. I led Molina to them and he took the bait like the fool that he is."

"And Danvers?"

"I put the blame on him. Now they're both heading back to Earth in disgrace."

"You've deliberately ruined their careers."

"They deserve it. They destroyed my life, the two of them. They took everything I had."

He's insane, Yamagata told himself. The tractor was dwindling slowly, lumbering off toward the disturbing close edge of the horizon.

"Message for Mr. Yamagata." He heard the voice of the base controller in his helmet's earphones. "From the captain of the freighter *Xenobia*."

Alexios spread his gloved hands. "We can't reply to them."

"Then what—"

The controller didn't wait for an acknowledgement. "Here's the incoming message, sir."

Yamagata heard a soft click and then a different voice spoke. "Sir! I apologize for interrupting whatever you are doing, illustrious sir. The captain thought you would want to know that one of the passengers aboard ship has committed suicide. Bishop Danvers slit his throat in the lavatory of his cabin. The place is a bloody mess."

Yamagata stared hard at Alexios, but only saw his own reflection in the heavily tinted visor of the spacesuit's helmet.

"Thank you for the information," he said, in a near whisper.

"They can't hear you," Alexios reminded him.

The base controller's voice returned. "Is there any reply to the message, Mr. Yamagata? Sir? Can you hear me?"

Alexios walked to the rim of the rift. Damn! he said to himself. If they don't hear anything back they'll start worrying about us.

"Mr. Yamagata? Mr. Alexios? Reply, please."

If they send out a rescue team they'll go after the tractor, Alexios thought. It won't be until they find that we're not on it that they'll start hunting for us.

He gripped the arm of Yamagata's suit. "Come on, we're going to take a little walk."

Yamagata resisted. "Where do you want to take me?"

Pointing with his free hand, Alexios said, "Down there, to the bottom of the rift. With the Sun coming up you'll be more comfortable sheltered from direct sunlight. It'll be cooler down there, only a couple of hundred degrees Celsius in the shade."

"You wish to prolong my execution?"

"I wish to prevent our being rescued," Alexios replied.

Yamagata stepped to the edge of the rift. Inside the spacesuit it was difficult to see straight down, but the chasm's slope didn't seem terribly steep. Rugged, though, he saw. A slip of the foot could send me tumbling down to the bottom. If that didn't rupture my suit and kill me quickly, it might damage my radiators and life support pack enough to let me boil in my own juices.

He looked back at Alexios, standing implacably next to him. "After you," Alexios said, gesturing toward the edge of the rift.

Yamagata hesitated. Even with only the slimmest arc of the Sun's huge disk above the nearby horizon a flood of heat was sweeping across the barren ground. Dust motes sparkled and jumped like fireflies, suddenly electrified by the Sun's powerful ionizing radiance. Both men stared at the barren dusty ground suddenly turned manic as the particles danced and jittered in the newly risen Sun. Slowly they

fell to the ground again, as if exhausted, their electrical charges neutralized at last.

They looked out to the horizon and gazed briefly at the blazing
edge of the Sun; even through the deeply tinted visors of their helmets
its overpowering brilliance made their eyes water. The Sun's rim was
dancing with flaming prominences that writhed like tortured spirits in
hell.

Yamagata heard his spacesuit groan and ping in the surging, all-
encompassing heat. He looked down into the chasm again, and the
after-image of the Sun burned in his vision. Turning around slowly in
the cumbersome suit, he started down the pebbly, cracked slope back-
wards. Alexios followed him. It was hard, exhausting work. Yamagata's
booted foot slipped on a loose stone and he went skittering down the
pebbly slope several meters before grinding to a stop. Alexios came
skidding down beside him.

"Are you all right?"

It took Yamagata several panting breaths before he could reply,
"What difference does it make?"

Alexios grunted. "You're all right, then."

Yamagata nodded inside his helmet. The suit seemed intact; its
life support equipment still functioned.

Both men were soaked with perspiration by the time they reached
the bottom of the rift. Yamagata looked up and saw that the edge of the
chasm was ablaze with harsh light.

"Sunrise," said Alexios. "You come from the land of the rising sun,
don't you?"

Yamagata decided he wouldn't dignify that snide remark with a reply. Instead he said, "The message for me was that Bishop Danvers has
committed suicide."

Silence for several heartbeats. Then Alexios said, "I didn't expect
that."

"He slit his throat. Very bloody, from the description."

"I imagine it would be."

"You are responsible for his death."

Again a long wait before Alexios replied, "I suppose I am, in a
way."

"In a way?" Yamagata jeered. "You planted false evidence and accused him falsely. As a result he killed himself. Murder, it seems to me. Or was that an execution, too?"

"He was a weak man," Alexios said. His voice sounded tight, brittle, in Yamagata's earphones.

"Weak or strong, he is dead because of you."

No reply.

Yamagata decided to twist the knife. "I am not a Christian, of course, but isn't it true that in your religion killing one man is just as hideous a sin as killing millions?"

Alexios immediately snapped, "I'm not a Christian, either."

"Ah, no? But do you feel any guilt for the death of Bishop Danvers?"

"He destroyed my life! Him and Molina. He got what he deserved."

Yamagata nodded inside his helmet. "You feel the guilt, don't you?"

"No," Alexios snapped. Then he raised his hand and pointed to the steep wall of the chasm. Yamagata saw that the slim line of glaring sunlight made the rift's edge look molten, so brilliant that it hurt his eyes to look up there.

"In five or six hours we'll be in the direct sun. A few hours after that our life support systems will run out of air. Then all the guilts, all the debts, they'll be paid. For both of us."

VALLEY OF DEATH

lexios could not see Yamagata's face as they stood together in the bottom of the fault rift. I might as well be looking at a statue, he thought. A faceless, silent statue.

But then Yamagata stirred, came to life. He began walking down the rough uneven floor of the chasm, heading in the direction opposite to the path of the unoccupied tractor. Alexios realized he was heading back toward the base.

"You'll never make it," he said. "The base is more than thirty klicks from here. You'll run out of air long before then."

"Perhaps so," Yamagata replied, sounding almost cheerful in Alexios's helmet earphones. "However, I find it easier on my nerves to be active, rather than standing by passively waiting to die."

Despite himself, Alexios started after him. "You don't expect to be rescued, I hope."

"When I was in Chota Lamasery the lamas tried to teach me to accept my fate. I was a great disappointment to them."

"I imagine you were."

They walked along the broken, stony ground for several minutes. The walls of the rift rose steeply on both sides higher than their heads, higher even than the fins of the radiators that projected from their life support packs. The ground was hard, cracked here and there. Pebbles and larger rocks were strewn along the bottom, although not as plentifully as they were up on the surface. The planetologists would have a field day here, Alexios thought. Then he grinned at his inadvertent pun.

Yamagata stumbled up ahead of him and Alexios automatically grabbed him in both gloved hands, steadying him.

"Thank you," said Yamagata.

Alexios muttered, "*De nada.*" Sweat dripped into his eyes, stinging. He felt perspiration dripping along his ribs. "I forgot to put on a sweatband," he said, wishing he could rub his eyes, mop his brow.

Yamagata made no reply, but Alexios could hear the man's steady breathing through the suit radio.

"I think the lamas made some impression on you," Alexios said, after almost half an hour of silent, steady, sweaty walking.

"Ah so?"

"You're taking this all very stoically."

"Not at all," Yamagata replied. "I am walking toward the base. I am doing what I can to get myself rescued. I have no intention of dying without a struggle."

"It won't do you any good."

"Perhaps not. But still, one must try. You didn't accept your fate when you were exiled, did you?"

That brought a flash of anger back from Alexios's memory. "No, I guess I didn't."

"Yet now you are committing suicide," Yamagata said. "You could have thrown me out of the tractor and returned to the base alone. Why give up your own life?"

"I have nothing left to live for."

"Nonsense! You are still a young man. You have many productive years ahead of you."

Thinking of Lara, of the skytower, of Danvers lying slumped in a ship's lavatory splattered with his own blood, Alexios repeated, "I have nothing left to live for."

"Not even the stars?" Yamagata asked.

"What's that supposed to mean?"

"The reason I came to Mercury, the real purpose behind building these power satellites, is to use them to propel a starship. Perhaps many starships."

Without a heartbeat's pause Alexios countered, "The reason I lived, the real purpose behind *my* life, was to build a tower that gave the human race cheap and easy access to space. You destroyed that. Finished it forever. They'll never build another skytower. They're too frightened of what happened to the first one."

"And for this you would deny the stars to humankind?"

"I'm not interested in humankind anymore. The stars will still be there a hundred years from now. A thousand."

"But we could do it now!" Yamagata insisted. "In a few years!"

"We could have been riding the skytower to orbit for pennies per pound by now."

Yamagata grunted. "I believe you have a saying about two wrongs?"

"You're a murderer."

"So are you."

"No, I'm an executioner," Alexios insisted.

"A convenient excuse." Yamagata wondered what Alexios would say if he revealed that Nobuhiko had destroyed the skytower. He shook his head inside the bubble helmet. Never, he told himself. Nobu must be protected at all costs. Even at the cost of my own life. My son has done a great wrong, but killing him will not make things right.

On they walked. With each step it seemed to grow hotter. Down at the bottom of the fault rift they were in shadow, yet the Sun's glaring brilliance crept inexorably down the chasm's wall, as slow and inescapable as fate. They could see the glaring line of sunlit rock inching down toward them; it made the rock face look almost molten hot. The heat increased steadily, boiling the juices out of them. Alexios heard his suit fans notch up to a higher pitch, and then a few minutes later go still higher. Even so he was drenched with perspiration, blinking constantly to keep the stinging sweat out of his eyes. He licked his lips and tasted salt. Wish I had a margarita, he thought. Then he realized how foolish that was. Maybe I'm getting delirious.

Yamagata kept moving doggedly along.

"Let's rest a couple of minutes," Alexios said to him.

"You rest, if you wish. I'm not tired."

Not tired? Alexios thought that Yamagata was simply being macho, unwilling or perhaps unable to show weakness to a man he took to be an inferior. He's older than I am, Alexios told himself. A lot older. Of course, he must have had all sorts of rejuve therapies. Or maybe he's just too damned stubborn to admit he's tired, too.

The heat was getting bad. Despite the suit's insulation and internal air conditioning, Alexios was sloshing. His legs felt shaky, his vision blurred from the damned sweat. He could *feel* the Sun's heat pressing him down, like the breath of a blast furnace, like a torrent of molten steel pouring over him. Still Yamagata plowed ahead steadily, as if nothing at all was bothering him. Blast it all, Alexios thought. If he can do it, so can I. And he trudged along behind the older man.

Until, hours later, the harsh unfiltered rays of the Sun reached the fins of his suit's radiator.

DEATH WISHES

Yamagata stumbled, up ahead of him. Alexios reached for the spacesuited figure but he was too slow. Yamagata pitched forward and, in the dreamlike slow-motion of Mercury's low gravity, hit the ground: knees first, then his outstretched hands, finally his body and helmeted head.

Alexios heard him grunt as if he'd been hit by a body blow. The rift was narrow here; there was barely room for him to step beside the fallen man without scraping his radiator fins on the steep rocky wall of the chasm.

"Are you all right?"

"If I were all right I'd be on my feet," Yamagata retorted, "instead of lying here on my belly."

The bottom of the rift was half in sunlight now, the huge rim of the Sun peering down at them now like a giant unblinking eye, like the mouth of a red-hot oven. Alexios was so hot inside his suit that he felt giddy, weak. Blinking away sweat, he peered at Yamagata's backpack. It looked okay. Radiator fins undamaged. No loose hoses.

"I can't seem to move my legs," Yamagata said.

"I'll help you up."

It was difficult to bend in the hard-shell suit. Alexios tried to reach down and grasp Yamagata by the arm.

"Put your hands beneath you and push up," he said. "I'll help."

They both tried, grunting, moaning with strain. After several minutes Yamagata was still on his belly and Alexios sank down to a sitting position beside him, exhausted, totally drained.

"It's . . . not going to . . . work," he panted.

Yamagata said. "My nose is bleeding. I must have bumped it on the visor when I fell."

"Let's rest a few minutes, then try again."

"I have no strength left."

Alexios turned his head slightly and sucked on the water nipple inside his helmet. Nothing. Either it was blocked or he'd drunk the last of his suit's water supply. It's all coming out as sweat, he said to himself.

"There ought to be some way to recondense our sweat and recycle it back into drinkable water," he mused.

"An engineer's mind never stops working," said Yamagata.

"Fat lot of good it does us."

"You should record the idea, however," said Yamagata, "so that whoever finds us will be able to act on it."

"A tycoon's mind never stops working," Alexios muttered.

"This tycoon's mind will stop soon enough."

Alexios was too hot and tired to argue the point. We're being baked alive, he thought. The suits' life support systems are running down.

"What do you think will kill us," Yamagata asked, "dehydration or suffocation, when our air runs out?"

Squeezing his eyes shut to block out the stinging sweat, Alexios replied, "I think we'll be parboiled by this blasted heat."

Yamagata was silent for a few moments. Then, "Do you think the base has sent out a search team?"

"Probably, by now. They'll follow the tractor's beacon, though."

"But when they find the tractor is empty . . . ?"

Alexios desperately wanted to lean back against the rock wall, but was afraid it would damage his radiators. "Then they'll start looking for us. They'll have to do that on foot, or in tractors. We'll be dead by the time they find us."

"Hmm," Yamagata murmured. "Don't you think they could hear our suit radios?"

"Down in this rift? Not likely."

"Then we will die here."

"That's about the size of it."

After several silent minutes Yamagata asked, "Is your sense of justice satisfied?"

Alexios thought it over briefly. "All I really feel right now is hot. And tired. Bone tired. Tired of everything, tired of it all."

"I too."

"Vengeance isn't much consolation for a man," Alexios admitted.

"Better to have built the starship."

"Better to have built the skytower."

"Yes," said Yamagata. "It is better to create than destroy."

"I'll drink to that."

Yamagata chuckled weakly. "A bottle of good champagne would be very fine right now."

"Well chilled."

"Yes, ice cold and sparkling with bubbles."

"That's not going to happen."

"No, I fear not."

"Maybe we should just open the suits and get it over with. I'm broiling in here."

Yamagata said, "First I want to record my last will and testament, but I can't reach the keypad on my wrist. Can you assist me?"

Alexios let out a weary breath, then slowly rolled over onto all fours and crawled over the gritty ground to Yamagata's extended left hand. It took all his strength to move less than two meters. At last he reached his outstretched arm and pressed the RECORD tab on the wrist keypad. In his earphones he heard a faint click and then a deadness as Yamagata's suit-to-suit frequency shut off.

Lying there on his own belly now, head to helmeted head with Yamagata, Alexios thought, Last will and testament. Not a bad idea. With his last iota of strength, he turned his own suit radio to the recording frequency and began speaking, slowly, his throat dry, his voice rasping, offering his final words to the woman he had loved.

When the rescue team finally found them, some twelve hours later, Alexios and Yamagata were still lying head to head. Their gloved hands were clasped, Alexios's right with Yamagata's left. It was impossible to tell if their hands were locked in a final grasp of friendship or a last, desperate grip of struggle. Some of the rescuers thought the former, some the latter.

The team argued about it as they tenderly carried their spacesuited bodies back to Goethe base. From there they were flown up to *Himawari*, still in orbit around Mercury. The medical team there determined that both men had died of dehydration. They were only five kilometers from Goethe base when they died.

The recording found on Yamagata's suit radio was sent to his son, Nobuhiko, in New Kyoto. Alexios's recording was sent to Lara Tierney Molina, in her family's home in Colorado.

EPILOGUE:
LAST WILLS

L ara sat alone in her old bedroom in her family's house in Colorado, listening to Mance's grating, bone-dry voice forcing out the words that would clear her husband. He confessed to everything: to assuming the identity of Dante Alexios, to spiriting the rocks from Mars and planting them on Mercury, to luring Victor to Mercury and making him the victim of the hoax.

Victor can clear his name with this, she thought. He'll never outlive the stigma entirely, but at least he can show that he was deliberately duped, that he's not a cheat. He can rebuild his career.

She looked out the bedroom window and saw that evening shadows were draping the distant mountains in shades of purple. Victor would be coming home soon, she knew. She briefly wondered why she felt no joy, not even a sense of relief that Victor's ordeal was at last finished. But she knew why: Mance. Mance is dead. That's finished, too.

Tears misted her eyes as she thought of all the things that might have been. But a chill ran through her. Victor was willing to send Mance to hell because he loved me and wanted me. And Mance fought his way out of exile and died on Mercury because he loved me. He gave up his revenge on Victor, he even gave up his life, because he loved me.

She began sobbing softly, wondering what she should do now, what she could do. She felt surrounded by death.

Then she heard footsteps pounding up the stairs and before she could dab at her eyes with a tissue the bedroom door flung open and Victor, Jr., burst in.

"Daddy's home!" the eight-year-old announced, as if it was the most glorious event in history. "He's parking his car in the driveway."

Lara got to her feet and smiled for her son. Life goes on, she told herself. Life goes on.

• • •

Sitting alone in the dim shadows of the small, teak-paneled office of his privacy suite, where not even the oldest family retainer dared to interrupt him, Nobuhiko Yamagata listened in stony silence to his father's gasping, grating final words.

He knows that I caused the skytower to fall, Nobuhiko said to himself. He blames himself for teaching me to be ruthless. How like my father: credit or blame, he takes it all for himself.

". . . four million deaths," the elder Yamagata's voice was rasping. "That is a heavy burden to bear, my son."

Nobu nodded. Unbidden, a childhood memory rushed upon him. He was six years old, and he had run down one of the house's cats with his electric go-cart. His father loomed before him, his face stern. Young Nobu admitted he'd killed the cat, and even confessed that it was no accident; he'd deliberately tried to hit the animal.

"I thought it would get out of my way," he said. "It was too fat and lazy to save itself."

Father's face showed surprise for an instant, then he regained his self-control. "That creature's life was in your hands," he said. "It was your responsibility to protect it, not to kill it. The world is filled with fat and lazy creatures. You have no right to kill them simply because they get in your way." And he walked away from his son. No punishment, although Nobu drove his go-cart with greater care afterward. For a while.

"Four million deaths," his father's voice rasped from the audio speaker. "And mine, too. I'm dying because of the skytower."

Nobu's eyes widened. Father! I've murdered you!

Aloud, he cried, "What have I done? What have I done?"

As if he could hear his son's sudden anguish, Saito Yamagata gasped, "If you have any . . . feelings for me . . . come to Mercury. Finish . . . my work. Please, Nobu. Give us . . . the stars."

His father's voice went silent. Nobuhiko sank back against his desk chair. The intimate office was lit only by the lamp on his desk, a single pool of light against the shadows.

Nobu fingered the controls in his chair's armrest that turned the office ceiling transparent. Leaning his head back, he saw the stars glittering in the dark night sky.

Father went to Mercury to atone for his sins, Nobuhiko thought. Now he expects me to do the same to atone for my own.

His lips curled into an ironic smile. Leave everything and traipse off to Mercury to build power satellites that will propel a starship. How like Father. Always trying to make me live up to my responsibilities.

Nobu got to his feet. I suppose I could direct the star project from here, he thought. I can visit Mercury but I don't have to remain there permanently.

He knew he was fooling himself. As he left his office and rejoined his family, he wondered how long it would take to travel to Alpha Centauri.

ACKNOWLEDGMENTS

My thanks once again to Jeff Mitchell, who really is a rocket scientist from MIT; to Steven Howe, as bright and innovative a physicist as I ever met; and to David Gerrold, whose description of a "beanstalk" in his novel *Jumping Off the Planet* is the best I have seen—true friends in need, each one of them.

The epigraphs heading the prologue and main sections of this novel are from William Shakespeare, Sonnets 29 and 123; Edgar Allan Poe, "The Conqueror Worm"; John Dryden, "Absalom and Achitophel"; and Shakespeare again, *Titus Andronicus*, Act II, Scene 3.

Look for

TITAN

BEN BOVA

Available February 2006

turn the page for a preview

24 DECEMBER 2095:
ON THE SHORE OF THE METHANE SEA

t was nearly dawn on Titan. The thick listless wind slithered like an oily beast slowly awakening from a troubled sleep, moaning, lumbering across the frozen land. The sky was a grayish orange, heavy with sluggish clouds; the distant Sun was nothing more than a feeble ember of dull red light smoldering faintly along the horizon. No stars in that smog-laden sky, no lightning to break the darkness; only the slightest hint of a faint glow betrayed where the giant planet Saturn rode high above.

The ice-covered sea was dark, too, with a brittle, cracked coating of black hydrocarbon slush that surged fitfully against the low bluffs that hemmed it in. At their bases the bluffs were ridged, showing where the feeble tides had risen and then fallen back: risen and ebbed, in the inexorable cadence that had persisted for eons. In the distance a methane storm slowly marched across the sea, scattering crystals of black hydrocarbon tholins like a blanket of inkdrops swirling closer, closer.

A promontory of ice suddenly crumbled under the relentless etching of the sea, sliding into the black waves with a roar that no ear heard, no eye saw. Slabs of frozen water slid into the sea, smashing the thin sheet of blackened ice atop it, frothing and bobbing in the water for a few moments before the open water began to freeze over once again. All became still and quiet once again, except for the low moan of the unhurried wind and the ceaseless surging of the waves. It was as if the promontory had never existed.

Titan rolled slowly in its stately orbit around the ringed planet Saturn just as it had for billions of years, as dark and benighted beneath its shroud of ruddy auburn clouds as a blind beggar groping his unlit circuit through a cold, pitiless universe.

But this slow dawn was different. A new kind of day was beginning.

A sudden thunderclap boomed across the ice-topped sea, so sharp and powerful that shards of ice snapped off the frozen bluffs and tumbled splashing into the dark crust below. A flash of light lit the clouds, casting an eerie orange glimmer over the shore of the sea.

Through the clouds descended a thing utterly alien, a massive oblong object that swayed gently beneath a billowing canopy. It descended slowly toward the rounded hillocks that edged the dark, turbid sea. As it neared the icy surface another flash of brilliant, searing light burst from beneath it with a roar that echoed off the ice mounds and across the wavelets of the murky sea. Then it settled slowly onto the uneven surface of one of the knolls, squatting heavily on four thick caterpillar treads as its parachute canopy sagged down to droop over its edge and halfway to the black encrusted sea.

The creatures living in the ice burrowed deeper to escape the alien monster. They had neither eyes nor ears but they were delicately sensitive to changes in pressure and temperature. The alien was hot, lethally hot, and so heavy that it sank through the soft surface mud and even cracked and powdered the underlying ice beneath its bulk. The ice creatures moved pitifully slowly; those directly beneath the massive alien were not fast enough to avoid being crushed and roasted by its residual heat. The others nearby wormed deeper into the ice as quickly as they could, blindly seeking to escape, to survive, to live.

Then the black tholin storm reached the cliffs and swirled over the alien monster. Silence returned to the shore of Titan's frigid sea.

PROFESSOR WILMOT'S ORAL DIARY

Today Urbain and his science chaps land their probe on Titan. The real work of this habitat will begin.

Ten thousand men and woman locked inside this orbiting cylinder. In the two years it has taken to arrive in orbit around Saturn we've survived one murder, one execution, and an ugly spot of police brutality. We've had an election, of sorts, and established a government—of sorts.

The scientists are happy. They've been studying Saturn's rings and even made some startling discoveries. Now they're sending that ponderous landing vehicle of theirs down to the surface of Titan. Bloody monster's going to trundle around the place under control from up here in the habitat.

I've been moved out of power, of course. It's better that way. If Eberly hadn't pushed me I would have removed myself. Nasty bit of blackmail, though; not pleasant at all. Nevertheless, my task here is to observe these people and see what kind of a society they ultimately produce for themselves. An anthropologist's dream: watching a new society being created.

Ten thousand men and women. No children, of course. Not allowed. Not yet. Exiles, most of our population. Political dissidents and disbelievers who ran afoul of their faith-based governments back on Earth. Locked into this artificial world, this man-made habitat. It's pleasant enough, physically. Better environment than most of them had on Earth, actually. But I wonder. Many of these people will live here permanently; they won't be allowed back to Earth.

Ten thousand hotheads and nonconformists. Physically they are adults, but they behave much like teenagers. Few of them accept responsibilities; they live to play, not work. Except for the scientists, of course. And the engineers, I suppose. Actually, one shouldn't be surprised by their adolescent attitudes. What with their long life expectancies and the rejuvenation therapies that can stretch their life spans into centuries, why shouldn't their adolescent years extend into their forties and fifties?

But it troubles me. It would only take a few of these aged adolescents to cause enormous troubles. They could spread dissatisfaction and rebellion through the whole population, like a viral infection. A few malcontents could wreck this habitat. A handful. Perhaps only one. How can they protect themselves against the outbreak of that kind of disease?

It's going to be interesting to observe what happens.

Titan Alpha has landed!" the mission controller sang out. "She's down safely."

With a loud howl of triumph he yanked the communications plug out of his ear and tossed it to the steel-beamed ceiling of the crowded control center. For the past six days the teleoperated *Titan Alpha* had spiraled through the radiation-drenched vacuum between the massive habitat *Goddard* and Saturn's giant moon, cautiously orbiting Titan a dozen times before attempting to enter its thick, smoggy atmosphere. Now it had landed safely, and it was time for celebrating.

Eduoard Urbain felt an urgent need to urinate. He realized that he had been standing in front of the mission control center's main console for more than six hours, and now that the controllers were whooping and pounding each other on the back, he felt he could breathe again. And pee.

But it was not to be. Not yet. Standing beside him was Jacqueline Wexler, president of the International Consortium of Universities, from whom funding and promotion and prestige either flowed or was withheld.

At this moment of triumph, Dr. Wexler was all smiles and accolades.

"You've done it, Eduoard!" she enthused over the bubbling chatter of the elated scientists and engineers. "A successful landing. It's going to be a happy Christmas for us all."

Urbain heard champagne corks popping, the laughter and the raucous horseplay that comes when nerve-twisting tension is suddenly released. Although he felt the same joy and satisfaction, he had no desire to celebrate, no urge to behave foolishly. All he really wanted at this particular moment was to get to the urinal.

Wexler was not about to release him, though. She grasped his forearm with fleshless talonlike fingers, hard enough to make Urbain wince, and began to introduce him to the other Important Persons who had flown all the way out to Saturn for this momentous occasion.

She was hardly an imposing figure. Dr. Wexler looked hard, brittle, Urbain thought: a short, bony woman with an intense birdlike face and plain brown hair cut short, wearing a tailored tunic and deep blue slacks designed more to disguise her skeletal figure than to make a fashion statement. Yet she had power and the ruthlessness to wield it. Back on Earth she was often called "Attila the Honey." Not to her face, of course.

Urbain himself was quite elegant. He had given a lot of thought to his wardrobe for this morning's event, and—with his wife's help and eventual approval—had selected a trim gray business suit with a soft Persian blue silk cravat.

Jeanmarie was in the crowd of onlookers, he knew. Searching for her, he finally saw her watching him, her eyes glowing with his success. She is beautiful, Urbain thought. Beautiful and happy, at last.

Thirty-seven university and news media VIPs had flown on a high-velocity fusion torch ship to this habitat in orbit around Saturn, courtesy of Pancho Lane and Astro Corporation. Normally, the men and women who directed the International Consortium of Universities preferred to remain on Earth and spend their money on research or teaching. Normally, news network executives sent their reporters afield while they remained in their opulent offices. But Pancho Lane was heading for habitat *Goddard* and had invited the ICU and the news media to send a contingent along with her, so here they were.

Urbain suffered through what seemed like an endless round of introductions. Wexler even introduced him to Professor Wilmot, who had been aboard *Goddard* from the outset as its chief administrator—living and working with Urbain for nearly three years now.

"Good show today, Eduoard," said Wilmot jovially, as they clasped hands while Wexler beamed approvingly. "Hope everything goes this well tomorrow."

Tomorrow, Urbain thought. Christmas day. When they begin to turn on *Titan Alpha*'s sensors and start the exploration of Titan's surface.

"Have some champagne, Eduoard." Wilmot proffered his own untouched plastic cup. "You've earned it."

"Er, not just yet, thank you," Urbain replied. "There is something I must do first."

```
┌─────────────────────────────────┐
│     23 DECEMBER 2095:           │
│     THE DAY BEFORE              │
└─────────────────────────────────┘
```

The successful landing of *Titan Alpha* on the cloud-shrouded surface of Saturn's largest moon was not the only startling event aboard habitat *Goddard*. A day earlier, Pancho Lane had provided fireworks of a different sort.

Although she had officially retired as CEO of Astro Corporation, Pancho still had enough clout to commandeer the fusion torch ship *Starpower III* for a six-week flight to distant Saturn. And to bring a gaggle of ICU bigwigs and news executives with her, as well as her personal bodyguard and lover.

Pancho made her way up *Starpower III*'s paneled central passageway toward the bridge to watch the torch ship's approach to *Goddard* through the bridge's glassteel ports. Once an astronaut herself, she had no patience with sitting in her compartment and staring at a video display of the approach and docking. Nor was she in a mood to mingle with the passengers in the central lounge: flatlanders, most of them. Earthworms who had never been farther than the comfortable cities on the Moon and only traveled deeper into space in the luxury and safety of this commodious torch ship.

If the ship's captain or crew members felt uncomfortable with the retired head of the corporation poking around their bridge, they did their best to hide it. Pancho sat at the vacated life support console, where she could gaze through the bridge's sweeping windows of heavily tinted glassteel as *Starpower III* neared *Goddard*'s main docking port.

It took an effort to keep her eyes off Saturn. The planet bulked huge and looming, nearly ten times bigger than Earth, striped with soft tan and muted yellow clouds whipping along at hyperhurricane velocities. White clouds circled the pole. Or was that an aurora? Pancho wondered. It's summertime down there in the southern hemisphere, she thought. Temperature's prob'ly gettin' close to a hundred and fifty below zero. They must be clouds, ice formations.

The rings were tipped so that Pancho could see them in all their dazzling complexity, glittering, glistening broad bands of gleaming ice chunks hanging in emptiness, stupendous rings many thousands of kilometers across, yet so thin that the stars shone through them. This close, Pancho could see that the rings were braided, countless individual rings woven together like a rich circular tapestry made of brilliant diamonds. Some of the scientists claimed that there were living creatures in those ice particles, extremophiles that thrived at temperatures near absolute zero.

Compared to gaudy Saturn and those radiant rings, the man-made *Goddard* was not much to look at, Pancho thought, as she watched the massive habitat growing larger. It was a thick, ungainly cylinder, twenty kilometers long and four across, rotating slowly to produce an artificial gravity for the ten thousand men and women living inside it. It reminded Pancho of a stubby length of storm drainpipe hanging in the emptiness, although as they neared it she could see that its surface was pebbled with observation bubbles, docking ports, antennas and other projections studding the cylinder's curving flank. And at about two-thirds of the way along the cylinder stood the ring of solar mirrors standing like a collar of flower petals, drinking in sunlight for the habitat's farms and electrical power and life support.

Susie's in there, Pancho thought. Then she remembered: Mustn't call her Susie anymore. She changed her name to Holly. And it damned near killed her.

Despite her best intentions Pancho couldn't help feeling a simmer of resentment about her sister. Sooze was only three years younger than Pancho, as far as calendar age was concerned. But while Pancho had allowed her hair to go stark white and was taking rejuvenation therapies to stave off the encroachment of age, Susan was physically no more than thirty. And mentally, emotionally—Pancho grimaced at the thought.

Susan had died while she was a teenager. Pancho had administered the lethal injection herself, once the medical experts had woefully assured her that there was no hope of saving Susan from the drug-induced cancer that was ruining her body. So Pancho pushed the hypodermic syringe into her sister's emaciated arm and watched her die. As soon as she was pronounced clinically dead the medics slid her body into a heavy stainless steel sarcophagus, a coffin-sized dewar that they filled with liquid nitrogen, steaming white, deadly cold.

For more than twenty years Pancho guarded Susie's cryonically preserved body as she herself climbed the corporate ladder of power from hell-raising astronaut to CEO and board chairman of Astro Corporation. Pancho directed Astro's side of the Second Asteroid War, and once that tragedy ground to its exhausted, blood-soaked finish, she had formally retired from Astro to start a new life of—what? she asked herself. What am I doing here, all the way the hell out at Saturn. What am I going to do with the rest of my life?

Her immediate plans she knew. She was going to see her sister for the first time in nearly three years. Spend the holidays with the only family she had. The thought made her tense with apprehension.

Once Susan had been revived from her long years of cryonic suspension and her cancer removed by therapeutic nanomachines, she was like a newborn baby in a young adult's body. The years she had spent bathed in liquid nitrogen had saved her body but destroyed most of the synapses in the cerebral cortex of her brain. She had practically no higher brain functions. Pancho had to feed her, teach her to speak again and to walk, even toilet-train her.

Slowly Susan became a mature adult, yet even when the psychologists happily proclaimed her training to be a complete success, Pancho was disturbed. She wasn't the same Susie. Couldn't be, Pancho realized, yet the difference unsettled her. She looked like Susie, talked and laughed and flirted like Sooze, but she was subtly different. When Pancho looked into her sister's eyes, it was somebody else in there. Almost the same. But only almost.

And the first thing Sooze did, once she was fully recovered, was to change her name and traipse out on the space habitat *Goddard* on this wild-ass mission to explore Saturn and its moon, Titan. She picked up and left Pancho behind, with a smile and a peck on the cheek and a perfunctory, "Thanks for everything, Panch." She ran off with that slimy son of a bitch Malcolm Eberly.

That was why Pancho was not in her most chipper and cheerful mood as *Starpower III* docked with *Goddard* and began to disembark its VIP passengers. She felt sullen resentment and an anger she believed to be completely justified. And she was more than a little apprehensive about how Susie would receive her. How's she gonna react to having her big sister drop in on her, after she's flown almost a billion and a half kilometers to get away from me? Merry Christmas, now go home: that's what Pancho feared her sister's attitude would be.

Stewing inside, juggling these emotions, Pancho made her way down the ship's central passageway to the main docking port after the skipper had announced they'd mated with *Goddard*. All the big muckety-muck scientists and news execs were gathering in the port's waiting area, chatting and buzzing impatiently. She saw Jake Wanamaker easily enough; he towered over the others. His craggy face broke into a smile as he spotted her and Pancho couldn't help but grin back at him.

"Hi, there, sailor," she said, once she had sidled through the gathering crowd to stand beside him. "New in town?"

"Yes, ma'am," answered Wanamaker, falling into the old routine. "Thought maybe you'd show me the sights."

They both laughed and Pancho felt better.

Until they finally stepped through the airlock and into *Goddard*'s reception area. The crowd was arranging itself into a straggly line as personnel from the habitat checked names and assigned the visitors to living quarters. Then Pancho spotted Susie, tall and lean as herself. She looks okay, Pancho thought, her heart leaping. She looks fine.

"Panch!" Sooze yelped, and she pushed through the line of notables toward her sister.

Mustn't call her Susan, Pancho reminded herself. She's Holly now.

Her sister threw her arms around Pancho's neck and Pancho knew it was going to be alright between them. No matter what, it was going to be okay. She introduced Holly to Jake, who took her hand in his meaty paw and said hello almost solemnly while Pancho beamed at them.

"C'mon, let's go to my place," Holly said. "You can find your apartment later, after the crowd's thinned out."

Pancho happily followed her sister as far as the hatch that led out to the corridor beyond the reception area. Standing there was a handsome, youngish man, hair the color of straw swept in thick waves, strong cheekbones, thin straight nose, chiseled firm jaw and piercing sky-blue eyes. His face was sculpted so perfectly that Pancho guessed he'd had cosmetic therapy. What was that word the old-time racists used? she asked herself. The answer came to her swiftly: *Aryan*. That's what he looked like: the ideal Nordic hero. Yet below the neck he looked soft, a slight potbelly bulging his loosely draped tunic. As if his face was all that mattered to him.

"Panch, this is Malcolm Eberly, *Goddard*'s chief administrator and—"

Pancho lashed out with her right fist in a lightning punch that caught Eberly's smiling face solidly on the jaw and knocked him backward onto the seat of his pants.

"That's for damn near killing my sister, you no-good son of a bitch," Pancho snarled at him.